"Jane Gabin's *The Paris Photo* fascinated me. Being sensitive to how some of her characters suffered often made my heart tremble. But then my feelings would soar and my heart could stay open because in plunging into it I could see how well the author's characters faced the City of Light's dark past."

—Dr. Alan T. Marty, author and historian

# THE PARIS PHOTO

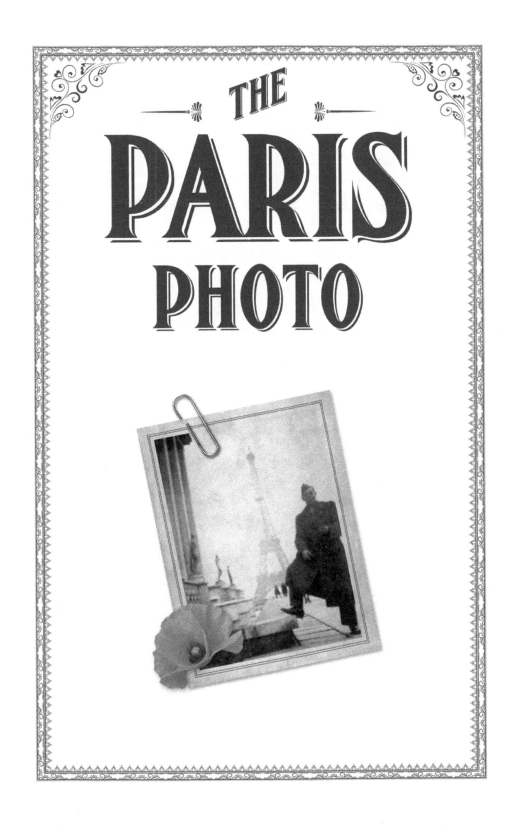

# THE PARIS PHOTO

## A NOVEL

*Jane S. Gabin*

# THE PARIS PHOTO

Copyright © 2018 by Jane S. Gabin
All rights reserved.

No part of this publication may be reproduced, stored in a retrieval system
or transmitted in any way by any means, electronic, mechanical, photocopy,
recording or otherwise without the prior permission of the author except
as provided by USA copyright law.

The opinions expressed by the author are not necessarily those of
Wisdom House Books, Inc.

Published by Wisdom House Books, Inc.
Chapel Hill, North Carolina 27514 USA
1.919.883.4669 | www.wisdomhousebooks.com

Wisdom House Books is committed to excellence in the publishing industry.

Book design copyright © 2018 by Wisdom House Books, Inc. All rights reserved.

Cover and Interior design by Ted Ruybal

Published in the United States of America

Paperback ISBN: 978-0-692-09751-9
LCCN: 2018959918

1. FIC014050    FICTION / Historical / World War II
2. FIC046000    FICTION / Jewish
3. FIC027200    FICTION / Romance / Historical / 20th Century

First Edition
14 13 12 11 10 / 10 9 8 7 6 5 4 3 2 1

The excerpt from Murder on the Rue de Paradis,
copyright © 2008 by Cara Black,
is reprinted by permission of Soho Press, Inc.
All rights reserved.

The old, sad stories of the Occupation. One never got away from them, she thought . . . The past clung to these cobblestones and buildings as if it were just yesterday.

—Cara Black,
*Murder on the Rue de Paradis*

# Merci à

ver the past few years, while doing research for this book, I traveled to Paris several times and found many individuals who assisted me, and some have become friends. I wish to thank them for their help and encouragement: Myriam Dubois, Carol Gillott, Michel and Brigitte Gurfinkiel, Dr. Laura Hobson-Faure, Dr. Alan Marty, Dr. Georges Stroz, Catherine Stroz, and Nicolas Stroz. I am especially indebted to Mme. Ariel Sion and the library staff at the Mémorial de la Shoah for their gracious assistance. Thanks in addition to Philippe Landau and Jean-Marc Levy of the Consistoire de Paris for providing access to their archives, and to Jean-Claude Kuperminc and Guila Cooper of the Library of the Alliance Israélite Universelle.

Many others in Paris have been supportive of my work, including Terrance Gelenter, Wally Chalmers, Serge and Beate Klarsfeld, Gilles Primout, and Sarah and Georges Wojakowski. In New York, I found valuable information at the library of the Jewish Theological Seminary, and I wish to acknowledge the librarian who assisted me, Dr. Sarah Diamant.

My thanks to other individuals supporting my efforts and inspiring me: Martha Hauptman, Sharon Halperin, Shoshana and Hugo Kaufmann, Carol and Neil Offen, and Ronald Rosbottom. Organizations providing me with knowledge and inspiration: the Rosenthal Library at Queens College of the City University of New York, and the European Association of Jewish Studies, at whose 2014 conference in Paris I was able to participate.

To my good friend Susan Bright, whose gift made it possible to jump-start my study of the French language.

As always, to my family, Richard Cramer, Philissa Cramer and Benjamin Resnick, and Will Cramer, for their steadfast support.

Jane S. Gabin
Chapel Hill, North Carolina

# PART ONE

## CHAPTER ONE

## AUTUMN 1943:

# In the French Mountains

Gray shadows have already fallen on the western side of the slopes above the École Bellevue, while the roof of the large chalet and the treetops behind it are burnished by the late afternoon sun. Classes, such as they are, are over for the day. The lessons are not strongly academic; there is just enough writing, reading, history, and mathematics to keep the boys from falling too far behind at their regular schools. Bellevue itself specializes in skiing and other winter sports. It is before dinner, and a group of boys is kicking a ball around on the unpaved parking area in front of the house.

M. Fremont, who runs Bellevue, is a former national champion athlete himself, still muscular and trim as he nears the age of fifty. He was part of the French national team at the first Winter Olympics in 1924 at Chamonix and never seems to tire of telling the students about this. In fact, they started to do a tally over the past months, and he seems to have averaged one or two mentions a week. But the boys don't mind, really, because M.

Fremont is also an excellent teacher, and their skiing and speed skating skills have improved tremendously.

As M. Fremont is happy to tell prospective students and their parents, the school started in the mid-1930s as a wintertime sports camp, then expanded to offer hiking and orienteering in the summers. After the war began, Fremont left his regular job at a school on the north coast, deciding it would be safer up in the mountains, ten miles from the nearest village, than in a manufacturing city near the sea. Having factories nearby made the area vulnerable to bombing, and Fremont cherished safety. So he worked out how to transform the camp into a boarding school, poached a few teachers from his previous employers, and quickly printed notices advertising the school and sent them to families who had come to the sports camp.

One day, early in the autumn of 1943, he had received a telephone call from a woman named Louise Boissiere, who said she had seen information about the school on a notice board in the public library near her workplace in Paris. She said she was looking for a good place for her son to study, safely away from cities. Fremont told her the price of tuition and reassured her about the school's safe location. He asked few questions but urged her to bring the boy soon, before winter weather set in.

Now, near the end of October, Simone and Guy arrive in the village late on a Saturday. Fremont has gone to meet them but is unsure of exactly when they will arrive. Bus schedules are unreliable these days. He waits for a couple of hours, first in a café where he can watch the bus depot, and then he sits on a bench outside, pretending to read a book. Because of the fuel rationing, there are few trains to the large towns and fewer buses from there to the villages. Finally, Fremont hears the chug of an approaching motor and watches as a bus pulls in and passengers descend. When he spots a woman and an adolescent boy emerge, he walks over to greet them and extends his hand.

"Madame Boissiere? I am pleased to meet you and . . ."

"Guy. My son, Guy Boissiere." The boy reaches out, and Fremont greets him hurriedly.

"Yes, yes, we need to go right now," says Fremont, urging them over to where he has left his car and ushering them into the back seat. "We need to get there quickly, before dark," he explains as they set off. He does not state the real reason for his hurry: to get away from the bus station and out of the village before anyone too curious notices them.

"It has taken us all day to get here," says the woman. "We had to wait over two hours for the bus."

"Yes, the rationing," agrees Fremont as he navigates the narrow road.

Guy has never been to the mountains before—the sea, yes, but not the mountains, and he stares out of the car's window as it rattles up the road, trying for a glimpse of the valley below in the setting sun.

"Just wait till these hills are covered in snow, Guy," Fremont says cheerily from the front seat of the car. "Just four to six weeks from now. That's when the fun begins! How well do you ski?"

Guy looks at his mother, who shrugs. "Sir," he begins slowly, "I have never been skiing."

There is only a moment's quiet, and then Fremont responds, "Really! Well, this is not a problem for us! Many city boys do not know how to ski. We will teach you." Fremont sounds agreeable. Simone wonders if he has encountered this situation before. But whatever Fremont thinks about a child who has never skied coming to a ski school, he keeps it to himself.

The old car puffs slowly around the many turns in the road. With all the winding, it takes almost an hour to reach the school chalet. It is becoming hard to see in the dark. When they arrive, Fremont takes Guy's bag, and they all ascend the chalet's wooden front steps. Guy looks back but sees no lights from the distant village. Or from anywhere—the dark is solid. But inside, there is a fire in the hearth and heavy blackout curtains on the windows.

"Two more for dinner tonight, Marie!" calls Fremont, and a middle-aged couple comes to greet them. "Marie and Paul, this is our new student, Guy, and his mother. They come from Paris."

Everyone shakes hands and soon Guy meets the other students. It seems to be a small school, only about thirty boys. Simone looks them over quickly. It is hard to tell, just by a quick glance, where they are from, who might come from a comfortable family, and who might be on their level. She looks down and glimpses their shoes; some are very worn; several boys have the wooden soles cobblers began to use after the leather supply had run out.

No one here wears the cloth star that the Germans have required the Jews to wear since the late spring of 1942. Are they all Christians, or are some perhaps secret Jews? She knows better than to ask and actually does not want to know.

Supper is simple, a thick vegetable soup with hunks of rabbit meat, with fresh bread and cold milk for the boys.

"You can see, Madame," Marie tells Simone, "The children get plain but nourishing food. Up here, we can occasionally get a little meat or milk from one of the farmers. Your son will eat better here than in Paris, for sure. And the air is fresh!"

"I am happy he will be here," Simone says quietly. She would not see him for . . . for months, probably. And she hopes he will indeed be safer here than in Paris or its outskirts.

As for Guy, he thinks this school looks nice enough. The bookshelf in the large front room has some of his favorites, like *Les Trois Mousquetaires* and *Les Contes du chat perché*. But now he will have to start all over again with making friends, just as he had started to really like the children back at the village school he had attended with Armand and Pierre. At least he was home with his mother and grandmother for a few days. He wants to stay with them, but his mother says Paris is dangerous now, and it will be better for him to be away, up in the mountains. She will stay in Paris and keep working and taking care of Gran'mère until . . .

"Until Papa and Gran'père come home?"

"Yes, I hope so," Simone tells him wistfully. "You have been wonderful and brave, Guy."

After dinner, she puts her arm around Guy's shoulders and draws him to the far side of the room. A large framed poster advertising a skiing resort adorns the wall in a corner. No one can hear what Simone murmurs to Guy: "Please listen to M. Fremont and the teachers. I know you will. And also . . ."

"Yes, Maman, your rules, too." The boy nods obediently and sighs. He has heard this before. "No speaking Yiddish—but I think I have forgotten it anyway. No talking about anything Jewish."

Simone gives him another hug. "Good! And what else?" This is not pleasant, but she has to be sure he remembers this because his life could depend on it.

"I know, Maman, when I go to the bathroom or take a shower." He thinks it is better not to tell her how much this rule frightens him.

"And what is my name?"

"Louise Boissiere."

She gives him an extra squeeze. "You are a wonderful boy. You

7

remember everything. I know this is not easy for you, but we will get through all of this."

Later that evening, after all the boys are in their rooms, M. Fremont speaks with Simone. "So, Madame, now you see how we live. The boys have lessons in the morning and then outdoor activities until dinner. After dinner, they can read, or study, or we play charades, or act out stories, either from books or ones the boys have written." He pauses. "I will need a way to contact you, in case of emergency. But in general, this is an isolated place. We get very, very few visitors." He looks at her meaningfully. "In case we do, we have a drill. Our teachers are prepared. The children are safe."

Simone nods. He speaks in clues and much is unsaid. She knows not to ask too many questions, but her throat aches. In normal times, which these are not, she would never leave her child in the middle of nowhere with strangers. She would want to know everything about the circumstances surrounding her child's safety. But now, such a vast charade! She is desperate to trust someone yet knows she cannot completely trust anyone. She wishes that someone courageous and strong would come along to protect them. But she is also aware that the only real protector her little family has is herself.

Fremont asks nothing about her family, about her husband's work, about their religion, about their source of income. He does not want to know anything. Just as long as the tuition is paid. And that is Simone's job.

In the morning, Guy waves to Simone as she and M. Fremont leave for the village. He watches the dust from the road rise behind the car, then settle and disappear. He blinks and bites his lip. He cannot let himself cry, he cannot. After all, he is now eleven years old.

## CHAPTER TWO

# AUGUST 1944:

# Northern France

ust is everywhere—the surface of the narrow road, the abandoned fields on either side. Evidence of fierce fighting is all around, in shattered tree trunks, bomb craters pitting the road, torn fences, remnants of buildings. When the wind blows a certain way, the GIs smell burning vehicles and houses. They pass a couple of blackened Panzer tanks and the charred frames of smaller vehicles. Smoke still rises from some of the piles of rubble in towns that have gotten blasted. Towns that look like they have been beaten up.

Corporal Ben Gordon is entering France with a mixture of excitement, relief, and guilt. From a convoy of boats crossing the Channel, he is now in a convoy of trucks with thousands of men and their supplies rolling through the battered French countryside. He sits next to the driver, studying a map as they rumble south and then east toward Paris. The late August sun beats down on the soldiers' heavy helmets, and their collars are soaked with sweat. Some of the men had wanted to remove their helmets for the ride.

"Negative," said their CO, "We don't know where Jerry or his friends may still be hiding, and if they decide to take potshots at us, you want your brains protected."

Ben is relieved he hadn't been one of those troops who'd had to throw themselves onto the beaches and then advance under fire. Then he feels remorse for even having this thought, knowing that guys just like himself, most of them probably younger, kids just out of high school, had died so that he could be in this truck.

He already feels guilty for not being in a combat unit. He had volunteered for the infantry mostly because he felt he should. But he was secretly relieved when he flunked the physical. He knows he's not chicken; it's not that. As much as he hates the enemy, he doesn't relish the thought of aiming at guys while they aim at him. But the docs had settled this question, this question. "With *your* feet, Gordon?" one of them had exclaimed. "You'd never be able to carry a pack and march for miles. Uncle Sam will find another way to use you." And that way was to send Ben to serve in a military post office. Piece of cake.

Ben starts to think about Pop and wonders if Pop would be proud of him now. He'd probably be prouder if Ben shot a few Nazis. But so far Ben hasn't even seen one. Actually, Ben reflects, his father was the one who taught him to talk first, try to reason, and only fight if you have to. But then fight with everything you had. Ben remembers when he was a kid, maybe eleven or twelve, helping his father one summer at that factory in the garment district of Manhattan. Ben had to push a wheeled rack of dresses from his father's building to another one a block away. He had to go down a short alley to the other factory's door—but found his way blocked by a group of tough-looking guys a few years older than he was.

"Hey kid, ya can't go through here."

Ben remembers trying not to look scared. "I have to deliver this stuff, OK?"

"No, you gotta pay a toll. You wanna pass by, you pay."

"I don't have money. I'm just trying to help my dad. C'mon, let me through, please."

"Hey, guys! He said please! Should we let him go through? Naw—go on back to Daddy." They laughed as Ben turned the rack around and headed back.

A few minutes later, Ben returned with the wheeled rack to the entrance of the alley. He had brought Abe. The toughs were still there.

"Oh, I'm scared," cried one in a fake whine. "He's brought his daddy!"

"Let my son through, please," said Abe calmly.

"Ooh, another polite one," sneered the guy who appeared to be the leader. He approached Abe, standing very close. He was a head taller than the older man. "We told the kid, he gotta pay a toll!"

"Look," said Abe evenly. "Step aside. I don't want to hurt you."

"*You're* gonna hurt someone, old man? *You?*"

Abe's fist shot out so fast that Ben didn't even see it until it connected with the guy's face in a cracking sound, sending him backwards yelping in pain as his nose spurted blood. He and the others fled down the alley and out of sight. Ben delivered the dresses, and that evening his father took him up onto the roof of their apartment building. "If you're big enough to be threatened, you have to be ready to defend yourself. I'll show you how," he said. Abe started to teach Ben some boxing moves, and from then on they sparred frequently on the roof, where Ben's mother and sister could not see them.

Ben had not known before that his father had been a featherweight champ. That belonged to his pre-marriage life. For Abe, boxing was not about showing off or being able to beat someone up; it was about discipline and skill and preparedness. Ben thinks about this now as the convoy rolls through the French countryside. He hopes he is prepared for the unknown challenges ahead. He does not know what they may be but hopes at least a couple involve smashing Nazis into the ground.

⤞⤝

Ben Gordon was one of the first boys in his neighborhood to sign up. True, he wasn't exactly a boy—he was almost thirty. But he had kept himself fit with sports on the weekends and hadn't become soft around the middle like some of his married buddies. He was still upset with himself for initially reacting, when Pearl Harbor had been bombed and war declared, with excitement. Then immediately he thought of the sailors, all those burned and drowned guys, dying before they could even fight.

He knew his obligation—to get in there and have his chance to do something, finally. It was heartbreaking to listen to rumors and read the letters from Mom's relatives in Europe. "Things are getting very difficult here," a cousin named Meir had written years earlier from Vienna, "so if you could sponsor us we might be able to get a visa. Please, could you write a letter? We would be forever in your debt." Ben's mother had crumpled the letter decisively. "What do they know about debt? Debt is what your father left me. We have enough problems—let them take care of themselves."

"But, Mom . . ." Ben began.

She cut him off. "I remember Meir. He laughed at my parents and me when we wanted to leave for America. He said we would never amount to anything here; we would just be illiterate foreigners. My mother begged

Meir for a little passage money. But no. So now I say no to him."

"This is different. The Nazis . . ."

"*You* want to sponsor somebody, Ben? You can barely take care of yourself, on your salary. Let the rich people in Manhattan sponsor more refugees. I have other worries."

There was no point pursuing this. His mother actually had fewer worries than most, even though Pop's life insurance policy had not been very much. She didn't need to go back to work at some factory. Ben's job at the post office offered stability, benefits, security. His kid sister Franny'd had decent-paying work as a bookkeeper in Midtown with the same costume jewelry company since she graduated from high school. She was a smart girl. Her skill with numbers had shown him how they could make ends meet without their mother having to go to work. Not that that would have been such a bad thing—Mom was a skilled seamstress, but she hadn't had a real job since before Ben was born. If she worked now—well, it would sure give her something to do besides complain, and it would take some pressure off him and Franny.

Ben did not have to think for a long time about what he wanted to do. Right after Pearl Harbor, he and Franny sat on a bench in the lobby of their apartment building. It was the usual place they met when they needed to talk without Mom overhearing.

"Franny." Ben hesitated, thinking that his sister would feel he was deserting her. Then he just plunged in: "I want to join up."

Her round face beamed at him, "Of course you do! I knew you would say this, right from when we heard the news. I'd be disappointed if you *didn't* want to go."

Ben's shoulders relaxed, and he grinned at his smiling, bespectacled younger sister. "You're not mad at me? You will have to do everything if

I leave."

"Jealous, maybe, and worried about you, but not mad. Gee, Ben, this is your chance for adventure! Try not to get shot though, okay? And we'll manage, don't worry."

He grabbed her hand. "You're a swell sister, Fran! I should have known you'd back me up! Listen—you'll have money, of course; I'll be sending you most of what I make. Mom is sure going to make a fuss when she learns."

"Mom always makes a fuss. So she'll fuss. At least, going off to war, you'll have a good excuse for moving out!" They both laughed, and Ben felt a bit better.

Ben and his friend Solly told each other they would sign up right away. But then Ben hesitated for a moment.

"Hold on a minute, Solly—you're married. *You* won't be drafted."

Solly grinned. He was the same age as Ben, a few inches taller, but looked older because he was already starting to lose a little hair on top. "No kids yet, so why not? Anyway, I'm not waiting to be drafted," he had said. "If I volunteer, I have a better chance of going somewhere good. Europe. I want to kick Kraut ass. I don't want to end up in some hellhole jungle."

Ben thought about Solly's wife Myrna and wondered if she had objected to Solly's plan. But why would she? She was an easygoing girl and pretty much agreed to whatever Solly wanted. They had only been married two years, and Ben had been their best man. Sylvia, now that might be another thing.

"Have you told Sylvia about your plans?" Solly always seemed to know what Ben was thinking.

"I'm having dinner with her and her parents tonight," said Ben. "They're good people, I think they'll understand." And they will certainly not echo my mother, Ben thought to himself.

"What about Sylvia?" Mom had asked, in her habitual, accusatory tone. "Some boyfriend you've turned out to be! She'll probably use this as an excuse to part ways with you." Again, Ben had thought it easier not to argue. But he did have his concerns. Sylvia's confidence was a bit fragile, although she sure was one sharp girl. She even tried to hide her terrific figure with big cardigan sweaters. She didn't smile very much and always seemed to be on the outer edge of groups. Maybe because her brother Morty, a successful salesman and the star of the family, was boisterous and social. A freshman in high school when Sylvia was a senior, he was a handsome kid, with dark eyebrows and black hair that often flopped forward. He was great at basketball and handball—all sports really—and while he'd always had a girl or two following him around, everyone had known that Lillian was his true love.

Now twenty-five, Morty was married to Lillian, and they had a cute two-year-old boy named Jack. So Morty wouldn't be drafted. Ben had played handball with him for a long time, and one Sunday morning about a year ago he had gone home with Morty after practice. "Come on up, have a cold drink," Morty had said. They were both sweating from the game. "Maybe my sister will be here. You remember my sister Sylvia?"

They were riding up in the creaky elevator of Morty's building.

"A little," answered Ben. "She was usually holed up in the library, reading! She was always at the top of the honor roll at New Utrecht." He actually remembered a little more, that Sylvia was known as a "brain" who would always have the answer. And she had taken Latin—only the really smart kids took Latin. The other part of her reputation was that she was . . . Ben had heard the word "cold." "Sylvia Stern?" commented one guy he knew. "Nice legs, but you won't get to first base with her."

Now Morty responded, "Yeah, yeah, that's Sylvia, studying—she was always studying. She's a great girl, though. Has a really good job in the city now, a bookkeeper."

Ben smiled to himself, sensing a setup. People had done that for a while, but not in the last few years. He knew that folks liked him, and they liked Franny, too. But no one liked them enough to marry them.

Lillian opened the door. In her arms she was holding Jack, who screeched with pleasure when he saw his father.

"Little man!" cried Morty as he grabbed Jack. He kissed Lillian and said, "Hey, Lil, Ben thought he'd stop in with us for a while, get a drink."

"Nice to see you, Ben," said Lillian, smiling as she welcomed the men. She was a bubbly type, with piles of auburn curls on top of her head, and she always had a smile on her round pink face. She was wearing a flowered yellow-and-green apron over her dress because she had been baking. Ben caught the scent of sweet, warm dough emanating from the kitchen. Someone else was in there, opening and shutting the oven door.

"Your sister's here, Morty—don't know what I would do without an extra pair of hands, now that Jack is getting into everything!"

Another young woman came out of the kitchen with a plate of warm sugar cookies. She had the same dark, curly hair as Morty, but her eyes were serious—Morty's were always amused. "Hello, everyone," she said quietly.

"Hey, sis," said Morty, hugging her while taking the plate from her hands. "You remember my buddy Ben from high school? Ben, this is my sis, Sylvia." He jammed a cookie into his mouth. "Mmm."

"I think I remember you," Sylvia said softly to Ben, "Weren't you on the baseball team?"

"You have a great memory! I sure was! And that was, what, ten years ago?"

Ben quickly realized his blunder. He had reminded this poor girl that, a decade after high school, she was still unattached. Of course, so was he.

But it was different for a girl. He knew that as a post office clerk, he was not a huge "catch" like an accountant or a teacher. And he was average-looking; he was aware of that, too. Being handsome would've helped. But, because he was a guy, nobody made sad little *tsk*-ing sounds about him or said he'd been "on the shelf" too long.

He recovered himself just as quickly by adding, "Well, hardly any time for sports now. I work at the post office near Borough Hall, so I keep pretty busy. But on some Sundays I let your brother beat me in handball, just to keep in shape."

Lillian set a glass pitcher of lemonade on the coffee table. It was warm in the apartment despite the open windows and the May breeze. Lightweight yellow curtains wafted inward cheerfully. Beads of cold water ran down the outside of the pitcher. Ben remembers this especially, because he had been staring at the pitcher to keep from staring at Sylvia's legs. They were great legs: long, shapely. Sylvia would have been really pretty if she had just laughed or acted like she was enjoying herself. But she smiled with her lips closed. Morty was doing his regular job of entertaining people, but Sylvia just smiled slightly. Ben figured she was so used to her brother's shtick that she didn't even react.

By the end of that week, Ben had phoned Sylvia to ask her out. It had just seemed like the right thing to do. Besides, if he stayed home every evening after work, he would end up playing cards with his mother and Franny. More likely, with just his mother when Franny went to the movies with her girlfriends.

Ben didn't have many friends. Well, yeah, he did have Solly and Harry. They had been really close during high school and for years after. But now they were both married, and Ben was the last holdout. He tried not to think about the fact that pretty much everyone he knew was already paired off. All their old crowd—married or engaged. Alice Benjamin had married Stuart Cohen, and they had moved to Jackson Heights. Ron Hooper and Beth Estrin, who had been an item since tenth grade, had gotten married right after graduation and lived in Canarsie.

He wondered why he had never paid attention to Sylvia before, but it was probably because she had kept herself in the background so much. Now, they started spending time with each other on the weekends. She loved music, so one Saturday they went into Manhattan for a recital at The Town Hall, then walked over to the Horn & Hardart Automat in Times Square for coffee and pie. Ben and Sylvia found that they both loved the movies. Ben confided in her that film was his true love, that he had worked part-time for Paramount Pictures for a while in Queens and hoped to move up—but that was before his father died and he had to find steady, guaranteed work. "Well, there went that dream," he said, stirring some sugar into his coffee. "But it's okay working at the post office—I get to meet so many different people."

"We're lucky to have our jobs," Sylvia responded. "I wanted to finish at Brooklyn College, but my family really needed me to work. So here I am, keeping the books for a furniture maker. It's not exactly what I planned, either—I wanted to be a math teacher."

"Maybe later, after things pick up, you can go back to college," Ben offered sympathetically. What a waste, he thought to himself. All that studying and getting up there on the honor roll, and for what? He had never been an outstanding student, though he loved taking pictures and people said he had a good eye for camera work. Maybe he really would have had a future at Paramount, he thought wistfully. But Sylvia, she was smart.

That last summer at home—1941—passed slowly. It was hot in the post office, despite the fans that had been set up in the lobby to keep folks cool.

Ben and the other guys working there still had to wear ties, but they also wore short-sleeved shirts. Ben, Solly, Frank, and Vito took turns eating their lunches in a nearby park and trying to catch a stray breeze. They chatted without much energy about the Dodgers and about whether the US would get pulled into the war in Europe.

"My dad says we saved Europe last time," said Vito, "and we don't need to do it again."

"Look how many countries Hitler has taken over in just two years," Ben shot back. "Do you think he's going to stop any time soon? What if they try to come here?"

"*Then* we'll fight them off."

Ben talked about this with Sylvia, too.

"I thought the last war was supposed to prevent all this," she said to Ben one evening as they waited in line to see *The Grapes of Wrath*. "Weren't the Germans disarmed in 1918?"

"I don't know who has been checking on them. The War was only a little more than twenty years ago, and now they're attacking the same countries all over again! Have you heard any of Hitler's speeches on the radio?"

"I can't catch any words," answered Sylvia, "even though my Yiddish should help me with German. All I can hear is his screeching. He doesn't give a speech: he just yells."

"And they hate the Jews there . . . It's frightening how their prejudice is taking over," added Ben.

"A refugee family just moved to my block. Jewish, of course. They said they were lucky to get visas. They waited for a year to get out of Europe. And then it was years before they got to New York."

"My mom's cousins in Austria used to write, and now we haven't heard from them in a while. The papers say a lot of folks over there have been getting arrested."

Then it was their turn to get tickets and enter. Afterwards, over ice cream, they spoke again of the possibility of war. "Just like in the story we just saw," mused Sylvia thoughtfully. "When life gets tough, people have to move. They just can't stay where they are, or they'll suffer. We have a huge country—I don't see why the US can't take in more refugees."

"Because it's already hard here for a lot of people," answered Ben. "At least that's what they say. The US says it can control the *kind* of people they allow in with those quotas. Most of the people wanting to come here now are European Jews, and we know how much this country loves the Jews."

Sylvia looked straight at Ben. "You know what's strange?" she asked. "Some of the people who don't want too many Jews coming here are Jewish themselves! I heard someone from my *shul* saying that too many immigrants right now might create more anti-Semitism here. But why? No one gave our parents trouble when they arrived."

"True, but that was a long time ago. Before the Depression. You have to admit, the past dozen or so years have been pretty bad. If a lot of refugees come here, and unemployment increases, people will blame the Jews. That's how their thinking goes. Personally, I think we should save people first, then figure out what to do with them."

"But if Americans pledged in advance to take care of a family, then refugees wouldn't be a burden on the economy, so why can't the US give more visas? Isn't this an emergency?"

This was one of the reasons Ben liked Sylvia's company. She thought outside of herself. In fact, she thought, period. They could talk about almost anything. One time, they went to a game at Ebbets Field, and she knew everything about the players and even the other team. He grinned to himself, remembering that "first base" comment. True, she was a "good girl," the kind who wouldn't fool around. She smiled with her lips closed and, as Ben had learned, kissed with her lips closed, too. She seemed to care about him, but when it came to anything more than a kiss on the side of her neck or caressing her arm, Sylvia stopped him.

Ben knew what that meant. Sylvia was holding out for marriage. That was obviously her choice, and he respected her for it even though he was personally very frustrated. He thought about his situation. He was not naïve. He had been with girls who had not been "cold." But after the fun was over, there wasn't much else. Marrying Sylvia would be a sensible option. They had a lot in common. They had similar backgrounds, and he felt truly welcomed by Sylvia's folks. She was smart, pretty, and had a sense of style. He could relax with her. And face it, neither of them were spring chickens—here he was, still living at home at twenty-nine with his mother and kid sister. Getting married would sure give him a good reason to move out of his mother's apartment. He thought about it. But he didn't do anything.

Autumn came. The leaves turned red and gold, then brown. The post office was not as hot, and the world news got worse.

Then on December 7, the Japanese bombed Pearl Harbor and everything changed.

Ben had told Sylvia that he wanted to join up and worried that she might object. But she didn't. "Of course, I'll worry about you, Ben—but I think it's great that you want to go over there and help smash the Nazis! It's about time America did something!"

Ben felt he had to decide other things quickly, too. And that would mean proposing to Sylvia very soon.

He discussed this first with Franny. "Object? Are you kidding?" She laughed. "I'll get your room and won't have to share the bed with Mom anymore!"

"But—you won't feel like I'm deserting you?"

"No, and anyway, I'm only twenty-one. I'll get my chance! Except that all the great and eligible guys are gonna go overseas. But I just have one question, because—well, you've been spending a lot of time with Sylvia, and with her parents. But I haven't seen you being all lovey-dovey. So, do you *love* her?"

Ben paused and looked seriously at his sister. "I really, really like her. I think she will make a terrific wife! She just needs a little more self-confidence. I think our being a couple is good for her."

"You didn't answer my question."

"Aw, quit it, Fran. You know I've made up my mind."

Ben decided to be old-fashioned about it and asked Sylvia's parents first. If they had hoped for someone with higher aspirations than a postal clerk, they hid it. They liked Ben, who had always been respectful, and besides, he was buddies with Morty. Morty, that ball of energy, had already quit his sales job and was helping to build warships in the Brooklyn Navy Yard.

Ben's mother did not seem surprised or excited. "Huh! So you are progressing from boyfriend to fiancé. Do you *have* to marry her?" she asked him.

"Mom! It's not like that. Sylvia is a really good girl!"

"She's no girl, Benjamin," his mother continued, hardly taking her eyes from the newspaper she was holding. "She's been on the shelf a while."

"She's only twenty-eight! And admit it, she is quite a looker."

"You know best, Ben. If you think Sylvia Stern is worth leaving home for, fine."

"I'm leaving home anyway, Mom. I'm volunteering for the army."

She looked up from the paper upon this reminder from her only son. "But you have a mother and a sister to look out for."

"Franny has a great job and can take care of herself. I also have a country to look out for."

"Fine, suit yourself. Just be careful, Mr. Patriot, and try to come home in one piece."

At least his mother had nothing actually negative to say, either about the army or about Sylvia. She had really lit into him about some of his past girlfriends. Irma was too poor; she would be a drain on Ben. Rebecca had an asthmatic sister; surely there were weak genes in that family, and Ben would probably end up caring for an invalid wife. Oh, and that Ruthie Ben had been seeing? He ought to know that people were already talking about her—did he really want someone with that kind of reputation?

Ruthie Bloom, now he had liked her a lot! And she sure was fun. She had a gorgeous figure that Ben had enjoyed running his hands over. They would head down to Brighton Beach and go for a dip in the water, have a picnic dinner on the sand, and then fool around under the boardwalk on Ben's blanket after dark. But when Ben had suggested that they might want to formalize their closeness, Ruthie had laughed. "Oh, Benjie! Come on, this is so much fun; why spoil it by getting married?" Ben wanted to have fun, too, but he also wanted something more. They had gone out for almost a year but broke up soon after that. That was about three years ago. His mother had exulted. "Good! Why would you even want to get mixed up with a hussy like her?" He heard Ruthie was now married to a guy in Jersey who was presumably more fun and probably made a lot more money than he did.

Yes, this was the right thing to do. Ben needed to claim Sylvia as his. She would be vulnerable to every guy who managed to evade military service. Ben had a vague idea of what a code of chivalry demanded and felt somehow that being engaged would offer Sylvia protection. If people asked her or her parents why she wasn't attached, they could say her fiancé was overseas in the military. And when Ben asked her to marry him as they walked home along 15th Avenue in the light, mid-December snow, Sylvia agreed without any hesitation.

She even suggested that they could marry soon, before Ben had to leave. But he said it would be too rushed and besides, what if she got pregnant and he didn't return? He didn't want her to be left with a baby to raise on her own. They compromised with an engagement dinner a week before Ben left for basic training. Now that the United States was in the war, they reasoned, things would probably get resolved in a year or two. Then they could get married when he returned.

Sylvia smiled at him and straightened his collar and tie, which had gone askew when he kissed her. A few snowflakes glistening in her hair, she said, "Having the wedding later will give you something to look forward to when you come back."

In a way, Ben had been relieved with this decision. He didn't actually have to do anything immediately, but meanwhile he was somehow protecting Sylvia against predators in his absence. He didn't really understand why, but he considered proposing to Sylvia an act of patriotism.

In the convoy, Ben's thoughts travel to one morning just before the Christmas holiday—the first one since the US had declared war. It was a cold, gray day, and the tan-and-brown linoleum on the post office floor quickly got wet and muddy from slushy galoshes, despite the black rubber mats Solly had put down. A few people, bundled in overcoats against the cold, came in. Mostly they wanted stamps or aerograms, and a few had parcels to mail. Everyone was animated and had questions. The same one came up several times: now that America was in the war, would any letters get through to Germany, France, Italy? Ben had to disappoint them all.

"Great Britain, Ireland, Switzerland . . . that's about it, folks. You think they're going to let the Clipper land with letters and parcels?"

"Hey, maybe they'll let in our B-17s!" cried Joe, coming over from his hardware store across the street.

"Yeah, and maybe I'll be flying one!" said Ben.

"You're going, kid?"

"Both of us," said Solly. "Soon as we can."

"Bless you, boys!" Joe reached under the grille to shake Ben's hand, then Solly's.

That's the way it went all day. All the talk was about the war. Who was joining up, and who had switched to wartime work. Women, too, especially mothers, were concerned about all the young men who would now be in danger.

Around lunchtime, Ben created a couple of signs reading "No mail delivered to enemy countries" and put them up.

Almost at closing time, late in the afternoon, Ben was straightening up the lobby, collecting bits of paper and mopping up the wet floor again. A young woman in a long gray coat came through the revolving door and stamped her wet galoshes on the rubber mat. Ben recognized her as Anne, the French girl. She had been in a few times before, and he knew she was from somewhere near Paris. Last time she was in, she had told him how lucky she felt, having come over to live with family friends about six months before the Nazis invaded France.

"Ah *bonjour, mademoiselle*!" Ben had taken four years of French at New Utrecht High School and liked to try it out on Anne when he could.

She looked troubled. "*Bonjour*, Ben, I hear you are going overseas in the army?"

"Wow, word spreads fast in this neighborhood! Yes, my friend Solly and I plan to go down to the local induction center at the end of this week."

He hesitated, then asked if she had heard from her cousins in Paris.

"No. Nothing since the Germans took over."

She has to be worried sick, Ben thought to himself.

"Will you go to France?"

"No idea, Anne. The army sends you where they want you to go. I'd rather go to Europe than the Pacific, but I don't think we get a choice. And I won't find out until later."

Anne bit her lower lip and reached into her purse, pulling out a slip of paper. "I want to ask a favor. I don't know anyone else who might be going. But if you do get to France, would you check on my cousins and see how they are?"

Ben took the slip and read the name "Daval" and an address on the Rue de Turbigo in Paris. "I'll check for you, Anne, I promise. Only I just don't know if I am really going, or exactly when."

He felt sorry for her. She was young—maybe twenty-one or twenty-two—and had told him that both her parents were dead. So she was already an orphan and now had no idea what might have happened to her remaining family back in France.

She looked up at him sadly. "But you'll try, and you'll let me know? *Merci.*"

He nodded affirmatively. "*De rien*, Anne, I will."

She kissed him lightly on both cheeks and left the post office quickly. Ben watched her leave, putting the slip of paper into a separate compartment in his wallet. He had no idea where the army would send him or how long anything would take.

❧

And now here he is, in a truck headed straight for the heart of France. With that slip of paper in his wallet. Ben has always kept his promises, and he will look for Anne's relatives as soon as he can. But it has been years since he left home, and he has no idea what he'll find in Paris.

## CHAPTER THREE

## AUGUST 1944:

# Arriving in Paris

everal times, as Ben's convoy goes through small towns, they pass groups of civilians who wave and cheer. He waves back at a girl who is carrying a homemade American flag. To her and her friends, the guys in Ben's truck are all liberating heroes, even though they have not had to fight yet. Of course, the girls don't know that. All they know is that the Germans are gone.

When he had arrived in England, Ben had been a PFC, but within six months had been promoted to corporal. His postal experience back in New York had helped him organize and streamline the military mail system in the UK. He liked having his hard work noticed and was quick to write home about his promotion. So far, army life had been agreeable, aside from his having narrowly missed being bombed in London. He enjoyed London itself, though life in a blacked-out city had its limitations. And despite the high demands of strict officers, Ben stayed calm and got things done. Certainly, he felt less criticized than at home, and laughed to himself as he imagined his mother in an officer's uniform, barking orders.

The drive to Paris takes all day. There is little traffic other than military vehicles. A couple of times they slow to pass a farmer's wagon pulled by a horse, or a bicyclist. The air is dry and dusty, and the men's throats are quickly parched. When there is a breeze, it brings a smell of burning.

"Where are all the cars, Corporal?" the driver, PFC Strickland, asks. Strickland is a kid from Tennessee, just out of high school. "You think Jerry stole them all?"

"Well, he probably stole all the gas," Ben replies. Strickland is pretty naïve, but Ben decides to treat his comment as a joke, and he answers with a joke.

They are going through suburbs now, slowing as they come into more populated areas. On one side of the street are four- and five-story buildings with tall narrow shutters; on the other, half-walls stand amid piles of strewn masonry. The area has been blasted by the Nazis or the Allies—maybe by both, it was impossible to tell. The place is a mess, with piles of rubble on nearly every corner. Several buildings have been sliced open, and Ben can see a cross-section of rooms with torn wallpaper as they rumble past. The overwhelming impression is of tan and gray dust everywhere.

Their road runs at right angles to the Seine, and when they cross the Pont d'Issy, they see the first outlines of Paris. Ben is surprised to see how low the city's skyline is compared with Manhattan's. The new Empire State and Chrysler buildings would dwarf the Eiffel Tower; even a lot of the office buildings in Midtown are bigger. Still, this first glimpse thrills him. As they get a bit closer, he sees a hill off in the distance—and thinks he recognizes the white dome of the Sacré-Cœur Basilica from pictures. Yes, the war is still on—but this is exciting, and Ben is excited to be here.

"Okay," says Strickland, "Here's where we split up."

Ben's truck and several others keep going straight on the Rue de

Vaugirard, into the heart of the city, while others peel off to the south and east. Command has decided that the major train stations still in decent condition will serve as distribution points. This was Seine Section, responsible for supporting all the American troops who would be fighting through to Berlin. The trucks carry communications equipment, medical supplies, fuel, rations: everything the forces will need.

Shortly after crossing the Boulevard Pasteur, several trucks turn right onto the Boulevard du Montparnasse. Here, at the grimy Gare Montparnasse, Ben and his men will set up one of the military post offices. Once the multitude of mail sacks has been sorted, once the trains are back on a decent schedule, letters and packages can start going out to the soldiers in the field. The morale of the GIs will zoom up then, Ben knows.

Their small convoy pulls up at the departure roadway, organized in a row next to the archways of the ramp leading up to the sooty and boxy station. There is no problem finding a place to park because there are few vehicles of any sort to be seen. Ben leads the way through a flimsy door under one of the arches; it opens into a cavernous area that looks as though it had been used formerly for storage and as a garage. It is almost dark at street level, with dirty windows higher up. Enough light filters in for the men to see thick motes of dust floating in the air. As they get used to the semi-darkness, they can see heaps of empty crates, broken baggage wagons, stacks of wood, old tires, and piles of refuse.

"Here we are, men," calls Ben, "Let's start setting up our base."

It takes the soldiers nearly a week to transform the cavernous space under the station's archways into a working military post office, and the storage loft along one end is now habitable—though not luxurious by a long shot—as sleeping quarters. Each soldier has an army cot and a small wooden crate, which functions as a nightstand and a place to stow his gear.

They have telephones connected to the other military lines, running water, and a couple of toilets. The newly scrubbed windows let in whatever natural light comes down from the sides of the Gare Montparnasse. Downstairs in the large main area, long lines of rolling racks of canvas mailbags are already being filled with letters and parcels for the occupying forces, all illuminated by strings of electric lights suspended across the vast room. Army trucks rumble to the large door at the far end twice a day with incoming mail and parcels.

Signs in French and English outside their building indicate that this is a US Army post office, but civilians come in anyway, out of curiosity or with letters in hand.

One morning, a couple of days after they have opened, a young woman with a parcel enters. PFC McDonald at the front desk tries to explain to her that she cannot use this post office, but she does not understand English and he speaks no French.

McDonald calls over to Ben. "Corporal Gordon! You know French—can you please come over here and explain things to this young lady?"

Ben walks right over. An attractive, dark-haired woman of about twenty—who would've been prettier if she hadn't looked so anxious—stands at the counter.

"*Bonjour, mademoiselle*," says Ben, "*Comment puis-je vous aider?*"

She shows him the package, and he takes it in his hands to examine it. It is addressed to M. Paul Stein in Marseille. A German name, but also possibly Jewish. The return address: "Famille Gryn" in Paris. Not a French name—immigrants to the US with this surname probably became "Green." Ben decides to take an educated guess and asks, "*Parlez-vous yiddish?*"

As soon as she hears the word Yiddish, the woman's face brightens. A Yank who speaks *mamalushen*, the "mother tongue!" What a miracle!

"You're Jewish?" she asks in rapid Yiddish, firing questions at him. "Where did you learn to speak Yiddish? How did you know I could speak it? Where are you from? Where is your family from?"

"It was a guess," says Ben, also in Yiddish, "When I saw the names on your package. My parents came from Poland, and I'm from Brooklyn, New York. But my first language was Yiddish. It's what we spoke at home. You are French?"

"Yes, and my parents, too. But my grandparents came from Russia about fifty years ago. So I grew up hearing Yiddish because we, too, spoke it at home." She pauses and lowers her voice. "I don't know how much you know, but the Occupation here has been a nightmare, especially for Jews. Thank God you are here!"

Ben is not sure what to say. She is the first Jewish civilian he has met in newly liberated territory. "We are happy to be here to help, *mademoiselle*. We have heard—only rumors."

She shakes her head and continues speaking in a lowered voice. "It has been bad, very bad. We have had to live very carefully, in secret. Thank God for some kind people." She pauses and raises her voice a bit: "I have not mailed or received a letter in four years. So tell me, why can't I mail my package here?"

Continuing to converse in Yiddish, Ben explains: "This post office is for the American military only, sorry. But you can go to the civil post office that has been set up just inside the Gare. Go inside and you'll see it."

"*Merci*," she says, pulling a slip of paper and pencil from her purse. She writes something down and gives the paper to Ben. "Listen, you must come to our apartment for dinner. Can you come Friday evening around seven? Here is the address. We have no telephone. If you have any Jewish friends, bring them, too! We will have a real *Shabbos* dinner!"

She takes the parcel back from Ben, kisses him in the French style, on both cheeks, and then sails out of the office in the direction of the main station.

McDonald and the other men have been watching Ben, impressed, the whole time.

"Golly," says McDonald, with admiration. "I knew you spoke French, sir, but not that you speak it so *well*!"

With a grin, Ben does nothing to dispel the impression that he is fluent in French.

## CHAPTER FOUR

## AUGUST 1944:

# In the French Mountains

"Pascal! Pascal! Come quick!"

A young man of about twenty is about to toss a soccer ball to the boys circling him when he hears Jean-Claude's shout. He glances up to the high window near the roof of the chalet and sees Jean-Claude beckoning energetically.

Pascal runs into the building and sprints up the several flights of stairs to the small triangular room at the top. A tall teenager is looking steadily through binoculars at something in the distance.

"What do you see?"

"It looks like a military truck, coming on the road from town. Here." Jean-Claude passes the binoculars to Pascal.

He adjusts the focus a bit before saying anxiously, "Yes, it's military for sure, a dark color. Doesn't seem to be in a huge hurry. We have a little time. Keep your eyes open, Jean-Claude, and shout as soon as you see them get closer. Well spotted!"

Pascal runs back down the stairs, calling loudly: "Visitors! Visitors!"

Everyone knows what to do. That top window of the main school building offers a good view of the road from town, about ten kilometers away. The vantage point can last a few minutes, and then any vehicle disappears into the forest. With the many turns in the road approaching the school, they might have thirty or forty minutes before the truck arrives.

"Visitors!" Pascal calls out and claps his hands as he enters the main room on the first floor. Some of the boys from outside are already coming in and running upstairs. The boys and the staff know the drill. Maria, the cook, comes out of the kitchen, saying calmly, "I'll have pitchers of cold water ready and will get out a plate of biscuits." Her voice is more controlled than she feels. She bustles back in to prepare. Maria knows it is never a good idea to hurry the German soldiers away; they will be invited inside and offered something to eat and drink. They do not come often, so far only twice in four years, for the area is remote and not on the way to the border. Still, they do come.

M. Fremont emerges, frowning, from his study. "What did Jean-Claude see?"

"Not sure, *monsieur*. But to both of us, it looks like a small military truck."

"Good lads. You've done well!"

The teachers take turns watching at night. But during the daytime, the older students—the ones with the best eyesight and strongest voices—take turns.

Pascal rejoins the group of boys on the flat gravel area in front of the school.

"Paul Camus, get inside *now*!"

A dark-haired boy who has been bouncing a soccer ball from knee to knee rushes past, mumbling "sorry, *m'sieur*" and charges up the steps.

The boys with dark hair or darker skin all rush upstairs with a teacher.

Pascal returns his attention to the rest of the students outside the front steps. "All right, fellows. We know what to do, because we have practiced. We smile. We are happy to have visitors! Remember, you are the only students here!"

He glances at the group. He should have eight boys: Franck, Alain, Jules, Guy, Jean-Pierre, Georges, Nicolas, and Lucas, the headmaster's son. They are all between nine and twelve years old, and they are all flaxen-haired.

All the other boys should now be safely in the attic space. Pascal thinks about little François Peretti from Paris; although his father was born in Paris, his grandparents came from Sicily, making the child look definitely non-Aryan. Peter is up there with the boys, making sure they keep absolutely silent. A few of the older students should be in the front sitting room engaged in a discussion with M. Fremont. It is an ordinary Friday afternoon in the summer at the École Bellevue.

"One final thing to remember," Pascal calls to his group. "Never let your hands touch the ball!"

He tosses the soccer ball to Jules, who bounces it off his head to Jean-Pierre, who kicks it across the gravel to Guy. Just as Guy deflects the ball from Alain's outthrust foot, Jean-Claude calls from the upper window: "Here they are!"

"Keep playing, boys!" shouts Pascal. But the kicks and cries of the students slow down as they all hear an approaching engine and tires crunching gravel on the road.

An olive-green truck pulls into the drive and stops. The front doors open and two soldiers hop out. Three more come out of the back of the truck. They carry rifles, but they point them down.

"*Bonjour, tout le monde!*" says the first. His accent is foreign. But he is not wearing the familiar gray-green of the Germans.

Pascal steps forward to greet the soldiers. "*Bonjour, monsieurs. Je suis le professeur*. I am the teacher of these boys."

The first soldier takes off his helmet, wipes the sweat from his forehead, then extends his hand to Pascal.

"I'm Sergeant Joe Cooper, United States Army, and this is my squad. We are here to give you the happy news that you free!"

No one moves.

Sgt. Cooper switches to his American-accented French: "*Vive le France! Vous êtes libres!*"

It doesn't take more than a few seconds for the boys to understand as the officer speaks the precious French words. One runs into the house, and a few seconds later, the rest of the students and teachers come pouring out into the yard.

Maria, in tears, comes down the steps with a pitcher and some glasses on a tray. She cannot speak at all. A student is behind her with a small folding table. Another boy carries a plate with biscuits.

M. Fremont approaches the soldiers. "I am Jean, the principal here. I can speak English. Welcome! The boys say you have news for us."

"Yes, sir," says Sergeant Cooper. "Paris is free! The French forces under General de Gaulle, along with other Allied troops, have retaken the city. The war is still on. But the Germans are on the run." Now the boys are yelling, the small ones jumping around as well.

"Please, stay for some refreshment."

"Much obliged, sir. We can't stay long. There are two more places further up on this road where we need to go." He looks at his men and nods. The other soldiers take off their helmets, too, and help themselves to the cold water. They stay half an hour, a couple of them joining in an impromptu soccer game with the boys. A few of the older students use this time to look over the road-worn and dusty but still intriguing jeep.

By the time the soldiers leave, the students are exhausted and happy. Some want to leave for Paris immediately. "Of course not," M. Fremont tells them, "First we need to contact your parents. But soon, soon."

Guy runs up the stairs inside to the room he shares with two other boys. He hears the celebration going on downstairs, but this is time he can be alone with his letter. He pulls his small suitcase from beneath the bed and takes a folded paper from the top of a stack of envelopes bound by a ribbon. Sitting on the edge of the bed, he re-reads the letter, even though he knows well what it says:

*My dearest Guy,*

*We hope to see you soon, but we do not know exactly when. I am well and so is Gran'mère. We both love you very, very much. I hope you are not getting too fat at school! That is a joke, Guy. Of course, I mean that I hope you are getting enough to eat. Now that the weather is warmer perhaps there are more vegetables for you. You must grow strong!*

*It is difficult to know when this will end. But you must not leave the school, even if you hear that our city is free. You must stay there and wait for me to come get you. This is very important! Please be patient and wait. I will come for you.*

*Kisses,*
*Maman*

Guy re-folds the paper and slips it back under the ribbon. It cannot be long now. He will do as he has been told and will be patient, although he can hardly wait to see his mother and grandmother. And maybe, once they are together again, they will find out about his father and grandfather.

From another side pocket in the suitcase, Guy takes a small piece of wood he has been whittling. When he found the piece under a tree, it looked to him like a bird, so he has been shaping it, a little bit each day. Now he takes his pocketknife and continues to work away at what will be the tail feathers. This will be a present for his mother when she arrives.

## CHAPTER FIVE

# EARLY SEPTEMBER 1944:

# Paris

Impressive what thirty men could accomplish in such a short time, thinks Ben, as he leaves the building and begins to stroll down the Boulevard Montparnasse. The postal station is up and running, letters have gone out, and the military censors have a secure place to work. This is Ben's first day off since arriving in France, and he is tired but pleased.

He smiles to himself as he walks down the broad boulevard. He's actually in Paris! Blue-red-and-white bunting still hangs from many of the apartment windows, a reminder of last week's ecstatic victory parades. Some of the shop windows, also, are decorated with French, American, and British flags. He passes a couple of large cafés where both civilians and Allied military personnel sit at small tables facing the wide sidewalk. He waves to a couple of guys he knows and stops and salutes officers of higher rank.

The streets are still relatively empty of vehicles. A few military trucks pass, but most of the French people who go by are pedaling bicycles. It's not crowded; Paris remains off-limits to American soldiers unless they are stationed in the city. Ben feels like he has the whole world to discover. He notices young women looking at him and smiling; he smiles back and raises his military cap slightly to acknowledge them.

Reaching into his uniform pocket, he fingers the paper, now soft, with a Paris address that Anne had given him in Brooklyn almost three years earlier. This is where he is now heading. He's checked on a map of the city and knows he has about an hour's walk. At the Boulevard Saint-Michel, he turns left and heads north, passing the Jardin du Luxembourg, where he hears bursts of laughter from children on the other side of the hedges. And so he continues, until he comes to the Pont Saint-Michel. Ben is tempted to stop and explore the Latin Quarter because he has read about it. But he has given his word that this would be his first errand.

However, he allows himself the luxury of standing at the railing of the bridge for a few moments, taking in the view of the gray-blue Seine, the gray towers of Notre-Dame rising above the streets and over the protective barricades that had guarded it from the recent shelling. He strolls to the west just far enough to glimpse the Louvre, whose stone façade is illuminated by the first sunny day in a week. Ben knows he is in a city that has suffered, yet he is suddenly flooded with happiness that he is here. If he squints just a little, blocking out evidence of recent fighting in the streets, it's almost like a postcard view. Despite this, the urgency of the day's mission floods back into Ben's mind, and he doubles back to the Pont Saint-Michel.

On the other side of the river, the thoroughfare changes its name to the Boulevard de Sébastopol; it is a wide commercial street lined with trees and shops, some even open. Yet everything is so quiet. Ben reminds himself that it is still before noon on a Saturday. Even a newly free city might like to sleep late.

It is only a couple of inches on the city map, yet it takes Ben a while to reach the Rue de Turbigo, crossing Sébastopol at an angle. Ben glances at the first few buildings to spot numbers on Turbigo, and they are low. So he has a way to go, but he doesn't know if it will be three more blocks or ten. A few lone bicyclists pass. There is no one, really, to ask, so Ben simply keeps walking.

He sees a number of things telling him that this is no ordinary morning, or ordinary place. Broken glass, boarded-up shop windows. Sandbags still stacked on street corners. Holes in the pavement where stones have been ripped out. Walls pockmarked with bullet holes. This is a city, a neighborhood, that has until just recently been under siege. Now it is resting, exhausted.

Ben stops in amazement when he comes to the place where the Rue de Turbigo crosses the Rue Réaumur. He has never seen a decoration like this, even on the most ornate buildings in New York. A white angel, a relief carved directly into the stone façade, stretches its beneficent wings high above the street. The building itself seems to be like others around it, a six-story apartment, but unlike others, this one has an angel more than three stories tall. Ben wonders if this kind of thing is typical in Paris. He'll have to read up in a guidebook—right now he cannot take any extra time to ask questions. But he does consider the irony of an angel, its wings outspread, blessing the intersection as its residents moved about under the eyes of the Wehrmacht and the Gestapo.

I must be in a garment district, thinks Ben, as he passes shops selling notions, fabrics, buttons, and ribbons. Glancing up, he sees signs for *mode* and *chaussures*—fashion and shoes—and wonders if this area is like the West 30s in Manhattan, with buildings housing dozens of small manufacturers. Again, he thinks about the factory where his father worked making leather belts for suits and dresses.

Ben continues northeast along the Rue de Turbigo, a wide, straight boulevard of balconied buildings with small shops and cafés on the street level, and, he assumes from the signs, workshops and apartments above. The gray six- and seven-story buildings on either side match the gray of the streets and sky. Some shops are open, but they are not busy at this hour. Other places are shuttered and look as though they have been closed for some time. A few blocks down on the other side of the street, he spots an imposing structure with a small tower at the center. As he nears it, Ben crosses the street to read the signs. The building turns out to be the Lycée Turgot, but no students linger on the wide sidewalk in front.

Ben pauses in his walk, taking out the slip of paper to double-check the building number. What are the chances that information given to him in 1941 is still accurate in 1944? What if no one is at the address? Things happen in a war. People move to where it is safer. Maybe, like Anne, they decided to leave. Or perhaps something happened to them. How will he track them down? He should have thought of all these things before, he scolds himself. He dreads having to give Anne any bad news.

Suddenly, just past the *lycée*, Been sees the building he seeks. A small apartment house of six stories, like its fellows on either side. A hardware store and a closed hair salon are at the street level; a large double door, presumably leading to the apartments, stands ajar. Ben pulls the door open to see a tiled hallway leading to a staircase curving around a narrow elevator cage. Just then, a woman emerges from an inside door marked *Concierge*. "May I help you?" she asks in French.

"*Bonjour, madame,*" answers Ben as he lifts his military cap. "I am looking for the Daval family, please."

"Third floor, middle door," says the *concierge*.

Ben prefers the winding staircase to the elevator. At the next landing there are several doors, none with any identifying name. He assumes the next landing is only the second floor but doesn't know if the building counts the ground floor as zero or one. No one at the middle door answers his knock. So he goes up one more floor and approaches the middle door. Again, no name. No *mezuzah* on the doorpost—but of course, why advertise one's faith to the occupiers?

Ben raps on the door, at the same time calling out, "*Bonjour*? Madame Daval?"

From within, a hesitant voice: "Non!" Then, in French: "Who is there?"

"*Je suis un soldat américain. J'ai un message de votre cousine à New York.*"

There is silence. Ben wonders if he has the right door. Or perhaps his French was incorrect. He thought he had said, "I'm an American soldier. I have a message from your cousin in New York."

The apartment door opens a crack, and a woman peers out anxiously. The light is behind her and it is hard to see her face. "This cousin," asks the woman nervously in French, "What is her name?"

"Anne."

The woman begins laughing and pulls open the door. "Anne! You saw Anne in Brooklyn? Come in!" Her French is accented, and Ben thinks he can hear eastern Europe. He steps inside the apartment and smiles at the woman. She is certainly older than he is, but whether she is fifty or seventy he cannot tell. She is very pale, thin, with grayish, shapeless clothing draping her frame. Ben wants to explain everything, but he knows he does not have enough French words for this. He decides to try Yiddish—it worked at the post office. So when he next addresses the woman, she beams.

"Oh, you speak so well!" she responds in Yiddish. "Sit, sit, I'll make you some tea!"

The apartment looks small and is sparsely furnished, but seems airy, with three tall windows along one wall that admit milky light from the street.

"My daughter will be home soon. She is Mme. Daval. Her name is Simone. I am Mme. Meransky, Miriam, but everyone calls me Mira. I am sure you can tell from the way I speak French that I come from elsewhere. I was born in Russia, and so was my husband. Paris is . . . Paris was . . . full of people from other places in Europe."

Mira flutters over a pot of boiling water and then pours it into a teapot. "I hope this tea still has some flavor," she says, "It's from before the war."

She places an old flowered teapot and two china cups on the small wooden table and sits across from Ben. He notices that one cup has a small crack running down its side.

"You must tell me everything," she says, "How you met Anne. Where is she living? What does she do? When did you last see her?"

Ben wants to explain and tell about the post office, and how Anne had come in soon after arriving in New York and could barely speak English. But he has hardly spoken when Mira begins to weep.

"So many people came here . . . but I don't know, I don't know," she murmurs.

Ben has no idea what to say. He has brought news that at first seemed welcome. Something is not right. He reaches across and hesitantly touches the back of the older woman's hand. "*Madame*? Mira? I don't understand. What don't you know?"

She looks up at him, and her eyes are wet. When she speaks, her voice quavers. "I don't know where anyone is. I know where my daughter is—she went out to see what she could find in the food shops. I know where my grandson is—he is safe, at a school up in the mountains. But everyone else?"

"I . . . I don't know what to say," stammers Ben. "You need to tell me some more, please."

Mira dabs at her eyes with a handkerchief that she takes from her apron pocket. "I am sorry, I did not plan to sit here crying," she says. It's obvious to Ben that she is overwhelmed. "It's just . . . you are an American, here, and you turn out to be a *landsman* . . . such a miracle."

Ben nods sympathetically, but he still doesn't understand exactly what's going on. He decides to wait until Mira says something else to reply.

"My husband, and Simone's, where are they? My neighbors—most of them are gone. I went for a little walk yesterday—this is my old neighborhood, but I didn't see one familiar face. Not one. The buildings are here—but it's so different, and I am frightened!"

Again, Ben feels unprepared and awkward. People seem to be missing, but he has no idea of what has happened. He is part of a liberating army, but the army seems to have had little knowledge of the condition of the liberated people. What had life been like for them under German control? He has seen propaganda films, he has read things reported in the papers. He is aware of rationing and a vague sense of fear—but in generalities, not specifics. Their CO had told the men: "The French will be happy to see you—remember that they were under the fist of the Nazis for four years. Be kind, be polite, and remember that your uniform stands for the United States of America. All that you do and say represents our country and our people."

What exactly had "under the fist" really meant?

"Forgive me," says Mira, dabbing at her eyes. "I haven't had anyone to talk to—other than Simone, and sometimes Guy—for, what, three years now? We only returned to this apartment two days ago. I am very confused."

"It's all right," says Ben, in what he hopes is a comforting tone, "Take your time." He is confused as well. Family members have disappeared. Simone and Mira have apparently been living elsewhere. He doesn't know who Guy is. But Mira obviously wants to talk, so he just nods and says, "Just tell me when you are ready."

Mira is quiet for a few moments, then begins again.

"I came here, to Paris, from Russia with my parents and brother, many years ago. Years before the Revolution, of course. Russia was a bad place for the Jews—rich, poor, it didn't matter when a pogrom came. If you were Jewish, they would kill you."

"This is exactly what I heard from my parents, too," agrees Ben, eager to latch on to something he actually knows about. "Russia, Poland . . . it was all bad for the Jews. I think that's where most Jewish immigrants to the States came from."

Mira continues, "My father said we'd be safer in France, even with the Dreyfus case so recent. So we left."

The name Dreyfus sounds familiar to Ben, and he scrambles through his memory. But at New Utrecht High School, history had not been one of his best subjects. He'll have to look up 'Dreyfus' later.

"Now Anne, who you know," adds Mira, "She is the daughter of my older brother. He moved to Marseille but died when Anne was still young. Anyway, growing up, we were very poor. Our father was a tailor. A very skilled tailor, like Sam and Yakov."

"Mira, excuse me—who are Sam and Yakov?"

"Of course—if Anne did not tell you, you don't know. Sam is my husband and Yakov is my son-in-law, Simone's husband. But he wants to be called Jacques. He wants to be French, although he comes from Poland, same as Sam."

"But the name—Daval sounds French."

She smiles, though Ben thinks he sees a certain sadness in her expression. "Yes, it does. That was not Yakov's name originally. It was Davidov.

I am sure in America, people change their names, too?"

Ben laughs, "Exactly right! My father did this, too—many years ago."

"What was it before?"

"I'm not exactly sure—Gorodetzky, something like that. He said no one could spell it, they got it wrong at Ellis Island, and anyway he just wanted to be more American."

Mira nods in understanding.

"The same reason Jacques came up with Daval," she continues. "It sounds nice, no? Very French. But Yakov—Jacques—he was always working and never got around to making this new name legal. And then the Germans made it illegal for us to change names. I wonder what name Jacques gave them when he registered."

Registered for what? Ben feels agitated and uncomfortable and has even more questions now but needs to wait. He hears a key turning in the lock.

## CHAPTER SIX

# Simone

The apartment door opens to reveal a younger woman, who rushes in to embrace Mira so quickly that Ben can hardly see her.

"Simone, a big surprise—this is an American soldier who knows our Anne!"

For a brief moment Ben is motionless. Simone, too, startles at these words from her mother, clearly taken aback by this unexpected visitor. As she turns to greet him, Ben sees a trim, strong-looking young woman with masses of beautiful dark hair piled on top of her head. A few strands have worked loose and trail down over her ears.

"And Ben, this is my daughter, Simone!"

Ben quickly remembers his manners and steps forward, trying to speak his best French, immediately reassuring her: "Don't worry, my French is weak, but I also speak Yiddish well!"

Simone sets her tan cloth bag on the dining room table, sits, and, exhausted by the heat, wipes her forehead with a kerchief she draws from her pocket. She still does not seem completely relaxed to Ben, however. Her pale printed dress is clean but worn-looking, as though it has been washed many, many times. Ben notices that it also seems a bit large for her frame. She is thin, too—but it is not the *chic* Paris thin he has heard about; it is the look of undernourishment. Both women, he realizes, have probably lost weight because of the food rationing. He knows about that. That was another thing their CO had told them; he instructed the soldiers not to eat too much if grateful civilians offered them anything, as it might be all they had to eat for the moment.

Simone stares blankly at Ben for a moment, then regains her composure. "It is good to meet you. Forgive me, for a second I wondered, 'why is this soldier in our home?' and then I heard what Maman was saying. Your name is Ben?"

"Yes, Ben Gordon, from Brooklyn, New York."

"Please, children, sit and talk," says Mira. "I'll make more tea."

Simone and Ben sit on opposite sides of the table, and Simone says, "I'm sorry—I was just a bit startled. I know the American uniform—we see you all around the city—but to see one in our apartment!" She speaks with some hesitation, like someone who has just been roused from sleep.

"Don't worry about it," says Ben, as he shifts slightly in his seat.

Simone continues, "Ben, I'm sure you have already told Maman how you know Anne. But do you mind repeating the story to me?"

So Ben tells the story, about meeting Anne in the post office and learning that she was from France, that she had, in fact, arrived in New York just a year before the Germans invaded Paris.

"I decided to practice my French from high school," says Ben. "I was pretty rusty. Anne lives near the post office, and we got to talking when she would come in. She was living with friends of her mother's family. She told me her father's sister and family lived in Paris—so that would be you, Mira?"

"That's right," Mira responds. "Anne is my niece, but unfortunately I haven't seen her since about 1935. She was lucky, though. She got out of France in time. She told you about us?"

"Not at first. We spoke a few times—she said she would make me practice a little French each time she came to the post office. After the invasion, she was very worried. She told me she received a letter from you—but it had been opened and then re-sealed."

Simone comments, "They must have spied on all the mail going outside France."

"I bet they spied on all letters, even the ones sent inside France," Ben continues. "Then right after Pearl Harbor, Anne came in to see if I was going to join up. When I said, yes of course, she asked if I would look for you in Paris and check on you. So here I am—but it has taken me almost three years since she gave me this note!"

"You're here; that's what matters," says Mira, patting Ben's arm. "And you know someone from our family—it's such a blessing."

Ben nods, but his brow is deeply furrowed. "Could've been sooner if the US had just done something earlier, gotten into the fight. But a lot of Americans just didn't want to be involved in Europe's war. Of course, that all changed when the Japs bombed us."

There is a long silence. They are all thinking about what might have happened differently. Ben looks at Simone; she is biting her lower lip. He imagines this has to do with the missing men and does not wish to ask too much yet.

Finally, Mira speaks. "So tell us, how did she look, Anne?"

He smiles with the memory, relieved to say something upbeat. "Oh, she's a cute kid—well, not a kid, a young woman. She always looked smart, with a scarf or colorful beads! She told me she had a job in trimmings—you know, buttons and lace and ribbons, that they would sell to the dress houses."

"Dress houses?" asks Mira.

"Places where they made dresses and skirts. Fashion, you know. Her company is in the garment district."

Mira and Simone both laugh a little. "Even across the ocean," says Simone, with a smile, "We Jews work in the garment business! My husband and father are both very good tailors."

"So your mother was telling me."

Simone still looks a bit puzzled. "Ben, you were born in America?" When he nods, she continues, "Then how come you speak Yiddish so *well?*"

"It's funny, really. Just like I told your mother, even though I was born in America," he says with a smile, "Yiddish is my first language. It's all I heard at home and around the neighborhood. I didn't even know English until I started grade school. All the Jewish kids I knew spoke at least some Yiddish, because all our parents came from Europe."

"When did your parents go to America?" Simone asks.

"Around 1900, I guess. Probably about the same time your family came to France, Mira. Same thing—anti-Semitism. In Austria, where my mother's family comes from, it wasn't as bad as it was in Poland, where my father came from, but still, America was the 'promised land.'"

"In some places it was very dangerous for Jews," adds Mira. "Many people left Russia, Poland, other places. I was a young woman when my parents came to Paris. They must have thought about America—maybe they didn't have the money to get there. Or maybe they felt Paris was safe enough."

"Well, it was . . . for a while," muses her daughter, who nervously rubs one hand with the other.

Ben glances down at Simone's hands—they are unadorned except for a slim gold wedding band. He notices that her nails are clean, straight, and unpolished—but her hands seem rough and chapped, the hands of a working woman. He also notices that when she isn't clasping her hands, they shake slightly.

They are all quiet.

Ben is uncomfortable—something is waiting to be said.

"So then," he says, "*Are* you well? I know things have been difficult here. Anne said she has an uncle . . . and there is a child." He speaks hesitantly.

Mira and Simone shift uncomfortably in their chairs.

"We two are all right, thank God," says Mira, shifting her eyes downward, "But the others . . . we don't know."

"Guy is safe," says Simone as she clasps her mother's hand. She turns to face Ben. "He is my son. He is away at a school in the mountains, many miles from Paris. He is twelve. But my husband, Jacques, and my father . . . "

Mira's voice has gone almost dry, and she whispers, "They were deported."

"Maman, we don't have to whisper anymore!"

"Deported to where?" asks Ben.

"We have no idea," Mira continues with some effort, "Although we have heard stories. Rumors. Work camps, some people said. First, Yakov and Samuel went to the local police station, as they were instructed. Then the police sent them to a detention point."

"It was just outside Paris, a place called Drancy," adds Simone. "It's not too far. I went there, to look for Jacques and Papa. But the guards wouldn't let me in."

"When did this happen?" asks Ben.

"1942, in the autumn," whispers Mira. "It was when they started rounding up people."

"No, Maman," says Simone gently. "1942 was when Jacques and Papa left Drancy, remember? The police started arresting people the autumn before that."

The older woman nods, "Yes, yes, you're right."

"And then, after a while, I stopped going," continues Simone, glancing over at her mother. "There was no new information. Ben, this is hard for Maman and me. At the beginning, it was all we talked about. This, and how to protect Guy."

Mira covers her eyes with her hands, bending forward in despair: "If we had known, we would have said nothing . . . part of this is our fault!"

"Maman, stop! We've been over and over this. How could we have known? Jacques and Papa felt it was safer to cooperate with the police."

"Please," Ben steps in. "I'm sorry. You are upset. We can talk about other things, or I can come back another time. I want to know things, but I am bringing back bad memories."

"No, you need to know this, if your army has not told you," responds Simone, "And seeing you is a wonderful surprise. We just . . . it is hard to sit and talk, just *talk* to someone. You cannot understand right now. For years we have hardly spoken to anyone. You don't know whom to trust. So you trust almost no one."

Mira adds, "And Simone was the *only* one I talked to. She could speak with the people at the factory—well, she could have a conversation. She didn't trust them, either. But all day when she was there, I had to stay inside and be silent. People might be listening."

"Perhaps another time," says Simone, looking purposefully at Ben as Mira begins to tear up again. "Come to see us again soon! We will be more prepared. This is . . . a bit of a shock to us. We have felt so alone."

They all rise, and Mira is the first one to hug Ben. "Thank you, thank you, for coming to see us. Our very own American!" She kisses him in the French manner, lightly on both cheeks.

"I can come back tomorrow afternoon, if you like," says Ben, and Simone kisses him the same way her mother did. As she leans forward, her hair brushes his face, and he catches the faint scent of lemons.

Now, as Ben walks back down the Rue de Turbigo toward the center of the city, he tries to absorb what he has just seen and heard. He realizes just how little he understood about what to expect in Paris. The American troops knew they would meet a population that had been under oppressive rule for four years—but, according to what they were told, the French had been resilient.

Although he knows about the rationing, Ben now has a better idea of just how little food Mira and Simone have. Simone's bag, he observed as she unpacked it, had contained only a bunch of carrots, a few beans, two potatoes, and some tired greens. "Now that the locusts have gone," Simone had said to her mother, "There will be more food coming to the markets. But it won't happen overnight."

As he walks back, Ben notices the neighborhood picking itself up. An older man in a long blue apron sweeps the broad sidewalk in front of some shops. Pieces of broken masonry lie everywhere, chipped off by flying bullets. Workmen wearing thick gloves are pulling shards of broken glass out of window frames and dumping them in a wheelbarrow.

Three young women—maybe even older teens—are walking in his direction, laughing to each other. They are wearing bright cotton dresses; he can hear their giggling before they cross his path. As they do, one calls out, "Ooh, American soldier!" Ben smiles back at them, tipping his cap. They giggle and look away. They are so young and happy, Ben thinks, and if their families are intact, they will be all right.

Ben looks at his watch—almost 18:00. Suddenly he feels completely exhausted and hungry. He needs to sit quietly and think for a bit before he goes back to the Gare Montparnasse. A café just past the giant angel stands open, and Ben drops into an outside seat. It has gotten very warm. He pulls off his army cap and sets it on the small marble table in front of him. A middle-aged waiter, white apron tied smartly over his trousers, approaches quickly.

"Welcome, sir! May I help you?"

"*Merci, m'sieur*," Ben responds. "I speak a little French. *S'il vous plait, un verre de vin blanc?*"

The waiter smiles and returns quickly with Ben's glass of white wine. He sits and sips slowly, thinking about how long it will take Paris to clean up, rebuild, and move on. From what he has seen, the bomb destruction has been nothing like that he saw in London, especially the eastern part, where entire streets of residential neighborhoods had been obliterated. Even so, from what he read in the American newspapers, he knows that the Germans bombed many areas in France before they actually invaded. He also knows that Allied bombing raids have targeted industrial plants on the outskirts of Paris. Officers have said that the Germans turned local industry into their own war machine. Paris has taken a real beating.

Ben sees damage and destruction here in the center of the city, some from bombing and some, he presumes, from the intense battles that preceded the Liberation. He assumes it's probably worse in other areas. Sometimes, he is glad not to be part of anything larger—all he has to do is help the military mail run smoothly.

Yet he really cannot think like that. He knows he has a vital part to play and is more than just a small cog in a big machine. How was the city of Paris going to begin feeding all of its residents again? He knows there are still lines in front of shops, and grocery stores and bakeries he passed along the way this morning were only partially stocked. Until farmers have enough to bring to market, and until they have the gas to transport their produce, things will move slowly. What can he possibly do?

All of Paris isn't your problem, Ben, he tells himself. But Mira and Simone, maybe you can help them a bit. He thinks of all their problems: living on inadequate rations, not knowing the whereabouts of Sam and Yakov, assuming but not knowing that the boy is all right. And why did Mira say she had to be silent all day long? He suddenly remembers the young Jewish woman at the Gare Montparnasse post office, who said many people had to live in hiding. He is in the dark himself, about so many things.

Ben finishes his wine and leaves some coins on the table. He heads back toward the Rue de Sébastopol and decides to make a detour for the PX.

Suddenly he realizes he hasn't thought about Sylvia all day. He really needs to write to her tonight, tell her what he has seen in France. Then he looks again at his watch and knows he needs to step up his pace. By the time he arrives at the PX, it is almost closing. "What can I get you, Corporal?" asks the soldier at the makeshift desk, noting Ben's stripes. "Not that we have much left."

"Well, what do you have? Any coffee? Cans of anything?"

"Okay, let's see . . . I got a coupla cans of coffee. Some boxes of soap flakes. Juicy Fruit. Life Savers. Hey—there are two cans of tomato soup. Not much here, buddy, till we get re-supplied."

"How much can I have?"

Ben ends up with a small box containing soap, two cans of coffee, the tomato soup, some gum and Life Savers, and then adds a few Hershey bars. Kids always like Hershey bars. When he gets back to the post office, he goes up the stairs to the guys' quarters and stashes the box under his bed.

"Where ya been, Gordon?"

Rizzolo and Thornton are at the other end of the room, polishing their shoes before going out. Soldiers are under orders to look smart when moving among civilians.

"I went to find a family for someone I know back home."

"Find them?"

"Some of them. They've had a tough time. They survived—but they have nothing! I mean nothing—not even enough food. I got them a few things at the PX."

"From what I hear, Jerry ate his way and robbed his way through this city."

Rizzolo chuckles, "And from what I hear, you can now buy anything you want in Paris."

"Hey, Gordon, come with us? We're going over to Rainbow Corner and then, I dunno, see what Paris has on offer. Come on!"

"Thanks, guys, but I'm beat. I think I just want to write a couple of letters and then go to sleep."

The other soldiers stroll over to where Ben is sitting. "You have to be kidding, Gordon!" says Thornton. "It's Saturday *night*, pal, and you're in Paris, France!"

"Rest later, Gordon! You haven't come all this way just to lie on an army cot!"

"Okay, okay, you're right," Ben agrees. Staying back here with his gloomy thoughts will not solve anything. He might as well go out on the town a little bit with the guys. He washes up, runs a comb through his dark hair, splashes on a little aftershave, and then heads down the stairs with his buddies. He'll write to Sylvia, he promises himself, as soon as he gets back.

## CHAPTER SEVEN

# Gifts

As soon as he is released from his duties the next day, Ben retrieves the box of PX items from under his bed. He decides to save the sweets for Guy and puts them into his locker. Then he takes the box and goes downstairs to see if he can grab a ride from anyone going out on a military errand. He doesn't relish the thought of another long walk up to the Rue de Turbigo with a heavy load.

He is in luck. Bill Thornton has to take a load of supplies to another postal unit out past the Place de la République. Ben hops into the jeep and rides with him almost all the way. Aside from the bicyclists and a few military trucks, there is little traffic. Occasionally they pass a horse-drawn wagon lumbering slowly down a street. The war has sent Paris decades into the past.

When Ben gets out of the jeep near the Temple Métro station, he is right across from Mira and Simone's building. This time when he knocks and calls out "*Bonjour! C'est* Ben!" the older woman has no hesitation in opening the apartment door.

"It's so good to see you again!" she says in Yiddish, welcoming him inside. He notices that she is wearing the same shapeless dress as the day before.

"I wanted to come earlier," he says, putting the box down on a chair, "But I had to do some army work first."

"Ben!" cries Simone, coming from the kitchen, wiping her hands on a towel. "We are going to sit down for a cup of tea soon. Please, join us!"

He remembers what the troops have been told: if you accept hospitality, take very little. The French have been living on tight rations.

"Oh, that reminds me—I've got some treats," he says, opening the box. He tries to sound casual. "I brought a few things you might be able to use. Just some items they had at the PX—that's the army store."

The women exclaim over the tins of soup and the soap, holding up each item as though it were a treasure—which, to them, it is.

Simone squeals, "Look, Maman! Coffee, *real* coffee!"

"Did you have to wait in line long for these?" asks Mira.

Ben shakes his head, "No lines at all. It's from the US military—they let you get this if you are in the forces. Maybe next week there will be other items. I'll see what I can find for you."

"You have no idea what getting a package of food means, Ben," Simone says quietly. "We have not been able to get so many of the things we needed. Coffee? That might mean a two-hour wait in a line, just to learn that the grocer has run out. And many times I couldn't even wait in those queues, because I had to be at work. And, of course, at the other apartment Maman couldn't go because no one knew about her. Life has been so difficult for us, so . . . precarious. And having the rationing to deal with, that just makes it even tougher."

"These things," adds Mira, "They're like gold to us! Thank you!"

Ben frowns. "There's a lot here I don't understand. There was rationing in England, too, but they were dealing with a wartime economy, and people *wanted* to help. But here it seems like a punishment. When the Germans arrived—is that when the rationing started?"

Simone laughs, but not with amusement. "The Germans were superior, of course, so they had superior appetites. They took what they needed . . . bread, cheese, meat, milk, fruits and vegetables. Everything was diverted to them, and we French got what was left."

"In other words," says Ben, "They just took whatever they wanted, right?"

Simone nods. Her voice has a kind of metallic edge to it. "Very smart, the Germans. With rationing, they gained many things. They got to eat and drink only the best. And they made the French people weaker. They made food into a . . . a sort of bargaining tool."

"What do you mean?"

"How would you like some nice, fresh beef? Good steaks. Enough for your whole family. Just tell us which apartments in this building are occupied by Jews."

For the briefest second Ben reacts with stunned silence, then he attempts to speak with some understanding.

"So they used the promise of food to get Parisians to rat on each other? Charming," he says slowly. "I know that in war people suffer. But here it seems like the Germans *purposely* made civilians suffer. There are so many things I simply don't understand. Like why Sam and Yakov—you called him Jacques?—were sent off to that prison, and why you haven't heard from them. And what was the other apartment you mentioned? There—where no one knew about your mother? I am not sure I understand."

Ben looks from Simone to Mira and sees their pained expressions. He realizes he might have said too much, asked too much about many distressful things at once. He feels his face get hot.

"I'm sorry," he murmurs. "I just blurted out all the things that I want to know at once. I don't want to cause you hurt or bring up things you'd rather not discuss."

Mira says sadly, "You are kind even to worry how we feel." She gets up to heat more water for tea.

Simone sighs. "Ben, with many things, you probably have more information than we do. You can get normal news from America and from the BBC, right? Not us. We only got partial news, or information the French government—which ran away—wanted us to have. And after the Germans took over, all the 'news' was censored. I assumed that anything we heard was propaganda."

"We got propaganda, too," responds Ben, "Just from a different source."

Mira returns from the kitchen, and the three of them sit silently at the worn wooden table. Ben absently stirs his tea.

Simone speaks first, beginning with a sigh. "There are so many things you don't know. And we still don't know. But I suppose we have to start somewhere. So we will tell you what it was like when the Germans arrived."

## CHAPTER EIGHT

# The Invasion

"When we heard about Germany attacking Poland," Simone continues, "A lot of people here talked about leaving. We would hear things at the street market, or in the shops. Some did go, like Anne. But we thought, we are French, and if France is attacked, the French army will defend us. The French won the last war, didn't they? We kept hearing about the Maginot Line and how our army was strong."

Mira adds, "What did we know? There were so many rumors. Then we heard that the Germans were preparing to invade France. We did not take it that seriously. But, some said, look what happened to Poland! Still, a lot of French people didn't worry that much about the Germans. They didn't think they could really harm France. And then just before they marched in, there was a panic. People tried to leave Paris any way they could. The streets were jammed."

"And not just the Jews," cries Simone. "Everyone! We heard that the

Germans were out for revenge, because of the last war, and they would kill everyone. As Maman said, there was panic. Complete panic. Even our government leaders fled. People who chose to stay in Paris were left to take care of themselves."

Ben asks, "What happened right around here, in this neighborhood?"

"Oh, here!" responds Simone. "You should have seen the boulevard in front of our building. It was filled with Parisians trying to get out of the city. Everyone tried all at once, it seemed. Cars, trucks, bicycles, people walking carrying luggage, others pushing handcarts or baby carriages. So many left at the same time—everything blocked up. One of our neighbors— Maman, remember Mme. Steinglas?—tried to take a train and came back from the Gare du Nord later that night crying—it was packed, she said, and there weren't enough trains. They had nowhere to go. So they returned to their apartment here."

Mira, nodding sadly, pours the tea she has made into the cups on the table.

"We heard about people with automobiles," she says. "Of course, not any of our neighbors. But some people, rich ones, had cars. They thought they could get on any road leading south, away from Paris. We heard they drove until their petrol ran out. Then they just had to leave their cars at the side of the road, wherever they were, and walk."

"From what we could tell," continues Simone, "No one was in charge. People were frightened."

Mira says quietly, "We watched from in front of our building. The only ones who did not try to run away were those, like us, too poor to leave."

"Maybe some," murmurs Simone, "Were so sure that they would be all right with the Germans in charge. I don't think any Jews felt that way, but some other French people did." She shrugs her shoulders. "They should have known. The Germans are bastards."

Ben listens and tries to imagine the chaos they describe. What if everyone in Brooklyn tried to leave at the same time, and the subways weren't running? Those with cars could drive toward the Midtown Tunnel or the 59th Street Bridge to get into Manhattan, but the traffic jam would be hideous. Any cars that went east to avoid the bridge and tunnel and headed out to Long Island would eventually end up at Montauk Point with nowhere to go. And on foot? Forget it.

"Where would we have gone?" sighs Mira. "We had no money, and my husband was not well."

"Jacques was usually calm, so he tried to be the voice of reason," explains Simone. "He said, 'Look, I have been in Paris for fifteen years. I have a much better life than I could have had in Poland. The French are good to us, no? We work hard, we pay our taxes, I even take a French name. So we don't have the money to run. Why should we run? This is France! *Liberté, égalité, fraternité, non?*'"

Mira adds quietly, "Maybe for some. We were so foolish. We thought it applied to us, too." Simone places her hand on Mira's arm, and the older woman touches her gently.

Mira continues. "There were rumors about what the Germans did in other countries. We heard they had been especially vicious to the Jews. But Poland has *never* been a good place for Jews. Thousands and thousands of our people left Poland over many years, before the Germans even thought of invading it. We agreed with Jacques—we have been here in France for a long time. We like it here. And Simone was born here, she is *really* French!"

Simone takes up the narrative. "So, we stay. The Germans march in. Thousands and thousands, under a big swastika banner they hang from the Arc de Triomphe. Everyone is frightened, but—nothing happens."

"So your lives just . . . continued?" asks Ben, incredulous.

"Yes, at first." Simone nods to Ben meaningfully.

They are all silent for a moment, knowing—in different ways—what is coming.

"They put up their street signs in German, they hung their ugly red-and-black banners everywhere. The Germans came with trucks and tanks and men on horseback. If they wanted to impress the Parisians, they did. They even gave concerts on the streets. Of course, it was all German music."

"I haven't come across any German soldiers yet, not even prisoners," says Ben. "But we've been told they are arrogant and cruel. You must have been terrified."

"We were—but strange to say, the invasion went almost smoothly," Simone continues. "Mostly, it was calm. People here were asking, 'why were we so scared?' This is when I started to hear some Parisians say, 'Oh they play their music so well, they look so handsome.' And someone else says, 'a group of German soldiers came into Galeries Lafayette, and I thought they would be horrid, but they were so polite. Some could even speak decent French!' Some thought being occupied wasn't so bad after all. And many who ran away from Paris, they actually came back."

"And how long did this 'nice' period last?" asks Ben.

"Not too long, a few weeks," answers Simone. "Most people soon realized, the Germans are not tourists. They are an occupying army. And the Germans let us know very quickly who was in charge. At the end of the summer, they put the whole city under a strict curfew."

Simone goes quiet, and Mira pauses to drink a little tea. "We Jews were frightened, of course. We had heard stories about terrible things in Germany and Poland, people being beaten up, forced out of their jobs . . . But here in Paris, yes, many people had been good to us. I have lived in Paris since 1909. Samuel and I have had to work hard, but it had been all right. We felt safe in France."

A slight breeze stirs the thin white curtains at the window.

"However," Simone interjects darkly, "Remember, Maman, things started to change here even before the Germans came. In the thirties. Jobs were difficult to find. All the people coming in, that made it harder."

Of course, Ben thinks to himself. The Depression. It wasn't just in the States, and it was only a few years ago. My father picked a really bad time to die. Ben's plan to work part-time while staying at Brooklyn College crumbled when he had to become the chief breadwinner. He tries to imagine what it had been like for the Davals, and asks, "And Jacques, he was one of those people, right? An immigrant who came to Paris and got a job. Did he feel, well, resented at work?"

Simone laughs a little, "No, of course not! Because he worked right here"—she gestures toward another part of the apartment—"He had a workshop in this flat. He was a very skilled tailor! He made the trousers for a suit manufacturer a few streets away. A lot of the things he made are worn by fine gentlemen in the 16th, I am sure. A lot of Polish and Russian people work to make clothes."

Ben can't help but laugh, "Just like in New York!"

"And nobody minds it," adds Mira, "Except once in a while you hear things."

"Such as what, Mira?"

"I would hear in other parts of Paris: 'There are so many foreigners here,' or 'Have you noticed all the Jews moving into this neighborhood?' 'If they want to be French, then why don't they learn to *speak* French?' That sort of thing."

"Gosh, it's *exactly* like in the States!" Ben exclaims. "The time when my parents came to America, and my friends' parents, there were big waves of immigrants. But America is different—we are expected to be a melting pot. Still and all, some Americans were nervous. And some are, unfortunately, bigots. So our government set up quotas."

"What do you mean?" asks Mira.

"There was a limit from each country."

"So the great melting pot wasn't so happy to see all those immigrants, right?" Simone's smirk tells Ben she is aware of American xenophobia.

Mira continues. "Aside from the humiliation of being invaded, it did not seem so awful at first. The Germans told us that France would be run by the French, but from Vichy. People thought this was a good sign. Pétain would lead this government, and everyone loves Pétain. He is our hero from the last war. That war, France won—but the price was so, so high."

"Families are still suffering," adds Simone.

Her mother agrees: "Do you know, many soldiers are still missing? Their families don't know where they are. No one knows. Probably buried in the mud of the trenches. That is part of why France did not want another war."

Ben nods. This makes sense.

"So the Germans tried to lull the French into acceptance," says Simone quietly, "And it worked at first. Then after the rationing and the curfew"—her voice rises in volume— "the fist comes down." Her own fist pounded hard on the table. "They took away French citizenship from Jews who came here from other places. Only the Jews. Polish Catholics were fine, Italian Catholics fine. Just the Jews. As it turned out, however, this didn't affect us directly."

"Why not?" asks Ben.

"Jacques never actually filled in the papers to apply for citizenship. And neither did my father. He always planned to, he said, but never got around to it. So even if he and my parents had become citizens, the Germans would have taken that away. I was born here, in Paris; my citizenship has always been French."

"So *you* were safe, right?" asks Ben.

Simone laughs, but it is bitter. "Are Jews ever safe? Do you feel safe, Ben, at home in America?"

Ben hesitates. He remembers avoiding certain streets on the way home from school in Brooklyn because a gang of kids would run after him and his friends, yelling "Hey kike!" or "Christ-killer!" while throwing stones and garbage. Then he remembers the sign on a restaurant door down at the Jersey Shore when he was four or five; he had just learned to read so he read out loud: "No dogs or Jews." His parents had pulled him away fast. But today, in New York, would Ben be beaten up by the cops and thrown in prison just for being Jewish? No. Had he ever been denied a job because he was Jewish? No—in fact, he had a government job. Still, he decides not to mention those ads in the New York papers for "Christian Only" clerical staff or the friend of Sylvia's who had gotten a job only after starting to wear a small cross she'd bought at Woolworth's.

"I do, Simone. Really, I do. Sure, there are some Americans who don't like Jews—but that's a personal thing, it's not the law."

Simone nods but appears to be losing some patience, "Yes, here also it was not the law. In fact, we had a number of Jews in the government. We had Crémieux in the 1800s. Then we had Léon Blum, Georges Mandel . . . wherever they are, God help them. But some French have made us always feel not *quite* French, even if, like me, we are born here and French is our mother tongue."

"And of course," Mira intones, "The law can change."

Simone nods sadly as her mother continues, "The Germans, they made more rules, just like the Russians with their ukases, their decrees.

Always new rules. New rules, more rules. Special rules, just for the Jews. Jews could not have radios, Jews could not have bicycles, Jews could not have certain jobs, Jewish children could not play in the parks, Jews had to ride in the last car in the Métro."

Finally, Ben finds himself incredulous. "But how could anyone tell, in the Métro, for instance, who was Jewish and who was not?" He tries to imagine this happening in the New York subway—impossible! Only Orthodox Jews, with their distinctive clothing, would even stand out.

"The Paris police would check the riders' identification papers," Simone explains. "They would ask to see your identity card, and registered Jews had a special mark, so they knew. If you were Jewish and not in the last car, they would take you off the train and God knows what would happen. Later, of course, they made things easy for themselves with the stars."

"What stars?" asks Ben.

"That was after we left," says Simone.

Ben is very confused now. He thought the Davals did *not* leave. But now Simone says they did. Jacques and Samuel have been deported, and no one has heard from them. And they are saying that the Paris police would check out people—he thought it would be the Nazis.

He waits to learn more, but the women appear trapped in their own thoughts.

"We should have known," repeats Mira quietly, "We should have known. All through the thirties, refugees had been coming to Paris. More came as things in other countries got worse. We read the papers and listened to the radio. We heard that man screaming to his followers. But that was *there*."

Ben nods and reaches up to loosen the knot of his army tie. The apartment has begun to feel quite warm.

Simone continues with the story. "Of course, we heard about *Kristallnacht* in Germany, and other things, too. When Poland was attacked, we were thankful that Jacques had come here in '31. But on the other hand, we worried about his family back there—we used to get letters from his parents or his sister, but after '39, nothing."

Ben understands that "nothing" meant so much. His mother had heard "nothing" more from her cousin Meir or anyone else in his family. Maybe they had found another American sponsor and gotten out. Or not. Ben had never heard this discussed this at home. But some of his Brooklyn neighbors had also mentioned having relatives in Europe, from whom they used to hear. And then they didn't hear.

"This is all so upsetting, Ben," says Mira heavily, "But in a way it feels good to say these things. We have not been able to talk about . . . about *anything* to anyone for . . . for years."

Ben hastens to reassure her, "Please, go on. You can tell me your story. I really want to know what has happened. We've—that is, soldiers—have been given only the big headlines. We don't know the details. We don't know what happened to actual people. You lived it."

He reaches out and takes Mira's bony hand in his. Her eyes fill with tears.

After a few moments, Mira says, "This is the first we have heard about *anyone* we know. So maybe we can write a message to Anne? Is the post going to America now?"

"Not yet. But I can toss this into an army mailbag."

It is mid-afternoon and they can all feel the day growing warmer now. Simone rises to open the windows a little more, and some faraway sounds— the clatter of dishes, a child's laugh—float through the air. Distant voices drift in—hardly anything is moving, it seems, on the side street below.

Simone rummages through the desk. "There is no paper here—the drawers are empty. They took everything."

"I have a small note pad," offers Ben, "In my pocket." He brings it out, along with a ballpoint pen. "You write it, and tell me the address, and I'll put it in tomorrow's pouch."

The two women lean over the slip of paper on the table and Simone writes. Ben, watching them, is still filled with questions, and now he has even more. He wonders who the "they" are who took their possessions, but he has a good idea. He still doesn't know what Simone meant when she said no one knew about her mother. And he still doesn't know why only Jacques and Samuel were deported. He wants to look into the Davals' kitchen cabinets to see if they have enough to eat. But he also knows the laws of good manners require him to stay where he is. It is so quiet that he can hear the scratching of pen on paper as Simone writes. Another strand of hair has worked loose and just touches her shoulder.

Finally, the note is finished, and Simone passes it to Ben. "When will it get there?"

"Probably in just a few days," he answers, "Now that the Atlantic is safe again."

"Atlantic!" laughs Mira, "That is funny, because Anne lives on Avenue Atlantic!"

"Atlantic Avenue," corrects Ben. "That's a major street in Brooklyn!" He glances down at the address on the corner of the paper. A low number on Atlantic—he knows where this is, right outside Brooklyn Heights, but with much lower rents. "I'll take care of this first thing in the morning."

He stands up to go, sensing that it's time for him to leave. He puts the note in his shirt pocket, which he pats. "You know I keep my promises. First thing tomorrow!"

Mira and Simone hug and kiss him.

"Thank you so much, Ben," says Simone, sounding slightly apologetic. "It is so good to have you here—we . . . we just can't talk any more now."

"Perhaps tomorrow?" asks Mira.

"I have to work until five, but I can come by in the early evening."

For the first time since opening their package, the two women smile, and then Ben is out the door and down the stairs.

## CHAPTER NINE

# A Way Out

That night, Ben does not sleep well. He tosses on his cot, thinking about everything Simone and Mira have told him. Waiting for an invasion but believing that the French army would protect them. The mass panic after people learned their army had surrendered and government leaders had left for the south. The Germans invading, but their evil reputation belied by their early behavior. Then their cruelty revealing itself, bit by bit. He still doesn't understand why Jacques and Samuel were deported but knows he will learn soon. Finally, he falls asleep.

In the morning, as soon as he is dressed and ready for work, Ben takes the note written by Simone and Mira, adds a message of his own, and addresses an envelope to Anne in Brooklyn. He takes it over to the desk of the censor, who looks at it briefly then stamps his approval. Once the envelope is in the next military mailbag going to the States, Ben reports to his work station.

At five in the afternoon he leaves and heads to the Rue de Turbigo.

When he arrives, Simone opens the door, wearing an apron. "Ah, Ben, it is lovely to see you!" She gives him the Parisian greeting, a quick little kiss on each cheek. He thinks this is a charming custom, and knows it's just a custom, but he feels his face grow warm anyway. She heads for the small kitchen, where Mira is adding something to a pot.

"*Bonsoir*, Ben!" she says, offering her kisses now. "We have been making a special soup. And I think it is now ready."

Ben remembers what he's been told.

"Thanks, but I haven't come here to eat! I just want to visit with you."

Mira is insistent. "Please, just try a little! I hope you like turnips!" She ladles out a small portion for him.

Ben has never eaten a turnip. But he thinks the thick soup, served with a hunk of bread, is very good, and he says so.

Mira laughs, "Ah, my secret spices!" They all laugh a bit, dispersing some of the tension they feel.

After they eat, Mira makes tea and Ben asks Simone to continue her story.

"That is kind of you, Ben," she says. "I think it is actually good for Maman and me to talk about these things, because we have kept so much inside for so long. You know, we did not live in this apartment during most of the Occupation. We lived in a small studio, in the 12th arrondissement. That's south and east of here. It's a long story."

Ben wants to say "I'm all ears" but doesn't know how to translate this to Yiddish—and it wouldn't make sense anyway. He imagines a person made up entirely of ears, and simply says in Yiddish, "Please, tell me."

"After the Germans came to Paris, things went on for a while as they always did. The Germans took over the best buildings for their officers. We started seeing German uniforms in the cafés as we walked down the boulevards. All those soldiers had to be fed—and where did their food come from? Stolen from us. But that's another story.

"When the Germans invaded, I had a job in a coat factory, and Jacques worked right here. Maman and Papa had a flat nearby and helped look after Guy when he was small. We had less food than before, and Maman spent many hours in grocery queues, but we could cope. There were many new rules—all aimed at Jews, as Maman told you yesterday. Many Jews lost their jobs, and businesses owned by Jews were taken over. Jacques continued to make his trousers—but the suit company was not owned by M. Silber anymore. It was owned by M. Silber's Christian foreman. The same thing happened at the factory where I worked."

Mira brings the flowered teapot and sets it down on the table along with three cups and saucers.

"One Sunday," Simone continues, "There was a knock at the door and it was my old school friend Hélène Hutin. Like me, she worked in a clothes factory. She is a Catholic, but it is not a problem, we were always great friends, and stayed friends even after she married a policeman and moved away to another town.

"We were all happy to see her—but this was a surprise. It was strange for her to show up without writing first. You know, a lot of Paris is not as modern as New York! We don't have a telephone—we write letters. That's what Hélène usually did before making a trip. She said Jean-Marc—her husband—felt things will get worse. She was worried for us. Hélène could not stay, just asked for a small photo of me, saying she would be back in Paris the next Sunday, to go to church with her mother. I was puzzled by all of this, we all were. Hélène was gone so fast I couldn't even ask her.

"Next Sunday, she returned, very early. And she gave me an identity card for Louise Boissiere—but with my picture. It was made by someone Jean-Marc knew. She begged me never, ever to say where I got it. The card was real, but the actual Louise had died. Hélène said she was about my age, from a farm somewhere. Hélène said, you are Louise now. Guy does not need a card because he is a child.

"Then she looked straight at Jacques and said she was sorry—Jean-Marc could get only one card. Jacques told her not to worry, and we both thanked her. We understood the danger she was in. We both wept—we knew we would not see each other for . . . a long time. Perhaps we'd never see each other again."

Mira strokes the back of Simone's hand. "Later, *kind*, we'll check on her."

"Maman," Simone is crying as she speaks, "If it were not for Hélène, who knows what might have happened to us? Or to Guy? Having that card—it saved us."

Ben decides to break the silence, as he is still trying to work out the timeline. "You mean," he asks, "You lived under German rule for a year, without anything really terrible happening?"

"Yes," responds Simone, "It was not good, but it was not *terrible*. And what did I know? I was a young mother and a seamstress. I just did what I needed to do each week to help us get by." She drops her voice and looks vacantly out the window.

"But then this new decree," Mira intones. "This was different. The French police put up notices saying that all Jewish men in Paris, born outside France, need to register with their local police precinct. Just that, to register."

Ben knows this story will not have a happy ending. Simone's eyes are brimming. But he cannot say or do anything else without interrupting the story.

Simone continues the narrative: "We had a big discussion at the dinner table. I say not to do it—if they don't have information about us, we are safer. Papa says yes, we need to register, because it is not the Germans asking us, it is the French. And the French have usually been decent to the Jews. If we cooperate with the French authorities, it will go better for us than if we ignore the notice and *then* they find out.

"As always, Jacques was the reasonable one. 'Simone will be all right,' he says, 'she speaks French like a native, because she is a native. But Papa and me, all they have to do is ask us to speak and they'll *know* we are immigrants. So what's the point of *not* registering? Come on, Samuel, we'll go together, it shouldn't take long.'"

"Shouldn't take long . . ." echoes Mira, who is weeping by now.

Tears spill down Simone's cheeks. "So the next morning," she says quietly, "They went . . . and we never saw them again."

The room is silent and breathless.

"We thought they would be back soon, at the most a couple of hours. Maybe there was a long line, we didn't know. Guy was asking, 'Where's my *papa?* Where is Gran'père?' My mother was here to stay with him, so I walked the few streets to the police station. There was already a long line. But I could not see my father or Jacques anywhere. They were gone. They had been sent on a bus to Drancy."

"What is Drancy?" asks Ben. "You mentioned it before. Was it a prison?"

Simone nods. "Drancy is a town outside Paris. A lot of workers live out there because rents are lower than in Paris. It's a poor area. I didn't know why people had been sent there.

"So I went there by train the next morning to look for them. I brought food for Jacques and Papa, and also Papa's medicine. I asked where people were sent by the police, and I was sent to this ugly place—plain boxes of buildings and lots of mud. The government was building apartments for workers, but they weren't finished yet. So they put barbed wire all around, and made this into, yes, a kind of prison."

Ben asks, "You mean the Germans, right? When you say 'they?'"

"You would think so. But no," responds Simone. She pauses and stares fiercely at Ben: "It was the *French!* Guarding the gate with guns were many *gendarmes*, French police. There was not a German uniform in sight–these were all *French* policemen doing this!" She clenches and unclenches her fists, and finally bangs one hand on the table.

"So many women!–I recognized a few from this neighborhood. We were all trying to see our husbands, sons, brothers . . . it took a long time just to get to the table at the gate to ask questions. We were not permitted to see anyone. I was frightened but also very angry–I was a French citizen and I had rights!"

Ben sees Simone's anger escalate as she relates this part of the story.

"*Our* policemen! Locking up good people who obey French law! Finally, I got to speak to a police captain. 'My husband and father haven't done anything wrong,' I said. 'Why can't I see them?' He said the police had to obey the directions of the government at Vichy. I said my father needed his medicine. The captain said to put my father's name on the parcel, and he would see that it was delivered. He told me to come back in three days."

"What was wrong with your father?" asks Ben.

"Diabetes. So it was important that he take his daily medication. He would have brought it if he thought he would be kept overnight. I returned three days later, as instructed, and got the same treatment. This time, there were even more women outside the gates. So many rumors were going around in the crowd–the men would be processed and released in a week, the men would be going to a labor camp in Germany, some would be released but not all. We were given no actual information. Was my parcel ever delivered? I don't know."

Simone pauses in her story. She is quiet, and Ben sees that her hands are tightened into fists again, the knuckles almost white. He gets the feeling that they haven't spoken about these events in a long time.

Mira speaks, very quietly. "Ben, time has allowed us to . . . adjust. But sometimes it's like these things happened yesterday."

When Simone is able to speak, she continues. "My mother and I thought we would lose our minds. We felt so powerless. I even went back to see the *gendarmes* at our local police station, to see if they had any information, but of course they were no help. Maman and I needed to be strong for Guy. We told him, 'Try not to worry, Papa and Gran'père are good people and have done nothing wrong. Maybe they will come home soon.' But in our hearts, we were very afraid. It seemed that a lot of men were gone, from our building, from our neighborhood. Women with small children were worse off—where would their income come from? How would they pay rent and buy food?

"At work, I told you, things had already been taken over by a Christian manager. The owner, a Jewish man, disappeared. Now, instead of coats for women, we had to make uniforms for German soldiers. The workers were mostly women, Jewish women. They told us if we did this work, maybe it would help our men—you know that all French soldiers were now prisoners of war?—get home faster. At first, I believed this."

The tea grows cold in the china cups.

"A voice inside me was screaming, 'Get out! Get out!' I had to make a decision, act quickly. I could stay and continue to work in the factory with the possibility of getting my husband and father released. But I didn't believe this promise. Maman was already living here with Guy and me. So I say to her, 'What are we to do—just wait for them to come and arrest us? The police have our names and addresses. They know where immigrant families live. They will come here, looking.' If there was any time to use my new identification papers, this was it. I determined to go to the other side of Paris, where we knew no one, and rent a flat."

"But how did you know where to look?" asks Ben, trying to follow all of this new information.

Simone stares at him. "I *didn't*. I just wanted to find a place for us in a neighborhood where no one knew us, away from here, and where rents might be low."

Mira nods, adding, "But I ask her, 'What if Jacques and Samuel come back here, and we are gone?'"

Ben shakes his head, trying to imagine what it must have been like for Simone and Mira on their own and facing a dangerous situation.

Simone continues, "I told Maman, I could keep checking at Drancy, but we had to think of our safety and of Guy. We must leave—but not in any way that would cause suspicion. This neighborhood, it used to be so friendly, people would chat on the street, exchange news. But now we were all frightened. Who was arrested this week? What happened to the family in Apartment 5? Shops closed. Offices were abandoned. I looked on the streets around here—some people seemed to just keep on with their daily lives. I saw children with their satchels going to school, women waiting in lines in front of the *fromagerie* and the *boucherie*. Maybe they thought, 'If we just cooperate, and don't make a fuss, we'll be all right.' This made me want to scream! I didn't want to think 'maybe.' I didn't want to sit around. I had to pay attention to that voice inside me."

Ben is very uncomfortable listening to Simone's story. It was one thing to read the newspapers about reported conditions in occupied countries, but this is the first time he is hearing about them from the inside. "There wasn't anyone you could turn to?" he asks quietly.

"No. No one." Simone's face is sad, and she looks down. "We were always a close family. We did things together. And even though we'd been in France many years, we didn't know a lot of people. We knew this neighborhood—Ben, you know what it's like to be from an immigrant family! It's easier to be with your own people and speak your own language. Also, we are not *frum*, not very religious, and do not belong to a synagogue. So we know some people, mostly Jewish and a few Christians, but we don't have many very close friends. All the information we had was what we read in the newspapers or heard on the street." She stops, coughs, and looks at Mira. "Oh, Maman, please, can you make us some more tea? My throat is so dry!"

"Before Jacques and your father went to register," asks Ben while Mira is boiling more water, "Were there protests against all the new rules?" He hopes his question isn't insensitive.

"Of course!" Simone frowns and answers immediately. "Mostly students, I think, and communists, who aren't afraid of anyone. They staged protests. We are French—passionate about injustice! Especially young people!"

Mira returns and pours more tea for everyone. Simone takes a couple of tentative sips of hot liquid before resuming.

"You think the Germans cared? Students from some of the *lycées*—they were arrested and beaten by the Germans. That was early. Many people were shot. Oh, there was resistance for sure. And the Germans would punish anyone for breaking their rules. Later, in the new neighborhood, I would sometimes see a V—for *Victoire*—chalked on a wall. I knew that someone risked his life to do that!"

She twists her mouth in an expression of disgust, saying, "But a lot of people, they just kept their heads down."

They all pause for a while. No one breaks the silence. Then Simone resumes:

"This is what I had to do. I left the apartment and walked to the Métro. On the way there I kept telling myself: I am Louise Boissiere. I got out at Porte Dorée, south and east of here, near the Bois de Vincennes, where there is the zoo. I walked around, looking, and thinking of what I would say when anyone asked. My story would be that I was from a village looking for work and a cheap place to live. My husband was in the French army, and I have a little boy named Guy. I told myself that this was my role and planned to act convincing. If I hesitated or acted unsure, people would be suspicious."

Simone pauses to take a sip of tea.

"How did you plan this all so fast?" asks Ben. "You had a whole story concocted."

Simone shrugs, "I don't know . . . I just *did*. I had to act fast. Maman and Guy were depending on me. Later I thought about all the danger. But inside, I knew it would be more dangerous not to go through with this."

Ben nods in agreement, though he notices that her eyes are a bit unfocused, as if she is lost in her story. Deciding any question will disturb her, he remains silent.

"I felt like . . . like a character in a play. I knew that if anyone who looked at my papers suspected they were false, well, that would be the end of me. And my mother and child would never know what happened to me. So while inside I was frightened, I had to act assured. I needed a small flat, and then to find work."

Ben leans forward attentively, waiting for the next part of the story. Obviously, he thinks, the worst did not happen—yet he is still anxious.

"I looked for a small place," Simone continues, "Where we would not attract notice. Furnished, because we would not have anything. I found a small place that was cheap, but the bath was shared with two other flats. That wouldn't do."

"Why?" asks Ben, who immediately realizes the innocence and igno-rance of his question.

"The police were told who was living where, how many. Everyone had to be accounted for. I was the only one with papers. My mother did not exist, do you understand? So we needed total privacy. If she was seen and reported . . . I found a suitable place, a studio. The *concierge* told me a couple had lived there but left very suddenly; I didn't ask why. Everything looked worn in this room, but clean; there was a WC and a tiny kitchen. It was bright and sunny, on the fourth floor, and the window overlooked the street.

"Then I had to get home; the Métro ran erratically and I had to be certain to return before curfew. Curfew was for everyone, not just Jews. I didn't feel safe until I got inside our apartment and bolted the door."

The three of them sit quietly around the table. Full of questions that crackle in his brain, Ben looks from the younger woman to the older. How had all three of them lived for years in a small, one-room apartment? How had Mira managed without papers? And the chief mystery—what happened to Jacques and Samuel?

## CHAPTER TEN

# Living In Secret

"There were some close calls," continues Simone, "And we had to be careful all the time. You must have so many questions, Ben. My mother, of course, knows all this."

"It sounds like you took on a lot of worries. And there was no one, besides your friend, who could help?"

"Yes, just as I told you. There was no one we could trust totally. I am sure there were many good people—but at that time, we did not know who they were. For instance, the *concierge* of this very building."

"The young woman downstairs?" asks Ben.

"No. An older one. She is not here now. Anyway, when I returned that evening, back in 1941, I had to explain to Guy. Maman already knew what I was planning. I knew we must leave in case the police come back. I was sure they would, eventually. But I also knew if we left this apartment with suit-cases, as though we were moving or trying to escape, *someone* would report us. So we took small bags only, and if anyone asked, we'd say we were going to visit friends in Créteil. Of course, Ben, we had no friends in Créteil.

"I told Maman and Guy—let me do all the talking. Maman's accent would betray her. She could point at her neck and I'd say she had a sore throat. Guy, he was just eight then, and he was small. He could just act shy. Maman put some clothes into the large knitting bag she always keeps with her. We both wore extra clothing—no one would notice that two women seemed bundled up in November. But these would be the only clothes we had! Guy packed up his school satchel. He took his favorite book, some colored pencils, and a soft rabbit. Maman, he must still have that rabbit! I took my purse and my big cloth shopping bag. That's all. We didn't look like we were running away, so no one stopped us. When we got to the Métro, I led the way to a front car."

"Is that why you had to be so quiet, Mira?" asks Ben. "Because of your accent?"

"My accent wasn't the only problem," the older woman explains. Her voice is small, and Ben realizes she might even feel guilty. "Remember, I actually didn't exist. All my papers were back in my own apartment, which I had left to be with Simone and Guy. I had no identification card. Or ration card. Simone had to make her rations for one adult and a child stretch for another adult. I was not even supposed to be in her apartment."

Simone explains, "The police only had the names of Louise Boissiere and her son in this flat. My mother had to be—well, invisible. She is the one who suffered the most. I worried for her health. You see, Maman has a weak heart. She could never see a doctor when we lived secretly. Someone was sure to report us, if not the doctor, then someone he knew, or a nosy neighbor."

Mira speaks quietly. "For almost three years, I did not leave that room. If I were seen in the corridor, someone might report me. During the day, when Simone was at work and Guy was in school, I had to be so, so still.

Silent. If a neighbor heard noise, well, it was risky. So I would read, and knit. And knit. Simone says the *concierge* turned out to be nice, quite friendly, but maybe that is because she thought Simone was a hard-working mother married to an imprisoned soldier."

"Maman is right," adds Simone. "I could never let on to anyone that I was a Jew. Ever. Even if someone confided to me that she was a Jew pretending to be Catholic, I could act sympathetic but never confess anything. It was so tempting—you *want* to reach out and trust someone. But you cannot. And I had to prepare Guy very carefully and gently."

"It must have been the hardest thing," says Ben quietly and thoughtfully, "To teach a child not to tell the truth."

"You are so correct," sighs Simone. "He had already lost his father and his home and his school. I told him we would be safe in our new apartment, and he would go to a new school. But there were important rules to follow. His story would have to be the same as mine. I tried to keep things as simple as possible.

"His name is still Guy, I said to him, but his last name is Boissiere. His mother's name is Louise. His father is Jacques. Where is his father? In the French army. So everyone would know: captured. He was never, ever, *ever* to say that he was Jewish. He was not to speak Yiddish, ever. But he had heard us talk. He was old enough to remember going to *shul* once or twice with his father."

She laughs, "And then he asked me, 'What is Jewish?' You see, I told you we are not *frum!* I said Jewish was the way people pray. It is different from the Catholic way. And I said we would follow the Catholic way. Also, he could never say his *grand-mère* lived with us."

Ben stirs the liquid in his teacup absently. It is so quiet in the apartment that he can hear a woman's voice in the street below.

"It must have been so difficult for him," Ben muses. "Kids are just natural babblers."

"I know," answers Simone. "I started out with just a couple of rules, but the list grew. No wonder he started to become so quiet." She sighs. "There were two more rules: he could never invite any child back to our apartment to play. And he had to be sure, when he went to the bathroom, that no other boy could see him down there. I didn't want Guy to feel ashamed. I just said some boys and men are a little different, there was nothing wrong—but if anyone saw they would ask questions."

Ben nods his understanding. His wonders how much the boy had actually been able to remember. "You asked a lot of Guy. How old was he then?"

"He was eight. A little boy, but old enough to be smart. And he knew, deep down, that everything was different. From the time his father and grandfather disappeared, he was a changed boy. It was like he inhaled the worry and distrust that Maman and I felt."

"That boy is a child but not a child," says Mira softly.

"The first couple of months were not so bad," adds Simone. "I registered Guy at the local *école maternelle*, and he seemed to like it. But he was shy, his teacher said, and slow to make friends. That was probably because of the rules I had given him. I told her, I am sure he is worried about his father. He needs time. There was a church, Saint-Éloi, a few streets away, and we started to go to mass there. I wanted Guy to be comfortable with this, to learn to cross himself. It was more lying—but it was for safety.

"There were jobs available at several small clothing workshops in the area, and I found a place at one just two Métro stops from the apartment. They asked me to make something on a sewing machine, and it was so easy for me. I am really very good at my work! When the foreman asked to see my identity card, I had it ready."

"Wait," asks Ben, "What about your old job? What happened when they saw that you weren't coming anymore?"

"My old job?" Simone laughs, but without any humor. "I simply stopped going. Maybe the manager thought I had been arrested or moved away. Why would he care? Hasn't that happened all over Paris? A lot of people have simply . . . disappeared."

In response to this observation there is only silence.

After a moment Ben asks, "So the three of you managed, in one room, with your working and finding enough food?"

"Yes," Simone answers, "But I was always on the lookout for extra food because of the rationing. I learned to barter—I would mend someone's worn clothing at home, and in return I received a jar of jam. Or I could exchange a little sweater that Maman had knit for a couple of eggs that someone at work had gotten on the *marché noir*." She laughs a bit as she says, "When Parisians were not denouncing each other, they were looking out for each other!"

"And then I would take whatever food Simone brought back," adds Mira, "And transform it into a meal. Turnip stew, barley bread, sometimes a carrot omelette. I needed to be creative!"

"But then—" Simone's voice darkens, "There was something else. I told you I was not able to see Jacques or my father when I went out to Drancy. I tried once again, before we moved. The French guards looked very impatient but said they would check the files. This *gendarme* came back after a few minutes and said, 'They are not here.'

"I tried not to act shocked. I asked, 'What do you mean "not here?"' I was just told they were taken elsewhere, by train. 'But where?' He just shrugged and said, 'Madame, the people here are criminals who have broken the laws. Take my advice, and do not come back looking for anyone.'

And he turned away.

"They are still missing, Jacques and Papa. We have heard rumors about prison camps in Germany, and labor camps where Jews and others are being worked to death. Rumors, of course, but we don't know, so we imagine terrible things. One of the women at work, her husband was a prisoner of war, and she got a postcard from him. But we heard nothing— and of course, if any letters or cards went to our old address, we were not there. Not knowing, not being able to communicate—sometimes Maman and I just wanted to scream!"

Ben wants to say something, anything, helpful. But he has not the remotest idea of what to say. The picture taking shape inside his head, of a grim, hungry Paris where no one could trust anyone else contrasted sharply with those cheery, colorful guidebooks the army had prepared.

Simone's voice commands his attention. "What Hélène said when she came to our apartment back in 1941 was true: things would get worse. Later in the spring, it got much worse. A new rule. A terrible rule, the worst one yet: the stars."

"I think you mentioned stars before?"

"Jews had to wear a yellow star on the left side of their clothing, on their chests like a badge. This was so they could be identified as Jews on the spot. I'm sure you have seen one of these stars?"

Ben shakes his head no.

"By this time the Germans and police had their lists. They knew who was Jewish in the neighborhoods. They knew who should be wearing a star."

"Wait a second," Ben interrupts. "Paris is a big city! How could they know who *all* the Jews were? There must be thousands!"

"I'm sure there are. But think about it, Ben. If some country invaded the US, and wanted to find all the Jews in New York, could they do it?"

Ben is startled and has not anticipated this question. "I suppose," he begins, thinking on the spot, "If they were organized, they would already know the names of all the synagogues and Jewish organizations. They could have sent spies before the invasion to go through the telephone books." Ben pauses for a few moments to think. "And then they could send soldiers to those synagogues on *Shabbos*—they'd find thousands of Jews right away. But they couldn't get to all the *shuls*. And then people would warn the other Jews."

"A good thought," answers Simone, "If everyone had a telephone. And what about people like us, who don't go to a synagogue? Who are not members? How would these people learn what was happening? How would people be warned about the invaders?"

Ben considers this and shakes his head slowly. "I don't know. This makes me think about my own family back in Brooklyn. After my *bar mitzvah*, that was it. My Jewish education stopped, and we hardly ever attended services. I really didn't pay much attention to religious things."

"Like us," Mira chimes in, "We knew we were Jewish, but we really didn't do that many Jewish things. Now, all of a sudden, that was all about us that mattered."

"Ben," asks Simone, "Do you know who in your neighborhood is Jewish?"

"Well, sure—most people probably. But we're not that *frum*. We go to services at Rosh Hashanah and Yom Kippur, mostly.

"So a visitor at Rosh Hashanah would see a lot of regular Jews, correct? More than the usual number?"

Ben thinks he sees where this is going. "I guess so."

"But if the invaders came at a different time, and didn't find that many Jews in the synagogues, they could just check in the nearby neighborhoods, correct? They could look for every door with a *mezuzah,* yes?"

"Sure, but not everyone puts up a *mezuzah.*"

"All right then. So let me ask: could you tell someone who wanted to know, who is Jewish in your apartment building?"

"But I *wouldn't* tell! What's anyone's business?"

"Maybe *you* wouldn't tell, Ben, but someone would. For a certain amount of money for each name? Or more ration cards?"

"No Jew would turn in another Jew!"

Simone gives him a bitter smirk. "You innocent boy. Maybe it hasn't happened a lot, but it has happened. Let me ask you: who knows everyone in your building in Brooklyn?"

"The super."

"What is a 'super?'" asks Simone.

"Oh, sorry—the superintendent—we call him 'the super' for short. He's the guy in charge of taking care of the building, you know, checking on the boilers, tossing out the trash, that sort of thing. It's his responsibility to know who lives in each apartment, how many people there are. For safety reasons. Like your *concierge . . . no!*"

"Oh, yes! If the *concierge* is sympathetic, she can hold back information. She can warn residents. She can hide people in empty apartments, for a while—but she would risk being turned in by a pro-Vichy resident. And if she herself leans to Vichy, or doesn't like Jews, or takes bribes, or just doesn't want trouble—she cooperates. She points out which apartments are rented to Jews, and then the police know exactly where to go."

"Do you think that happened here, in this building?" Ben asks.

"Maybe, maybe not. We're not sure. We went to the new place pretty quickly. I don't know what happened here. I just heard rumors here and there."

"Wait—if you left here, how did you keep this place? After all, you're back now."

"I used to put the rent money in an envelope and give it to the *concierge* each month. Sometimes I had enough for two months' rent. So I would mail it, never with a return address. Once or twice, I would travel here and go up to our apartment, move things around to make it looked lived-in, and leave an envelope in the *concierge's* mailbox. I was just lucky; I never saw her or anyone I knew. I left as fast as I could. It was risky."

Ben nods, "All right, I understand. But go back to where you were telling me about the stars people had to wear."

Simone nods, "Try to understand, Ben. I learned about things only little by little. I read the notices and looked and listened. I don't know how many Jews the police deported. I know they started with foreigners like Jacques and my father. Some people who wore traditional Jewish things like *yarmulkes*, who looked poor, who sounded like foreigners, they must have been easy for the police to spot."

Ben remains quietly listening and wonders if Simone ever gets news about the missing men.

She continues, "But I guess they must have kept going, looking for more people. I learned about this the same way everyone did: by seeing posters on the street. Jews had to wear cloth stars. There were all kinds of rules about how one was supposed to stitch it to an outer garment, how visible it had to be, and so on. To me, this meant the police—or the Germans, because they were the real rulers—were having trouble identifying Jews on sight. So they had to label them. They must have been going after French Jews, too, not just immigrants."

"When did this happen?"

Simone and her mother look at each other and shrug.

"I don't remember. Last year? The year before? It's all a jumble. I just read the signs—they were put up all over. Yet another law against the Jews meant that the noose was getting tighter. Now it wasn't just the Germans who could see the Jews—everyone could."

"But *you* didn't have to wear a star. You were supposed to be a Christian, right?"

"Yes, but I still had to prepare Guy for what he would see. First, I told him that if some children came into school wearing stars, he must not say that he is Jewish, too, and should have a star. He must say nothing about being Jewish. He should just continue the same behavior; if a child is someone he usually plays with, he should continue. But don't talk about the star. In my heart, though, I knew I should get him out of Paris—things were being stepped up, it was getting more dangerous."

"Did you tell your mother all of this?" asks Ben. He can't imagine that Simone would wish to burden Mira with yet another worry, but he is curious.

Simone looks at Mira and smiles weakly. "Not everything, I didn't want her to worry even more. I told her a little bit about work and what I saw on the streets. For instance, at the factory, things went on—with a difference. When the star decree took effect, two women showed up wearing them. One was at the table right next to mine. No one would have guessed she was Jewish—she had blonde hair that she wore in braids. I was as friendly to her as I had always been. But that week she seemed quieter than before. By the middle of the next week, she was gone. Two days later, another girl—no star this time—was at her sewing machine.

"I wrote to Hélène. I—well, 'Louise'—usually wrote to her once every six weeks or so, and she wrote back. We assumed our letters were being checked, so we never wrote anything personal or political. I never mentioned my mother being here, of course, or my husband and father at

Drancy. I just said I wanted to come visit with my boy. Two weeks later, 'Louise' got an answer, saying we could come out on a Sunday."

"Then your problems were over?" asks Ben, although he knows this is not the answer. After all, why is the boy at a school in the mountains if this village had been a good refuge?

Mira shakes her head "no" in his direction.

Simone continues: "I told Guy that we would visit Hélène and her family, but that he would stay longer so he should say good-bye to Gran'mère. They both cried, for they were devoted to each other. Guy was the bright light of her days. And next morning, we went to the train station. Guy had his school satchel all packed. I had my market basket plus some clothes for Guy, pieces of extra fabric I had found at the factory, and money to give to Hélène. She had not asked for it, but I knew feeding an extra person cost a lot, especially a growing child. I knew Hélène would enjoy the fabric and would easily snip and stitch it into things for her family.

"The trip took only an hour, yet it seemed much longer to me because I expected guards to ask for my papers. But they never did.

"Hélène's town, Dreux, was just the way I pictured a French country village—there was a fountain and a well, a few small shops and a café with a blue-and-white striped awning. The tallest point was the clock tower of the church, and it struck the hour just as Hélène came running up. I remember that—such a normal sound! The first thing she said to me was that I had lost weight—I suppose I had noticed the way my dresses fit. But I didn't realize that others could see the difference. The rationing. Hélène said not to worry, that in the country there was more food than in the cities.

"Pierre and Armand, Hélène and Jean-Marc's two little boys, looked healthy and happy, and after a little shy period, Guy was playing with them and their dog. There were hardly any automobiles, of course, and it seemed that the streets were filled with scampering children. The air itself felt lighter in the village."

Simone takes a sip of tea while Ben and Mira listen attentively. Mira has heard this before, Ben realizes, but he is on edge because this is all new to him. The words of the woman in the post office come back to him: *We had to live in hiding.*

"We had a lovely day together," continues Simone, "And then I had to go back so as not be caught on the Paris streets after curfew. I took Guy aside and reminded him of the rules: he would do all the same things as Pierre and Armand. When they went to school, he would go; when they went to church, he would attend. He was never to say he was Jewish. That is when he asked me, 'What does Jewish mean again?' I told him it wasn't important—except that he needed to make sure that no one saw him when he went to the bathroom. I am sure this frightened Guy—but it was to protect him from too many questions.

"That night was so painful. It was the first time I had ever been away from my child, and his first night without me.

"In Paris things went as smoothly as they could. I brought home books from the library, also newspapers. The newspapers were all controlled by the Germans, so we knew it was just propaganda. But it was something to read. When I had a little extra money, I bought wool and Maman knit sweaters for all the boys, and I brought them next time I visited Dreux. I saw Guy several times over the spring and summer.

"Some girls at the factory invited me to go with them to a film on our day off. I felt guilty because every minute I was not at work or doing necessary errands, like waiting in those damn lines for groceries, I felt like I should be with Maman. I was her lifeline. But I also knew keeping too much to myself might make me look suspect. So a couple of times I went, but it was hard for me to enjoy myself."

Ben shakes his head in disbelief. "I just can't imagine how tough it was for you. You had to work and not let your guard down. At home, you had to pretend things were all right so your mother wouldn't be frightened. You had to find enough to eat. And you were so isolated."

"True," Simone answers, "I always felt on guard. Always. But the summer passed. I sewed uniforms for the occupiers, because that was my job. I imagined I was leaving pins in, to stab them. Just the thought spiced up my days! But really, I thought if the war went on for years, Maman and I would just wither.

"At a flea market I found an old record player and some recordings, Beethoven and Mozart, and in the evenings I played them loud enough so she and I could talk to each other. We made sure to speak only in French, in case anyone heard us. Remember, Maman?"

Mira smiles, "It was actually a little bit fun. Dangerous fun, because some neighbor might complain about the noise, but fun. It was our own way of rebelling. But also, things were unpredictable—sometimes we had electricity for lights, and to play records, sometimes not."

"And also," adds Simone, "The streets were so quiet at night. It was weird, Ben! A major city—and nearly silent! There were definitely fewer people in Paris, and this had nothing to do with normal summers, when many leave the city for their annual *vacances*. No, people had left or . . . were taken away. We read about arrests in the newspapers. Sometimes posters were put up on the streets listing 'traitors' who had been arrested or had been executed. If Jews were listed as being arrested, I knew we were still vulnerable. Often Maman and I wondered: why is this so important to them? Isn't there a war going on? Why do they spend time and resources on hunting down Jews?"

Mira speaks up, "The only good thing about these arrests and 'traitors' was that it meant the French were fighting back. I pointed that out to Simone when she reported hearing about this."

"We received little notes from Guy," says Simone, "And read them over and over. He started at the village school with Pierre and Armand and liked the games they played. Sometimes they had a rabbit or chicken for Sunday dinner. He sounded happy. But then in the spring Hélène wrote, asking me to visit. I knew something was wrong."

Again there is silence in the apartment.

"When I arrived, I learned the Germans were now going into the villages, hunting for Résistance members and Jews in hiding. The Germans would be nice at first, said Hélène, but they kept coming back, asking more and more questions. Then they started pressing. The rationing would continue, and still their army expected villagers to provide produce and livestock for them. And they wanted men to volunteer for work service in Germany. I wondered to myself: didn't they deport people to labor camps? Or had they worked everyone to death and now they needed ordinary Frenchmen? Then they said that it was a crime to help or hide a Jew. Anyone found doing this would be punished. The Germans threatened to execute the entire family of anyone sheltering a Jew or a foreign soldier."

Ben is aghast and sits up even straighter. "This is like all the worst propaganda about the 'Huns' that went around during the Great War! They couldn't mean that!"

Simone stares at him. "Oh, they were saying this just to scare the civilians? Well, it worked. Hélène told me she could feel the fear that fell over her neighbors. I thought I would faint. But we could not take a chance, and I couldn't expect her to risk her children's lives. So I brought Guy back to Paris that very evening."

"You never told me all of this!" cries Mira, clutching at Simone's arm.

"Of course I didn't, Maman," responds her daughter, patting her mother's hand. "I knew it would frighten you to know what was happening in Hélène's village. So I just . . . did what I needed to do. I had heard of a school up in the mountains. They didn't ask many questions. If I could pay the tuition, Guy was welcome. I just wanted him to be safe from . . . oh, the atmosphere in Paris was stifling!" She sits back in her chair, drawn and pale.

Mira steps over to her daughter and kisses her forehead. "You are even braver than I thought!"

After a few moments, Mira returns to her seat. "Oh this city!" she exclaims. "Paris used to be such a lovely place, even for people without money." She looks at Simone with a weak smile, and Simone returns her gaze.

"Oh yes, Maman, I remember! When I was a schoolgirl, Paris was a great place. We had fun, we could ride on the Métro, or visit a museum, or go to the bird market near the Hôtel-Dieu. Ben, I am sure you have heard of Paris as a great city, yes?"

Startled, Ben looks up. He has been lost, thinking of squads of Nazi soldiers bursting in on village homes, opening closet doors to look for cowering Jewish children.

"Oh, yes, definitely!" he says. "I used to see posters in the windows of a travel agency, or a book in the library. They call Paris 'the city of light,' don't they? Of course, people like me, we thought of Paris as a place that rich people visit, or writers, poets. It's a place to dream about visiting. Honest, Simone, I never thought I'd get here. It's just a shame that it took a war to get me out of Brooklyn."

Simone looks at Ben sadly. Ben, returning her look, is not sure if she is sorrowful, or just thinks he is ignorant.

"The City of Light! Well, it's dark now," Simone comments, her voice bitter. "Poor Ben, you did have your storybook vision, didn't you? A fantasy for some, a horror story for others. Paris has been a frightening place. It's not like the last big war—of course, I was just a little child then." She looks intently at his face.

Mira, silent, watches them both.

Then Simone asks, suddenly, "Ben, exactly how old are you?"

"Thirty-two. I was born in 1912." He wonders where Simone is taking him in this conversation.

"The same year for me—1912! But I think," she adds gently, looking a bit dejected to his eyes, "That I am older than you."

Ben is not sure if he is being criticized but feels he may be starting to understand. "Well," he starts tentatively, "You are a mother, and had to be responsible for your child after your husband was deported, and you had to work at the same time."

Simone shakes her head. "Many women, I am sure, face the same difficulties in normal life. But if they have the support of a family, or a group, it is a little easier." She looks at him steadily. "Life here has not been normal. Maman and I have been cut off from everyone. We have had only each other for three years."

Ben is suddenly ashamed of himself for all of the times he has complained about life back in Brooklyn to his fellow soldiers.

"Anyway, I took Guy up to the mountains by train and then by bus up to the small village near the school. They didn't ask if we were Jewish. I wouldn't have told the truth anyway. The director met us with his car, since the school is actually some kilometers from the village. He promised me Guy would be safe."

"Have you heard from him?" askes Ben.

"A few times, yes," Simone responds. "He told me how terribly cold they were during the winter but said not to worry because he is having a good time and learning to ski. I guess children find ways to amuse themselves."

Simone rises to take the plates and utensils back to the kitchen. Ben gets up quickly, picks up the remaining dishes and follows her. In the kitchen, she turns back to him, and speaks with her voice lowered: "I assume he is safe. I don't tell my mother everything. I have sent Guy many letters but have only received a couple from him. So I worry."

"Maybe the Germans didn't let all mail go through," he offers.

"Perhaps you are right," she answers quietly, and looks back at him with a smile. "Maybe I do fret too much."

Simone brightens up a little as she and Ben return to the main room. "I am going this weekend to get him. I wrote and told him that he would need to stay a little bit past the time when Paris would be free. I said there would be fighting, and it would be too dangerous. But now I can go!"

"It will do us all good," adds Mira, "To be together again at last! When I see that child, I will be able to breathe!"

"It is a long trip, and Maman needs to rest, so she will stay here."

Ben knows this is his cue to depart. He knows both women must be exhausted, but he wants to leave them with a promise. "Mira, you don't have to be alone here all the time. I'll come this weekend, when I'm off duty. Maybe I'll bring a buddy from New York. We'll take you out!"

"That would be lovely," says Mira. "You are welcome anytime, Ben."

Ben takes his army cap and stands. He feels exhausted and sad from listening to their stories. "Thank you for telling me what you did. I know this is very, very difficult for you."

"What is hard is not knowing," says Mira. "I'll feel better when Simone comes back with Guy. The last three years have felt like twenty."

Ben stops at the apartment door and turns around, saying, "Try not to worry, both of you. I'll stop by on Sunday, Mira, and Simone, I'll see you and Guy soon!"

But as he descends the wide wooden steps to the lobby, Ben doesn't feel enlightened; he feels burdened.

## CHAPTER ELEVEN

# Visiting Mira

en likes waking up a little before the others in the morning, before the rush for the washroom and the frantic minutes of grabbing coffee before having to report for duty. Ben wants to collect his thoughts before facing the day. He fluffs his pillow up a little higher. He can see Davis sitting up on his cot against the far wall, working on a letter in the half-light. He hears a couple of the guys snoring gently.

He can't stop thinking about the Davals and how much fear and uncertainty they have had to deal with. Above all, Simone's courage and strength fill Ben with awe. She doesn't know where her husband or father are, he thinks, or even if they are still alive. She's had to live a double life while moving her child from place to place to protect him. She has had to earn enough money to provide food for three, rent on two apartments, train tickets, and tuition for this school in the mountains. All this without anyone to turn to! He thinks about his own life and how easy he has had it. Even ten years ago, when his father died and Ben had to give up the work he really wanted to do in order to pay off his family's debts, he still never had to scrounge. And he has never lived in fear. Simone, in contrast, had to fight fear, hunger, and danger for several years.

Solly has agreed to go with Ben to visit Mira later in the day. Ben has told Solly everything he knows about the Davals and what they have had to deal with.

"Imagine," Ben said to him, "The only person she has been able to talk to, really talk to, for the last few years is her mother. And I'm sure she hasn't told her everything."

"I hope they get along well!" Solly had commented. Ben was being very serious, and Solly was making one of his jokes, so Ben had pretended not to hear. Instead, he tried to imagine what his own mother would do in the same circumstances. He can't. His mother is a whiner, and Mira is not.

When it's time to leave, Ben and Solly, looking sharp in their dress uniforms, stop at a little flower stand on the Boulevard du Montparnasse. Solly thinks a cheerful bouquet of pink, orange, and yellow blossoms will delight the older woman.

The men have free time until 18:00, so they are in no particular hurry. Ben wants to point out the huge angel he saw the other day. They look into shop windows and smile at the pretty girls sitting in groups at the sidewalk tables in front of cafés. Occasionally an army vehicle passes, but most of the traffic they see has two wheels.

"Bicycling seems to be the preferred method of transportation," observes Solly.

"It's not preferred, it's all there is," says Ben. "You haven't gotten out much, Solly, have you? There is no gas here, well, except for military vehicles. The Germans took it all. People here don't have cars, either. Vehicles have been used for their parts or stolen. Or maybe they are garaged somewhere. So people *have* to use bicycles. Or that." He points to a wagon, pulled by an old horse, lumbering toward them from the direction of the Place de la République.

"Wow, this city has been sent back a hundred years," Solly remarks.

"Yup, and it will take some time to get everything up and running again. At least some of the Métro is working."

They stroll along the wide pavements, trying to stay on the shady side where it is a little cooler, when they hear screams and shouts coming from a side street. They run to the next corner as the sounds grow in volume. Turning left, they see a small crowd surrounding two barefoot and weeping women clutching torn clothing around themselves. The men and women in the crowd hoot and shout; a few in front carry large scissors. Ben sees that the women's hair has been roughly shorn. Just at that moment, two French *gendarmes* and two American military policemen rush up and yell at the crowd. One of the military policemen gives his jacket to the woman whose shirt has been nearly torn off.

"What's happened here?" Solly asks the other American policeman after most of the mob has been chased away.

"A little vigilante justice, it seems," he answers.

Ben nods silently. Still curious, Solly asks for more information. The American tells them about the ruthless reprisals doled out to French civilians, by other civilians, suspected of being too "friendly" with the Germans. He explains that when active collaborators—the ones who actually worked with the Germans—were caught, they were beaten to death. Or simply shot. This is different. Here the women have been accused of "horizontal collaboration," then tried and punished by the mob.

The French policemen bundle the two women into the jeep belonging to the Americans, who then get in and ride off in the direction of the Rue de Turbigo. A couple of men from the crowd spit in their direction and yell something in French. Solly and Ben assume it is obscene.

The men turn back and see the two American soldiers.

"You think, why we do this, hah?" yells one of the men in English. "Whores! That's what they get for sleeping with the *Boches*."

Solly and Ben do not want to get into an argument. They just nod and turn around.

"Maybe they did, and maybe they didn't," says Solly, who is still holding his bouquet.

Ben is quiet for a moment. "I'd like to know what those two guys are doing in Paris. There aren't many male civilians of military age running around."

"Think they do that to every woman who had sex with a German soldier?"

"Maybe, if it wasn't a big secret. Who knows? Maybe those women were just turned over to the mob by someone jealous."

In a few minutes they arrive at the Davals' apartment building, where by now Ben is well known by the *concierge*.

"*Bonjour*, Corporal Gordon!"

"*Bonjour, Giselle, ça va? C'est mon ami, Corporal Lipman.*"

Solly gives Ben a friendly punch on the arm. "Say, you're doing pretty well with your dozen words of French, Ben!"

"And the longer I am here, the more I learn. I'm up to two dozen now!"

They ring Mira's door, and she welcomes them both with the French light kisses on each cheek. Ben introduces Solly, who doffs his military cap, saying, "*Enchanté, madame!*" and proffering the bouquet.

Mira exclaims, "*Merci!*" She immediately looks for a small vase and arranges the flowers artfully.

"Actually," Sol says in Yiddish, "I'm a Brooklyn boy just like Ben, and I speak Yiddish even better than he does!"

They all sit down around the dining table. "It's a beautiful day, Mira," says Ben. "We'd love to take you out, come on! Go out on the town with two American soldier boys!"

They all have a laugh, and Mira agrees to a little walk and then dinner.

"You must be very anxious, with Simone gone," Ben offers.

Mira leans forward a bit. "Yes and no. Of course, I would like to see both Simone and Guy safely back here. But actually, I do not mind this time alone. I do not have the same worries I did earlier, before the Liberation. Then, yes, I was nervous all day, because I was supposed to be, as Simone said, invisible.

"I came alive at the end of the day when Guy would return from school and Simone from work. Then I could move about. Of course, having Guy there was a joy. We helped him with his lessons. It will be exciting to see how much he has grown."

She looks apologetically from Ben to Solly. "I am boring you?"

"No, go ahead, Mira. I have told Solly a little bit, but we also want to hear things from your point of view."

"I never said some of these things to Simone." She pauses and looks down at her hands. "But I was so afraid when she was at work. What if something happened and she didn't come back in the evening? I could not go out to look for her. I was a prisoner in two ways: living in an occupied country, and having to stay in that room. Without papers, it was very risky to go out, too risky. Anyone hearing my accent would know immediately that I was born elsewhere, and soon I would be denounced and arrested.

"I couldn't even look out the window during the day for fear that I would be seen. So I read whatever I could, and I knitted. After Simone told me she could barter knit goods for some food, finally I was at least somewhat content—it gave a purpose to my days. Simone found yarn somewhere, enough for me to make little sweaters and hats for children."

"Did you ever hear any of the other people in that building?" asks Solly.

"Oh, of course," she responds quickly. "But what they were doing, I didn't know. I didn't want to know." She pauses and mimes looking up. "But I could imagine. The little apartment above ours, it also must be small, and I would hear low voices and a bed squeaking on many afternoons.

"But the really frightening noises came at night, from outside. We would hear the footsteps and voices of the German soldiers on patrol. And then sometimes we would hear a car motor. There are very few cars in Paris, so hearing one at night was truly startling. A couple of times, just before dawn, Simone and I would hear a car come to a stop outside a building on our street. We would peek carefully from behind our window curtains, in time to see someone being pushed into the car, which would speed away. A couple of times, very late, we heard boots stomping up the stairs. It wasn't anyone avoiding the curfew—*those* people would tiptoe."

Mira clutches her thin gray sweater a bit tighter around herself.

"Even now, remembering those sounds . . . boots pounding on stairs. I just get chills. We could never be sure if the next sounds would be fists banging on our door. Or other sounds. Mostly, there were no sounds at all. A city at night should have a little noise, at least before midnight. The cafés used to stay open—we'd hear music coming up to our windows. But when the Germans were here: silence. Maybe you might hear a motor in the distance. It could only be Germans, prowling around. I would lie awake at night, listening. If a motor came closer, if it stopped . . . but it didn't, and thank God our Guy slept through it all."

Now Solly leans forward and tries to sound reassuring. "Mira, we are almost there. Allied forces are pushing through. This war will end soon. Things will get back to normal."

She gazes at him sadly with a knowing look that says he can never understand. "It would be nice to think so, Sol. Maybe they will get back to normal for you, and for you, Ben. You will go back to New York and things will be the same. For us, things will never be normal. Never.

"If Paris had simply been invaded by another country, that would be one thing. All French people would have suffered the same. We would be united in our fear, or our anger. But no, there were two enemies: the Germans *and* the French. I cannot forget what Simone told me about Drancy. French uniforms. My own country! If I cannot trust my own country . . ." Her voice trails off.

There is silence in the room, and finally Ben says, "You are correct. We cannot imagine at all what it has been like here. Our own parents came to New York from Russia and Poland—but they *fled* those places. France is our ally, it's supposed to be a good place to live. There's a lot we do not understand."

"It will take a long time to repair all the damage done by the war," adds Solly, "But it will happen. Come, let's go out and you can tell us about this neighborhood, or we can go somewhere else if you would like."

Mira looks down at her sturdy brown leather shoes. "I think these will survive a little travel, don't you?"

"Actually, Mira, compared to a lot of the shoes we've seen Parisians wear," notes Ben, "yours look pretty good!"

Mira laughs. "That's because mine have hardly been used! In the apartment I just wore stockings, heavy ones in the winter. Other people's shoe leather wore out, that's why so many shoes now have wood soles! Simone told me that the cobblers ran out of leather, so they used wood instead."

"Okay, so *that* explains what we've seen!" exclaims Ben.

"We haven't had real coffee either—which is why we treasure the coffee you brought us, Ben. We used leaves, acorns and chicory to create ersatz coffee. We adapted our recipes. And we adapted our clothes as well."

Ben interjects, "It has to be so frustrating—the Germans are gone but there are still shortages, still rationing. But they will end after a while."

"I hope so," Mira responds. "The food situation was actually better during the time Guy lived with the Hutins, our friends in the countryside. They could always manage to find a little extra, and when Simone came back to Paris from a visit, the bottom of her big shopping bag held some fresh carrots or greens from the Hutins' garden, maybe some eggs or rabbit meat. It depended on what was in season. But Simone still had to be careful—she could not afford to be caught with any black market goods, even though apparently everyone got extra food that way."

"Some folks are always going to find a way to get forbidden things," says Ben.

Solly sits up, suddenly remembering something. "My father told me that during Prohibition, he got a flask of whiskey from someone, and he stashed it in a pocket inside his coat. But when he was riding the subway home, something happened—the bottle broke, and everyone on the train could smell the booze. People were looking around. My father had to get off at the next stop and ditch the coat so he wouldn't get arrested!"

Mira nods. "Yes, exactly. German rules for rationing were very strict, yet some people could get around them. But people like us, we had to keep our heads down and just keep going. We managed but were always hungry. Have you noticed that if you look around, most people are very thin?"

"That's true," says Ben, "Really, the only people I've noticed lately on the slightly stout side are some Americans and Brits! Officers, mainly."

"Yes, Parisians are lean these days, and not just the chic fashion models. You want to find the people who 'adjusted' to the wartime economy?" asks Mira. "When we go out, look for those who are not skinny. Either they are rich and could afford black market prices, or they collaborated in some way. The Germans ate well. The Vichy leaders ate well. Not everyone in Paris went hungry."

Mira stands up and reaches for her purse. "You know where I'd like to go? To the Jardin des Tuileries. But that is too far for me right now," she muses a bit sadly. "Let's just go up to the Place de la République and watch Parisians being free!"

"That sounds great!"

"All right then. It will be nice to go there again, and with you!"

Solly holds open the door of the apartment, and Ben lowers his voice to say conspiratorially: "And let's keep our eyes open for the well-fed!"

## CHAPTER TWELVE

# Guy

s soon as his shift ends on Monday, Ben goes to his locker up in the barracks to retrieve the sweets for Guy he had placed there. He adds them to the two tins of condensed milk he has in a small bag. Then he heads down the stairs and out the side door, heading to the Métro stop by the Gare Montparnasse. By this time, he knows the route to the Davals' well.

Mira opens the door to Ben's knock and pulls him inside the apartment. He notices that she is wearing the same worn dress he has seen her in before, but this time a bit of lipstick gives her face some liveliness. "Ben! It is good to see you again!" she cries as she gives him a little kiss on each cheek. He places his bag on the floor.

Simone comes forward with her hands on the shoulders of a boy in front of her. "I want you to meet my son, Guy."

The boy is slight, with light-colored hair combed back from his forehead. His skin has been tanned a bit from being outside so much, and his dark eyes are fixed on Ben. Ben extends his hand. "I have heard a lot about you from your mother and grandmother," he says in French.

Guy is a bit shy and formal as he responds in stilted English, "I am happy to meet you, sir. It is to our honor that you visiting us, sir." He still sounds like a boy, for his voice has not changed yet. After he delivers his little speech, Guy shakes Ben's hand and finally smiles.

Simone laughs. "Guy wants to show you the English he has learned in school."

"I study English for one year!" says Guy proudly.

Although of medium height, Guy seems already to have outgrown his short blue pants. Ben observes that Guy's white shirt is clean and freshly pressed as if for a special occasion. And although he is thin—like the majority of French people Ben has seen—he is not pale like his mother and grandmother. His clothing is worn and drab, but Guy smiles from a face that looks sun-warmed and thriving.

"Do you speak Yiddish?" asks Ben in French.

"He has forgotten almost everything," sighs Mira. "We told him not to speak any Yiddish while he was living with the Christians, and he didn't. He is a good boy, but as a result he has lost his language."

"But I have French!" exclaims Guy. "And now English! Maybe I practice with you, Corporal Ben?"

"Sure thing, kid. And if you want to speak French with your mother and grandmother, don't worry about me! My French is improving, so perhaps I'll understand."

"Ben, how can we be so rude?" Simone speaks up. "We were just about to sit down for a light meal. Please join us!"

"Oh, that reminds me," says Ben quickly, picking up his bag. "I brought you a few more treats."

He hands the tins to Mira and Simone, who exclaim over them and immediately start debating what dish they should make using the condensed milk. "And this is for you, young man," says Ben, reaching into the bag and bringing forth the gum and Hershey bars.

Guy cries, "Sweets!"

"Guy!" chides his mother.

"Oh! Thank you, sir!"

"I know you are excited to have your own treat, Guy, but you must never forget to thank someone who gives you something," Simone reminds him.

"Yes, Maman."

Simone thanks Ben and puts away the tins in the kitchen cabinet. Everyone takes a place at the table, and Simone brings a pot of soup, then returns with another place setting and a loaf of bread. "Just think—one of the neighborhood *boulangeries* will soon get flour from a mill outside the city. It will be wonderful to have good bread again!"

Everyone takes some soup, which has carrots, parsley, a potato, turnips, and cabbage. Mira slices the bread and gives some to each person.

"The bread is a bit dry," says Simone, "But dipping your slice into the soup will moisten it and add to the taste."

Ben does as Simone suggests, and she is right. "This is really good!" He smiles at Simone, and she seems truly happy as she smiles back. Ben looks around at their little group and feels the tentative beginning of contentment. The trio—mother, son, grandmother—together again for the first time in a free Paris. He is glad to be with them.

He asks, "Guy, tell me, what was the school in the mountains like?"

"Oh, it was wonderful even though it was so cold! We all stayed in one room at night to keep warm. Gran'mère knit me woolen socks and Maman sent them, also a sweater. Sometimes I had to wear my sweater to bed and socks too. How is that? Do you understand all I say?"

"I think so, Guy. But may I ask you to speak a little more slowly for me?"

The boy nods in agreement. "When the weather was bad, we stayed inside and had lessons and read stories. My favorite was *White Fang*. Do you know that story?"

"By Jack London? Yes, I read it at school also!"

"When it stopped snowing and the weather was fine, we went out to ski. I learned all about skiing. I am very good at it! Can you ski?"

"No," says Ben. "I have never skied."

"It is so much fun! You should try. And when the snow was gone, we went on hikes and learned the names of wildflowers and trees."

"That explains the healthy color in your face," says Ben.

"What do you mean?"

"Well, your skin is darker than your Maman's or Gran'mère's. It's from being out in the sun, running around. You get a little sunburned being outside. But it's much better than being cooped up inside all the time."

Everyone is quiet, and Ben realizes his mistake. He turns to Mira and Simone and apologizes.

"It's all right, Ben," Mira says, dismissing his concern with a wave of her hand. "What matters is that staying inside kept me alive and protected Simone, and being outside on the mountain kept Guy healthy and strong."

"And it's not like I was outdoors a lot," adds Simone. "Just walking to the Métro and back."

"Sorry, I wasn't thinking," adds Ben.

There is a pause and Ben seems to be searching for something to ask, something that will bring up happy memories and not bitter ones. He knows that Guy is listening, and even though the boy has forgotten much Yiddish, perhaps he might understand some words.

"So you lived in another part of Paris, right?" begins Ben. "How did you know when you could come back here—when it would be safe to do this?"

Simone sighs, puts down her spoon and napkin on the table, and sits back. "We knew that something was going to happen, but not exactly when. It was just a feeling at first, but by early this summer we started to hear things. Then we observed. There were fewer German soldiers on patrol in our neighborhood, and the ones we saw seemed older. What had happened to the younger men? Where had they been sent?"

"Simone and I could only guess," adds Mira. "Of course, we couldn't believe anything that we read in the newspapers she brought home. If there was an article about another great German victory, we really paid no attention. We had no radio, so really, we knew nothing."

Simone adds, "But one of the other women at work said she had heard on a neighbor's radio that the Allies would be coming soon. Of course, I just listened and nodded. First of all, maybe it was just a rumor. Second, how did I know she wasn't a planted collaborator? Though why the Germans would plant someone in a clothing factory was beyond me. She may have been hiding an escaped RAF pilot in her apartment for all I know. We heard about such things. But I could never become involved because I could not afford to stand out. I just kept sewing."

"But didn't you hear the guns, the bombs, as the fighting came closer to Paris?" asks Ben.

"Yes, of course," responds Simone, "*Eventually* we could hear all this. At first it seemed like a distant rumbling, thunder perhaps—but then it continued, for days, growing louder. Many people tried to leave Paris, to go a little further south, to be safe from fighting."

"Are you talking about storms?" asks Guy. "We had thunderstorms in the mountains!"

Mira laughs, "No, *yingele,* we are talking about a different kind of storm. We'll explain to you later."

Adds Mira, "If we thought we were going to be rescued by American or English soldiers rushing in by the thousands, well, we were soon disappointed. The sound of guns continued for many weeks! But no one seemed to be coming to Paris."

Simone continues, "We wanted the Allies to roll into Paris and drive out the Germans. We knew we would be in danger"—she looks over at Mira, who nods in agreement—"because there are always civilian casualties in a city. But we were still eager for an invasion. On the streets, I could feel the tension. The Germans kept threatening to kill civilian hostages. I could ask no questions or even look too curious. But I knew something was happening."

Ben has been listening carefully. "You must have been full of hope as well as tremendously afraid," he says.

"Yes, exactly," agrees Simone. "We had no idea how things would go. So I wrote to Guy and told him, you stay at the school until I come for you. Even if other students go home, please stay there and wait for me. I knew that even if most of the Germans left Paris, some would stay and fight. The city wouldn't be safe for Guy until all the violence ended."

Guy, hearing his name, looks up, but the rapid Yiddish is moving too fast for him.

Ben nods. "And there was indeed fighting in Paris—we heard that it was incredibly fierce. Ferocious. There were barricades in the streets, lots of sniper action. I didn't see any of it, of course—my unit came in afterwards."

"I wish I could have had a chance to fight, too," says Simone. "I would have loved to shoot some Germans for what they did to us. But I had other duties, for instance staying alive." She smiles weakly, but it is not a smile of amusement. "At any rate, after the fighting did end and it was safe to return to this neighborhood, that's what Maman and I did. I remember when we came out of the Métro at République. There was the statue of Marianne, same as ever, and I thought, you have survived, and we with you!"

Simone pauses to rest and remember. They hear the jingling of a bicycle bell from the street.

Mira continues the narrative. "We came to our building—you can see that we are not far from the Place de la République. The door downstairs was open, the tiled floor was the same. The names were off the directory, though. When we approached our old apartment, we heard noise inside, and knocked. Someone came to the door and asked—in French—what we wanted. What we wanted! Our apartment!"

"'We live here!' I said. 'This is our place!'" Simone continues angrily. "And this man opens the door a crack and says, 'Oh no, this apartment was abandoned, so it's ours now.' And he slams the door. So what do I do? I went to look for the *concierge*, surely she would remember me, that I had been paying rent. But she was gone. So—I went to the prefecture of police."

Ben is startled. "You mean the same police who . . ."

"I had no choice, there was no one else to help us! Where would we have slept that night—on the street? So yes, exactly! The same police who took away Jacques and Papa three years ago. Perhaps not the same exact men, although I think some were. I just tried not to think that this was the place where our troubles started, where Jacques and Papa went to 'register.' But now I needed the police to help me. So I showed them—I had the lease with me, and some old mail. I could prove that we had lived at this address, in that apartment. I told the police we had been visiting friends in Dreux for a few weeks, to get away from the violence."

Guy has been sitting quietly, his eyes moving from his mother to his grandmother and then Ben, trying to follow the conversation.

"Obviously, you did get the apartment back," says Ben.

"Yes, and only because of the police! Imagine, instead of being the enemy, they were now our helpers. They came over here, and they threw out the squatters!" She smacks her own head in frustration. "And to think—the same police who had destroyed our lives a few years ago. I wanted to hit them and hug them at the same time."

Simone reaches out to her mother, and they clasp each other's hands.

"Such a relief," adds Mira, "That at least one piece of our old life was back. And Ben, this happened just the day before you came looking for us!"

She looks straight at him and her eyes are brimming.

"If I had been a day or two earlier . . ." Ben begins.

"That's right," Mira nods. "You would have missed us, you would not know where we were, you would write to Anne and say, 'They are gone!' So in a way, we are lucky."

Ben feels a little shiver. He had been so incredibly close to never finding the Davals at all. But he had, all due to Simone's persistence. And perhaps something else, some force that wanted him to find them. But no, he doesn't believe in such things; it had just been a coincidence or plain luck.

Instead, he simply says, "Mira, Simone—what a story! I can hardly believe the timing of my visit!"

Mira adds quietly, "And here we are, back where we started before the Germans invaded."

Ben knows they will talk about the missing family members. But for right now, he wants to keep things a bit lighter, for the boy. So he decides to rush in with a question.

"Guy, you've had so many adventures in a lot of places," begins Ben in

French. "Can you tell me a little about them?"

The boy looks quickly at his mother; Simone nods her approval and then he responds. "Yes, Corporal Ben. People were pretty nice to me. I especially liked the mountain school because we were a whole bunch of boys together. And I liked taking care of the rabbits when I lived in the village. But—" he pauses, then takes a deep breath, "It was hard being without Maman and Gran'mère."

"I'm sure you were very brave the whole time," says Ben kindly.

The boy looks up at him sadly. "I tried to be brave," he says. "But I was scared, too. And what scared me the most was"—he looks nervously at his mother and grandmother—"what I couldn't talk about."

"What was that?" asks his mother.

Guy looks down at his plate. Ben wonders if the boy is about to cry. But Guy continues quietly: "What happened to my father and my grandfather. I learned some things like that happened in other families."

Simone looks startled. "Who, Guy? You haven't said anything about this."

"At the mountain school. One boy, Pierre, told me his father and mother were arrested while he was away visiting his grandparents in Nîmes. Also Marcel, from downstairs. In this building. It was right after Papa and Gran'père left. Marcel said his father went to the police station too and never came back. This morning I went and knocked on the door of Marcel's apartment and a strange man answered. I asked for Marcel, and he just said, 'They do not live here,' and shut the door."

"A lot of people are gone, Guy," says Simone quietly. "That happens during a war. People move around, or they go to a safer place . . . or they get"—she pauses slightly, as if searching for a word that does not sound too harsh—"captured."

"And good things happen too, at the end," says Ben. "The bad guys lose. We're here to help, and so are the British, and the Canadians. And we'll all help to straighten things out before we go home. We'll be here for a while. And France will go back to being France again." In his head he hears an echo of that popular song he'd heard in England, where "Jimmy will go to sleep in his own little room again."

"There is still something I don't understand," continues Guy, speaking slowly, not for Ben's sake but because he has been thinking about all this for a long time. "Maman, you told me never to talk about being Jewish. And I didn't. But sometimes, at the school in Dreux, I heard some of the boys say 'Jews are evil' and 'Jews don't belong in France.' If I told them I am Jewish, I would still be the same person they play soccer with, but would they hate me? Would I have gotten in trouble?"

Simone's face has a very serious expression, but her voice is kind. "Guy, those boys probably did not even know any Jewish people or what they are like. They heard their parents say things. So they repeat them, without understanding. It must have been so hard for you to hear things like that. You did the right thing by keeping quiet. I don't know if you would have gotten in trouble. But Hélène would have gotten in very big trouble. That is why I had to take you away from there, do you understand that? I couldn't even explain this to you on our way to the mountain school—because I did not know who might be listening in the train or the bus. But Hélène and her family really love you."

Guy looks at her with puzzlement.

"Then why couldn't I keep staying there? I liked her house and the little school. And I did everything right! I even learned to kneel in church and cross myself."

"It was nothing you did, my sweet. The German rules got harder. A lot of the police were working with the Germans. So I had to get you even further away, to a place where the Germans and the police did not go."

"We had hardly any visitors at the mountain school. And we never went to the town. M. Fremont said it was too far away. But really, it wasn't *that* far. The boys at the school were different from the boys in Dreux."

"How so, Guy?" asks his mother.

"They never said things like 'This is all because of the Jews.'"

All of a sudden Guy asks Simone directly: "Maman, was M. Fremont hiding us?"

Simone looks right back at him and nods her head, "Yes, Guy, I think so. But he never said this. I think it was just . . . understood."

The conversation is making Ben uncomfortable as he watches Guy struggle with questions and imagines his having to hide the truth for so long. At the same time, he is full of admiration for Simone, who is explaining things calmly to Guy and assuring him that he is not to blame for anything.

Ben tries to ask something to lighten the mood a bit. "What was it like around here, in this neighborhood, when you came back?"

Mira answers immediately, as if she, also, wants to turn the mood to something brighter. Her face becomes animated, and Ben thinks he sees some of her youthfulness returning. "It was so colorful in the streets, so joyous," she begins. "Everyone we saw was very excited. There were French flags everywhere! Those horrible Nazi banners were gone. Everything looked familiar, yet . . . strange. Some buildings—well, it felt like we had never been away."

Then she stops, remembering, and gazes out the window. "We saw shop windows that had been boarded up, places closed. There were many people on bicycles, and some wagons pulled by horses. Very few cars. A couple of American army jeeps came by, with soldiers driving and French young people sitting on the hood or standing inside, screaming and yelling—but happy screaming."

"Most people were very happy," adds Simone. "It just depended on what happened to them during the Occupation."

"What a miracle it would be," murmurs Mira, "if each day, we could get back some of our life. If Samuel and Jacques could just step out of the lift . . ."

Ben raises a new subject, partly to distract the Davals. "I hear there is going to be a service at the big synagogue. This Thursday, to celebrate the Liberation. It's for everyone, and they are inviting soldiers, too. An American rabbi will lead some of the prayers. Do you want to attend? We could go together."

Mira and Simone look at each other. "We are not very religious," says Mira, hesitating. "But perhaps we ought to go. What do you think, Simone? We might see people we know. So much must have happened in Paris that we don't know about. Maybe we can learn something."

Simone agrees with her mother and asks Ben, "Which synagogue? The big one on Rue de la Victoire?"

"I'm really not sure. I'll check and will come back Wednesday to tell you." He turns to Guy: "You'll come too, right?"

The boy, who has been listening quietly, looks up. "Yes, if Maman and Gran'mère also go. It might be good, Maman! Maybe I'll see some other boys there!"

Ben gets up to leave. They all have something to anticipate. Maybe there will be some shred of good news for the Davals.

On the long walk back to his quarters, Ben has time to think about Sylvia back in Brooklyn. He has been writing her regularly, once a week, since he left New York. And she has been sending him letters faithfully, first to the APO in London and now to Paris. At first, he told her nearly everything that he was allowed to: about his work setting up the mail services, about the famous places he visited, about an interesting book he read or an unusual food he tried. He told her about the new camera he'd gotten, and all the places like Piccadilly Circus and the Tower of London where he'd taken pictures. He'd enjoyed explaining some of the funny words he'd heard in London, such as the loo, or bangers and mash. "Bonnet" was strange, too, because the word didn't mean a hat at all, but part of a car.

Ben realizes he hasn't been writing much to Sylvia lately, however. Well, he's been so busy, he tells himself. Does he care about her? Of course. She's a swell girl, and her parents have been great to him. He really enjoys being with her whole family. He had proposed to her because—well, he liked her, he felt relaxed with her. He tried not to think about the fact that getting married would give him a good excuse to get out of his mother's apartment.

All of his friends were living like the adults they were. He wanted that also. He had found a steady job that promised more security than his interest in photography, and now he was involved in a great, and potentially dangerous, adventure. Everyone, with the exception of his mother, seemed to be proud of him and praised his action. For the first time in his life, Ben Gordon felt like he was doing something meaningful.

Then why isn't he feeling happy? Why is he feeling burdened as he walks down the gray Paris streets?

Ben had made a promise, and as soon as he gets home he will have to fulfill it. But does he, really? Engagements are broken all the time. Things don't always work out. But if he does this, Sylvia will face the indignity of being jilted. Jilted and over thirty—and if she doesn't find someone else fast she'll never have the baby he knows she wants. Ben tries to sort and absorb and analyze everything crashing about in his mind, and by the time he approaches the Gare Montparnasse, he has a raging headache and just wants to hit the sack.

## CHAPTER THIRTEEN

# The Synagogue

The Rue de la Victoire is much narrower than Ben expected. Its name seemed so majestic that he thought it might be wide and imposing, like Eastern Parkway in Brooklyn or Fifth Avenue in Manhattan or the grand Avenue de l'Opéra here in Paris. But instead it is rather narrow, and he can see that about halfway down the block, some people are already assembling. Ben walks down the street toward the group, who are starting to gather in front of the synagogue itself, a large and ornate structure. It is the tallest gray stone edifice on a street of gray stone, with carved Tablets of the Law atop the central of three arches.

Ben arrives at four in the afternoon, an hour before the announced time of the service, because he does not like to be late to anything, especially if he is unsure of the address. This is the 9th *arrondissement*, he knows, and just northeast of the Palais Garnier opera house, a great landmark to remember. The streets seem to run every which way in Paris, unlike the navigable grid of Manhattan. But if he could learn London, he can certainly learn Paris!

He knows he is west of the Davals' apartment, and Mira, Simone, and Guy will meet him here in half an hour. "I'll go to the service," Simone had said earlier to Ben, "But not for any religious reason. Only to see if I know anyone there, or if someone has heard anything." She had looked at him fiercely: "You think I can believe in a God who could let this kind of war, this kind of evil, take place?"

As Ben approaches the space in front of the synagogue, he sees small groups of men and women talking animatedly with each other. Ben sees a number of British and American soldiers, too. The civilians are chatting with these soldiers but glance nervously—and sometimes angrily—at the French police guards standing on the periphery of the area.

An older man in a worn gray suit comes up to Ben, saying "*Bienvenue, monsieur l'américain, et merci!*" Ben shakes his hand and responds in French. He tries his Yiddish, but this man is only French-speaking. Still, he takes Ben by the arm and pulls him to another knot of people who are speaking quietly off to one side. "*Voilà, ce soldat parle le yiddish!*"

The two women and a man, all middle-aged, brighten and begin speaking to Ben in Yiddish, all at once: "Where in America are you from? Can you help us locate missing people? Will your military help us? There isn't much food in Paris!" Ben notices that these people seem to have dressed up, the women wearing bright scarves and large earrings. They want to look good, maybe for themselves, maybe for foreigners. After a few minutes, though, he sees that their shoes are worn, with wooden soles and heels, and their clothes are patched in places.

Overwhelmed, Ben tries to give as much information as he can, but what he actually knows is limited. So he tries to explain, in Yiddish: "I am with an army postal unit. I have only been in Paris a few weeks. Really, I don't know what the military is planning. So far, I have met only a few

Jewish citizens. I know one family where the father and grandfather disappeared. They have heard nothing. You need to tell *me* what has happened!"

More come over to join their group, and Ben can see that other American and British soldiers in front of the synagogue are similarly engaged in conversations. As people clamor for information, the volume of speech on the street rises.

Ben observes a couple of old men, thin and bent, standing at the edge of the crowd. As they move closer, Ben sees that they are not all that old. Maybe they are a few years older than he, but they carry themselves like men twice their age.

A gray-haired woman in a tweed suit clutches Ben's arm and speaks in rapid Yiddish: "Paris has been a frightening place. At first, we heard that the police were interested only in foreigners who were here illegally. And only adult men. Then the search got wider. Any Jew was hunted down. Do you know about the *rafles?*"

Ben shakes his head. No, he does not. He only knows what he has read in the American newspapers, in the *Stars & Stripes*, and things he discussed with Simone. Apparently, there are many more details of which he is totally ignorant, and he feels apologetic and guilty. Simone might not know, either. He doesn't know what a *rafle* is—he cannot imagine it is anything like the type of "raffle" places have in the States.

"I am sorry. There is a lot I don't know yet. What is a *rafle?*"

"The *rafles*—they are the roundups—the summer of '42 was awful."

"What happened in the summer of 1942?" Ben asks. "Did something change?"

"Yes, it got so much worse," adds a middle-aged woman with dark circles under her eyes. "The police could not tell which French people were Jewish. So they made us wear the yellow stars. Easier to pick us out that way."

"And there were terrible punishments if they caught you without the star on your coat or jacket," chimes in a teenage boy.

"In the middle of the summer of '42," continues the woman, "The police surrounded neighborhoods and then pushed whole families onto city buses and took them to a racing stadium in the center of the city. They locked them in there—for almost a week! Then the people—women, children, babies!—were taken away to God knows where. No one has heard from anyone who was captured that day."

"But many people were not captured, right, because you are all here," Ben comments.

"You are seeing just the lucky ones," says a man with gray hair and a thin mustache. "The ones who were tipped off by good policemen, or heard warnings and hid, who had some outside connection, like decent neighbors."

"Yes," says another man. "We know of many people were helped by Christians, good Christians. They offered hiding places to Jews."

"Here are two of them," says one of the bent-over men, who walks over slowly and speaks up. "My neighbor Jean-Pierre let my brother and me stay in his attic. Right here in Paris. We were completely dependent on him. And here we are!"

"But what happened to you?" asks the gray-haired man, "Why are you both stooped like that?"

"We could sit up, but not stand in that attic," responds the brother. "At the beginning, no one knew how long this would last. Turns out we spent two and a half years without walking or standing—well, it had its effect. But as Alain says, we are here!"

"Many Jews left the city; they managed to get out before the Germans invaded," adds another woman.

"Some joined the Résistance, we hear," adds another man.

A woman points out, "I heard that some priests and nuns in many churches hid Jews."

Ben is now at the center of a clamoring group of men and women of various ages. He sees no children. People are desperate to talk to him and the other foreigners. One haggard man is particularly voluble, speaking so quickly that Ben cannot discern what he is actually saying. He decides the best thing to do is listen, and when he listens he looks at the speakers' eyes, many of which are wet.

"I am sorry, I am sorry," murmurs Ben. There is nothing else he can say.

"Many people lived in hiding," says another man, "and others went underground."

This was exactly what Simone and Mira had told him about their own situation—to survive, Simone had to become someone else, and Mira had to disappear.

A young woman tells him, "Jews who lived in neighborhoods together, they were more likely to be picked up. The police searched areas near all the synagogues, like this one."

"Are there many synagogues in Paris?" asks Ben in Yiddish.

"Oh yes, quite a few," responds one man. "You know, Jews have been in Paris for two hundred years! But a huge number arrived within the last sixty years, getting out of places like Poland and Russia."

"I understand," says Ben. "That's exactly when most Jewish immigrants came to America."

"The French police, I curse them," adds another, spitting on the ground for emphasis. "They went building by building. Sometimes the *concierges* pointed out all the apartments where Jews lived. That made it so easy to arrest them."

"But some *concierges*," says the first woman, "Did the right thing.

They protected residents and warned them. I heard that some policemen, too, warned about the arrest raids."

"This is true!" responds another woman, who wears a brown hat. "A friend told me, the policeman on her street came to her apartment and told her to leave, just leave, that very day—but to put on lipstick, look happy, and to walk confidently, so no one would think she was frightened and running away." She pauses momentarily, then sighs, "But most policemen just did whatever Vichy told them to do."

"Vichy took their orders from the Nazis."

"We had two enemies: the German occupiers and the French anti-Semites. And you could also be turned in by ordinary people who were bribed."

"Hungry people are easily bought. Also, you should know, it was not only Jews who hid, not only Jews who were arrested and tortured."

A man in a dark blue suit, who has been silent, now speaks. "My name is Émile. My family name looks French. I speak fluent French. A lot of French Jews are not religious—I include myself. I never went to synagogue and never told anyone about being Jewish. So no one came looking to arrest me." He pauses, then starts to cry. "But my sister is married to an observant man. When I went to their apartment, to check on them—it was empty. It had been looted. My sister and her husband and two little children, they had all been deported. Gone. Overnight."

"Maybe we will learn something today, Émile," says a woman to the man in the blue suit and clasps his shoulders.

Ben listens to all these vignettes of loss, and hiding, and disappearance, and wants to know more. "You say the police hunted down and arrested the Jews, but not for any supposed crimes, just for being Jewish?"

"That's right."

"But they did it at different times and in different places?"

"They had many different 'roundups' called *rafles*. No one knew who would be next. The one in 1942 was the biggest. It was so big that many Parisians took notice—you couldn't ignore the thousands of police in the streets that day. I think that's when people here *really* started hating the Germans."

"And after the Jews were arrested," continues Ben, "They were deported, right? But where did the French send them? Or were they sent away by the Germans? And how many people did this happen to?"

"This is what we want to know," answers Émile. "We know many people went to Drancy, the camp. You have heard of it?" Ben nods. A few weeks ago, no, he hadn't, but now he certainly has.

"After Drancy," continues Émile, "Well, we have heard many stories. All kinds of rumors. Work camps, prisons, slave labor factories. The exact number, no one knows. But everyone knows someone, or of someone, who has disappeared."

Ben feels a sick heaviness in his stomach.

"I heard that the head rabbi in France will speak today, and also an American rabbi," says a woman in a pale dress, approaching the group.

The tall, heavy synagogue doors open, and people quietly start to enter. Ben wishes his group well, explaining that he has to wait for his friends. Soon he spots the Davals walking down the street toward the synagogue.

They greet each other warmly, with a kiss on each cheek. Mira seems a bit out of breath; this is the longest distance she has walked since the arrival of the Americans. "I have passed here many times over the years," she tells them all, "but I have never been inside. It's such an intimidating building!"

They edge their way through the large, high foyer into the sanctuary. Ben notices that Simone and Mira are looking about, searching for any familiar face. Guy is looking around as well; there are no children to be seen, although there are a few young adults. The interior of the synagogue is dark and tall, the ceiling higher than at any of the synagogues Ben has been to in Brooklyn. The high arches are almost church-like. A slightly musty odor, the smell of disuse, enters Ben's nostrils. It reminds him of his first day in Paris, when they opened the space under the arches to set up the post office. With enough help, he thinks, the dinginess could be swept out in a week.

People file into the sanctuary past heavy, worn, burgundy velvet drapes. The vast synagogue is filling quickly with both civilians and soldiers. Ben finds three seats together for the Davals about halfway toward the front, whispering to them that he will stand at the side with other American soldiers. As he moves to his place, Ben notices a very old man seated on the raised platform facing the congregation, next to several younger men in uniform. More dark curtains hang from the tops of the tall windows; everything is lit by a central chandelier and electric lights flanking the platform.

Ben's eyes scan the assemblage, including the crowded balcony—there must be two thousand people here, he thinks. Two thousand people, silent. Then one man rises from his seat on the platform, comes forward, and begins a plaintive chant. Ben recognizes the ancient words of *El Malei Rachamim*, the prayer for the souls of the departed. He hasn't heard this since the day of his own father's funeral in 1934; he closes his eyes and immediately sees his weeping mother, his throat tightening as he remembers having to appear strong. He opens his eyes. Here are hundreds and hundreds of people, all of them in mourning. His own past sorrow seems small.

The cantor sits, and the old man rises slowly and approaches the lectern. He begins with a prayer in Hebrew and then speaks to the group in French. It is difficult to hear him. The man is very frail. Then a tall, slim young man in glasses wearing a US Army uniform rises to address the congregation. Ben is surprised when the man begins to speak in very fluent and comfortable French. Then he speaks in English, to the soldiers.

"We have only been here a short time," he says, "But we can already see the suffering that has befallen France, and especially the anguish of our Jewish brothers and sisters. In the days just before this service, twenty to thirty Jewish civilians have come to my office at the Hôtel Majestic to ask for one kind of help or another. The stories we have heard are chilling but also heartening. We have heard about many deportations, but we have also heard about children being smuggled to safety in Switzerland, about Jews imprisoned at Drancy who seized lists of people sent away from there."

Then the American rabbi alternates his sentences, first in French, then in English. Whenever he pauses, just for a moment, sounds of weeping fill the spaces.

"We are here to help," he continues, "In any way we can. It will take a long time for the Jewish community here to recover. But with God's help, this will happen. We will work together with you to bring light back to a darkened Paris."

The rabbis then lead the assembled congregation in prayers of thanksgiving for the liberation of France, and then they say the *Kaddish* for the dead. Ben thinks to himself: do they know for certain who is dead and who is presumed dead? He joins in the steady, low chant of the prayer, thinking of his father. Thousands of people are chanting together, the sound occasionally broken by sobs or a cry.

As he looks about, Ben sees many soldiers in uniform; there are many Americans as well as British, and also some French. From where he stands, Ben cannot see Mira, Simone, and Guy, but he knows they are also filled with grief and for the first time are surrounded by people who share their sorrow. They are certainly not alone.

When the service ends, the synagogue foyer and forecourt are filled with people trying to greet the rabbis. As he makes his way back toward the doors, Ben asks some French civilians about the old man.

"Why, that is *le grand-rabbin*, Julien Weill! He is the chief rabbi of Paris!"

"It is a miracle he is even here at all," adds another man, "because he was tortured by the Nazis. But he lives; he never deserted us!"

Ben squints against the light as he emerges from the synagogue. In the forecourt, clusters of people are gathering around the tall American rabbi, clasping his arms, reaching for him. Ben sees a woman take one of the rabbi's hands and kiss it. She is crying, and Ben hears the rabbi speaking softly in French, his voice cracking: "*Merci, merci. Mais je n'ai fait rien*. Thank you, but I have done nothing."

"Isn't that Rabbi Nadich?" Ben asks another American soldier standing near him. "He led services when I was stationed in London."

"Yup, that's him, Judah Nadich—from New York, just like me! Joe Berger, infantry."

"Ben Gordon, APO. And I'm from Brooklyn!" They shake hands.

"Infantry! So were you there, on the beaches?" asks Ben. Immediately a wave of remorse hits him. Why did he even bring this up?

"Absolutely! But my platoon came in the second wave. If I had been in the first, I would probably not be here chatting with you today. Those guys were hit hard . . ." his voice trails off.

"I know," says Ben. "They got creamed." He and Joe are silent for a moment. Then Ben speaks up: "I volunteered for infantry and was turned down. Sometimes I feel very guilty for having gotten off so easy."

"You're in uniform, though, right? So you are doing something for America." He places his hand on Ben's shoulder.

"Thanks, Joe."

Then Joe reflects, "That first day, Gordon, when we marched into Paris, people were screaming and yelling, they were so happy. But this is different—so much sadness. All the Parisians were pushed around by the Germans. But from what I've been hearing, the Jews were especially terrorized. From the things I've heard, I think a lot happened that we don't even know about yet."

"News will trickle in, I am sure. Where are they sending you now, Joe?"

"I have a few days here, then I'll go"—he shrugs—"wherever Uncle Sam tells me."

The men shake hands again, wishing each other well, and Ben moves ahead to the street, where he spots Mira and Guy among the large crowd of milling civilians and soldiers.

Guy comes running up. "Maman saw someone she knows!" he shouts. "From before!"

A few minutes later, Simone hurries over to join them. "First, I was upset because I had no information," she says in a low voice, "and now I am learning too much. Too much." She takes a deep breath. "I met a woman I knew from school. Maman, do you remember Genevieve Lerner? She was in the Résistance. She and I will meet again next week." She pauses and puts one hand over her eyes. "Oh, the things I heard!" she continues, her voice breaking. "I cannot speak. Let's go home."

"I'll walk with you," offers Ben.

Guy is standing, mesmerized, in the middle of the Rue de la Victoire, looking back at the front of the synagogue, where groups of people are still clustered. He has never seen so many American soldiers in one place. They look wonderful, he thinks, big and strong in their clean, pressed khaki uniforms with shining buttons. They look you right in the eye and smile. They fought their way into Paris to save everyone! He hopes they will stay in the city and keep him safe.

"Guy, *allons!*" calls his mother.

Then he turns and joins Ben for the walk back home.

Later that evening, Ben takes the Métro back to the Gare Montparnasse. Standing and watching his reflection in the glass windows, he thinks about all that he has heard. Everything he heard the rabbis and the civilians say was very alarming. More news—news about the unknown—is coming. He is very fearful.

Ben knows that all civilians suffer under an occupation. But the idea that Jewish Parisians had it far worse than their neighbors, and had to live *so* surreptitiously in order to survive, that was new. The *only* group of people who had to turn in their radios! The *only* people who had been kicked out of jobs! Everything he heard people tell him today corroborated Simone's stories. From what he has pieced together from her, and from what he heard today, the Jews had been hunted down like prey animals. And they had been hunted all through the whole city of Paris. Putting all the stories together created a terrifying picture.

Only now were the American soldiers even starting to hear stories about resistance efforts. Ben imagines that many French civilians had actively resisted the Nazis, but people with dependents like small children would have been too fearful. Other Parisians, wanting to be on the winning side, had collaborated with Vichy and the Germans. Probably, as Mira had said, most people had just kept their heads down and muddled through.

Ben thinks about the tins of milk and the cans of coffee and other things he has brought to the Davals. What a small effort, so pathetic! It's all he has been able to do, however. He wants to do more, for them and for others like them. His uniform means something very important to Ben—and he wants it to mean something positive to these Parisians. The rest of the way back, seated in his train car, he thinks about how he can accomplish this. He is so caught up in thought that he almost misses his stop.

## CHAPTER FOURTEEN

# A Plan

en wakes up in the soldiers' quarters above the post office. He has had a restless night, dreaming of walking down a darkened street. The street didn't look familiar, so it could have been New York or Paris or anywhere. What was creepy was the sound. As he walked, he heard footsteps behind him; when he stopped, the footsteps stopped. If he turned around to look, he saw nothing. But if he moved again, the steps started up, clicking softly in the shadows. Ben had taken a couple of psych courses at Brooklyn College before he had had to drop out in '34, after his father died. But even without those vague classroom memories, he doesn't need a textbook to figure out what was chasing him in the dream.

Now he is relieved to open his eyes and see Solly's profile on the cot next to his chest, rising and falling gently. Ben sits up and takes a look at his wristwatch: 0500, plenty of time. He swings his feet out of bed and pads softly down the hall to the WC. When he is dressed, he creeps quietly down the wooden stairs and outside, where the gray city is starting to wake up.

Sitting on a bench overlooking the Boulevard du Montparnasse and the Rue de Rennes, heading toward the Latin Quarter beyond it—so much he has yet to see here!—he reaches into his coat pocket for his pipe and tobacco pouch. He fills and lights the pipe, settling back on the bench and watching the dark blue night gradually lighten to dark, then a paler gray. Gray sky, old gray buildings, a few gray people pushing thumping handcarts across the cobbled pavement toward the train station.

He still hasn't mentioned Sylvia to Simone or her mother. She isn't an off-limits discussion topic, so he doesn't know why he hasn't brought up her name. It would have been easy enough when Simone was talking about her fears for Jacques. He could logically have said, "I also know how it feels to be separated from someone I love. I have a fiancée in Brooklyn. We are 4,000 miles apart, and anything could happen." But he hadn't. Well of course, Sylvia was safe at home with her mom and pop. But why is he acting like it's a big secret?

Ben pulls on the pipe thoughtfully. He is not hiding anything. His buddies, like Solly from home, know very well that he is engaged. The guys in his unit know; they have even teased him about it when he has balked at going with them to dance places up in what they call "Pig Alley": "C'mon, Gordon, *Syllllllvia* will never know!"

It just hasn't come up naturally in conversations with Simone and Mira; probably, he reasons, because they have done most of the talking, because they had so much pent up for so long. He has been a sympathetic ear with a connection to their family. And really, he has known them for only a short time: a couple of weeks. Probably, the postal units will get even busier the more American troops pour into Europe, and he won't have as much time to see his new friends. And once things settle down, and everyone returns home, things will normalize, right?

Ben tries hard to convince himself that eventually, all will be well. Still, he has no idea if Paris, or anywhere else in Europe, will be "normal" again.

His pipe finished, Ben knocks out the ashes on the low wall where he has been sitting and heads back inside. He can smell sweat and the spicy shaving lotion some guys use to cover the sweat. Everyone is getting ready to go for breakfast and coffee. "Hey, Ben!" calls Solly, walking over to him followed by two others, PFC Jack Einhorn and PFC Al Davis. "The boys and I were just talking—you were at that service on Thursday with Rabbi Nadich, right?"

"Sure. I was over by the left-hand wall."

"Yeah, I thought I saw you. Listen, the three of us were talking a little to him after most of the crowd left. There were Jewish people telling him how little food there is in Paris, no kosher meat of course, and because they were living in hiding they didn't even have ration cards. The army has got stuff, and the army has a great postal service."

Jack chimes in, "So why don't we get together to find things for them, and ask our folks at home to send more parcels to us?"

"That's just what the Rabbi said," Ben responds. "The US Army is here to help the French, but the Jewish soldiers can put in some extra effort."

"And remember what they told us in that brochure they gave out?" says Al. "The French will be happy to see you and will offer you hospitality but try not to eat too much!"

"I brought some things from the PX to this family I met," adds Ben, "And they were thrilled with it, even though it wasn't that much."

"So do we go through army channels with the chaplains, or through the synagogues?" asks Jack.

Ben thinks for a moment, then says, "We know where that synagogue is, so let's gather things here and bring stuff over there. Next week is Rosh

Hashanah—it would be great if we could take care of this by then."

At the canteen, they sit down together with breakfast and mugs of hot something-close-to-coffee. The shortages are starting to affect everyone. The men plan to gather whatever they can at the PX and store it upstairs under their beds. "Don't forget to ask for cigarettes," Al reminds them.

"I don't smoke, so I'll get other things," says Jack.

"No, if you can get cigarettes, get 'em. They're great for bartering! Just don't sell them on the black market and get yourself arrested!"

Solly is quiet and then brings up a new subject. "A couple of the Jewish civilians I spoke to at the synagogue," he says, "told me some pretty horrific stuff. People disappearing. I heard about some mass arrests and deportations of Jews—including kids. Kids! What threat were they? I thought the Germans were fighting a war. Rounding up women and kids?"

Ben thinks for a moment, then says, "Remember how at home, before America got into the war, how we heard all those stories about Nazi persecutions and anti-Jewish laws in Poland and Germany? Has anyone here gotten news from relatives in Europe and then not heard anything else?"

Jack and Al shake their heads no.

"A cousin of my mother," Ben tells them, "in Vienna, begged her for help. But she didn't take him seriously. We never heard from him after that. This family in Paris that I mentioned? Two men were deported, and they have heard nothing."

"I wonder how much anyone knows," muses Solly. "I mentioned all this to our CO when I saw him yesterday. He said, not our job, Corporal Lipman! You know how 'by the book' he is! He just puffed himself up and said, 'Our job is to handle the mail, and the mail is pouring in. If there are problems in other areas, they will be dealt with. Understood, Corporal?' He just wanted me to salute and leave him alone."

Jack says quietly, "Yep, that's the Service."

"Okay fellas, so we have our orders," says Ben. "Doesn't mean that on our own time, we can't take care of our own people! Let's see how many items we can gather here by the end of the week."

By then, they have stockpiled soap, sweets, canned vegetables, peanut butter, jam, condensed milk, cigarettes, and gum. Ben and Jack get hold of an army jeep and lug the boxes downstairs on Friday afternoon. They make three trips up and down the wooden steps, then zip over to the Rue de la Victoire with their haul. They ask the small group of volunteers staffing the synagogue to give the items to anyone who needs them. They feel that, for the time being, they have helped at least some families and survivors. At least it's a start, thinks Ben, as he feels the gloom he's been wearing like a rucksack begin to lift from his shoulders.

## CHAPTER FIFTEEN

# A Suffering City

It is the end of September. Paris has been liberated for just over a month, and while the initial euphoria has diminished, there is still an atmosphere of celebration and relief in the air. Except, of course, in families with missing members—people who have been deported, captured, or executed.

For Jewish residents of the city, the solemn High Holy Days have just ended. Ben has never really enjoyed religious services on these holidays, basically because they are so long. He does like some of the melodies and hymns that he remembers from his childhood, when he went to *shul* with his father. After his *bar mitzvah*, though, he gradually stopped going; he preferred to play baseball with the other guys in the neighborhood on a Saturday mornings. When his father died, however, Ben went to prayers every morning for a month, and then once a month for almost a year, to say the *Kaddish*, the prayer for the dead. Now he goes four times a year, when the memorial *Yizkor* prayers are said.

Hearing *Yizkor* during wartime was—Ben isn't even sure of how to define this experience. His father's death, from a sudden heart attack, in the ambulance on the way to the hospital, was terrible. But it did not come as a huge shock; Ben's father had health problems and didn't take care of himself. But here—people were shot on the street or dragged from their homes to be tortured before being killed. He had heard about a group of Résistance members—including a teenage kid—who were shot by the Germans just a week before Liberation. Ben doesn't understand this cruelty—the Germans must have known they were losing, so why didn't they just *leave* instead of killing people for as long as they could?

Almost worse, he thinks, is the condition of families that just don't *know*. Parents, children, sisters, brothers simply disappeared, and no one seems to know where they were sent. And no one has heard from them in two, three, even four years. Ben heard many people weeping during the Yom Kippur services. Some may have known definitively that loved ones had died. Others didn't know if they had survived or not. The Davals are in exactly this situation. Just where are Jacques and Samuel?

"But what about the good people?" Ben had rationalized to Simone one day when she had been extremely angry. "If your friend Hélène hadn't gotten you those papers . . ."

She had agreed on that point, though her exasperation was clear. "Yes, you are right. What Hélène and Jean-Marc did allowed us to survive. They are two people. And there were other good people working to help. But there were *more* people doing horrible things."

She paused, but when she resumed speaking, her voice was quiet and angry. "There was also a large, very large, network of evil here. It must have been carefully planned. It would have taken *hundreds* of people, maybe thousands, working together, to round up a huge group of mostly women and children and keep them in the Vel' d'Hiv for almost a week. It had to be stifling in there! And then to ship them off to some godforsaken place. Ben, I have heard story after story from people here—Catholic and Jewish, but mostly Jewish—of people who were arrested and deported. Innocent people! Not soldiers—ordinary families!"

"Brutality in battle is one thing, but if the Germans . . ."

"That's it! If it were *just* the Germans, marching in here, taking over, and persecuting the French, we could all be angry together! But I didn't see *any* German officers when I visited Drancy. And I went more than once. It was run by the *French*. Who ran all these roundups that I heard about? *French* policemen!"

"Are we being given some kind of mixed-up story?" Ben had asked her. "Wasn't it the French policemen who started the battle for Liberation by turning against the Germans running Paris?"

She had looked at him scornfully. "Some people just want to be on the winning side, whichever one that is. The police didn't rebel in '42 or '43. Oh no—they waited until they heard the gunfire approaching Paris and then figured that the Germans were going to lose. Sure, then they realized they had better stand with the French if they didn't want to get their eyes torn out by angry citizens!"

Ben had sighed and remained silent. He always tried to find a positive aspect in any situation, but in a war that was nearly impossible. He had had it easy, he knew, and the closest he had come to danger was during the Blitz, just missing being hit one night in London.

Ben did not tell Simone that one day, a couple of weeks ago, he had visited the Hôtel Majestic on Avenue Kléber, not far from the Arc de Triomphe, when he had a Thursday afternoon off-duty. The building had actually not been a hotel for many years. It had been turned into offices by the French in the thirties, then seized by the Germans to be their military headquarters. Now it served as the HQ of the United States Army. As he had hoped, Rabbi Nadich was there, working on his sermons for *Shabbos*, but he had graciously given Ben some time.

"Have you heard anything further," Ben had asked, "about the Jewish civilians deported from Paris? I've become friendly with a family from which the father and grandfather were taken to Drancy and then sent . . . somewhere." He sighed.

The Rabbi nodded. "We've been compiling all the records. Deportations continued right until the time Paris was liberated! The Nazis seem to have been, well, obsessed with finding every Jew in this city."

"But they didn't."

"Correct. But they found so, so many," said the Rabbi sadly.

Rabbi Nadich and Ben discussed the Vel' d'Hiv roundup and the order to wear the cloth stars marked "Juif."

"We have some lists of the missing," said the Rabbi. "We're putting things together, but right now no one knows exactly how many people are unaccounted for, or where all of them might be. Thousands of people, thousands!"

Ben nodded in agreement. "There are rumors, Rabbi. There were even rumors about what happened to Jews in Holland, in Belgium, and in Poland before France was invaded."

"Yes, rumors. And I hope that we can put some of these rumors to rest soon, and that we get some hard facts. But I have a feeling we're not going to like what we learn."

"Perhaps, sir," Ben had answered. He decided he would not say anything to Simone about what he had heard from the Rabbi.

Now Ben thinks about that visit while sitting here with Simone. He knows she has every right to be enraged. The two most significant men in her life had been taken away, she had to live undercover for almost three years, and she felt betrayed by her own country. Mira, who dealt with the same losses, was simply quiet. Except for when she was with her grandson, who made her eyes shine with delight.

Ben is at the Daval apartment again for dinner and has brought another large box filled with goodies from the PX.

"Ben, you are too generous!" Mira had exclaimed as she opened the door for him.

"It's courtesy of Uncle Sam!"

"Your uncle sends you these things?"

Ben had laughed, "US. Uncle Sam—it's a nickname for the United States government. These are all things it provides for us soldiers. And we are happy to share with you."

After the dinner dishes are cleared, Ben helps with the washing up and then suggests that they all go for a walk. After all, he says, he has not seen very much of Paris yet, and he would love a little tour with actual Parisians. Mira says that she is rather tired and will stay home reading with Guy, but she encourages Simone to go out with Ben.

"Get out a bit, Simone, breathe the free air. I know you will be safe with an American soldier to protect you." She and her daughter laugh, and Ben is not sure whether he is really seen as a protector or has been given a warning.

"Don't worry, Mira. I will deliver Simone to your doorstep unharmed in a couple of hours."

They set off in the direction of the Place de la République, two blocks away. Many others just like them are also out walking, enjoying the freedom of open streets and the ability to be outside without a curfew.

Simone and Ben are silent as they approach the long plaza with the dramatic white stone statue of Marianne, the symbol of France, at its center. "There was fierce fighting here just before the Liberation," says Simone quietly. "One of the women I met in our lobby told me about it. She said the Germans used a building on the far side of the Place as a barracks, and they holed up in there, shooting hundreds of Parisians from the windows. Look—you can still see where crosses and bouquets were set out at the spots where people died."

Indeed, Ben now notices the small crosses still visible in the fading light, set up in various sections of the plaza. "It's so lovely here—it's hard to imagine that just a few weeks ago the war was being fought right in this very location," he says.

They walk to the center of the plaza, picking their way past rubble, and find seats on the stone bench beneath Marianne. In silence they watch lights come on in Paris as the western sky darkens. The city becomes more twinkly each minute. It does not look like what it has been for the past four years—a dark place of fear and death.

Simone is very quiet, and Ben is afraid to speak.

"I wish I could speak to you in French," Ben finally says in Yiddish, "but you speak so fast."

"Ah, because you have schoolboy French."

"Well, I *was* a schoolboy when I learned."

Simone laughs. "Technically, I was the same. Maman and Papa came here from Poland, and aside from Yiddish, they spoke Russian only when they didn't want me to understand. I learned French when it was time for school. Maman and Papa learned French also, but they speak it with Polish accents." She stops abruptly. Then, after a moment: "Spoke . . . I don't know if my father still speaks. With his illness, I can't imagine he has survived all this time."

They are silent again for a few minutes.

Ben pulls a pack of Luckies from his jacket pocket. "*Voulez-vous* a smoke?"

She shakes her head. "I am happy I never took up that habit. People who smoked, during the Occupation they had a hard time, unless they could pay the black market prices."

"Well, they must be happy now that they can get their hands on American cigarettes."

"Only if the Americans are nice and give them away. I've heard that some of your soldier friends have created a little black market of their own."

"Selling stuff from the PX? That's completely against regulations. A soldier could be court-martialed for that!"

Simone laughs briefly and makes the little derisive French *pfff* with her lips. "Regulations! People do what they want." She pauses, concentrating as she stares ahead at the dark sky. "And they do what they need to do."

The pain in this last statement makes Ben wonder what exactly Simone had needed to do to get by during the war, and if she has been holding something back. He has met relatively few civilians so far and hesitates to ask too many questions. To survive under occupation, one had to keep a low profile, or fight back, or go along with things. From what he has heard, there were only a few kinds of Frenchmen: those who fought in the French army and were captured; civilians who had been killed; those who were in the Résistance; and those who had collaborated in some way with Vichy and/or the Nazis. How had people managed who were just trying to get by? What about old people, on pensions? Or students, preparing to graduate but without employment ahead? Women left on their own to work or to look after children were vulnerable to the occupiers or collaborators. His mind goes back to the shocking event he witnessed with Solly.

He wants to break the silence that hangs in the air. He needs to say something, but he does not want to upset Simone further.

Simone sits quietly next to him, her shoulders slumped in exhaustion. She looks off into the distance and then slowly begins to speak in a low voice. "It's almost impossible to describe what it's been like, Ben. The last four years have been nothing but rumors and gossip and fear. We were afraid of the Germans but not of the French. We trusted 'the hero of Verdun'—how could we not believe the reassurances that came from Pétain? Everyone revered him. '*Maréchal*, we are here, *Maréchal*, we are here.' They made the kids sing that in school. *Merde*. There was only one thing we knew for sure—things would go badly for the Jews. If things were bad for the French, they would be worse for the Jews."

"Did all the Jews feel this way?"

"Not at first." She pauses, thinking. "Well, how do I know? I only knew my family and friends, and the people in our neighborhood. I was born right here in Paris, so I am used to French ways. But my mother and father and Jacques all came to France to avoid the hate and the danger and the beatings. They thought, 'France! Liberty for all!'" Simone's voice breaks, as she quotes the words Ben has seen engraved on every public building: "'*Liberté. Égalité, Fraternité*'—*pfff*."

She leans forward on the steps, arms around her knees, and weeps softly.

Ben does not know what to say. Simone's bitter outburst makes him think of his own Pledge of Allegiance and its concluding words "with liberty, and justice for all." Not the way *that* worked out, either. Even the great, liberating US Army was segregated. But what good would it do to tell Simone that other countries, too, were hypocritical? He wants instead to stroke her arm, to remind her that the French really *were* free now, that things *would* improve. But he does not want Simone to think that he is using her sadness as an excuse to touch her.

And after all, she is a married woman, and he is engaged. He has still not told this to Simone or her mother. No, he will do the right thing and wait for the right moment, but this certainly is not it. Now the best thing he can do is simply listen.

"We were so blind. I think Jacques knew that things would go badly, but my father was more optimistic. He really believed the French people would protect us."

"It sounds like they didn't at all."

"From what I've heard from some others since Liberation, yes, actually, many did. Even some of the police." Simone's tone has perked up a bit with this relatively hopeful response, but Ben hears the acidity of her indignation quickly seep back into her voice. "But others were all too happy to denounce Jewish neighbors and see them dragged away . . . Maybe they are just bigots full of hate. Or maybe they want your apartment. Or your wife. Or the money they'll get paid for providing a name or two."

Ben shifts uncomfortably on the hard stone step.

Simone speaks to him slowly and deliberately: "You have never had to make a choice in order to survive, have you?"

Ben shakes his head. No, he has not.

"You have no idea, no idea." She looks silently ahead at the city growing darker as the sun continues its descent. Then she turns back to Ben, her expression grim. "Yes, without those papers from Hélène, Maman and I would very likely be dead. Maybe Guy, too."

Ben merely listens, feeling ignorant and ashamed. Why hadn't the Americans believed all those early rumors? Why hadn't America tried to intervene and help? He struggles to recall details of the congressional

debates about military action. And he remembers reports about the perse-
cution of European Jews not being treated seriously.

"With the papers," Simone continues, "I had a new life and could
hide Maman and Guy myself. But the stress was incredible. I don't think
I can even give you an accurate idea. I was afraid all the time, all the time,
constantly. Only when I slept did I get a little relief, and even then, the
dreams . . ." Her voice trails off.

Ben has heard all of this before, but tonight, Simone's story seems much
more personal and intimate with just the two of them than it did with her
mother and son in their apartment. Still, he is not sure of what to say to
comfort her. "It must have been very hard to stretch your ration coupons."

"Ration coupons? They were the least of my worries," Simone replies,
her voice somewhat derisive, but again beginning to crack under the
emotional pressure. It seems she, too, feels this particular conversation
to be different somehow, even though the subject is, by now, well worn.
Ben decides to stay quiet, sensing Simone's need to vent her emotions
but also worrying that he might say the wrong thing. "Well, no, because
worrying about food became a total preoccupation in Paris. I could never
do anything that would get me into any kind of trouble—no gossiping, no
complaining, no buying a few extra eggs when it was possible on the black
market. I couldn't have my identification card scrutinized. What if I were
caught? I couldn't alert Maman—she didn't exist, as far as the authorities
were concerned. If I did—she would be off to Drancy, too, with me not far
behind. And then what would happen to Guy?"

Ben feels chagrined, even though nothing that Simone describes is his
fault. A cool breeze ruffles Simone's tresses, and she shivers slightly in her
thin cotton dress. The temperature has definitely fallen in the last half hour.
He thinks he can see her shaking, but he is not sure if it is because of the cold.

Ben takes off his light wool khaki army jacket and drapes it over Simone's shoulders. "Here," he says.

"Thank you, Ben. Look, I am sorry to make you listen to all of this. But I've really had no one to talk to! Yes, I had my *maman*, and we love each other very much. But I could not tell her *everything* and make her fret even more. About how frightened I was on the Métro because the police would arrest people at random to hold as hostages. Or about the foreman at the workshop who offered me black market bread and cheese if I would . . . oh, don't look so shocked! A lot of women accepted offers like that, because they had children to feed. Have you seen some of the women who've been accused of sleeping with Germans?"

Ben nods, remembering that scene near the Rue de Turbigo.

"Well, some did. The Germans, after all, had the very best: wine, cheese, eggs, meat. They requisitioned the best hotels, the nicest houses. So if Parisians wanted to eat well, they collaborated—in different ways."

"Yes, I have heard about this." He does not want Simone to feel like she has to give him any more details. Maybe, also, he does not want to know. Small tears have begun to appear on Simone's cheeks, tiny droplets reflecting the glittery city lights.

"I had to be so careful all the time. All the time! We knew the newspapers were really controlled by the Germans, but we took them seriously when they mentioned regulations and punishment. After a German was assassinated in the Métro, that's when they started taking civilian hostages. Anyone. They said if a German were attacked, a certain number of hostages would die. Later, they would print the names of those who were shot. So I had to keep my eyes open and avoid being trapped anywhere."

Ben desperately wants to be able to say something, to make her pain go away, to fix it. But he knows there is nothing he can do. Deeper guilt sets in on him, and he squirms in his seat, trying to ignore the aching void shaping inside him.

"I never wanted to be first out of the Métro, or last. If I saw they were checking identity cards ahead, I just kept going, because I knew they looked for people turning back. I never missed curfew. I worried about Maman because her health is not good, but I could not bring a doctor to her. I felt relieved about Guy when he was in the village, because he could eat better there, but I worried that someone would see that he was circumcised. We are finally safe, but I am so, so tired from being on alert all the time! I am tired from having to be two people!"

Simone finally lets her tears flow freely, and her whole body shakes with sobs. Trying to remain strong for others all those years has come at a huge price. She leans against Ben and continues to weep. He shifts slightly on the bench so that his body is turned toward her, and he wraps both of his arms around her. After a little while her crying slows, and she presses closer. He places one hand reassuringly on her shoulder, while with his other hand he begins to stroke her back gently and rhythmically. He bends his head into her thick, lemon-scented hair. They remain like this for quite some time.

## CHAPTER SIXTEEN

# LATE SEPTEMBER 1944:

# Paris

It takes Guy a while to learn to navigate the streets of the city. He knows the importance of not being lost and not having to ask strangers for directions. When he left Paris he was a little boy, and until then he had stayed very close to home. But now he is twelve and a half, and his mother and grandmother agree he must have some freedom. So each time he has gone out to explore, he ventures a little bit further. The streets seem to go every which way, and the long stretches of six-story gray buildings at first look all the same to him. Still, he always gets home when expected and has proven trustworthy. Now he is leaning against the broad stone balustrade of the Pont Neuf, so intent on his map that he does not hear the man approach behind him.

"Are you lost, boy? Can I help you?"

Guy quickly spins around and sees the policeman's uniform. He manages only a brief "*Non, m'sieur,*" clutches his map, and walks away as quickly as he can without running. Never run, unless you are in real danger. If you run they will know, like an animal knows, that you are prey.

Guy knows he is no longer prey. But years of habit are hard to change. He still reacts by instinct and training. His mother and grandmother told him, over and over: avoid the police. Don't talk to any policeman, to anyone in a uniform. If you sense trouble, don't run—that shows panic and fear. Say nothing and keep your face blank. Just turn and walk away.

Guy looks younger than his age because he is small. He is thin, like most people in Paris these days. There is never quite enough to eat, even with the extra things Corporal Ben brings them. At home, he does not complain. This is another thing he has gotten used to—never complain; you don't want people to think you are not grateful. He knows Maman and Gran'mère try their best to keep him fed and happy, but the only thing he enjoys about meals is that they are finally all together again. Sometimes there is an egg or two if Maman has been lucky, or fresh beans or apples if a truck has come from the countryside, and some potatoes fried with onions. The next day, leftover food appears in a new form. By the third day it's not really good at all, but at least it's something. There was more to eat in the country—not much more, maybe a rabbit or some chicken if Mme. Hutin or Marie at the school had been able to get one. But in those places, although he was less hungry, he had been among strangers and without his mother.

It is hot, and the bridge walkway is dusty. Guy is sweating in his thin cotton shirt and would love to find a glass of cold water. He reaches the north side of the Seine and turns to where a couple of the *bouquinistes* have already re-opened their stalls, stocked with old books and magazines. Only now does he turn and look back. He does not see the policeman. No one is coming after him.

Guy sits on a bench under the sparse shade offered by a couple of thin trees and studies his map some more. His memories of Paris are still blurry, although he was born and grew up here. He knows the neighborhood around their apartment building, the long wide boulevard that stretches southwest to the center of the city. He knows the street of shops around the corner, where M. Guiland has his little grocery store and always has a friendly word for him.

When he was small, his neighborhood was small: a few streets over to where Gran'mère and Gran'père lived, the school where he and the other children lined up in their smocks every morning, girls and boys outside the doors marked GARÇONS and FILLES. He loved how the bright French flags always flew above the door and the carved words: LIBERTÉ | ÉGALITÉ | FRATERNITÉ. When he was little he really didn't understand those words. But his parents had told him they meant that France was a good place where everyone was treated nicely. This added to Guy's confusion when Papa and Gran'père were taken away by the police.

Guy remembers the baker's shop where Maman would buy a fresh challah every Friday morning and where the lady would often give Guy a sweet. He remembers vaguely the *shul* around the corner where he would go with his father, holding his hand as they stepped through the gate into the courtyard and then into the large dark room where the men would sit, speaking quietly in the other language. He thinks that maybe Maman and Gran'mère were sometimes there, smiling down at him from their seats in the balcony. Or was that someplace else?

He remembers the two boys who lived in an apartment downstairs, Marcel and Simon, and how sometimes they would kick a soccer ball around the building's small courtyard, until one of the upstairs windows opened and someone yelled down about the noise. Twice Guy has gone down the winding wooden stairs to Marcel and Simon's apartment door to see if they had come back, too. The first time there was no answer, and the second time a stranger opened the door and just said gruffly, "They moved," before quickly shutting the door again.

Guy wants to ask his mother where the family has moved to—maybe it wasn't far, and he could visit. But he knows better than to ask. Maman has too many things to worry about, like finding a job closer to home and trying to find a doctor for Gran'mère. And then Papa and Gran'père. They have not heard from them in a long time, more than three years. If he concentrates very hard, Guy can sometimes remember the voices of his father and grandfather. But they are fading. There is only one small photo of his father, which Maman put in a frame on the sitting room mantel. Without this, he might also forget his father's face. He cannot tell this, either, to Maman or Gran'mère.

Guy does not know what time it is because he does not have a watch as many grownups do. But he can sense the hour from what he learned at the mountain school. When the sun was straight overhead, it was the middle of the day, and as it moved lower in the sky, it became afternoon. He knew that direction was west, so each evening he turned to face north in order to whisper *bonsoir* to Maman and Gran'mère. His father and grandfather, he thought, were further east, maybe not even in France anymore.

When he stayed at their home, Guy had heard M. and Mme. Hutin whispering to each other when they didn't think he could hear, such terrible rumors. But he had been afraid to ask anything, because then they would know he had been listening. At the mountain school, he had trusted Pascal and wanted to tell him that he was so worried about his missing father and grandfather—but that would mean giving away his secret about being Jewish. So he just tried not to think about it too much.

Still, no one knows. He has already asked Maman too many times if she has gotten any letter or message from Papa. He does not want to upset her. So he no longer asks.

Guy's feet are starting to hurt. His scuffed brown shoes are too small. He has already cut away, with his pocket knife, the part of the leather that covered his toes; for a while he had a little more room, but now they are pinching again. He cannot say anything to Maman—her shoes are old and worn, too.

It feels like late afternoon, and as Guy walks along the Seine embankment, he scans the tops of buildings for any clock that seems to be working. He finally sees one—it's four o'clock, so that means Maman will be home in about an hour. Also, Gran'mère will start to worry if he is not back soon. There is still so much to explore, but Guy has been wandering since noon and he is tired. He looks at the stone wall running all along the river, sees fresh chips of rock where bullets flew across the pavement a few weeks ago. There are dark streaks on the wall, too, but he does not want to look at them too closely or think about them. Instead, he focuses on finding the shiny bullet cases he has heard about. He gazes down where the bottom of the wall meets the stone walkway. He looks carefully. There is one—lodged in a crack between two gray paving stones. It is hard to see gray metal except when a shaft of sunlight hits it. Only a few weeks have passed since the fighting stopped, so maybe most of the treasures have already been found. Guy will go just a little further, and then cross to the other side of the Rue de Rivoli. Maybe he will take a quick look; there might be more spent shells for him to discover.

Guy waits patiently to cross the road. There are only a few cars. No buses are running, but many people zip past on bicycles. Then two military jeeps come by, filled with American soldiers. He knows these are the "good guys." And he has learned to spot the differences in the uniforms of the Americans, the British, and the French soldiers. Now one of the Americans catches his eye and waves, shouting, *"Bonjour*, kid!"* Guy waves back and grins. They wear the same uniform as Corporal Ben.

He wonders if any American soldier in the jeep has a boy waiting back home.

After looking both ways after the jeeps pass, Guy runs across the road. He quickens his steps, but every once in a while looks down. It is something to do, a way to keep busy. By the time he is near the door to his building, he has four spent shotgun shells in the right pocket of his shorts. Guy is happy to be almost home but is still worried by the questions bouncing around inside his head. Why haven't I seen anyone I know? Where are our old neighbors? What happened to Papa, and will I ever see him again?

When he approaches the building, though, he tries to push these thoughts away so he can enter the apartment looking happy.

## CHAPTER SEVENTEEN

# Winter Arrives

y the end of November, the days are short and the weather noticeably colder. Parisian shopkeepers are already placing festive silver-and-red stars and other decorations in their windows. Little carved wooden carolers appear at the shoemaker's; newsagents and *libraires* feature cards with a cheerful *Joyeux Noël* message. The big department stores, like La Samaritaine, Au Printemps, and Le Bon Marché, start to dress their large windows with glittery pomp, mannequins sporting sequined holiday dresses and the latest knit suits amid the snowflake stars.

Parisians are pulled in opposing directions: this will be the first free Christmas since 1939; people can celebrate all they want and walk down the avenues without fear of being stopped by the Wehrmacht or the Gestapo. On the other hand, the war is not over. The German forces are no longer pillaging French livestock and agricultural products, but the unusually harsh weather hampers productivity. Little is growing; thinned herds and flocks have not recovered. Gas and coal are in short supply. The days grow shorter and darker and colder, and there is not enough heat. Grandmothers take apart their own shawls and knit the wool into sweaters for their grandchildren.

This is what Mira is doing when Ben and Solly arrive late on Sunday afternoon, December 10th. It is the first night of Chanukah. Simone welcomes them and then rushes back to the kitchen, where she is frying *latkes*, crisp potato pancakes.

"Chanukah is not that important a holiday," she says, "but my Papa always made us *latkes*, and we played dreidel. Do they celebrate Chanukah in America?"

"Same thing," answers Solly, "it's a minor holiday, really, but because it comes so close to Christmas, Jewish families make a bigger deal so their kids don't feel left out. But the food—food is really important! We came here for the *latkes*, because they sure don't have *latkes* at the soldiers' mess!"

"Do you have a menorah?" asks Ben.

"We had a small one, very old, at our apartment," says Mira. "But it is gone, like everything else."

"What do you mean by 'gone?'" asks Solly. "Stolen?"

"Samuel and I had an apartment on Rue Oberkampf, a few streets away from here. Everything was taken by—who knows?—the Nazis, the French police, looters. Simone took a look a couple of weeks after we got back—it was totally empty. Please . . . I don't want to talk about it."

Ben and Solly are silent. Then Ben prods his friend to lighten the atmosphere: "Solly, show everyone what you brought!"

Solly sits at the kitchen table, and Mira, Simone, and Guy come over to see what he is drawing forth from his kit bag. He pulls out something wrapped in newspaper, places it on the table, and then unwraps it.

It is a small menorah, crafted from strips of metal with eight empty bullet cases, and a larger one, welded on top. "A real soldier's menorah!" he claims proudly.

"Do all the Jewish soldiers get one?" asks Guy.

"No—I made this one for you!" Solly tells him. "And look!" He brings out other items from his bag. "My wife sent me a package with Chanukah candles and her special sugar cookies!"

"May I have one, sir?" asks Guy.

His mother answers: "Cookies are for after dinner. With tea."

Guy runs to the corner of the living room where he has a cot and pulls a small box from underneath. He brings it back to the table and opens it for Ben and Solly.

"Look," he says, "I have more empty bullets here. I found these on my walks, after I got back from the mountains. I had to look hard—I think other people got there first. But I still have a lot."

"Are they French or German?" asks Solly, leaning forward with great interest.

"Oh! I don't know," says the boy.

"Let's take a look," offers Ben. He and Solly examine the small spent shells, turning them over and over to find identifying marks.

"See this?" Solly points to some numbers at the bottom of a couple of the bullet cases. "Definitely French, yes—these are the kind the French use."

"Yup, Solly is correct," agrees Ben. "Guy, you should save these—they were fired by some very brave Frenchmen to set Paris free!"

"Guy?" Simone speaks up, alarmed. "You never mentioned that you were picking up bullets from the streets. Lucky you didn't pick up any live shells!"

"No, Maman, these are all spent. A live one still has the pointed end, and you can smash it with a rock and . . ."

Ben interrupts: "Now don't make your mother worry for nothing. You don't have anything dangerous in that box. But if you happen to see any live ammunition on the ground, just tell a soldier or a policeman."

"I don't talk to policemen."

"But the policemen now are all right," Simone says patiently, but her eyes settle on nothing in particular. "Remember—it was the police in our neighborhood who helped us get this apartment back."

"I forgot."

Simone explains quietly to Ben. "It's still hard for him—for my mother—and for me, too, to trust the police. You can understand why." She wasn't happy that she had to seek the help of the French police to regain access to this apartment; she would not have done it if she had had another choice. She actually detests them, marching right along with the forces of occupation and obeying whatever orders Germans gave them. How clever of them to finally choose the winning side so close to Liberation, thinks Simone. Were any of them the same men who took her father and husband away? Maybe, maybe not. But she keeps all these thoughts to herself.

"Hey, buddy," says Solly to Guy. "We like being here in Paris. But we are not going to be here forever. The war will end. We'll have to go home, and so will the Brits. Then you'll have the French army and the French police to protect you. So, remember that they are on your side."

"Thank you, Solly," says Simone. What a simplistic view this man has, she thinks. Loyalty, justice, security? She has seen who can truly provide these—very, very few. Yet she smiles at Solly and simply says, "I know you are trying to help."

After some *latkes*, they all share Myrna Lipman's sugar cookies. Mira makes a pot of tea. Guy wants a third cookie but sees there aren't many left on the plate. He reaches out, then hesitates. "Oh, go ahead, Guy!" says his mother, laughing.

"I almost forgot!" Ben exclaims, and he pulls two small parcels from his army pack. "Happy Chanukah!"

Flour and sugar, treasured commodities. "*Crêpes!*" exclaims Simone. "*Challah*," sighs Mira. Guy brightens up and cries, "Cake!"

"Well," says Solly with a chuckle, "it seems that there is no consensus here, so we'll let you deal with this decision among yourselves!"

"Anyway," Ben adds, "we have to get back to our quarters. Mondays are always busy at the postal station, and we need to be up early."

He and Solly get up and retrieve their coats.

"Before you go," says Simone, as she rises to see them to the door. "Remember my friend Hélène Hutin, who lives outside Paris?"

"The one who got you the papers, and let Guy live there for a while?" asks Ben, as he buttons up his coat.

"You have a good memory, Ben. Yes, and she has invited us to come for Christmas Day. Her husband, Jean-Marc, has a day off work and they will have a big celebration. They have invited us to join them!"

"That sounds great! Guy, I'm sure you'll be excited to see that town again!"

Guy, his mouth full of cookie, doesn't speak, but nods vigorously.

Then they all say good night, and soon the men are walking down Rue de Turbigo as snow starts to fall gently.

"We could take the Métro," says Ben. "It's right across the street."

"Ah, let's walk a little. It's traditional to do that after *latkes*, right?"

A couple of teenage boys wearing mufflers around their necks come running past them, yelling as they scoop up little mounds of snow, which they toss at each other.

Ben and Solly walk quickly to try and stay warm. As they do, Solly ventures, "Hey, Ben? I was watching your face tonight. You really like Simone, don't you?"

"Of course! She is phenomenal . . . but don't get excited."

Ben expects that there is a smirk, but he doesn't look at Solly and just wants to keep going without talking.

"Have you told them about Sylvia?" Solly's tone is gentle, but Ben can sense disapproval.

Ben maintains his silence. There is a long pause as they continue briskly down the broad sidewalk, feet crunching the packed snow. "Well, no—it just hasn't come up." Puffs of steam fill the air as he speaks.

Solly stops short. "Jesus, Ben! We've been in Paris for over three months! You have had plenty of chances to say something. It's one thing that you like Simone—but another that you are hiding the truth from her! What are you waiting for? The day before we ship out?"

Ben stops, too, turning to look at his friend. "It doesn't matter either way, does it?" he says, exasperated with Solly. "Nothing has happened between us, and nothing is going to. I'm engaged, and she is married, and . . . why have any other thoughts?"

"She was looking at you the way you were looking at her. I'm not blind. You're attracted to each other."

They resume their rapid pace down the cold street.

"Sure, Simone is an attractive woman, of course. And she is so brave—I told you all the things she did to protect her mother and Guy. Finding a place for them to live, moving Guy around to different locations so he'd be safe . . . she had to be another person for years and never let anything slip. You know all this. I admire her—she's gutsy! Resourceful. She acts on instinct, but she's smart, always thinking ahead. She had no one to lean on—she just *did* things. She's not like any girl I have ever met."

"So in comparison, Sylvia is really boring, huh?"

"Oh, shut up!" Ben shoves his fists deep into the pockets of his woolen army coat as they continue.

Solly is persistent. "Even without the comparison, Sylvia is boring. Am I right, Ben? Look, I'm sorry to nag you about this. But—I did want to see whether I was right. And I am right—you *really* like Simone. So, enjoy her company while you can, but tell her the truth."

Ben turns to Solly, looking very serious. "I don't want to hurt her. Ever. She has had to deal with enough. This is not like one of your little flirtations over here, Sol."

"What do you mean by that?"

"That red-haired WAC in London. I know you slept with her, and more than once."

"So what? That was in London. It was a distraction for both of us, OK? A distraction from being blitzed. It was just for then, and it was nice, but it was nothing serious. We both knew that, too. But if this is different, and you are serious, you're asking for big trouble."

It is much colder now. Ben pulls his right hand out of his pocket and looks at his wristwatch.

"Too cold to walk. The Métro is still running—let's go."

They hurry down the steps of the entrance of the Arts et Métiers station, past a cluster of people coming up, laughing.

As they wait on the chilly platform for the next train, something occurs to Ben, and he sees a way to change the subject. "Hey, Solly?"

"Yeah?"

"Those bullets. How did you know they were French? I couldn't tell."

"Neither could I. I just said that. I thought it would make the kid happy."

They see a light in the tunnel, coming closer slowly. The train will be here in a few moments.

"Sometimes you can be a nice guy, Solly."

"And I'm a good friend." He punches Ben gently on the shoulder. "I'm telling you—don't be a jerk."

Ben nods. He'll think about it. He has been thinking about it. He is weighed down with the thinking.

## CHAPTER EIGHTEEN

JANUARY 1945:

# Paris

At first, the new year looks hopeful to Ben. He has been recommended for a promotion for his excellent service record, and shortly after the first of the year becomes Sergeant Gordon. His pay will be somewhat higher, but what he really likes is the recognition and the additional stripe on his uniform sleeve.

Snow starts to fall, gently at first. It is already sharply cold, and many people walking in the street wrap scarves across their mouths. Inhaling the frozen air actually hurts. Still, the snow makes the Paris rooftops and chimney pots and neighborhood squares look charming. Like a scene from *La Bohème*, thinks Ben, before remembering that the opera ends tragically. But it's not far from the truth, he knows, especially in working-class *quartiers*, where fuel is scarce and enough nourishing food is still a dream. Four and a half months after the Germans were driven out of their city, Parisians are still hungry and very cold. Everyone wears coats and sweaters indoors.

The euphoria surrounding the Liberation has been over for a couple of months. Only children and teenagers find fun now, throwing snowballs at each other and at their teachers as they pass, or try to, on the pavements. This freezing January, if you are an American soldier in Paris, and not at the front, you are lucky indeed. Ben is guiltily aware of the great battle that has been raging miles to the north, in Belgium and Luxembourg, since mid-December. Brutal details have been filtering in on the radio and in the *Stars & Stripes*—surprised by a German offensive, American troops have faced the challenge bravely. Thousands of reinforcements were rushed in just after Christmas. In addition to fighting the German war machine, the Allies have had to deal with English-speaking Nazi spies who try to infiltrate their lines. Soldiers on patrol drape themselves in white bedsheets, seeking to camouflage themselves in the snow. All along the eighty-mile front, the fighting has been bloody and bitter.

Near the end of the month, the Russians liberate Auschwitz.

Ben hears about this late one night on the BBC as he prepares to go to sleep in his quarters. He keeps a small radio on the windowsill near his cot because it gets better reception there. He hears how the Red Army, advancing through Poland, found several thousand emaciated civilian prisoners and evidence of atrocities on a massive scale.

My God, it's true, he gasps. He sits up straighter in the dark, listening hard. All those rumors they had heard in London, that the Germans were going to do terrible things to civilians, especially Jews. Simone and others in Paris, like the people he had met at the synagogue, worried sick about relatives who had disappeared in the *rafles* or had been arrested—what if those relatives had ended up in a place like that? Echoing in his memory are the fears of anti-Semitism voiced back in New York by recent immigrants from Europe.

Ben is sweating despite the chill in their drafty quarters. He goes over to where Solly is lying on his cot, shaking him. "Solly!" he whispers insistently. He doesn't want to wake up the others. "Get up! I have to tell you something!"

Solly turns over on his side, opening his eyes. "Aw, Ben, I was just having the greatest dream." He never snaps awake, the way Ben does.

Ben crouches down near the head of Solly's cot, so he can whisper audibly. "Well, I was *not* dreaming, I was listening to the BBC. I heard some really awful news about what the Russian troops found. It's horrific!" And he relates, quietly, what he heard.

Raising himself on one elbow, Solly frowns and then responds: "What are you talking about? Were these POWs?" Either he hasn't heard every word or he is still half-asleep, or both.

"No, Solly. The report said 'civilians.' Remember what those people at the synagogue told us? About people disappearing? And what about Simone's husband and father?"

Solly frowns in concentration. He is awake now, and sits up, thinking for a few moments. "It's just a *report*, right, Ben? There is nothing in print, no photos?"

"No, but the BBC . . ."

"And these are Reds, so can we really believe what they say?"

"Why would they make this stuff up?"

"I don't know . . . to make themselves look more heroic? Look, we'll check tomorrow in the papers, maybe the *Stars & Stripes* or another paper has something more . . . definitive. We can't do anything about anything now. So let's get some sleep." Then he flops back down and pulls the blanket up to his chin.

Ben stumbles back to his cot. He is exhausted, too, but can't sleep. He keeps thinking about what he heard on the BBC. When he finally dozes off, he dreams of his father on horseback, wearing a Russian uniform and swinging a saber to his right and left to free the starving prisoners from the Nazis.

The next day Ben doesn't have more than a few minutes to listen to his radio, and there is no new information. There is nothing in *Stars & Stripes*. He asks their CO if he has heard anything, and he gets the same response he got when he asks about helping the civilians: "The mail is our priority, Gordon. You and your guys are doing a terrific job, so keep it up. Leave any possible war crimes to other divisions, okay?"

Ben bristles inwardly at his CO's indifference and advice to simply concentrate on his own job. But he knows he won't get anywhere, so just salutes and says, "Yes, sir!" He is actually quite proud of how smoothly his post office has been running. They are processing thousands of items each day, running them past the censors, and dispatching them to their destinations. Thousands of letters to anxious parents, wives, and girlfriends are now going back to the States from France. Meanwhile, letters and parcels are arriving here. Ben likes to think about the weary frontline soldiers getting loving notes from home. He tries not to think about the mail that cannot be delivered. He tries not to think about the letters he himself ought to be writing. Instead, he determines to find out what exactly the Russian troops have discovered.

⚜

Ben enjoys the comradeship of the other guys with whom he has worked since their first assignment together in London. A good little group has formed: Ben, Solly, Joe Rizzolo—another Brooklyn boy—and

Bill Thornton from Philly. When they have time off together, they explore what they can of Paris. At lunchtime, they often go to one of the many cafés near the station. Over the weeks, they develop favorites. When the weather was still warm, they adopted the Parisian custom of sitting at an outside table, chairs facing the street, to enjoy the passing parade. They tried Le Select and Le Dôme on the Boulevard du Montparnasse and other nearby places, but find themselves gravitating to La Rotonde, on the corner of Montparnasse where it meets Boulevard Raspail.

All the cafés welcome men in uniform. And all the French girls smile at the men in uniform, too. But some places seem warmer than others. Over the weeks, Ben has befriended the manager of La Rotonde, M. Jarreau, practicing and improving his French with him.

"I don't know why, *monsieur,*" Ben had said to him one day, "but I feel more comfortable here than at some other cafés."

Jarreau had nodded and smiled faintly. "Many cafés stayed open when the Germans were here," he explained. The tone of his voice was stern and disapproving. "Some were happier to serve the conquerors than others."

"Did you serve them also?"

"But of course! Did we have a choice? We could not actually refuse to serve them if we wanted to stay in business and, in addition, alive." He smiled, but not with amusement. "So we waited on the Wehrmacht soldiers and officers who sat where you are sitting now, sir. But we did not serve them with pleasure. We performed our duties and served drinks and meals as best we could. Our resources were very limited. How could we serve good coffee when there was no coffee? Or the freshest salads when there were few vegetables?"

Jarreau paused to speak quietly with a passing waiter, a man of about his own age whom he clasped warmly. Then he turned back to Ben, smiling.

"Paul has a son who has been a prisoner of war; they expect him home soon."

Ben had raised his glass. "To good news!" he toasted.

"I am sure there are other cafés in Paris," continued Jarreau, "that did not suffer from shortages, either of fine foods or wine or customers. But many Parisians, I can guarantee, will never again cross their thresholds."

꿏

Now Ben has a few hours to himself and has decided to explore part of Paris on his own, with a camera. He needs some time alone, to think clearly and to appreciate being where he is. Ben knows he is comparatively lucky. After all, his parents were poor immigrants to the United States, he didn't even speak English until he started at PS 16 in Brooklyn, and he was an average student at New Utrecht High School. Today he is walking down the Rue de Rennes in one of the world's greatest cities, in the uniform of a sergeant in the American army.

He pauses to take a picture when he sees something that catches his attention—a fanciful Art Nouveau gargoyle on the corner of a building, a beautiful marmalade cat sunning himself in a street-level window, an older couple in patched coats, moving gingerly but hand-in-hand down the snowy sidewalk.

But mostly he thinks. What is that other word for thinking about something over and over? Ruminate. Yes, he is ruminating over his situation. That brings him to the word 'ruminant,' that is, chewing its cud, and he remembers that all animals fit for kosher eating must be ruminants. Chewing his thoughts over and over again, that is what he is doing. He keeps covering the same territory. If he stays here he might be happy—but he will make a lot of people sore, really sore. If he goes home, he'll have the life he always expected to have. But there won't be any more adventure.

Ben turns slightly right when he reaches Rue de Vaugirard, and heads toward the Jardin du Luxembourg. It's a calm oasis. Maybe he will find a bench in the pale sun and warm up a bit. He knows he is being foolish and impractical. He hasn't even told Simone about his feelings; he has no idea how she'd react. He knows she thinks of him as a dear friend, almost a family member, someone to confide in. But more? After all, she is a married woman, and her husband might return. Then what? Ben will have revealed his emotions for nothing, and then he'll just feel embarrassed.

In a few minutes he can see the tall railings of the iron fence surrounding the Jardin. Only a few brave souls have braved the cold to walk inside the park, and Ben finds an entry gate. The statues, the empty benches, the symmetrical rows of trees against the white snow, all these will be excellent subjects for photography. He holds his camera up to his eye, sets the focus, and decides not to think about other things, at least not for a while.

## CHAPTER NINETEEN

# A Light
# In The Gray City

P ale icy winter still clings to the city like a worn blanket. Snow covers some of the rooftops and water that has dripped down the sides of many buildings has been transformed into rows of icicles. Here and there smoke drifts from a chimney pot. The white cloudless sky melds into the rows of gray-white buildings. If there are flowerpots on any building's narrow, iron-enclosed balconies, they are bare. There is little color in the streets. If he did not know he was in a great and beautiful city, thinks Ben, he would find Paris awfully drab.

But then there are bold flashes of color—in the tricolor flags fluttering over schools and government offices, in the red scarf whipping behind the bicyclist who zips past Ben on the street, in the bright green apron worn by the baker's assistant as she sweeps the sidewalk in front of her shop. These remind everyone that spring will be coming soon.

A few weeks later, Ben is on an excursion to the Bon Marché department store in search of gifts to send home to the women in his life. He finds beautiful scarves for Sylvia and her mother—one has a bright floral pattern, and the other a Parisian street scene. For his sister, who likes jewelry, he selects a Limoges porcelain brooch with enameled flowers. He finds a similar one for his mother, although he knows that she'll find fault with whatever he chooses.

He wants to buy something for Simone, something to bring a smile to her face, something to remind her that she is a beautiful woman. Should he buy her some perfume? Or is that too personal a gift? It also seems a little silly—he should get her something American, not French. But of course there are no American gifts to find in Paris. His American money will go further here, so anything he finds should be something that Simone would never get for herself. He wanders through the large store, noting that most of the customers seem to be American and British soldiers and officers. Emerging on the Rue de Sèvres, he walks toward the Hôtel Lutetia a block or so away, at the corner of the Boulevard Raspail. He has wanted to see this famous luxury hotel that was seized by the Germans.

He has heard about the Lutetia but has never seen it up close—it is certainly a beautiful building, with sculptured ornamental elements on its sides and a magnificent door facing the street. The Nazis used it to house their top brass, and he figures the Allied command have already gone through every room looking for anything left behind. As he approaches the front of the hotel, Ben notices some commotion on the sidewalk by the main door. A knot of excited people clusters around a large sign being set up by men he assumes are hotel employees. An American lieutenant stands off to one side, watching.

"Sir?" asks Ben, saluting.

"At ease, Sergeant."

"What's going on?"

"Some French soldiers who were POWs in Germany have returned. A guy working at the desk inside told me that the hotel has offered itself as a meeting place for anyone coming back, and these men can rest and eat here until their families arrive. The Lutetia is putting up a signboard with the names of the people returning."

"Hear about any others coming back?"

"You mean other POWs? Jerry sure captured a lot of Frenchies!"

"No, I mean civilian prisoners."

The lieutenant frowns. "Well, I heard there are some other guys, not soldiers, who were grabbed up for a work program in Germany."

"Jewish men?"

The other soldier shrugs, "I don't know if they were Jewish or not," he responds. "The Germans took French guys who were strong enough and sent them to work in Germany to replace German guys who were drafted."

Ben is puzzled and troubled. This doesn't sound right. From what Simone has said, Jacques sounded strong enough—but why would a sick older man like Samuel be wanted for any work program? And this American officer doesn't even seem concerned that the Germans took civilian prisoners. He is reminded of his own CO's indifference when Ben told him he heard on the BBC about the Russians liberating a prison camp in Poland.

"No, I'm talking about something else," Ben says. "All the arrests of civilians that the French made, when they sent men to Drancy and then deported them, and also women and kids. Some French friends of mine told me about this. I think a lot of civilians were deported, then sent to eastern Europe."

The lieutenant seems surprised to hear this. "I don't know about any of that. But these guys are pretty lucky, wouldn't you say? Four years as POWs, but they're alive to come home!"

Ben has had enough of this conversation. He thanks the lieutenant and then continues up Raspail to the Rue de Rennes, where he turns right and can follow the street straight back to his quarters at the Gare Montparnasse. He won't say anything to Simone or Mira about this meeting place for returnees. They have still heard nothing about the fate of Jacques or Samuel. Why build up their hopes?

Instead, he thinks about his weekend plans with Guy. The boy is back in school now, not too far from the apartment. At least this is some return to normalcy. Ben considers introducing Guy to the great American sport. He has heard that some of the Americans are planning to organize baseball games in the Bois de Boulogne. Maybe they could pack a picnic lunch and go to watch. And if Guy shows some interest, Ben can practice some pitching and catching with him afterwards. He's glad he packed a ball and glove in his duffel bag when he shipped out.

Now he thinks about standing in his bedroom at home, wondering which small but meaningful items to take with him in the army, and this makes him remember his obligations to the folks back in Brooklyn. He'll mail the scarves and pins, but he has promised to send cards as well. He stops at a newsagent's not far from the gare and buys a few postcards showing the Eiffel Tower, the Trocadéro, and Notre-Dame, not that he's even seen all of them. He figures who will receive each card, and then realizes he hasn't thought about Sylvia in . . . a few days? He is not sure, but he's been busy, distracted. Very distracted. There's still a war going on, after all.

Quickly, it seems, everyone in Paris knows about the rendezvous point at the Hôtel Lutetia. Some prisoners of war have now returned, as well as a number of young men who were sent to Germany as part of the STO labor program. They arrive at the Gare de l'Est to great excitement, met by relatives screaming with joy and other cheering Parisians, and are whisked off to the Lutetia. When anyone returns, his or her name goes upon a huge signboard set up in front of the building. Train after train arrives with returned military prisoners; most of these men, a bit unkempt and some needing a shave, are exultant, jumping off the trains as soon as they come to a stop in the cavernous terminal. Some soldiers, very thin and ill, are carried on stretchers by medics and are also taken to the Lutetia.

But about the other trains that left Paris, or the ones that had left Drancy, there is no information.

Many Parisians come daily to look at the board and scan it anxiously for familiar names. Simone and Mira tell Ben that they have traveled regularly to the other side of the Seine, to the corner of the Boulevard Raspail and the Rue de Sèvres, to check the message board at the Lutetia. They look for the names of anyone they know, anyone in the Jewish community. Because, from what they have heard here and there, the only civilians who were rounded up systematically were Jews. Mira and Simone thought that at the Lutetia they might see one or two acquaintances—and maybe they would know something about Jacques or Samuel. But they never see anyone they even vaguely recognize.

A few weeks after the first French prisoners of war return, other trains begin to arrive in Paris. The passengers look very different as, slowly and painfully, they descend from the cars to the platform. Women as well as men appear, pale and thin, some almost skeletal, survivors of forced labor. Perhaps some are recognizable as the people they were before the war. Many are not.

Parisians who come to the train station to meet a detained husband or aunt or sister look past the weak figures with sunken, dark eyes for the relatives they used to know. The survivors walk with difficulty; others are carried; they, too, go to the Hôtel Lutetia to begin their recovery. But they arrive without fanfare. People in the crowd at the station turn their faces at the sight of these wraiths.

Some joyful reunions do occur at the Lutetia. But not for Simone or Mira, or thousands of other Parisians who scan the lists of survivors.

It was now almost the end of March 1945, and the approaching Passover holiday took on special meaning for the Jews of Paris. They would celebrate the festival of freedom as free people for the first time in four years.

For Ben, this means receiving a parcel from his synagogue in Brooklyn with *matzos*, a small bottle of wine, and *Haggadahs* with the story from the Book of Exodus recited at the Passover *seder*. When he checks with the synagogue on the Rue de la Victoire, he learns that they have obtained Passover supplies through the American Jewish Joint Distribution Committee. He mentions their Passover service to Simone and Mira when they invite him to a small *seder* at their apartment.

"Oh," says Simone. "we used to love Passover, even if we were not that strict about looking for all the old bread crumbs! We didn't go to synagogue, but we always had a *seder* at home, with the traditional foods. Probably just as you had in Brooklyn!"

"When I was a kid," says Ben, "my father always led the *seder*. My sister and I always loved to search for the *afikomen*."

"Like here," adds Mira, "Samuel, as the eldest, usually led the *seder*. He loved to retell the story of the Israelites going out of Egypt." She pauses and looks sadly at Simone. "Whoever thought that last *seder* in our apartment would actually be our last one together?" She sighs.

"Did Guy ask the four questions?" asks Ben. He does not want to dwell on the sad moments.

"Oh yes, he was old enough to do that! He knew them when he was five years old," says Simone. "I am sure he has forgotten them by now."

But Guy has not completely forgotten. He has practiced. When Ben and Solly arrive at the Davals' for the *seder*, the boy is ready. Ben has brought the *matzos* and wine, and Solly has a huge bouquet of daffodils and pussy willow branches, which he gives to Mira. "You see," says Solly cheerfully, "spring is truly here!"

Even though it is the middle of the week, it is a holiday, and everyone looks their best. Ben and Solly wear freshly pressed dress uniforms and they have polished their shoes to a glow. Mira wears a dark blue dress with a striped vest, and her little touch of dark red lipstick adds some vibrancy. Simone, in a gray suit with a white blouse, wears her beautiful, thick hair piled high on her head. Like a crown, Ben thinks. And Guy looks very smart in a new brown tweed jacket, which he wears with a shirt and tie.

Simone has set a beautiful table and has arrayed a large platter with all the symbolic Passover items; their regular *seder* plate, an heirloom brought to France by Mira, disappeared along with their other things while they lived in hiding.

"*Ma nishtana halailah hazeh, mikol haleilot?*" chants Guy. "Why is this night different from all other nights?"

When he has completed all the questions, Ben cannot help commenting: "Guy, you sang the questions so beautifully! Did you remember them after all this time?"

"There is a boy in my class," says Guy. "He knows this better than I do. He and I have been practicing." He smiles shyly. "I wanted to surprise Maman and Gran'mère."

"Oh but you did, you did," says Simone, tenderly stroking the boy's hand. "It's a lovely surprise! Papa and Gran'père would be so proud of you!" And then, her chin quivering, she cannot speak any more.

Mira wipes her eyes with a corner of her handkerchief. "Samuel always used to practice the questions with Guy when he was little. Do you remember that, Guy?"

"I remember him being nice to me, Gran'mère. He never made me feel bad when I made a mistake."

After dinner, Ben asks everyone to sit close around the table so he can take their picture. Then Solly and Ben exchange places and Solly takes a photo of the four of them: Simone, Ben, Mira, and Guy. They are all smiling. Later, when Ben has the prints made, he notices that he is the only one looking truly serious. The Davals were the ones who had just come through years of deprivation and fear, but to look at this photo it was the American who seemed most preoccupied.

Why was that night different from all other nights, indeed?

## CHAPTER TWENTY

APRIL 1945:

# News at Last

Pale green buds float in the tree branches all up the Rue de Turbigo. The Sunday air feels lighter, and families walking to the various churches in the area seem cheerful as they pass. It's definitely been getting warmer, too, and Ben is wearing just his army shirt and khaki slacks. It's too warm for his jacket, especially if he's going to be playing ball. He is looking forward to this morning's outing with Guy. Guy had seemed genuinely interested when Ben had taken him to watch the Americans playing baseball, and afterwards Ben had showed the boy the fundamentals of pitching and catching. Guy had great coordination and a good sense of timing; Ben would enjoy honing the kid's skills.

At the same time that Guy has been recovering some of his Yiddish-speaking skills, Ben has been improving his own French, so they can now converse in an easy blend of Yiddish, French, and some English.

By now Ben is familiar with the neighborhood, and he greets Mme. Laforet, who lives above the Davals, as she exits the building. He holds the door for her and then crosses the tiled hallway to bound up the stairs.

Guy is sitting on the stairs a few feet from his door, holding a baseball listlessly in his hands. His light brown hair flops over his forehead. He raises his head when he sees Ben coming up the steps.

"Sergeant Ben!"

"*Bonjour*, Guy! Why the long face?"

"What?"

"Oh, sorry. It's an American expression. It means you look sad."

"I *am* sad."

Ben sits down on the step, next to Guy. "Why, what's wrong?"

"Now I know." He pauses, and then, "I have no father."

"What do you mean? What's happened?"

Guy answers slowly.

"A man came two days ago, looking for my mother. He looked very sick."

Ben can see that this is difficult for the boy. He is not sure where the story will lead, but he has an uncomfortable idea.

Just then the apartment door opens, and Mira is there. Lately she has been looking more animated—but that is gone now. She looks even older, her face pale and worn. Her eyes are rimmed with red—Ben immediately thinks she has been crying a lot or not sleeping, maybe both.

She speaks quietly, her voice tired. "We thought it might be you, Ben. We heard voices in the hallway. Please, come in, both of you."

Mira hugs Ben and draws him into the apartment, as Simone rises from a chair to greet him. She, also, looks worn out. Her face is pale. Ben notices that her hair has been put up somewhat carelessly, as straggling ringlets have escaped the pins and have fallen down to her shoulders.

"Guy started to tell me . . . someone came? What's happened?" Ben begins.

"Yes, late on Friday afternoon. Sit, I will tell you," says Simone. "Guy, you don't have to listen to all of this again, if you would rather go out."

"It's all right, I'll stay."

They all sit around the kitchen table and Simone begins. Her voice is quiet and slow, yet strong. "It's a short story, really. There was a knock on the door. We weren't expecting anyone, but I opened the door anyway. A man was there . . . I was so startled, I must have let out a cry, or something . . . I don't remember. This man, I had never seen him before. He looked very ill, thin and . . . his hair was short and wild, and his face was pale. Maman, right? His skin looked gray, or yellowish. But his eyes! His eyes seemed burning, fierce. And he was wearing . . ."

Mira jumps in, leaning forward in her chair, "Pajamas! Yes, pajamas! Striped, I think, loose and worn, dirty. Maybe this was someone who escaped from an asylum. I was actually frightened!"

"I was, too," continues Simone in her measured tone, "but also, I felt sorry for him. When he opened his mouth, I could see he had lost many teeth. And then he asked—in Yiddish!—'Where is Simone? I need to see Simone.'"

Simone pauses, placing her hand on her chest as if to control her heart. Her voice is steady, but, watching her eyes, Ben imagines a tempest inside her. Mira looks down, elbows on knees, shaking her head slowly from side to side, saying, "When we heard Yiddish on his lips, a Jewish man looking like a ghost, we both just froze."

Ben's mouth opens, but he chooses not to speak and lets Simone continue.

"'I am Simone, *monsieur*,' I said, and I invited him to come in and sit down. Maman made him some tea. And then he told us." Simone pauses, taking a few deep breaths. In the silence, a joyful laugh from the street below wafts in through their open window. "He said he met Jacques and Samuel in Drancy. He called Jacques "Yakov," you know, the Yiddish way. He had to be telling the truth, right, Maman?" She turns to Mira, who silently nods.

"He knew their names," continues Simone, "and he actually asked for me by name . . . He said his name was Josef. Maman and I could not say a thing. We just sat here and stared at him. He told us he came from Poland, too. Ben, he looked like an old man, but he was only around Jacques' age! He said they had many long talks, and promised each other that if either of them survived, he would find the other man's wife and tell her what happened. He explained how they memorized each other's addresses and the names of their wives and children. Josef knew that Samuel was my father and was very sick. But he also told me how Jacques tried his best to take care of him in Drancy."

Mira reaches over to her daughter, her hand trembling. Simone takes another deep breath.

"They were in Drancy a long time, months," continues Simone, dully, as though she has memorized Josef's story and is now reciting it. "He said no one knew what was going to happen. Suddenly one day they were told they were being deported to a work camp in Poland. Everyone was sentenced to hard labor. Josef said he had heard a rumor that if prisoners could do useful work, they might get better treatment. He was a shoemaker, and he knew that Jacques and Samuel were skilled tailors. But when the train arrived at this camp—a place called Auschwitz in a town called Oświęcim—the Germans started dividing the men into two groups. Strong and weak, younger and older. Josef said it all happened so fast . . . the guards were very rough and had these snarling dogs. The guards pushed older men, and anyone looking too weak or ill to work, to one door. Josef said Samuel was shoved that way.

"But Jacques wouldn't leave Samuel and tried to argue with the guards that Samuel was a good worker. Josef saw all this—he was in the other group. He saw a guard smash Jacques in the head with his rifle, and when Jacques fell—he shot him."

They all sit very quietly.

Finally, Simone continues, her voice now almost a whisper.

"Josef said he didn't understand how he survived years of hell in that camp. He thought Jacques might have survived, too, if he had just gone with Josef's group. But . . . Josef said he wanted me to know that Jacques had tried to help my father."

Mira nods silently, tightly twisting a handkerchief in her hands.

Simone sobs, "And that sounds just like Jacques! He loved my father." She leans on her mother, who puts her arms around the younger woman and rubs her back gently.

After a few moments, Ben speaks, if only to break the sorrowful tension. "This is the worst news you could have received," says Ben quietly, "but it also means that you . . . well, you know what happened."

Simone look up at him and asks, "It has to be true, right?"

"What reason would he have for making it up, Simone?"

She nods. "Yes, this is what I tell myself. And he came to *look* for me—in his condition!"

Ben really does not know what to say. He can't help it—his mind turns back a decade as he remembers his own father's death. He heard a report from the ambulance staff and then doctors at the hospital. He had to identify Abe's body at the hospital and make arrangements with the funeral home. Ben had evidence and his family had been able to say a formal goodbye. Simone and Mira have only Josef's word.

"It sounds," he finally says, "like Jacques did a very brave thing."

Mira adds softly, "Josef said his own survival seemed like a miracle, but he didn't believe in God anymore. He said to us, how can there be miracles if God lets some men turn into vicious beasts? He said he was liberated by the Russians. They came to this place Oświęcim in the winter—it took him all this time to get back to Paris! And then he had to leave, to see if his own family in Paris has survived.'"

"I still can't believe that Josef came to find us first, before his own people," says Simone, tears still streaming down her face and her voice picking up speed. "He would not stay to eat anything. He finished his tea and got up to leave. We told him about the message boards at the Hôtel Lutetia, and he said he would go there. Maman wanted to prepare a bag of food for him to take, but he was in a hurry. We said we would check on him in a few days, and we will, we will, won't we, Maman?"

Mira looks at her daughter with horror: "We don't know where he lives!"

Simone stares back at Mira, her hands rising to her cheeks. "Oh no!"

Ben speaks up, "We have some information—and maybe at the Lutetia we can find out, or perhaps Rabbi Nadich can help. Surely someone will know Josef."

Guy has not said a word, but sits motionless on the floor next to his mother's chair.

Simone looks down at him, slipping her fingers through his hair gently. "This is difficult for you to hear again, yes, Guy?"

He does not look up but stares down at the floor and shrugs. "It is what happened," he says quietly.

"So now, Ben, you see, we finally know," says Mira, raising her head to speak directly to the American. "It has to be true, we must take Josef's word for this. Why would a weak and sick man come looking to give this message, when he needed any remaining strength to locate his own people?"

"Maybe Papa could have gotten out," murmurs Guy from his place on the floor.

"Perhaps," responds Simone, "but we cannot know. We do know that he would not abandon Gran'père, so he was very brave." She pauses. "They were both very brave."

No one says anything.

Ben can hear the ticking of his watch.

Finally, Simone stands up and speaks. "Ben, it's a beautiful day. You and Guy should still have an outing. Go ahead, Guy. Gran'mère and I will keep each other company, and when you and Ben come back we'll have a nice dinner for you."

"I don't want to go out if you and Gran'mère are staying here and being sad," murmurs the boy.

"Guy," says his grandmother gently, "of course we are sad. But we are not surprised. Deep down, Guy, I think your mother and I both knew there would not be a good ending to this. But at least we found out, and we learned something . . . That poor Josef! I hope he finds his family."

Guy finally agrees to go out with Ben, and in a little while they descend the stairs and emerge onto the sunny street. "We don't have to play ball, Guy," says Ben. "We can just go for a walk, or I could show you the post office, or we could go to a park, whatever you want."

Guy nods. "All right. Let's go to the river and watch the barges."

"Whatever you say!"

They walk together silently. Ben knows he needs to say something comforting to Guy, and he figures he'll be able to do this because of his own experience—but it was so, so different for him. Over the past months, it has gotten easier for Ben to speak with Guy—linguistically, with their language mixture, but also emotionally.

They cross the Rue de Turbigo and make their way to the Rue du Temple, heading south. After going down several streets, Ben realizes that he is following Guy, and not the other way around.

"Guy, are you sure we are going in the right direction?" he asks.

"Of course! I know the best way," says Guy proudly, "from studying my maps.

"Do you know that this is one of the oldest streets in Paris?" asks Guy, looking up at Ben.

"They *all* look old to me, Guy," the soldier responds with a laugh. "Remember, America is new!"

Guy laughs in response.

"And it is named," he continues, "for the Knights Templar, you know, the Crusaders."

They walk together down the narrow street, stopping to admire the arched doors or worn wood, tall enough to admit a horse-drawn coach, with old carvings of animals over many entrances. Some shopfronts are boarded up, while others are brightly decorated for spring. For long stretches, Ben and Guy walk and say nothing. Ben tries to imagine the emotions flowing through the boy, but he can only guess. Suddenly the decade since Abe Gordon died in an ambulance on the way to the hospital in Brooklyn seems short. At once, Ben had become both the grieving son and head of the family. Losing his father changed everything for Ben. He wonders if it will be the same for Guy.

He also thinks hard about what he heard of Josef's story. Josef said he was liberated by the Russians during the winter—wouldn't this corroborate what he heard on the BBC back then? He remembers: the Russians said they found thousands of people—civilians, not soldiers—and evidence of real horror. POW camps were one thing—but the idea that huge numbers of ordinary people were being captured and killed, this was something new and terrible. Ben has a hard time absorbing this idea. He thinks about poor Josef, traveling from January until April to get back to Paris. What he must have gone through on that journey!

They are almost at the busy Rue de Rivoli, where Allied military vehicles pass and the broad sidewalks are crowded with civilians. Across this street is the Hôtel de Ville, the highly ornamented city hall adorned with statues of knights and soldiers, and beyond that, the Seine. Ben is startled just for a moment—his mind has been in Brooklyn and Poland, and the scene in front of him is a completely different world.

Groups of people are milling about, and some soldiers are strolling along, no longer the exciting novelty they were months earlier. A couple of cafés seem to be open.

"How about something to drink, Guy?"

The boy agrees, and they go into a small café where a young waiter approaches.

"*Bienvenus, monsieurs.* May I bring you something? We have Coke, sir!" And he smiles to Ben.

Sure, Ben thinks to himself, black market Cokes that were probably stolen from the US Army, and which you will try to sell me at an outrageous price. Because of course all Americans need to have their Cokes, yes? He smiles back at the waiter, asking if they have cold milk.

Ben orders two glasses of milk and two slices of chocolate cake. "You need to drink milk, Guy. It will help your bones to grow."

"Maman says it was very hard to get milk when the Germans were in Paris. But when I lived with Hélène's family, we had milk from their cow. Also at the mountain school. Sometimes we had goat milk."

Ben is distracted again. Why is this waiter young? He is not young enough to be a student—why wasn't he in the army? Perhaps he had been a collaborator or working in the *marché noir*. Ben feels guilty having these thoughts—for all he knows, the young man might be recently out of hiding. Or maybe he had worked with the Résistance.

"Do you have a father and mother, Sergeant Ben?"

Guy's question pulls Ben back to the moment. "What? Oh, oh, yes. I have a mother, but my father died ten years ago."

"What happened?"

"He was sick and never went to see a doctor, so when he finally went for help it was too late. But I remember him as a strong man. When he was young, he was a prizefighter. You know, a boxer. And he worked hard. He was like your father, in fact—he worked making clothing."

Guy brightens up. "Maman says Papa had a workshop in the apartment and made beautiful trousers for gentlemen. She says he was very good at his work."

Ben smiles at him—in fact, he realizes he is enjoying sharing these memories. "My father cut and attached leather trimmings to belts, coats, and suits. Before that he worked as a cutter in a dress factory."

"Do you remember your father?"

"Of course. But see, I was already an adult when he died. When I was a kid, he taught me how to fight, you know, boxing, if I had to." Ben takes a couple of mock swings at Guy, and they both laugh.

"He was very sweet to our mother," Ben continues, "and brought home flowers for her every Friday afternoon, for *Shabbos*. We used to go for walks together, on Sunday mornings, just the two of us, and talk about, oh, cars, baseball, other things. His English was not great, because he came from Poland, but I never laughed at him, I always tried to help him. He was very proud when he became an American citizen."

Ben speaks quietly, savoring the good memories. And Guy listens politely, nodding solemnly before speaking again.

"I don't remember much about my Papa. I feel very bad about this. I haven't told Maman. It would make her feel sad."

Ben looks at the boy—how awful for him, not even to have anything to remember. In a way, he's lucky, because there is less to miss. But then he must feel guilty because he *doesn't* miss his father. This is a tough one to puzzle out, and Ben isn't sure what to say. But he has to say something and try not to make Guy feel any worse.

He places his hand gently on one of Guy's shoulders. "Guy," he starts slowly, "there is a big difference in our situations. You were only seven or eight when your father was taken away, right? And you've had to move around a lot. The war, well, it's almost over, but it's still going on—I'm sure you were scared a lot. So forgetting—it's not your fault. I was a lot older—twenty-two when my father died. So I had saved up many memories. But I am sure your mother and grandmother have told you many good things about your father. And your grandfather, too."

Guy looks thoughtful and nods his head in agreement. But he does not speak.

"Their memories are very different from yours," continues Ben, "because they are adults. Ask them to tell you more things."

"*Oui*," Guy says, then sips his milk. He pauses, looking up at Ben: "Thank you, Sergeant Ben."

"You can just call me Ben."

"Maman says I have to show respect and address soldiers by their rank."

Ben laughs. "You are so right! Then you need to salute me!"

Guy's eyes open wide in surprise. "Really?"

Ben musses Guy's hair. "No, I am just making a joke! But I understand your *maman*. My mother taught me the same thing. I was always supposed to call people Mr. or Mrs. or Miss until I was an adult, and even then I was to do it until they gave me permission to use their first name. Your *maman* is very proper."

And smart, he feels like adding. And strong and brave. And beautiful. But he doesn't say those parts out loud.

# CHAPTER TWENTY-ONE

# The Truth Emerges

O n April 11, 1945, the US 6th Armored Division enters Buchenwald. The soldiers, unprepared for the reality of a concentration camp, are shocked and sickened to see stacks of bony corpses and survivors nearly as skeletal but somehow still clinging to life. Army photographers chronicle the event, even though they can hardly believe what they are seeing. In the next couple of weeks, other Allied forces liberate more camps. On the 29th of April, the US Army units liberate Dachau. General Eisenhower, touring the camps with the troops, tells soldiers in case they were uncertain what they were fighting for, they could now see what they are fighting against.

Word of these extensive atrocities against civilians gets back quickly to armed forces members behind the front lines. Reading reports in the papers, Ben realizes that all those rumors he had heard at home, years ago, proved true. And the upsetting radio report he had heard in January, that was true also. The Nazis had been rounding people up, all over Europe, and murdering them. Not just Jews. Other minorities. The disabled. Gypsies, political prisoners. These reports corroborate what he had heard from Josef's visit to the Davals. He feels sick inside. How many victims *were* there? No one seems to know.

At the same time, no one seems to know how many had been saved. The US troops had found survivors, but who were they and how many were there?

Simone and Mira no longer need to check on the message board at the Hôtel Lutetia. Other Parisians are still uninformed about what happened to their missing family members. Ben goes over to the hotel a couple of times in late April and early May to see if he can learn anything additional; maybe he will meet someone from the Davals' neighborhood, or perhaps he will find someone who knows something about deported Jews. POWs and others keep trickling into the city. As weeks pass and more survivors start to stumble back to Paris, the knots of people in front of the hotel and in the elegant lobby grow larger. Some more names are added to the message board. Occasionally there are shouts of joy as people are reunited.

Most people wait in vain.

One Sunday morning outside the Lutetia, Ben starts up a conversation with two French women, one older and one younger, both thin and tired looking. They hope to hear some word about their family's father and brother. "They were arrested during a *rafle* in our neighborhood," says the older one. "We were out, and some neighbors warned us not to go home. We have never heard from Max or Jean-Paul, and it's been over two years."

People see Ben's American uniform and assume they can speak freely to him—maybe they think he is some official who can assist them. Ben finds himself the recipient of much volunteered information. A young woman in a dark blue dress comes up to him and says, "My name is Lily. I have been living in a convent outside of Paris for over a year. The sisters have been wonderful, hiding a number of us Jewish girls. I've come here to see if there is any news of my older cousin. I heard from neighbors that she and her husband and two little children were taken in that big roundup, when they put people in the Stade Vélodrome."

"And where are your parents, Lily?" Ben asks her, although he is hesitant to do so.

"My mother died before the war. She was lucky to have missed all this. But my father . . . he was arrested in 1943 and then shot. The Germans put a notice in the newspaper and posted flyers around Paris. My father and others arrested at the same time. That's how I found out, from those posters."

Several people in the surrounding group nod knowingly.

"I'm sorry," says Ben quietly. Then he asks, "What is the Vélodrome?"

"It's a huge cycling stadium," a young man responds, "not far from the Tour Eiffel. They used to have races there. The Paris police arrested thousands of Jews, whole families, and locked them in there for almost a week. Then buses took them to Drancy, and from there . . ."

The young woman's dark eyes are wet and reflect pain. "The police missed me, because I was living on a farm, but my parents . . ." There is a pause, and the odd look on Ben's face prompts Lily to add, "The stadium is also called the Vel' d'Hiv."

"I am so sorry," says Ben. "I have heard about this roundup in the stadium, but only by this name you're telling me—Vel' d'Hiv. I've heard that thousands of Jews were taken, but also that many people had been warned and avoided capture." He feels he is getting battered by awful stories but is compelled to keep listening. Ben is reminded of the crowds from the memorial at the synagogue on the Rue de la Victoire, all gathered around him, the miraculous Yiddish-speaking American soldier. The pain in Lily's voice is the same as that in the voices of those who first told him of the Vel' d'Hiv. These people need people to hear them.

Lily nods. "True. Some police officers did the right thing and warned residents of what was coming. And there were other good people, like my neighbors. But most people—*most people*—just went along with the decrees. We still do not know how many Jews, exactly, were caught. It wasn't just one roundup. There were many." She pauses and her eyes narrow with anger. "And you know what else I heard?" She raises her voice, to make sure that many hear her. "That whole operation, at the Vélodrome, was run by the French. The *French! Our* people! They took mothers and little children. So who is the worse enemy—the *Boches* or our neighbors?"

The group erupts in angry outbursts and Ben has some difficulty hearing individual voices in French and Yiddish. He considers leaving, sensing that this familiar anger he has heard so much of from Simone has the potential to incite a riot. But he nods, saying, "This is not the first time I have heard about some of the French going along with the Nazis."

Another woman standing nearby, somewhat older with blonde hair turning to gray, looks at Ben with weary eyes. Her voice is soft, but her words are steely. "I hope your air force," she says, "pounds Berlin into powder." She pauses and inhales before continuing, "But you are our allies, so I don't know what you can do to the French."

Ben has no words.

Who *are* the French? he asks himself. The ones aligned with de Gaulle? Résistance fighters? The ones who went along with whatever Vichy said and helped the Germans? Or the ones who stayed quiet and kept their heads down?

Staff members at the Hôtel Lutetia try to be kind and helpful. One stands at the door to the lobby to answer questions from those coming to read the signboards, but he, too, seems overwhelmed by sorrow as he shakes his head sadly while responding to an inquiry.

Overcome with a new despair, Ben turns away and heads to the Métro. He has been invited to the Davals' this evening and has promised Guy to help him with his math homework. Math was always one of Ben's strong subjects, and he hopes his skills will blend with whatever math system the French are teaching.

Seated on one of the upholstered benches of the Métro, Ben observes the people in the car. They do seem more relaxed than he remembers Parisians looking during the winter. There are still shortages, but not as bad as they were. This will be their first spring without the oppressive presence of occupying soldiers. Or worrying about that man in the dark raincoat, the one staring at you. Or wondering if what you just whispered to your friend had been overheard and you were going to be reported. Now, colorful posters advertise new fashions and entertainment. Riders are smiling and laughing. A teenage girl wearing bright yellow beads to go with her yellow sweater is holding hands with a boy in a smart blue jacket.

Ben thinks about Guy and marvels that he does not seem more upset. Perhaps he is taking his cues from his mother and grandmother. At first, when they heard the news from Josef, they were saddened and shocked. But perhaps, as they had said, it was really what they expected. Only a few of the disappeared seem to have returned.

It is hot in the Métro car. Ben takes off his army cap and wipes his forehead with a handkerchief. Between learning about the German atrocities, worrying about the people deported from Paris, and his own crazy thoughts, his head is splitting. He knows that what he has been thinking is really not sensible. But he can't help thinking about it anyway.

He wonders if he can stay in Paris and . . . well, he could become part of the Daval family for real. He could marry Simone and become a dad for Guy. He has mentioned this a bit hesitantly, to Solly, because Solly has been his best friend since fourth grade. And he remembers how Solly had reacted. They had been sitting on a bench outside their quarters at the *gare* one evening. It was quiet, and they were smoking their pipes.

Solly had listened patiently as Ben hesitantly outlined why he loved being in Paris. But when Ben finally got to his central idea of staying here and marrying Simone, Solly took the pipe put of his mouth and exploded at Ben.

"Are you *nuts*, Ben? I had no idea it was this bad! Hey, if you don't go home, you don't have a job. If you stay here and try to get one, you'll be competing with all the French POWs who are returning, and compared to them, you are basically illiterate in French! Yeah, you're a big hero now, but you think you'll be able to land a job here? You think you'll be able to provide for a woman and a kid?"

Ben raised his hands in protest, trying to reason with Solly. "I know, I know. But it's not like others haven't come to France without strong French. All those immigrants! And you know I am quick to learn."

Solly leaned forward toward Ben and poked him in the chest with his index finger. "OK then, Sylvia will kill you. More likely, her parents will kill you. Your mother wouldn't kill you for not marrying Sylvia, because she doesn't want her sonny-boy to marry *anyone*. But she'd sure kill you for not coming home. And you know she'd take it out on Franny."

Solly rolled his eyes at Ben and took a few puffs as Ben rattled on: "And if I stay in Brooklyn, married to Sylvia, she'd take it out on Franny anyway, because Franny would be the one stuck living with Mom."

The two sat in silence for a few moments. Then Solly turned back to his friend, lowered his voice, and said slowly, "I can hardly believe you, Ben. We haven't even discussed the most important thing!"

Ben looked at Solly defiantly. "And that is?"

Solly had shaken his head and closed his eyes. "It's so obvious—which one do you *love?* Do you love Simone? And what does *she* want?"

Ben answered with determination: "Yes—yes! Simone is the most exciting woman I have ever met. The bravest. I know I have her up on a pedestal. I love looking at her, just being in the same room."

"And Sylvia?"

Ben sighed sadly. "Sylvia is Sylvia. She's a great girl, and smart. Frankly, we're comfortable with each other, okay? There's no . . . big excitement. But we get along." Ben stopped for a moment and then plunged on. "It's not just Sylvia. If I marry her—I know what the rest of my life is going to be. We'll get an apartment, live in Flatbush or Bensonhurst. Maybe, for a change of scenery, we could move to Queens. I'll stay at the post office. She'll work in an office. The end."

Solly smoked thoughtfully for a few moments, then removed the pipe and stared at Ben. "Have you *told* Simone how you feel about her?"

"Not in those exact terms."

Solly just stared at Ben.

Finally, Ben spoke again. "But here's another thing: that boy needs a father. I really care for him, Solly. I want to help guide him, do something to make up for all the lost father-son love he's never had. Yeah, I know it's crazy, but it's not so crazy, Solly!"

The fire had gone out in Solly's pipe and he tapped the bowl against the bottom of his shoe to knock out the tobacco ash. He turned to Ben once more.

"Look, genius-boy, no one would blame you for having a little adventure over here. Simone has had a difficult few years, she meets you, you are nice to her and attentive. Things happen. Fine. But this is not your world and you are not going to change your whole life for a fling in Paris."

"Shut up!" Ben jumped up from the bench and yelled at his friend. "How dare you say that Simone is just 'a little adventure' or a 'fling?' This is not like you and that WAC in London! I really care about Simone and I don't want to just . . . use her. No, they haven't kissed yet."

But Solly was still annoyed, snapping back at Ben. "Remember that discussion we had back in December, when I told you not to be a jerk? That was months ago! And you've still never let on that you are engaged?"

"It didn't come up, there was never a good time . . ."

Now Solly raged at him: "What kind of schmuck are you? I mean, I'm right, aren't I? You and Sylvia are still engaged?"

"We've never broken it off." Even as he said it, Ben knew he sounded weak. But he just didn't know what to do. He sat down again.

"Ben, you are asking for a lot of trouble," Solly said quietly. "Stick with your original plan. Why look for complications? Go home. Marry Sylvia, stay in Brooklyn, or move out to Long Island if you need to get away from your mother. Go back to your job or get a better one. Have a kid or two. Go to Ebbets Field and see the Dodgers with me."

"Aside from the Dodgers, Solly, that's not that thrilling. And what makes you the big expert?"

The other man shrugged. "I don't know. But judging from some of the kids we went to high school with, it's just easier not to mess things up with more problems. Stick with your own."

Ben shook his head back and forth. He had not been able to get through to Solly—but he also knew he was treading on thin ice here, thinking about ditching everything he had known. He slumped forward, putting his hands over his eyes and then up through his hair.

"I don't know what to do, Solly! Here I am, thirty-two years old, and this is really the first exciting thing that has ever happened to me. Living in Paris, meeting Simone, feeling like I can *do* something. Being here is like having a front-row seat to the start of something big."

Solly clapped one hand on Ben's back. "Just think, kid, *think*. Yes, I agree that you are a smart guy. Now prove it. You have to say something to Simone about Sylvia."

Ben nodded, "Yes, I know you're right, seriously. Soon—when it's the right moment—I'll tell her."

The Métro rolls into the Montparnasse station and a lot of riders stand up to get out. Ben has been lost in his thoughts and hasn't even noticed the number of stops they have passed. He rises from his seat and makes his way toward the exit stairs. What did he expect—an electric sign to come down from the sky with blinking arrows pointing to the words 'Tell Her Now?'

He climbs the stairs, one step at a time, without any energy.

## CHAPTER TWENTY-TWO

# Reality

**P**eople are screaming with joy in the streets. Tricolored banners flutter from the balconies of the buildings across from the post office on the Rue du Départ, and throngs are running down the Boulevard du Montparnasse to a giant celebration. Ben, while taking pictures in the plaza in front of the office, learns from a passerby that people are rallying near the Opéra. He joins the jubilant crowds hurrying there, threading his way through the packed streets to get a good view. It is May 8th, the day victory in Europe is declared.

Ben knows he should celebrate, too. But instead he sees his time in Paris ending. Not next week or the week after, but soon.

The war is still going on in the Pacific, and he knows that many fighting units will be sent there, if needed.

But he is too distracted by his own situation to think deeply about what might happen on the other side of the globe. Surely he is not the only American soldier thinking of staying in Europe. He will have to go home first. He is not going to be a coward and break up with Sylvia by mail. He has seen the results of guys getting letters like that from stateside sweethearts. It was wrenching for them—one of the worst letters a soldier could get. Ben will not be the kind of guy to send one.

Could he ask Simone to come to New York? Maybe Solly was right about the complications. She would have to learn English. But she would never leave her mother. So would all three of them have to be uprooted? Should he speak to Simone alone first, or to Simone and Mira together? This is the point where Ben stops thinking and his mind continues to spin on its own.

Surrounded by flags and noise and ecstatic crowds at the plaza in front of the Palais Garnier, Ben takes a few snapshots, then turns around and slowly makes his way back to the Gare Montparnasse.

Later that night, he goes to another celebration at the Place de la République with Simone, Mira, and Guy, and walks them back to their building afterwards. He and Guy sit outside for a bit to talk. Ben has loved spending time with Guy. The boy seems to have grown a bit taller, even in the eight months he has known him, and even despite the food shortages. Ben thinks that both freedom and the cans of American condensed milk he has supplied have played a part.

"Guy," Ben asks, "have you ever thought of having a *bar mitzvah?*"

"I don't know what that is, Sergeant Ben."

Ben smiles, saying, "Of course you don't—you haven't had the chance to see one. Usually, every Jewish boy has one at the age of thirteen."

"Did you have one?"

"Of course."

"And your father?"

"Yep. But I wasn't there." They both laugh.

"But what is it?" asks the boy.

"It's a religious ceremony where a boy makes the transition from being a child to being an adult, at least in the Jewish community. You do this by reading a passage from the Torah, the Jewish Bible, in Hebrew and saying a blessing. Then you are an adult."

"It doesn't sound too hard."

"It's not if you have heard others do it. And if you have heard people chanting from the Torah. You don't just read aloud, you sort of sing it. Can you read Hebrew?"

"No. But remember at Passover, I sang those four questions?"

"I do. And you have a really good voice!"

"I couldn't read the Hebrew letters. But a boy in my class at school wrote out the words in regular letters, and then I learned the words and the tune by heart."

"You could do this, Guy! I think it would make your *maman* and *gran'mère* very happy."

"Do you think my papa had a *bar mitzvah?*"

"I'm sure he must have! If he went to a Jewish school in Poland, he would have learned the prayers. Even in families that are not religious, the boys study for a *bar mitzvah.*"

"Does it take a long time to learn?"

"Depends on whether you read a long part of the Torah or a short one. You could learn this in a month. Some boys study for a year, but they are usually very religious and recite a long passage. I forgot to tell you that in America—I don't know about France—you also get gifts."

Guy's eyebrows rise a bit. "Like another birthday!"

When he brings Guy upstairs a little later, Ben mentions the idea to Simone.

"Let's talk about this later, Ben, after Guy goes to sleep," she says flatly.

She turns away abruptly and closes the apartment door. Ben stands in the hallway facing the closed door. Simone could not have made it any clearer that this topic is not welcome. He goes downstairs and outside the building to wait for Simone. Sitting on the bench that he and Guy had occupied, he slowly fills his pipe and lights it, watching a trail of fragrant smoke rise through the dark air. About twenty minutes later, Simone emerges from the building. For just a couple of seconds, as she opens the tall door, light inside the foyer illuminates her from behind, and she is a shimmering silhouette. Then the real woman is in front of Ben, seating herself on the bench.

"So what is this you are filling Guy's head with?" she asks.

"You disapprove."

"It's not that I approve or disapprove. It seems pointless. Being Jewish is what got Jacques in trouble in the first place. Being Jewish is dangerous. Guy doesn't need this extra study. And it won't help him get into a top *lycée* either."

"Why does it have to be a top *lycée?*"

"Because I am ambitious for Guy. You think I want my son to be a tailor like his father and grandfather? To sit all day at a sewing machine like them, and like me? He has learned French. With the Yiddish he has been hearing, it will be easy for him to pick up German at the *lycée*. And then he can learn English. He will have a chance. He is a smart boy, and in France he will be able to go to university."

Ben listens and then rushes in with a solution.

"Have you ever thought about educating him in America? Our schools in New York are excellent, and free—right through university." He knows he is pushing too hard, has said too much. He has played his hand, and now Simone knows exactly what he has been thinking about. And he fights the panic he immediately feels—what if she agrees?

Simone gives Ben a long look that begins with a frown and ends with a sad smile. She places her hand on top of his.

"I think I understand you," she says quietly. "But don't you think this boy has been uprooted enough? And my mother won't leave France. She isn't very well, you know."

"No, I don't know. She looks healthy to me."

"She has a heart condition and did not see a doctor for more than three years. Now, as you know, she has seen one. But although she seems fine, her heart is not strong. Paris is the only home she knows, even if for a while it was not a good Paris."

Ben hears a "no" in the making, so to save himself from possible embarrassment, he switches back to the earlier topic. "Well, what about the idea of a *bar mitzvah?* Wouldn't it be a good thing to keep this tradition? And Guy would be called to read by his father's name. In a way, that would make Jacques part of the ceremony, too."

Simone bends her head to one side, narrowing her eyes as she stares at Ben.

"Why are you so persistent, Ben, when you told me that you yourself are not religious?"

Now she is forcing him to defend himself, and he tries. "This isn't religious, really. It's . . . it's a tradition. All right, it's a religious tradition. But didn't you have a *bris* for Guy?"

"Yes," says Simone, her voice a stage whisper with an angry edge, "and that was another thing I constantly worried about—while he was living as a Christian, what if someone saw that he was circumcised? His life was at risk! Being Jewish made him vulnerable!"

Ben sees that she is not mad at him—she is scared, or has been. Even now, Ben thinks, though she has no reason to be frightened, those years of hiding and pretending are still taking their toll.

He responds to her gently. "Simone, I know I take some things for granted. I have never had to hide being Jewish in America. I've felt safe. And I don't know the kinds of things you and others here faced."

He suddenly seizes her hand and looks at her deeply. "But if you turn your back on all the traditions—then the Nazis and others like them have their victory."

She is quiet for a few moments, letting her hand rest in his. Then she withdraws it, slowly. "I need to think more about it," she says softly.

Now that Simone has calmed down, Ben doesn't want to ruin things by pushing. She will discuss this with Mira and Guy, and they will make a decision. Right now, he has to think about getting back to the post office; it's late, and he is on censor duty in the morning. He and Simone exchange quick Parisian kisses, and then he heads back.

On the way he passes jubilant people, couples with their arms around each other's waists, fathers carrying children waving French flags. Ben feels, oddly, just a tiny bit regretful that the war is ending. For despite all the deprivation and the horror and fear under which all Parisians lived, it's a beautiful and exciting city, and he has loved being here. And being with Simone.

## CHAPTER TWENTY-THREE

# Guy's Bar Mitzvah

On a warm Saturday morning in early July, six American service-men in dress uniform come up the steps from the Temple stop of the Paris Métro. They walk three abreast along the wide sidewalk of the Rue de Turbigo. Ben is proud of his uniform, and proud to be from the country that helped France stand up straight again. The presence of Allied troops in uniform is no longer a novelty in Paris, yet they still draw admiring glances because, as at least one of them realizes, they are so sharp and handsome. Solly Lipman winks at a pretty young woman who has jumped off her bicycle in the street to stand and gaze at the men in khaki.

The Americans turn left into the Rue Notre Dame de Nazareth, a narrow and quiet street of drab buildings. About a third of the way down the block on the left, however, is the Synagogue de Nazareth, named for the street. An arched gateway leads to its outer courtyard. While it is smaller, older, and less imposing than the synagogue on the Rue de la Victoire, it has a similar architectural style.

Past the courtyard is the entrance to the main sanctuary, with a stair-case to the side leading up to the women's gallery. This is an Orthodox, traditional congregation, unlike some of the *shuls* Ben has attended in New York, where men and women sit together. The soldiers move down the center aisle and take seats close to the front.

They sit down together, and Ben looks up to the women's gallery; Mira and Simone are already there, and they smile down at Ben. Solly Lipman is there, as well as Al Davis and Jack Einhorn, and two other Jewish soldiers Ben recruited from another unit. Most of the soldiers do not remove their military caps, but Einhorn has exchanged his for a dark *yarmulke*.

They are all present for the *bar mitzvah* of Guy Daval. The gathering is not huge, although, Ben notes as he gazes around, there is obviously seating for several hundred. He wonders, as he looks around at the many empty seats, how many members of the congregation were deported and killed. Perhaps some people were able to flee France or might still be living in other parts of the country. Ben also imagines that some may have lost their faith during the dangerous years. There could be a number of reasons for the empty pews.

The sanctuary itself looks worn, but clean. Dark blue velvet curtains, faded and patched in places, hang at the front, and the blue carpet is threadbare. But someone has polished the brass candelabra, and there are two large vases of fresh flowers in front of the *bimah*, the raised reading platform up front.

Ben and Solly look around for Guy, then realize that he is probably with the rabbi. A couple of women, about Simone's age, sit down in the row behind Simone and Mira in the women's balcony, greeting them. A few more men of various ages, all wearing dark suits and hats, enter quietly. One of them approaches the soldiers.

"Welcome to our *shul*. Thank you for coming today. I speak some English. My name is Jean-Pierre Keller."

The Americans rise to greet him, and they shake hands as M. Keller introduces the others. "This is Serge, and Léon, Guillaume, and Isaac. We are not many, but there are more here now than those who came in October and November. People are coming back from outside Paris, and from outside France." He pauses and lowers his eyes in sorrow. "We do not yet know all who are not coming back."

"We understand," says Solly. "The *bar mitzvah* boy—he has lost his father and his grandfather."

"We know. It is such a blessing to see young Guy here. To continue. You know, this is the first *bar mitzvah* we have held here since . . . things began. This makes us feel there is hope."

A few more people sit. A man with a boy of about six. Three more women appear upstairs. Ben notices there are no old people. He also sees, to his relief, that there is a *minyan*—the required presence of at least ten men.

Just then a door near the front of the sanctuary opens, and two men come out with Guy. Guy has a new suit for the occasion, including his first pair of long dress pants. He wears a new white shirt with a striped tie. Before, he wore the short pants and knee socks traditional for French boys. Today marks the beginning of his adult life, as least as a Jew. Solly smiles and nudges Ben, because the new suit has been their gift. The kid looks good.

They watch intently as Guy puts a *yarmulke* on his head. Everyone rises as the rabbi begins the prayer service, placing a *tallis* around Guy's neck. The other man, serving as the cantor, chants the liturgy. Holding the Torah in his arms, Guy follows the rabbi and cantor in a procession around the synagogue interior before returning to sit at the front.

Ben had forgotten how long a Sabbath service could be, but he is too focused on Guy, Guy's mother, and members of the congregation to be bored for a moment. When the time comes to open the Torah scroll and read from it, Ben finds himself biting his lip. He sees more than one man wiping away tears.

Several men are called up to the front to recite blessings over a portion of the Torah reading. M. Keller is the first. Then Ben is called, and he hardly has to glance at the prayer book; he remembers the ancient words as if he had recited them just yesterday. The next blessing is read by Solly. Being given these honors is a surprise to both of them, and they feel humbled to take part.

Finally, it is Guy's turn to say the blessing and then read a portion of the text in Hebrew. The rabbi guides him to find the right place in the scroll and gives him a small silver pointer so guide his way. Guy's voice is still a boy's—somewhere between a soprano and alto—and his chanting is melodic and clear. He has had about six weeks to prepare. Ben, Solly, and Jack Einhorn have each worked with him. And this rabbi probably has as well. It is not a long portion—there was not enough study time for that—but what Guy does read, he reads very well.

Afterwards, when the service is over, they all share lemonade and cookies in the front courtyard. Guy is accepting congratulations from people he knows and doesn't know. Ben hears one man tell him how much it means to see a young boy following the Jewish traditions, to hear his chanting in a building that had not heard voices at all for several years.

Ben approaches the young rabbi, who is wearing a dark suit rather than the long robe he remembers from his *shul* in Brooklyn, to thank him for assisting Guy. "Oh, but I am not a rabbi, sir," says the young man.

"Our rabbi, and his whole family, were deported. Only God knows what happened to them. I was studying at a *yeshiva* in London before the war, and just came back a few months ago to help."

"Is . . . your family safe?" Ben asks hesitantly.

The young man shakes Ben's hand solemnly, saying, "Thank you for asking. Most of us are all right. My mother and sister also got out, to London, just before the Germans occupied Paris. My father stayed behind to close his business and was supposed to meet us in England. But . . . he was caught in a roundup." Both he and Ben know what that means.

The Americans are taking Guy, his mother, and his grandmother out to lunch. They stroll down the Rue de Turbigo, past the Lycée Turgot, to a lovely small restaurant. Mira is chatting happily with Solly, and Guy has the attention of the other soldiers. Ben walks next to Simone.

"Thank you for agreeing to allow Guy to have his *bar mitzvah,* Simone."

"The decision, finally, was up to Guy. He thought about what his Papa and Gran'père would have wanted, and he said, 'I will do this for them.'"

"He is a smart young man, and wise. Thoughtful."

They reach their destination and enter the restaurant. Before the end of the meal, the soldiers give Guy special gifts to mark the event. Jack presents an official US Army Jewish prayer book, a small softbound volume with a military olive-green cover. Solly gives Guy a boxed set containing a Parker ballpoint pen a and mechanical pencil. From Al Davis, an army pocketknife. The other two soldiers, Bob Simon and Joe Shapiro, give him a compass and a military whistle.

Ben's gift, in a small box which he passes to the boy, is a Bulova wristwatch. He had written to Franny a couple of months ago, asking her to send it from New York. Guy's eyes widen, and he puts on the watch immediately. "This is the first watch I have ever had!" he exclaims with delight.

"*Merci, merci beaucoup!*" says Guy to the soldiers, as he shows off his gifts to his mother and grandmother.

"You have given Guy such a memorable day," says Simone gratefully. "And to give him gifts, too, really, this is beyond kind."

"I know that this *bar mitzvah* celebration would have been such a source of pride for his father and grandfather," says Mira as she dabs at her eyes.

Guy looks up solemnly to the assembled soldiers and nods. "Thank you for coming today, and for these gifts—I will always treasure them!"

For just about everyone, this is a happy and memorable day. After lunch, the Americans, except for Ben, go off on an expedition to the Louvre. Ben walks back to the apartment with the Davals. He asks if anyone wants to go for a walk up to Sacré-Cœur. It's already after five in the afternoon, and it won't be quite so hot.

"Not for me!" protests Mira. "I've had a long day, and think I'd prefer to stay here and knit."

"And I'll stay with Gran'mère. I need to rest and *not* study," says Guy, laughing. Ben knows the kid wants to examine his new treasures.

Ben and Simone start out, heading northwest along the Boulevard de Magenta at a leisurely pace. They are in no hurry. They stop and look in shop windows like any other couple. Eventually they reach one of those multipronged intersections where many roads converge.

"If I had to find my way around here," says Ben, "I would go nuts."

"Just remember that the sun sets in the west," responds Simone, and she takes his arm protectively, like a mother protecting her child from becoming lost.

They cross and turn left onto the Rue de Dunkerque. Ben's questions sit in his throat like rocks. If Simone doesn't bring up the subject, he will have to. "Have you thought any further about what I mentioned earlier?

About coming to New York?"

When Simone looks directly at Ben, it is with a gaze both tender and sad. She sighs before she responds. "Oh, Ben, I can't ask my mother to leave Paris. Really, this is the only home she has known. If I were on my own, maybe . . . but I'm not on my own."

They continue walking in silence. Then Simone speaks again. "I've been hearing," she says, "about some American soldiers who are planning to move here."

"Yes, I have too. But they have to be decommissioned first. Then they can come back. When you are in the military, their rules come first."

The street brings them out to another broad boulevard.

"Look up," Simone advises.

There, on a hill above them, rises the domed white church, the Basilica of Sacré-Cœur, just starting to turn orange with the golden rays of the early evening sun. Ben has read that the church is often described as a wedding cake, as it rises in ornamented tiers. They still have a way to go. Ben hates to admit that he is getting tired; they have been walking for almost an hour.

"Just a bit more," urges Simone, "And then we can take a cable car to the top. Or a huge stairway if you prefer!"

They opt for the stairs. It takes them another fifteen minutes to reach the top, but the view, when they turn around to see it, is absolutely worth their every step. Ben is entranced, looking down at Paris spread before them, starting to twinkle.

Simone points out what they are seeing. "Notice the dome, over to the right? That is the Panthéon. And further to the right, you can see it?"

"Yes! It's the Eiffel Tower!"

"From here, you can see everything in Paris! Look, to the left of where we are, you can see the outlines of the two big train stations we passed, on our way over. The Gare du Nord and Gare de l'Est."

"You know this well! Have you come up here a lot?"

"Oh, but of course! When I was a child, growing up near here, it was a favorite outing! My parents loved the view and enjoyed watching me run up and down the steps until I was exhausted. Then my father would lift me onto his shoulders, and we would walk home that way."

Simone smiles to herself at the happy memory. For a few seconds Ben sees a distance in her eyes, her face—as if this view has transported her to an earlier time.

"Jacques and I did this, as well," she continues. "We walked up many times before we were married, late on Sunday afternoons. We would stop at a café for something to drink if we had a little extra money. And then we would watch the sun setting, just as we have done tonight."

"You must miss him a lot."

She nods, but her voice is flat and unemotional: "I have gotten used to the idea. There is no use looking back."

They sit down on the next-to-top step and watch the setting sun in silence.

Ben is torn. Simone has basically said that no, she cannot go to the United States. The easiest, the best, the most logical thing to do right now is to accept that and forget anything else. He feels guilty trying to take advantage of the situation, to step into a dead man's shoes. But technically Simone is free, and so, in a way, is he.

How can he resist this moment? His sense of logic has wandered off somewhere. The air has cooled, and Ben sits high above Paris as it is silhouetted against the setting sun, a beautiful, warm woman sitting very close to him. He turns toward Simone just as she looks at him, and he places one finger softly under her chin. When he puts his other arm around her back and pulls her gently toward him, she presses her lips against his.

Then she sits back a bit, and gazes lovingly at him.

"Oh, Simone . . ." And they resume their kiss as the sun sets, leaving them embracing in the dark.

## CHAPTER TWENTY-FOUR

# Summer And Another Fall

"It's the time for *vacances*," says Simone to Ben. "Vacations. Summer holidays. French people do this every year, especially in Paris."

"Everyone gets a vacation at the same time?"

"Almost everyone. It is a tradition. Of course, during the war it was different, and last summer, very different. And some people must stay here in Paris, to run the hotels and museums and restaurants. But many places just close because all the workers leave the hot city. They go to the beach. Or the mountains. Paris gets so hot, and quiet."

"Well, no vacation for us," Ben responds. "The generals say no troops are going home anytime soon. In fact, some of our combat units may go over to the Pacific. Poor guys. It's rough there. And they have just finished a hard fight in Europe."

It is a Sunday morning, and they are sitting on a bench in the Jardin du Luxembourg. It is the end of July and already so hot that Parisians venture outside only in the mornings or evenings. Amazing what has happened in just one year, thinks Ben. Last year at this time, the Allies were blasting their way through northern France to Paris. This year, Europe is free and in Allied hands. And Ben is with people who feel like a second family, enjoying a beautiful, if hot, day in a gorgeous Parisian park.

"*Allons*, Sergeant Ben!" calls Guy from another bench. He is trying to teach Ben more French. "I have the boat ready to launch!" He and Mira rise and start to walk toward the round pond near the Palais du Luxembourg. Guy and Ben have worked on this smart-looking boat for several weeks, and it is freshly painted in red, white, and blue; they did this on purpose to show love for both of their countries.

Ben and Simone start to follow them. "The dress factory is giving us all some time off, which is perfect since there is still not enough fabric for us to use. But things are getting better. After all, how can you stop Paris fashion?"

"So what will you do?" asks Ben. He hopes the Davals will stay in Paris so he can spend more time with Simone.

"We all need country air, so we will go to Hélène and Jean-Marc's for the last two weeks in August."

"Terrific for you!" says Ben, smiling to conceal his disappointment. "And cooler weather, too, perhaps."

"Even if it's just as hot there, the buildings are lower, there are more trees for shade, and there is a stream where the children can play and cool off," says Simone. "But we will miss you, Ben."

Some children run past them along the park's tree-lined, pebbled path, also on their way to the boat pond. The walk is dappled with light as the sun shines down through the leaves.

When the time comes, Ben sees the Davals off at the Gare Montparnasse. He gives each of them a kiss on each cheek, and then an extra kiss for Simone, who blushes. Only after the train pulls out does he realize that he does not have their address, so he cannot write.

"Hey, Gordon!" Al Davis calls to Ben as he comes back into the post office. "Want to go to a show at the Folies Bergère tonight?"

"Sure, why not?" Ben tells himself he needs the diversion from the thoughts pinging back and forth inside his head. But he'll keep these thoughts to himself while catching up on the Paris scene he has been missing.

When he is out with the other soldiers, Ben picks up a small brochure called *Paris Spectacles*, and looks through it for ideas of entertainments to attend. *Boris Godunov* is playing at the Palais Garnier, with special prices for Allied soldiers; tea dances are going on at a number of clubs; there are programs at cabarets and music halls, and all kinds of films. There are plays in English produced especially for the British and American forces. And there are French shows; Ben sees an ad for one called *Rose-Marie* at the Théâtre du Châtelet, and although he has no idea what it's about, he wonders if Simone might enjoy it. He folds the brochure and puts it in his jacket pocket to discuss with Simone when she returns to the city.

When he has time, Ben explores other parts of the city, sometimes by himself, sometimes with Solly or a couple of the other boys. He discovers the marketplace at Les Halles at night, enjoying a serving of traditional onion soup, with gruyere cheese melted on top and dripping over the sides of the brown crockery bowl. He explores the offerings of the *bouquinistes*, the bookstalls lining the stone walls along the banks of the Seine, and finds some antique fashion prints to take home. He and Solly go to Les Invalides and gaze at the tomb of Napoleon. And in between all the sightseeing, they drop themselves into the sidewalk-facing rattan chairs at different cafés and admire the passing parade while sipping chilled wine or mugs of beer.

And still Ben avoids thinking about what he ought to do. Simone will not come to the US. Is he prepared to return to France as a civilian? What skills could he bring that would be desirable? His thoughts keep hitting a dead end here. Sure, he could do this if he were a famous novelist or a foreign correspondent, or worked for some big international company, or were simply rich. But he is just a postal clerk who can speak passable French, is good with numbers, and is interested in photography.

"Solly," he asks one day as they sit over glasses of white wine at the Café de la Rotonde, "What are we going to do after this is over? We can't act like Paris never happened to us."

"I think we're going to have a choice, sonny," answers Solly after a few thoughtful moments. "And that choice will be: to remember this experience and move on with our lives, or to remember this experience and be miserable because it's over. Remember that popular song from the last war—'How are you going to keep them down on the farm, after they've seen Paree?' We've been lucky. We've seen more of the world than most folks we know. And we haven't been shot! Let's just enjoy this, as long as it lasts."

Ben stares into his wineglass. Finally, he says, "There may not be anything as exciting as this ahead of us."

"Maybe, maybe not. You've got a wedding to look forward to, right?"

"I suppose so."

Solly is alarmed by Ben's resigned tone and defeated expression.

"What do you mean, 'suppose so?' A lot of people back home depend on you—Fran, your mom, Sylvia, Sylvia's folks—"

Ben cuts him off. "What about here? People depend on me here, too!"

Solly stares hard at his friend and clears his throat before speaking. "They got along before you arrived, didn't they? Simone is tough. The guts of that woman! She is a survivor."

"No, Solly, they *didn't* just get along. Sure, things are better for them now, but they have been through awful, horrific times. Yes, Simone is tough—more than any woman I know. But still. You know, when I'm not at the post office, I practically live over there."

"True enough. But you actually *do* live in Brooklyn." Solly pauses and looks closely at Ben. "Hey, what's with the face? You've explained everything to Simone, right?"

Ben doesn't answer, just looks fixedly into his wineglass.

Solly shakes his head from side to side. "You idiot! You *still* haven't told Simone about Sylvia? Oh, Ben, you have to be realistic. Simone lives in one world, you live in another. Wait—she's not pregnant, is she?"

"Solly!"

"Sorry, sorry! I had to raise the question, no? OK, so you haven't been *really* stupid. But come on, Simone could never live in Brooklyn. She wants to stay here, right? At least, she has to because of her mother and Guy. Listen to me, please. Leave it alone. She'll meet a Frenchie and will marry him. It's life. Stop your moping."

The beginning of September arrives, and everyone who has been away returns to Paris. The Davals have not told Ben exactly which day they will return, so he does not meet them at the train station. He visits them the next weekend. Guy is preparing for school and will soon be applying to a *lycée*. He has grown over the summer, taller, at least a couple of inches, but is still thin. He wears long pants all the time now, for he is not a child anymore.

For the second time, Ben celebrates the High Holidays with Guy and his family. The sorrow of losing Jacques and Samuel is still there, but somewhat muted. The family at least knows something about what happened to them. "We have been learning," says Mira sadly, "that they were just two among thousands, thousands of people taken from Paris."

Simone murmurs: "Including thousands of children—murdered. Young people in the Résistance—murdered. And not just poor immigrants—families who have lived in France for generations all lost people. But de Gaulle says—" Here she pauses and makes a derisive puff with her lips. "—We must act like one nation now. Heal. Ignore the collaborationists who may live across the hall. Yes, we all must work together to rebuild France."

Ben listens to the resignation in her voice. But it's preferable to, he reasons, and healthier than being consumed by bitterness.

"Ah," Simone continues, "there is nothing else to do. Guy has been saved, and that is what matters."

Later, Guy confides to Ben that this does make him feel lucky and special—but also burdened. "I *must* do well in school, Sergeant Ben, and get into a good *lycée*. Maman and Gran'mère depend on me. I am afraid of disappointing them."

"Just try your best, Guy. That's really all you can do."

Toward the end of October, Ben's commanding officer sends for him, Solly, and two others. They go to his office, and he asks them to shut the door. The CO looks serious as usual, and the men react in kind, wondering what their shortcomings might be. Ben was under the impression that their postal office was operating efficiently.

"At ease, men," says the CO. "Please sit down. First, I want to commend you on a job very well done. The Seine Section Army Post Office is running great. Both incoming and outgoing. No bottlenecks. This means a lot to the troops and to the families at home."

They relax a bit. Maybe there will be a promotion?

"Unfortunately, in Germany things are not going as well. So we need to send you there. Frankfurt is going to be the center of operations for the Army of Occupation under the leadership of General Patton. You four will report to Frankfurt on the first of November. You will take charge of their army post office and get things set up as you have done here. Any questions?"

Of course Ben has questions, but right now he cannot swallow. He should have anticipated this instead of deluding himself into thinking he'd be in Paris for his entire European deployment.

"All right—dismissed, gentlemen!"

Ben rises with the other men but hangs back to speak with his CO. "Sir," he begins, hesitantly.

"Yes, Sergeant Gordon?"

"As you know, sir, I was one of the first men here, and really took charge of this operation."

"I know, Gordon. This place is a terrific example. I am praising you—why don't you look happy?"

"I was thinking, sir, that for this reason I might be allowed to remain here to continue in a leadership role."

"You *have* a leadership role, Sergeant." The CO pauses and looks at Ben. Then he realizes something.

"Sergeant Gordon, have you formed any civilian alliance here?"

"Yes, sir, there is a . . . family I have become quite fond of."

"Your commitment to the army comes first, Gordon. You know that. And we need you in Germany. Frankfurt is not Paris. Here, in a little while, the French will be running everything. They are our allies; the Germans are not. Our men are in Germany as a force of occupation. It's a whole other ball game, and I'm sure you can appreciate that."

"Yes, sir."

"Tell your friends goodbye, and that you will write to them. You have your orders. Dismissed."

"Yes, sir!" Ben salutes smartly, and the CO salutes in return. And then Ben turns and walks out of the office. Three days, and then they have to leave. Three days.

Ben feels like he has been punched, hard, in the gut. He is angry with the army, and also with himself. He should have known this could happen! He should have anticipated. He was stupid, stupid to think he would spend the rest of his army duty in Paris.

The next evening after work, Ben goes to the Daval apartment for, as he believes, the last time. Or at least, as he tells them, the last time before he goes to Germany—in two days. It is painful for him to speak. Everything has happened so suddenly. He explains what the CO told him and the other soldiers. It's not his choice, not what he wants—it's a military assignment.

At first there is nothing but silence in the Daval apartment. Finally, Mira speaks, saying, "Ben, you have been a tremendous blessing to us. You came to us at a time when we needed help, and you have been a wonderful friend. We just didn't think you'd be leaving so soon."

"Neither did I," he answers.

"Why didn't they tell you earlier, or give you more time to prepare?" Simone wants to know.

Ben can hardly look her straight in the face because he feels so torn. He just shakes his head and says, "I tried to ask my commanding officer if there was any way I could stay. But he insisted. That's the army. If they tell you to do something, you can't argue. You have to do it."

Everyone has said something except Guy. He is sitting on a wooden chair with all of them, looking down and ripping a piece of paper into smaller and smaller pieces. When he finally starts to speak, his voice breaks.

"Hey," says Ben, helping to cover the boy's awkward moment, "your voice is starting to crack a bit—that means it's changing, it's the beginning of your getting a man's voice!" He shakes Guy's hand, and then clasps him in a hug.

Guy, still looking down, murmurs something about having to study for an examination and rushes from the room.

Ben has to leave, and he stands.

"I'll check on Guy and make sure he's all right," says Mira. "Have a safe journey, Ben."

"Thank you, Mira," he responds, hugging her.

After she leaves the room, Ben and Simone move slowly toward the apartment door. It is all he can do to control his voice as he turns to her.

"Simone . . . you are the bravest woman I have ever met. I think you are so special, and I wish I could stay here longer. I wish that, with all my heart!" He embraces her very tightly. "I'll write, I promise. And I'll let you know when I might be able to come back to Paris."

"Are you sure you know the address, for when you write to us?" asks Simone with a little lilt in her voice. She, also, is trying to sound lighthearted.

"After coming here so often for a year and a half? I have this address engraved on my heart!"

"*À la prochaine fois!*" she cries. "Till the next time!"

They give each other double kisses, then Ben is out the door and down the stairs, biting his lower lip.

**CHAPTER TWENTY-FIVE**

## NOVEMBER 1945:

# Frankfurt am Main

The large home on a grassy hill just west of the city, built in the early 1930s with a combination of modern Art Deco curves and half-timbered stucco, seems to Ben to reflect traditional German village architecture. It looks like many German buildings he has seen in American magazines. He and Solly learn that this house belongs—or had belonged—to a manager at IG Farben, the giant chemical company headquartered in Frankfurt. But it was requisitioned by the United States, so now American officers are billeted there. Corporal Carter, one of the young soldiers who takes them up to their rooms, gives them a brief overview.

"We take all our meals together," Carter tells them. "Army cooks, so we don't have to worry about being poisoned by the locals. Yeah, and another thing, get ready to hear from the servants here that none of them were Nazis." He raises his voice to a German-accented falsetto: "'Oh no, *I* vasn't a member of the Party—but *she* vas.' That sort of thing. Just assume they were all Nazis and it'll make things easier."

Ben and Solly smile at Carter and nod in assent, and then he goes back downstairs. The men look around their new quarters. A spacious second-floor bedroom with a modern, attached bathroom. Framed Alpine scenes on the walls. The large windows overlook the suburb of Höchst, which they cannot see now because it is dark. They have arrived after dinner.

"Hey, it beats a crappy roomful of army cots under a bridge at a train station."

"When you put it like that," notes Ben, "it's almost appealing."

They stow their gear in the closet and dresser, then head downstairs to the large living room, where a fire is blazing on the hearth. A couple of officers are listening to the radio, while others are sprawled, reading, on the large leather armchairs and couches. After the whole crew from the Paris APO have settled in, they introduce themselves all around. The new men get maps of Frankfurt and all the Armed Forces offices that have been set up. As officers, they are placed in the relatively calm Höchst instead of central Frankfurt.

Corporal Carter tells them a little bit about their new home. "This is a really nice section," he tells them proudly. "For one thing, we didn't bomb these buildings, so you have nice roofs and windows!" The men laugh a bit. "The folks at IG Farben knew how to take care of their friends, and so do we. So their 'Farben Kasino' is now the EUCOM Inn, a club for members of the Allied services. That's the center of all the post activities. Check it out on your maps and find some time to go. Tomorrow morning, we'll go on a tour of the main city and Armed Forces facilities. Be ready at 0830 hours."

Ben notices on his map there is a Jewish chaplain's office in Frankfurt as well as a synagogue. Now *that* will be interesting, he thinks, saying Hebrew prayers in Germany.

Around ten o'clock, Ben retreats upstairs, while Solly and many of the others stay downstairs to drink beer and talk. There is a small desk in the room, and Ben sits down with a pad of paper to write. Now here he has a problem. When he speaks to Simone, Yiddish is easiest, but he has never learned how to write using script Yiddish characters. In almost two years, he picked up a lot of French, but enough to write a letter? He doesn't think so.

He decides to write a draft in English and translate it as best he can. The salutation is the easiest, and he can do this in French: "*Chére Simone.*" But does the accent mark over the first 'e' go from right to left, or from left to right? Ben decides this is minor, and after all, Simone will be able to figure it out.

"I wish I didn't have to be here. I would much rather be in Paris near you. But my travels are courtesy of Uncle Sam, so I have to do what Uncle Sam tells me." He has explained about Uncle Sam, but what if Simone has forgotten? What if she thinks Ben is actually obeying an uncle of his? Or if she gets this name confused with that of her father, who was also named Sam? He crosses out the lines. "But my travels are for the army, so I have to do what the army tells me." That verb is a little weak. He changes "tells me" to "commands." That makes it sound like Ben absolutely did not have a choice, which, of course, he didn't.

At this rate, it will take him hours to write the letter, and all of a sudden Ben realizes he is totally, completely, flat-out exhausted. From the debriefing meeting early that morning in Paris, to the flight to Germany, to the check-in with the American authorities here, it has been a tiring day. He places the pad back in his kit, changes into his pajamas, and heads to the bathroom to wash. Laughter comes up the stairwell from downstairs, with some music (probably from the BBC) in the background.

Ben returns, closes the door, and eases into his soft, warm bed; just as he realizes it is much more comfortable than his bunk in Paris, he is asleep.

The next day is cold and sunny. As the officers polish off a hot breakfast of eggs, hash browns, and rolls, a young soldier enters the dining room to greet them. "Corporal Anthony LoMonaco from St. Louis, Missouri! I'm here to show you a bit of Frankfurt and then take you to your new posting." The men don their overcoats, board a small army bus, and head to the center of Frankfurt, about five miles away.

When they flew in last night it was almost dark, so they could not see the vast stretches of smashed and flattened city. For the first time, they have a close-up of the destruction the Allies have unleashed on their enemies. The skeletal remains of buildings remind Ben of what he saw on the roads into Paris in the summer of '44—but those were small towns, and here was a major city. Or what was left of a major city. Piles of rubble line the road. Parts of buildings stand on either side, parts of gray brick or stone walls here and there, half of a church steeple, the ribs of a domed roof. The destruction stretches as far as he can see, on both sides of the road. Only an occasional building is untouched.

Ben has heard that Frankfurt was considered quite a beautiful city. Well, it's not beautiful anymore, he thinks, and frankly, I don't care. You're the ones who wanted a thousand-year Reich, he says inwardly, so this is what you get when the world hits back.

As with Paris, there is little traffic other than military vehicles. An army jeep coming their way beeps a greeting. Ben notices that many civilians are riding bicycles, just as in Paris. But here and there he also sees trolley tracks, and some trams are even running. The bus slows to a stop as they approach an intersection where an American soldier with an MP armband is directing traffic. Other American soldiers stride briskly across the street, followed by individual civilians strolling, it seems, without purpose. An old woman pushes a baby carriage, but Ben notices as they pull away that the carriage is filled with framed pictures, candlesticks, and other household goods. Shattered people, he thinks, looking for shattered buildings.

The bus moves east into the heart of Frankfurt, close to the heavily bombed main train station. Across the street are two old, elegant hotels in decent shape.

"OK, boys, this is the Zeil, the main business street," LoMonaco calls out from the driver's seat. "See that building on the right, with the American flag? That's your post office. And to the left, in the park, is the HQ of our forces. We'll go up there now and walk around a bit."

They make a left and wind their way toward a large, hilly park dominated by a tremendous curved building with six jutting wings. Its clean, bold, modern lines contrast starkly with the architecture of the city. That is, the architecture of the old buildings still standing.

The men are awed by the sheer size of this building. "A marvel, isn't it," exclaims LoMonaco. "Over five hundred rooms inside. And as you can tell, it's pretty recent, only fifteen years old. The architect, Hans Poelzig, won a prize for the design."

"Hey, LoMonaco, you a tour guide or what?" laughs one of the soldiers.

"Just doing my duty for the USA! Anyway, this building was completed in 1930, and now it's ours. General Eisenhower requisitioned it for SHAEF headquarters. Let's walk around a little bit, and then I'll take you to the Palmengarten nearby."

"Pretty impressive," says Solly to Ben.

"Yeah," responds Ben. "And you have to admire that precision bombing, too."

"What do you mean?"

"The train station and tracks, just down the road, bombed into smithereens. And here, not a scratch."

"But this building isn't a transportation center."

"No, but it is the center of one of Europe's biggest companies. Bombing this would be the equivalent of someone bombing General Motors or US Steel or Texaco."

"Meaning?"

"Nothing. Just an observation."

They get back on the bus and drive a few blocks west over to the Palmengarten. "These gardens were set aside in the middle of the nineteenth century. Now there is an American Red Cross center here for us, so when you boys have some time to relax," says LoMonaco with a little laugh, "Come over and have tea. Our men are installing a nice fence around this whole part of the city, so you won't be disturbed by grumpy citizens!" Everyone laughs as they continue through the park and then onto some other streets. Everywhere in Frankfurt, there are the same battered piles of rubble and destroyed buildings.

After dinner, Ben goes back to his letter and tries to add some more. He tells about the house where they're billeted in Frankfurt, about all the destruction. He asks how Guy is doing in school. He knows Paris is only a two-hour flight, but he is not sure if the army will let him go. Maybe he ought to ask his CO first. Then Ben feels guilty for not writing to his folks at home—and not even remembering to write to them. When he thinks of the people he really misses, they are in Paris. To compensate, he tells himself that tomorrow, when he goes for his first day's work at the Post Office, he will buy some postcards to send back to the States.

The next morning, the army bus is again waiting on the Brüningstrasse, and it takes the men into Frankfurt. Several, including Ben and

Solly, opt to get off near the center of the city. Ben and Solly walk the rest of the way to see things at street level. Beyond a pile of rubble on the sidewalk, people line up patiently to wait for a tram. In the window of a bombed clothing shop, a mannequin wearing a tattered dress leans crazily against the cracked frame. A woman walks past them, pulling a small boy by the hand. Solly looks back at the child, who turns and shapes his free hand into the form of a gun, pointing at the Americans.

Then Ben remembers from their army guide that the Jewish chaplain's office is just a few blocks before the post office, so they decide to stop in. An army private working there greets them and takes them in to see the rabbi.

To their surprise and delight, the officer in charge is Judah Nadich, the same rabbi they heard speaking at the Synagogue de la Victoire in Paris. They have a friendly conversation with him. Nadich takes a second look at Ben, exclaiming, "Say, I remember you! From the postal unit. You came to see me at the Hôtel Majestic, correct?"

"That's right, Rabbi," says Ben, and they shake hands.

"How is everything going for you men? I hope you're remembering to take care of your spiritual needs while you're taking care of the army's mail. Please, come see me whenever you want!" Ben feels flattered that the rabbi, who must have met thousands of people in France and Germany, remembers him. All the men shake hands, and the soldiers promise they will be back one Saturday for Sabbath services.

Finally, he and Solly get to the post office and see firsthand how much they need to accomplish. The place has been understaffed, with insufficient security. Now that they have a larger workforce, all the problems can be tackled. The officers assigned to the Army Postal Unit meet and decide how to delegate tasks, drafting a plan that will have the office providing more efficient service within a few weeks. For the first step, they place more troops on security duty. Then they direct that all vehicles delivering the mail are to be repainted red, white, and blue in order to alert border guards that all contents are official.

Ben finds the distraction of this work rewarding. He loves making things run more smoothly and enjoys helping organize the postal service, bringing order to what had been a rather haphazard place. At the end of the day, the Americans return to their billets in Höchst, a good hot dinner, and then a relaxing evening on the comfortable leather couches in the living room, listening to music on the *Volksempfänger* radio that sits on the mantel over the brick-and-stone fireplace.

But Ben is restless. He stays with the guys for half an hour, then goes upstairs to the room he shares with Solly, where he can sit quietly and work on his letter. Mostly he sits. He knows just why he doesn't share the same upbeat attitude as the other men in the unit. The war is over, and they have won. But Ben, personally, doesn't feel like celebrating anything. Well, brooding doesn't help, and neither does talking to Solly, who has been listening to Ben's worries for a while. Maybe Ben needs to talk this out with someone new, someone who can be objective.

Ben stands up, screwing the cap back onto his pen. Rabbi Nadich, yes, he could go speak with him. He feels a bit better having set this small goal for himself. Ben gets into his pajamas, goes into the bathroom to wash up, and then crawls into the comfortable bed. By the time Solly comes upstairs, Ben is asleep.

## CHAPTER TWENTY-SIX

# Another Encounter In Frankfurt

Frankfurt is not nearly as interesting or comfortable as Paris. Ben and Solly are in complete agreement about that and realize that one difference lies in the attitude of the civilians. In Paris, they were liberators, and the French were overjoyed to see them. Here, people are either sullen or ingratiating. Both are annoying.

"I never liked those Nazis," says Helga, the chambermaid who takes care of their rooms, when she brings fresh linens, "No sirs, never. But what choice did I have? I have two small children to feed. My husband is on the eastern front." She lowers her voice as she bundles up their soiled towels. "But watch out for Inge, the girl in the dining room. A loyal party member, I am sure." She heads down the stairs to the laundry.

Ben sits at the desk in their room, thoughtfully puffing on his pipe and gazing out the window at the brown-and-gray yard in front of the house. It is clear no one has tended it in a while, and what must have been flower beds are now twisted tangles of dead leaves, weeds, and vines. Through the bare branches of a row of trees, he can see a few stone buildings and the round tower of the von Brüning castle, where the Armed Forces Network has set up their radio station. Ben has seen what there is to see in Höchst and is not particularly interested in the huge chemical factory. He doesn't even want to know what the Germans manufactured there—but he has heard stories.

Solly, relaxing in an armchair and leafing through an issue of *Stars & Stripes*, looks up. "Well, we knew from Carter that *that* was coming. But they're all bitches as far as I'm concerned. I don't trust any of 'em."

"Some of those girls may not have had a choice," offers Ben quietly.

"What are you, soft in the head? Unless they are really little kids, all the Germans are Nazis who put those thugs into power. Remember, they *elected* Hitler. We should have bombed more of their damn country."

*Bong.*

The wooden clock on the wall rings the half hour. It has a satisfyingly deep sound for a wall clock. Neither Solly nor Ben can make out the cramped German abbreviations written in Gothic letters on the enameled dial, but they enjoy marking the time by the clock's dignified peal.

"I like that sound," says Ben.

"You like the clock?" asks Solly. "You know when we finish up with Frankfurt, we're going straight home. Pack it."

"As in, take it?"

"Yeah, why not? Souvenir, spoils of war and so forth."

"You mean, steal it."

Solly stares at him. "You really care? These Krauts just murdered and pillaged their way across Europe. Take their damn clock!"

"Maybe."

"Come on," says Solly, getting up and stretching, "It's a Saturday morning, the weather is decent, and we can do what we want. Let's go explore this town, at least what's still standing!"

Ben agrees, grabs his camera case, and the men get their military caps and overcoats from the hall rack and head down the stairway to the front door. Outside, the air is crisp and brisk, the sky gray but not dull or cold enough to hint at snow. There is just a bit of wind, and the air is quiet. It's not that far to the city center, but when an army jeep passes they hitch a ride.

The main roads are becoming more navigable each week, but the side streets are still rubble-strewn and require pedestrians to pick their way through. "Looks like the air force was pretty thorough," comments the driver, a sergeant from Illinois.

"It'll take them years to rebuild," says Solly. "Just as it'll take London years to rebuild after what the Luftwaffe did."

Ben and Solly hop out not too far from where the post office stands, but they walk north and explore some of the streets that are not too badly damaged. Ben takes a few pictures of a tram passing, an elderly couple crossing a street, children at play in a pile of ruins before they are chased away by an American MP.

By midday they find themselves close to the Palmengarten and salute the GIs who guard the approach gates. This is now an American installation, and they remember what Corporal LoMonaco told them on their introduction to the city. They show their IDs, enter and stroll over to the main building with its huge glass conservatory. They enjoy lunch there, chatting with some other American soldiers. Ben takes a lot of photographs.

After about an hour, Solly sits up suddenly. "Hey, Ben!"

"What?"

"It's *Shabbos!*"

"So? We're doing what we usually do on *Shabbos*—relaxing!"

"But didn't we promise your rabbi buddy that we'd come to services?"

Ben nods, "Yep. And we haven't been back. Well, he knows we're not religious." Ben has been thinking about his dilemma, and has decided that no, he does not want to talk to the rabbi. In fact. he'd like to avoid the rabbi, who would probably end up making him feel guilty. Ben knows he has to do something, because he can't keep his mind on anything else.

Solly is already up on his feet. "Hey, let's stop by his office on the way back. Maybe it's open so guys like us can drop in."

"It's probably closed."

"It's not that far. Let's just see."

They go back down the hill to the intersection that will lead them to the Jewish chaplain's office. When they finally locate it, the door is locked, a note on it stating that Sabbath services would be held at the officers' mess on Saturday at 09:45.

"Well, we tried," says Solly. "Maybe next week, okay?"

Ben nods and they turn around to go back and see if they can catch a tram or a ride to Höchst.

A small group of GIs is moving down the street toward them. As they near the group, one of them sneers at Ben: "Hey, Jewboy!"

Ben turns to face the man, a private. "You have something to say?"

"Sir, I'm sorry about him," says another young GI solemnly, saluting with one arm, while trying to support the offender with the other. "He got an early start on drinking today, and he can't hold his liquor." Another soldier, probably still a teen, pipes up: "We're trying to dry him out before our sergeant sees him."

"It's not your responsibility," says Solly, looking directly at the laughing drunkard, while removing the other man's supporting arm, "it's *his* responsibility."

"Bet I'm right, huh?" smirks the first soldier, staggering a little and holding onto the brick wall next to the sidewalk. "You *are* a Jewboy! You're both kikes, or you wouldn't be coming outta that office."

"What's it to you, soldier?" Ben confronts him.

The drunken soldier sways a bit as he burbles, "Ahh, it's all your fault that we're even here with all these shitty ruins an' having to be in this rathole at all. My dad says the war is all the fault of the Jews. Yeah, you people always get others to fight so you can make a profit."

Ben says nothing, just suddenly grabs the soldier under both arms and hoists him off the ground, pivoting and smacking him hard into the wall. The young GI yelps and opens his eyes wide.

"Did that hurt?" asks Ben, his voice exaggerating the words. "Gee, I'm sorry." Ben quickly pulls the surprised soldier toward him, then smashes him back against the wall, just a bit harder this time.

The soldier starts to cry.

Solly grabs Ben's shoulders, "Stop it! The guy is a jerk. Just let it be. Come on, Ben! It's not worth a court-martial!"

Ben lets the soldier drop to the ground, then kicks him high up between the legs. The GI screeches, then moans as his buddies swiftly hoist him up and stagger down the street.

Ben is so angry he can't speak; he clenches his jaw and Solly can see the muscles working in Ben's cheeks. They start walking toward the place where the army bus will pick them up. Finally, after about two blocks, he turns to Solly and growls: "Good men died to fight the Nazis and punks like that still believe all the lying shit!"

"Nothing is going to get fixed overnight, Ben. And if that creep comes from generations of bigots, it's gonna take a while."

"And you know something? No matter *what* we do, fifty years from now there will still be anti-Semites."

"Just the way it is," murmurs Solly.

Ben knows that Solly is right. But he doesn't feel any better about it. He pulls out his pipe and stuffs some tobacco in the bowl, jamming it in with his thumb. He pauses for a moment and turns his back to the wind, lighting the pipe and drawing a few puffs. Then he turns back to Solly and they continue up the street.

After dinner, Ben goes upstairs by himself to finish his letter to Simone. It is difficult to add anything that he hasn't already said to her, and he stares fixedly at the growing darkness on the horizon. What does he expect, a magical answer written in the orange clouds? How can he promise something if he cannot deliver? The envelope, addressed, sits on the desk, waiting. All he has to do is sign the damn thing. It's already been eight weeks since he left Paris. By now, Simone will have gotten the idea. Maybe just as well. Ben stares out the window into the foreign night.

# PART TWO

## CHAPTER ONE

## AUGUST 2008:

# Florida

It is a sunny morning in south Florida. It is always a sunny morning in south Florida. But by the afternoon, the summer heat will build up and the skies will darken until they are deep gray. Then a huge downpour will drop a wall of water over the area for fifteen minutes. When it stops, suddenly, the sun will re-emerge, and steam will rise from the parking lots where there had been pools a few minutes earlier.

A framed sepia-and-cream photograph of a handsome man in uniform sits on the coffee table next to a black-and-white photo of the same man with a woman and two small children, a boy and a girl, standing next to a 1954 Studebaker.

The same children, now middle-aged, have been working in the apartment for almost a week, sorting and tossing and boxing.

It is not a large apartment—there's a sizable living-dining room connected to an enclosed patio, with a short hallway leading to two bedrooms and two baths. The Gordons, unlike many of their neighbors, resisted decorating in shades of aqua and peach; instead, their apartment is understated and elegant in neutral tones. The effect is calming. Judith has always admired her mother's quiet good taste: antique sconces on either side of an early American hutch, which showcases pottery collected over the years. A watercolor of a maritime scene on the New England coast. An original oil painting of a young girl reading—she remembers her mother buying that at an art fair in Connecticut.

A week ago, the place was packed with friends and neighbors after Ben Gordon's funeral, many staying for the evening prayers. The second night of *shiva*, the week of ritual mourning, was also crowded. By the fourth and fifth nights, the group was down to about a dozen, their father's closest friends.

Now Judith, relaxed in jeans and a dark gray t-shirt that picks up the tones of her hair, is sunk deep into the cushions of the cream-colored living room couch, going through the contents of a shoebox. "Oh look at this, Michael! A Mother's Day card I made for Mom when I was what, four? I could barely write. Dad must have helped me."

"If we keep reminiscing over each little piece of paper, Judy," says her brother, "This will take us a month, and neither of us has that much time off."

"Sorry, I'm keeping you from your billable hours!"

They both laugh, because they know that even though he loves his work in real estate law, Michael Gordon is not a fanatic about charging his clients for every hour (or fraction thereof) of his time. He is "doing very well," as their mother used to enjoy telling her friends in Florida. However, being a professor at a small college in Ohio that "no one had heard of" is apparently not "doing very well." Judith had once asked her mother, "Mom, do any of your friends tell you that their children *aren't* doing well? Or, if they have been unemployed or downsized, do you think they would *admit* it?" You're doing it again, Judith, she tells herself: arguing with a woman gone five years, may she rest in peace.

"The books? Earth to Judy!"

"Coming, coming."

Judith rises—pleased when she finds she can do this without holding onto the sofa's armrests—and passes where her brother is sitting at Dad's desk. Both her parents had used it, but they called it "Dad's desk" because he often sat there, working on his articles for the condo newsletter or reading the *Sun-Sentinel*. Judith had arranged more framed photos of her father, of her parents, and a couple of albums that visitors could browse through. She crosses the room to the two bookcases where her parents' modest library shares the shelves with travel souvenirs and framed photos of Sarah and Ian, Michael's grown children.

"A whole series of Howard Fast's novels, first editions," says Michael. "Think they are valuable?"

"Valuable to read—one of the greatest progressive voices in twentieth-century literature," Judith instructs him. "Ian and Sarah ought to read them."

"Ought to, but will they?" Michael thumbs through one of the books. Then speaks in a falsetto as he imitates his children when they were young. "'Aunt Judith, do you always have to sound like a professor when you discuss books?'"

"OK, give them to me," says Judith, laughing at him. "I'll take the art history books, too. Keep *A Day in the Life of Israel* for Naomi—there are probably a lot of photos that will remind you both of your trips." She sees the bound volume of *Spinning Sisters: Woman Factory Workers in 19th-Century American Literature*. Of course—the inscribed copy she had given their parents almost twenty years ago. It was the book that had gotten her tenure. What it should have earned her was a position at a larger, more prestigious school, in a major urban center. But it hadn't.

"I'll take a few more, Michael. Then let's pack the paperbacks for the used book store."

"Fine. Let's just finish with the bookcases and go out to dinner—quit for the day."

Judith and Michael sit quietly at an Asian restaurant in the nearby shopping center, exhausted by the day's activities. As they wait for their entrees, Michael starts to rip open sugar packets and pour the sugar into his little cup of Chinese tea.

"Four, Michael?"

He blinks at Judith and looks up. "Huh?"

"I didn't know you took so much sugar," Judith explains.

Her brother looks down and sees the little pile of ripped paper next to his cup.

"Oh, gee, I didn't even realize I was doing this."

Judith reaches across the table and squeezes his hand. "You *are* tired, Michael. We are both probably more worn out than we realize."

Her brother nods. "But Dad made it easy on us, didn't he? All his legal papers were in order. He prepaid the funerals. So many of my friends have gone through hell finding plots and making arrangements because their parents would never discuss plans. Imagine going coffin shopping when you're still shell-shocked from the news."

Judith sips her tea and responds, "Well, Dad was organized. That made it a bit easier for him—and us—when Mom died." She pauses for a few moments and continues with a small, if sad, smile, "So the chapter closes, as we knew it would someday. And here we are, Michael, at the point we feared for so long. But we've almost gotten through it."

"It's kind of a spectator sport down here," Michael answers. He sighs.

"What do you mean?"

"My partner Josh says—his parents live a couple of towns from here—they call South Florida 'God's waiting room' and just sit around for the phone to ring announcing another funeral."

"Think we'll also be obsessed with death when we get that old?" asks Judith.

"Ask me then. I know one thing—I sure as hell am not going to move into one of these geriatric ghettos." He pauses and randomly starts to play with a small china vase on the table.

"You know, Judith," he goes on, "some of the people who attended Dad's funeral—I don't think we'd met them before."

"You're right. We knew some of them, and of course a lot of their friends have already passed on. We knew a few from when we were kids, like the Lipmans. And then Dad mentioned his newer buddies—the 'kids,' as he called them. Guys in their seventies, like his card-playing group."

Her brother nods. "Yeah, I met a few of them. I got to hear some nice stories about Dad. He was highly thought of around here. People liked him."

Judith smiles. "'Ben was a lovely guy,' they said, 'a gentleman, always willing to help out when he could.'"

Michael sits back in his chair and reflects for a moment. "That was Dad. Really, I can't think of a single time he blew his stack at anyone. Can you?"

Judith thinks for a moment as she cleans her glasses on the blue cotton scarf around her neck. "Well, he did have some sharp words about visitors here who did not park in the designated visitor spots!" They both chuckle over this. Judith continues, "Other than that riveting issue, he always saw the best in others. Or maybe he ignored their faults. I used to think that was weakness—he never got bent out of shape over things. I guess he learned pretty early on that it's just easier to get along with people."

Michael looks straight at her. "I know what you're thinking: he was easier to deal with than Mom. Whatever we did was fine with Dad, but Mom . . . found fault."

Judith sighs and nods in agreement. "I know they both loved us. But with Mom—there was always some issue. Remember when you wanted to take a year off from college and work?"

"Oh, yes," says Michael, raising his voice to mimic their mother's: "'You'll never go back, Michael! You'll get some job and never amount to anything. Stay in school and finish your degree!'"

"And you stayed in school."

"I would have finished college even if I *had* taken a year off. But it was easier not to get her riled up."

"And she really pushed Dad to go to school at night and work on his degree so he could be a CPA."

"You have to admit that after he became a CPA and got a job at the accounting firm, he did make better money."

Judith muses, "But was he happy? Accounting has always seemed so boring to me. I wonder if he was bored. He never said."

"Mom was certainly happier and nagged him a bit less."

"It must have been tough on him in those years, working at the post office during the day and then going off to college classes at night. He was hardly home."

Michael laughs as he says, "That phrase you use, it reminds me of something Mom used to say: 'I raised you children practically by myself. Your father was never there.' As though he was some deadbeat dad."

Judith looks sad when Michael mentions this. "I wonder if Dad knew she said that. I heard that line, too. It really wasn't fair for her to blame him for being away several nights a week, when she was the one pushing him to take classes."

"If making more money was important to her, why didn't *she* finish college and become an accountant? After all, remember, she was the one who was good with numbers!"

Judith has a sudden memory of herself at about eight or nine, riding in the back seat of the family car as they drove up one weekend to visit Uncle Morty and Aunt Lillian in the Catskills. Slumping next to her, little Michael was already asleep. Judith had really wanted to look at the high rock sides of the road but instead had to answer her mother's drilling of the times table. "Four times five? Four times six?" It was a Saturday, and Judith had not wanted to do school things. "Six times four? Six times five?" But she couldn't protest then, so she just kept answering. To this day, of course, Judith knows her times table—but the interrogation is a painful memory.

She pulls herself back to the present. "Oh, Michael," she says a little impatiently. "You *know* that things were different for women when we were kids. When you think about it, how many of our friends' mothers worked? Hardly any. Mom was expected to be the traditional behind-the-scenes wifey and it pissed her off. I think that was the source of a lot of her stress, anger, whatever."

Michael nods as he reaches with his chopsticks for another piece of sesame chicken.

"You're right, Ju. It was the same story with Naomi's mom." He pauses and looks right at Judith, serious. "But you know, you really *do* sound like you're giving a lecture when you lecture me."

They both giggle, and it lightens the mood.

Judith remarks, "I'll bet Mom was proud of your Sarah, going to med school and becoming a researcher. Maybe one—one!—girl in my high school class went to med school. But back then, everything fell on the husband's shoulders. I think Dad would rather have used his evenings to play with his cameras!"

"Or play with us!"

They finish their meals and Michael pays. They alternate treating each other. As they walk to their car Judith spontaneously squeezes her brother's shoulder. They don't have to speak to let the other know how much it means to have their company.

The next day they tackle the clothes closets and more papers. Michael is busy packing Ben's clothing into boxes to be donated to the local Goodwill. He keeps a couple of sweaters for himself, and one for Ian.

Judith is seated at her father's desk, going through each drawer. She finds her father's checkbook and a stack of unused check refills. She keeps the book and one refill for paying bills, tearing the rest in half and discarding them. Then she stops in the middle of tossing papers, recalling something. "Michael? Remember when we were small—what we heard them talk about in the kitchen? The expenses?"

"What are you talking about?"

"At night, after we'd gone to bed. Their talks about money?"

Michael shakes his head. "I really don't remember."

"I guess you were too small. You were probably fast asleep. But I would lie awake, my door open a little, and I would listen to them."

"So?"

"I don't have very detailed memories of this, but enough. Before Dad became an accountant, Mom was the one who kept the books. That's the work she used to do, before we were born—just as you said yesterday, she was good with numbers. She made Dad account for everything he spent. She kept saying she needed to know because she had to watch their budget.

Most of what I remember is that she kept quizzing him, figuring out where little bits of money had gone. It made *me* worry about money, even though I was only seven or eight at the time. I never wanted to live like that."

"Is that when you decided to become a teacher?"

Judith frowns at him. "Oh, everything is such a joke to you!"

"Oh, come on, lighten up. Why are you mentioning this now? I mean, this happened over fifty years ago."

Judith waves her hand a bit dismissively. "Oh, I don't know, it just came into my mind . . . looking at Dad's bankbook and checkbook. Later, when things were easier, I guess it didn't matter as much. But when we didn't have money, Mom really controlled that budget."

"Of course she did—it's important to stick to a budget when you don't have money." He crosses the room and takes a seat on the other side of the desk.

Judith shuts the drawer and looks closely at Michael. "I think it was about more than just budgeting. I think it was about some way she had power over him. But as a kid I was frightened, hearing Dad have to account for every penny. It made me afraid of being poor. And of being interrogated about everything."

"You've never told me about this before."

"Well, I didn't think much about it before." She stops, gets quiet. "And then when I was in school . . ."

"Judith, stop. Don't upset yourself."

"I had to deal with it before you did. She remembered when I had a test, and always asked how I did. And then she wanted to know who got a better grade."

"Hey," says Michael quietly, reaching out and touching the top of her hand, "Sometimes you think too much. Let it go. Our parents did their best for us, and they had a nice life together."

"I guess so. But I keep thinking that Dad was, I don't know . . . weak, a pushover, and that Mom was controlling. Dad was just happy I was around. He wanted to play ball, teach me how to use a camera. He never grilled me about grades."

"Well, he didn't have to, did he?" asks her brother, laughing, "You always got top grades!"

"I was afraid not to!" Judith retorts. "Mom kind of drilled it into me that top grades determined everything."

"You eventually got over that, right?" asks Michael, grinning.

She smiles back at him, "Yes. Eventually."

"See, I think it's just a matter of perspective. You and I were different, so we just saw things differently. I think Mom was a great organizer; she got things done. She managed all of our activities, plus she did charity work. She was a troop leader for your Girl Scouts, and a den mother when I was a Cub Scout, remember? She always chaperoned school outings. And I had a great *bar mitzvah*—she did everything!"

Judith frowns at her brother, but not in anger. "Well, yes, I remember that she wanted everything to go smoothly for us and was really involved at our schools. But I think there was a competitive edge in her. She wanted us to be the best. Was she a troop leader because she really believed in scouting, or was it so she could keep an eye on us? Same thing with chaperoning. I used to think she was always watching me. Oh, I don't know . . . I think it bothered her that she herself was not a professional, so she tried to take on positions of authority."

"But however they managed things, it worked, didn't it? Everything was . . . just so in our house. You could eat off the floors. Mom did it all!"

Judith says sadly, "Yes, it was just so. You and I were forbidden from jumping on the couch, remember? When I think of the hours Mom spent cleaning. And ironing!" She laughs a bit. "Of course, that was before the perma-press era!"

"Gosh, I don't know. But once they retired to Florida, she was in some clubs, and she enjoyed life here. Didn't she?"

Judith frowns a bit, thinking. "I believe she did, mostly. But I remember one time, when I was visiting, and they had some friends over. Someone asked her, 'So, Sylvia, do you like Florida?' and she answered, 'Ben is happy, so I am happy.' Now what does that mean?"

"Judith." Michael speaks her name. It's not a question, but it is.

"What?"

"Stop. Stop looking backwards. They are gone. Let's continue in the now."

She nods. "You're right."

Every night, Michael phones his wife Naomi and tells her what he and Judith have accomplished during the day. Sometimes Judith says hello to Naomi, and other times she just gives her brother some space. Nothing bothers Michael—even when he was originally bypassed for partner—and Judith is happy for him that he has that personality. He just made partner at a different firm. He is easygoing, like their father. At night, Michael falls asleep quickly in the second bedroom.

But Judith lies in her parents' bed, watching the ceiling fan spin lazily, thinking about her mother and father before they became an old couple. She had gone to a therapist when her mother was first diagnosed with the cancer that would kill her within a year. "I feel so guilty," she had said, wadding the wet tissues in the therapist's office, "Because I'm glad my father might get a break. I should be thinking about my Mom's being so sick. Instead I'm thinking about how dad might get some relief from her criticism. Mom has really picked on him."

"Why should you feel guilty for wanting something good for your father?" her therapist had asked. "The next . . . well, you don't know how long, actually. What is coming will be difficult for both of them, and for you. Don't waste your energy feeling guilty."

What were her mother's criticisms? Small things. You didn't fold the laundry right. The coffee you made after dinner was too strong. You should have brought the mail in *before* you went to the meeting. Nothing big. But it seemed to Judith that whenever she visited, that's what she heard. It was a variation of what she heard when she was growing up: Why don't you defend me to your mother instead of making excuses? We could live in a better neighborhood if you would make more money. If you would speak up to your supervisor at work, maybe you could get a raise. To be fair, her mother never said these things in public, only in private. But her parents never knew that Judith, and sometimes Michael, listened.

Sylvia was a stay-at-home mother, like most middle-class mothers in the fifties. So Judith, when she was little, was closer to her. And she absorbed. What she absorbed was that her father was a basically decent guy who lacked gumption. He didn't advocate for himself. And the one who paid the price for this was her mother. If he had stood up for himself, he might have gotten a better job, and then she wouldn't have to scrimp. If he hadn't let his mother push him around, she, Sylvia, would have been treated with more respect.

When Judith, and then Michael (but mostly Judith) went to school, the focus shifted to them. Why are you satisfied with that grade? Next time, talk to your teacher *before* a test if you don't understand something. You're not going to drop Spanish, are you? Quitting a subject won't look good on your transcript. You're really going to wear *that* outfit to school?

Yet once Judith and Michael were grown and out of the house, their mother still didn't try to change her own options. She apparently preferred to complain. Judith knew it was no accident that she herself was married only briefly, and had avoided any other complicated attachments. Her mother was a living example of marriage being not such a great deal for women. Judith wanted to avoid developing her mother's PDS: Perpetually Dissatisfied Syndrome.

She didn't avoid it entirely. She was still dissatisfied. So she was the leading expert on Elisabeth Shuttleford. Who cared, really? She knew the second she retired, she would be replaced by another–younger–Victorian. Every year, armies of eager young scholars with shiny fresh doctorates would show up at conferences, hunting for employment possibilities. They wanted to discuss their research, or ask about hers, and she felt their warm breath on the back of her neck. Oh, it is exhausting to think of these things, Judith muses as she turns onto her side. Michael is lucky, does all right for himself, and he and Naomi have a sweet life. She is truly happy for them. And by producing the grandchildren, they had taken the heat off Judith.

A few days later, Judith and Michael have completed their inventory and have decided their next steps. They have emptied the refrigerator and freezer, making many trips to the dumpster behind the apartments. They will donate their father's clothing–all in good condition, for Sylvia had seen to it that Ben was a meticulous and dapper dresser. Judith will take the oak secretary, some books, her dad's cameras, the pink-and-blue-flowered china tea set her parents had bought in London in the seventies, and the dark wood wall clock their father had brought back from Germany. Michael wants his father's pipe rack and pipes, his grandfather's shaving mug, the antique brass desk lamp, some framed prints, and the golf clubs. "These are in super condition. Ian and I will fight over them!" he crows.

He will come back in a few weeks to meet with the real estate agent and arrange for the shipment of most of the larger items. They will each take a few small things now.

"Poor you," says Judith. "I don't know what you are going to do with that dining room set. No one wants early American anymore."

"I know. But maybe it will make a comeback just like fifties stuff is now 'mid-century modern' and commands high prices."

"Mom and Dad thought fifties design was tacky! They wanted something 'classic' instead. So now we have it—and Michael, if we sell it, Mom and Dad will kill us."

Judith and Michael say good-bye to Mr. and Mrs. Lerner and Sam Marcus, who live across the courtyard and were among their parents' closest friends. They do one more walk-through to ensure that the windows are locked, the shades drawn down. Michael sets the thermostat just a little lower. They are waiting for the car service to pick them up for the ride to the airport when Judith suddenly remembers. "Michael! The outside storage room, upstairs!"

Quickly, Judith looks inside the kitchen cabinet where their parents had kept keys on hooks. She grabs one and rushes out of the apartment. When she returns a few minutes later, she is carrying one large carton. "This is it," she says, puffing a bit. "It was the only item they had up there."

She drops the box heavily onto one of the kitchen chairs. It is sealed with packing tape and marked in their father's neat print: "Memorabilia."

"Could be anything," says Michael. "Let's open it up."

A quick but careful slice across the top of the carton with a box cutter reveals stack upon stack of photographs. They reach in and examine a few random piles.

"These are from all over, Michael. We can't look at them now. I wonder if these are extras that didn't go into the albums."

Her brother takes a brief look at the pictures piled into the carton. "It will take a lot of time just to sort!"

"Just look at these"—Judith holds up a group of cardboard-backed formal portraits from a century earlier—"from Europe, and none of them labeled!"

"Dead Victorians!" crows Michael. "Just your speed, Judith. Come on, you love a mystery. Take them home and find out who they were!"

A car honks its horn out in the parking lot. The car service. They have to go.

Judith takes the bait. She reseals the box and carries it out to the waiting car. The driver helps them stow everything in the trunk and on the back seat, and then they are off, heading east toward I-95. At the airport, Judith has to pay an extra fee to take the carton of photos. She and Michael kiss each other good-bye and head to different gates. Judith calls back to her brother:

"I'll let you know if I find any treasures among the dead Victorians!"

## CHAPTER TWO

JUNE 2009:

# Ohio

The academic year has been busy and exciting; all the stars had aligned, and Judith has been quite content, after a very trying spell. It wasn't really depression, just, as she told herself, existential angst. It settled on her shoulders every few years when she questioned the value of what she was doing. But then her classes filled with students who actually seemed interested in the Victorian age and always asked decent questions. Many wrote thoughtful papers that had not been poached from encyclopedias or, more recently, the internet. She had thought about retiring several times but always got re-energized by a new batch of students, so she kept putting it off.

But then last year Tom Bennett, one of the college librarians she particularly liked, had died suddenly, only a short time before he was scheduled to retire. She remembered having lunch with Tom and a few others sometime in the early spring, and he was excited about the plans he and his wife had for travel and taking part in community theatre. He was such a pleasant person and seemed healthy, and he was cheated of the rewards he had earned.

And then near the end of the summer, her own father had died. She remembered saying to Michael at the time that they were now orphans. It was sort of funny, and yet not. Weren't orphans sad little Dickensian waifs, hollow-eyed and ragged? And yet. Judith knew it was time to take stock, but she really didn't have the time for that. The new semester was starting, and as usual, plunging right into work was her best antidote for everything.

John Cummings from the Art department and Phyllis Hudson from History had worked with Judith to put together an amazing spring break trip to London. In March, the three of them embarked with twenty students on an intense interdisciplinary program on Victorian London. John had arranged for group tours of the Victoria & Albert Museum, the Dickens Museum, and the Linley Sambourn House. This last one was the most interesting to Judith, who had, of course, been to the others but yet not this one—a Kensington townhouse formerly inhabited by an illustrator for *Punch* magazine and maintained as it was left decades ago. It was a true Victorian time capsule that Judith had yearned to visit for years.

Phyllis had reserved various places to stay in university accommodations near the British Library. Their group had afternoon tea, all clinking china and strawberries and scones, in an 1898 hotel on Russell Square, and attended a concert in the Royal Albert Hall. Upon their return home, each student submitted an evaluative paper. Judith and the others felt that all their efforts were worthwhile when they saw the students' enthusiasm, but the entire experience, including making extensive logistical arrangements, had been time-consuming and exhausting. Judith didn't complain more than her colleagues, though—she didn't want to risk being thought of as too old to escort a student tour.

She fully intends, sometime soon, to examine the contents of her father's "memorabilia" box stashed under her bed, but between dealing with classes, preparing for the trip to London, the trip itself, then papers and exams—it is nearly the end of June before she can actually tackle the job. By the time she does, an embarrassing array of dust bunnies have assembled around the corners of the box.

Except for the summer session enrollees, students and most of the faculty have left town. Finally calm and quiet, with a free morning and a full mug of coffee, Judith sits down at her dining room table with the carton.

Where to start? As she works, Judith finds herself alternately fascinated and annoyed. "Dad, couldn't you be bothered to *label* anything?" The pictures seem to be mixed together randomly, although there are clusters that come from the same period—she notes the same group of people, or the same places. Several shots of Niagara Falls, vacation pictures from a place with cottages, spiffy cars with license plates from the 1930s. Most of the photos are in black and white; color shots are later ones, starting in the 1960s when film developers also noted the month and year on the reverse side of prints or along their edges. Well, *that* was a help.

You're the history buff, Michael had told her often enough. As though being an attorney, he didn't have to deal with historical precedents. She grumbles to herself as she decides to pursue a chronological review. She will divide the pictures into decades using internal and external evidence.

If the photos have dates printed on them, they are easier to identify—especially as many of the people are familiar: she and Michael as kids, photos from Michael and Naomi's wedding, Aunt Fran, Uncle Morty and Aunt Lillian. Even a few from her own wedding to Lawrence the Loser. She recognizes Dad's mother as a young woman but cannot find any of his father. Other pictures are also of people Judith knows, and she can guess the decade by clothing and hairstyle—so this shot of Solly and Myrna looks to be from the late forties or early fifties. She shakes her head—wow, those lapels!

One group of pictures is much older, some in sepia tone, glued to ornate cardboard cards engraved with the name and address of the photographer. Now here is a clue—someone has written in pencil "Benjamin 2yrs old." That has to be her father in 1914. He is cute and solemn-faced, sitting on a prop rocking-horse in a photographer's studio. There is a picture of a smiling older man holding a folded newspaper under his arm, with the notation "1927?" If she could see this enlarged, she might be able to make out the exact date on the newspaper. But she still doesn't know who it is. Maybe it is the grandfather who died so many years before her own birth. Perhaps his face will show up in other pictures.

There are no wedding pictures. Judith and Michael are the only people she knows without a wedding portrait of their parents. "I told you," their mother had once said, "we were married in a rabbi's study, and he wouldn't allow any photography at a religious ceremony." Judith had asked, "But Mom, what about at the reception afterwards?" Her mother had paused, then given an evasive answer: "Who had money for a reception?" So Judith had let the subject drop.

Judith remembers her father always having the latest in photographic equipment that he could afford and imagines he would have been tickled to have a digital camera. Then, instead of taking fifty pictures of an event, he could take 500. But after a brief flirtation with the Instamatic, he remained a steadfast 35mm man.

Judith decides to divide the piles into two groups, using the year of her own birth, 1948, as a dividing point. Of course this is egocentric, she tells herself, and not random. But she has a reason: there is my father's world before I entered it, and afterwards.

The color pictures all come after. She gets a second mug of coffee and comes back to the table to browse this stack.

She and Michael, as small children, fishing in a pond; Judith at seven, having a group of girls over for a birthday sleepover; Uncle Morty kissing Judith at some family event; a dozen pictures of Michael at his *bar mitzvah*; parents' day at Camp Greenwood. There are some photos of people she doesn't know from more "recent" occasions over the last thirty years, well after both she and Michael left home.

By the time Judith begins to tackle the first pre-1948 pile, it is almost noon. She has been lost in her own past as well as that of her family. And she realizes she has not been tearful at seeing images of her lost parents—on the contrary, she sees what full, happy lives they led. They lived not extravagantly, but comfortably; they had a lot of friends; they traveled; they had wonderful children, and grandchildren courtesy of one dutiful child. And they both lived to be old—what a blessing! Even their last illnesses were relatively brief, compared with what some others had gone through. When their mother had developed pancreatic cancer, she said—mellowed by medicine—"How can I complain? My health has been pretty good until now. And this is one of the quick ones!" She was gone six months later.

After a break for lunch, Judith starts to examine another batch of photos. In addition to late nineteenth century pictures—most unlabeled and undated, for which she cannot even blame her father—she finds a few that are dated, from the 1930s. One shows her mother, Sylvia, in front of a dress shop; a street number is visible, but no name. On the back: "Sylvia's 1st job, 1931." A group of young people are at a picnic, almost all of them laughing, some sitting on benches. At first, Judith thinks she knows no one, then spots her father standing behind an attractive woman who seems to be leaning back against him. He has one arm around her waist and the other . . . cupping her breast? The woman, in a smart summer outfit, is laughing as she looks up at him. *Dad!* Anyway, it's not Mother, since this picture is from 1937, and they didn't get married until late 1947. Judith has to grin—this is the first picture she has seen of Dad being, well, physical.

There is another large stack, and a quick flip through tells Judith these are from WWII. These have been taken with different cameras, she surmises, as there are several sizes of prints. Or perhaps they were processed by different labs. Many are repetitious—men in uniform on a ship, obviously a troop transport, but is it going over or coming back? Judging from the relaxed expressions on some of the men, Judith guesses it's a homebound run. But without notation or dates, she cannot know absolutely.

A group of people sits on the steps in front of what appears to be a shop or café; she has no idea where this is, but the name of the café is in French. Judith takes the large magnifying glass from her desk—the one she often uses to decipher cramped Victorian handwriting—and looks more closely. A group of men and women sit together, and one—no, two—men are in US Army uniform. One is smiling as he stands directly behind a seated woman. His hands are on her shoulders; her hands, reaching back, are clasping his, and she is smiling, too. Judith is fairly certain this soldier is Dad's friend Sol.

She flips through the pictures more quickly, looking for her father. Judith assumes that he has taken these pictures because he is not in any of them. She has seen pictures elsewhere of him in uniform. One, a formal portrait, was taken at a studio in Paris and inscribed to her mother. The other was one taken in London, in front of Westminster Abbey, of Dad and another American soldier—she and Michael had displayed photos like these for visitors who came to pay condolence calls.

Now these are pictures she has never seen before. Here is a shot showing Dad and a number of older men seated in what seems to be a meeting room—

who are they? There are no signs or decorative elements in the photo. The back of the picture simply says, "Paris '44, timed picture with local residents." The group is seated a few feet from a table on which there is a camera case, so her father must have used a camera with a delayed-action setting. However, most of these photographs have no notation at all on them. And here is another picture of Dad with two women and a boy. Who took this? Another soldier, or was it the self-timer again? She turns the photo over and, for a change, there is writing. It says, "Paris, April '45" and she notices names entered lightly in pencil. She reaches for the magnifying glass. One woman is "Mme M" and the other is "Mme Duval;" under the boy's picture she reads "Guy D."

Another puzzle! Civilians, obviously, but this is in a home, with a fireplace mantel in the background holding a framed picture on display. The only real clue is the name "Duval"—probably the French equivalent of Smith or Johnson. Not exactly unusual. Then Judith sees some street scenes in the snow, in the rain, one showing the French name of a large shop—but nothing is written on the back. If Dad took all of these, it seemed that he enjoyed roaming the streets and taking random shots of everyday life: children in a park watching a sword-swallower, a woman pushing a baby carriage, two American soldiers sitting at a café table, a cat warming himself on a windowsill.

Finally, here is one of Dad, in uniform, riding a child's scooter; some-one—it's not Dad's handwriting—has written on the back "Ben acting his age!" And there is another showing Dad, again in uniform, lounging on the grass next to a sign written in French. Judith decides to take any pic-tures that include French writing to someone in Modern Languages. She knows Claudette Benoit from a couple of committees; maybe she'll ask her. It would be nice to know what these words mean.

All of a sudden, Judith has a vision of herself as a girl, walking along holding her father's hand and listening to him whistle a tune. When she had asked, "What tune is that, Daddy?" he had answered, "I Love Paris."

## CHAPTER THREE

# The Photo

"Michael, you're there!"

"Why did you call if you didn't think I'd be here?"

This is usually the way their weekly phone calls begin. They have always gotten along decently because despite being only two years apart, they were always friends, never rivals. Possibly their parents had different expectations for a boy and for a girl, but they never compared the children. And perhaps now, having gone through the deaths of their parents together, Judith and Michael are even closer.

Judith asks after Naomi and the children, and then she starts to tell Michael about the photos she has examined.

"I just haven't had a chance to get to them until now. It's been very busy," she explains.

"Find any surprises?"

"Yes and no. There are a lot of people we know, and multiples of shots from events that should be in albums. Your *bar mitzvah*, for instance.

What I have must be extra that Mom and Dad did not include in the album . . . Yes, I know you have the albums. But is there an album from the war? There is a huge stack of wartime photos."

"I don't think they had any albums from before we were born. At least I don't remember seeing any."

"Then let me ask you this, Michael. Do you remember anything specific Dad said about his time in France?"

"Hey, you're the older one! Wouldn't he have been more likely to talk to you about those things?"

"He didn't talk much to me about the war itself. I remember that he used to talk about places he'd seen in Paris."

"Yeah, there was one funny story he used to tell," said her brother, "about working in the army post office when a civilian came in who didn't speak English. So Dad used Yiddish to speak to her and pretended to his buddies that it was French."

"Oh, I remember that story! He got a lot of mileage out of it—he mentioned it again just a couple of years ago, remember?"

"Right—he went to her family's apartment, and brought them food from the PX, and the father wanted to give him a piece of jewelry to take home?"

"Exactly. Dad turned down the jewelry—so instead the man gave Dad a yellow fabric star that said *Juif*. You have that, don't you?"

"Yes—Dad put it in a frame and gave it to me a few years ago. It's here on the study wall."

"Did Dad ever mention a family with a young son?"

"I don't think so. Why do you ask?"

"I found a photo of him with two women and a boy, sitting around a table. No men. It's dated 'Paris, 1945.' I'm just curious."

"Any names?"

"There are initials, but the only last name I can make out is Duval. I wonder who they are, or who they were. There are some other pictures of Dad in Paris, or at least in France, because there are signs in French."

"Can't help you there!"

"I know—we both took Spanish. I am thinking of taking these pictures to a woman I know in our language department for a translation. There are some other pictures from Germany, but those are easier. Dad wrote more information on the photos from—where was it?" She flips through a short stack of pictures. "Frankfurt. That's where he was stationed before he came home."

"Let me know what you learn! Listen, Judith"—she can hear him repressing his laughter—"are you sure you can handle this research? It's out of your realm—way after the Victorian era."

"You're a horrible, hateful person, Michael," she says, smiling to herself. "Talk to you next week."

On Monday, after her first summer session class ends, Judith crosses the quad to the Modern Languages building and goes upstairs to Claudette's office.

"*Bonjour*, Judith!" Claudette pronounces her name the French way, with a soft zh for J, a t in place of the th, and the emphasis on the second syllable: *ZhooDEET*. Claudette is about forty, slim and chic with a bright cotton scarf draped loosely over her pale ivory knit blouse. "It is good to see you here! I haven't seen you since before . . . your father . . . I hope everything went well?"

Judith collapses in the chair on the other side of Claudette's desk. "Ah, air conditioning! It's not that far from my office—just too hot today." Both women laugh a bit.

"Thank you for asking, Claudette. Yes, everything went well. We all

miss Dad, of course, but in the context of things, it's hard to be deeply
sad. He had a good, long life and passed away in his sleep. My mother used
to say that kind of death was a blessing, like being kissed by an angel."

"Such a comforting metaphor!"

Judith nods. "Claudette, I have a French question, or a French puzzle.
I went through a box of my dad's old photos, and there are many he took
during WWII. Some of them have signs in French, and I am wondering
what they mean. For instance, look at this one."

She passes to Claudette the one of Ben lounging on the grass in what
seems to be a park.

"Ha! The sign says, 'Stay off the grass.' A funny one, your father?"

"Oh yes, at times!"

"And did he speak French?"

"A little. Oh—I just remembered something!"

"Yes?"

"Just a flash—of going for a walk with my father. I was little, my brother
must have been home with our mother, and Dad tried to teach me to say
'hello' and 'good-bye' in French. There was snow on the ground. Why do
I remember that?"

"Perhaps your brain is connecting to old French memories! Did you
study French in school?"

"No. My mother insisted that in New York City, Spanish would be
more practical to learn. So that's the language I took."

"What else do you have?" asks Claudette.

Judith hands her a group of photos, and Claudette looks through
them, smiling. "Ah, *très mignon*—very cute, and in that uniform!"

Claudette continues to study the pictures. "My parents were both children in Paris during the Occupation. Of course that was long before they

met and married. When I was growing up, they spoke about it a good deal. The joy of being freed from the Germans—they said it was overwhelming to the adults around them. They grew up hearing that Liberation was like seeing the sun shine for the first time in years. And look at these pictures: taken on V-E Day! And your father was *there*. What an experience—did he speak about it?"

"About the Liberation, never," says Judith. She feels suddenly sad, like she has missed out on something. "I knew he had *been* in Paris, as well as London and Frankfurt. He made references to Paris. And there were things in our apartment he had brought back—a Limoges pin, some pretty dishes, a beautiful scarf for my mother, some prints. I knew he hadn't been in combat, that he served in a postal unit. That's really all. Aside from one or two anecdotes, no, he never really told us a lot about his time in Paris."

"Perhaps, like many soldiers, he just wanted to forget," Claudette ventures.

Judith shakes her head in puzzlement. "I could understand that if they had been in combat and had seen things they didn't want to remember. But as far as I know, my father didn't experience any kind of trauma. Well, he didn't have any lasting injury, as the fathers of a couple of my friends did. I guess Dad simply came home and moved on with his life." Judith feels this ignorance stabbing at her—she could have asked him about Paris so many times, and now any chance was gone.

"Why did your father write details on the backs of some pictures and not others?" asks Claudette, continuing to browse through the photos.

"Who knows? We all do that, I think. Here, look at this one, of my dad with some civilians and a disabled tank. Look—the tank even has some German markings."

Claudette takes the small picture, studies it, then turns it over.

"There's nothing written here."

"Exactly. Now look at this one." She gives the other woman a photo of a zebra.

Claudette looks at the reverse side, and bursts out laughing: "Really! As if we didn't know!" Ben had written: "1945, Zoo–zebra."

"Funny, right? You would think the picture of the people with the abandoned German tank would get more attention! Now I have a little puzzle I'd like you to help me solve," says Judith. "There is just one picture I have showing my father in a civilian home." She passes the photo to Claudette. "There isn't much to go on, but I'd be curious to know if this boy is still alive, and if I could find him, to see if he remembers my dad."

Claudette examines the writing on the back of the picture. "There is only one surname here," she observes.

"Yes, Duval . . . and you're going to tell me that my chances of finding the right Guy Duval in France today are small?"

Claudette shakes her head ad laughs a little sadly. "Ah, Judith, do you know *how* common is the name Duval? In France, it is like 'Smith!' And do you know if he *stayed* in France?"

Judith laughs and raises her hands imploringly. "I don't! I have absolutely no idea of what to do. That's why I thought perhaps you might advise me."

Claudette turns to the wall where a large map of France hangs. "Paris, Lille, Orléans, Rouen, Lyon, Marseille, Toulouse . . . and then hundreds and hundreds of villages. If he is alive, and stayed in France, he could be anywhere on that map. Unless he moved to London or New York. With the name Duval, you might have thousands of candidates."

"It's . . . it's overwhelming," says Judith, as she nods in agreement. "But I thought about this all night. Well, when I was awake. I am just so curious. What do you suggest I do?"

"First thing," says Claudette, "we can look online for French telephone directories. They still have phone books in some places in France, but this might be quicker." Her fingers tap rapidly over the keyboard. "Here, I'll email you the link. Now, just for fun, let's take a look for entries under Duval . . . what is the first name again?"

"Guy."

"*D'accord.* Guy Duval. Oh . . ."

Judith scans the walls of Claudette's airy and welcoming office while her colleague scans the computer. Posters from Air France advertising the Mediterranean coast, flyers for summer programs in Reims and Paris. A large poster of a nineteenth-century painting of fashionable strollers on the beach at Deauville.

A few minutes later, Claudette issues a long sigh.

"There are many, so many when you include listings for G Duval," she observes. "You can't possibly contact them all!"

Claudette turns the computer screen so that Judith, sitting on the other side of the desk, can see.

Judith is quiet for a moment as she scans the long list. "Oh. Well, it's just as you warned me, Claudette." She considers to herself silently—really, what are the chances? Should she even bother? Oh, how can she not? "No—I won't call. First of all, I can't speak French, but also they need to look at the picture to see if the boy is perhaps a relative. Maybe someone might recognize the women. I can have copies made of the picture, and I could write a letter—with some help, of course."

"Of course! But you know, Judith," advises the other woman, "the likelihood of your success is slim, if we are going to be realistic." She tries to sound gently discouraging, but Judith seems not to be listening completely.

"How old do you think the boy is in this picture?"

Claudette takes off her glasses and studies the photo. "I don't know. Certainly not high school age, but not a child. He's wearing a blazer or suit jacket–trying to look grown-up. Twelve? Fourteen?"

"That sounds reasonable to me."

Claudette thinks for a moment. She sees that Judith is determined. "All right then, we have a little research challenge here. You need to go to the online directory and make a list of all the possible candidates. Write what you would want to say in a letter, and I'll translate it into French. You'll keep it short, yes?"

Judith leans forward, animated. "Of course! That's great, Claudette, thanks so much! I know it's a long shot, but it might work."

When Judith gets back to her office, she sends an email to her brother about her plan to see if she can find the boy in the photo.

About an hour later, she gets a call from Michael: "Hooray–Judith Gordon has discovered the twentieth century!"

"Michael, you know very well that my past research has gone all the way to 1918!" she laughs. "Well, I'm curious about this–aren't you?"

"Maybe. I mean, I guess so."

"It could add to what we know about Dad."

"But how much, really? *If* you find this kid–well, he has to be fairly old now, and how much is he going to remember after all these years? Look, we know Dad served in the army post office. He met a lot of people in the countries where he was stationed. He helped out some civilians. And he came home with some souvenirs."

"You actually remember the souvenirs?"

"Sure," says Michael. "There was bunch of stuff in the house when we were growing up. Let's see . . . a couple of Limoges pins, some framed prints of people along the Seine."

"Yes, old pictures—there was one that always scared me when I was little —a man with a three-cornered hat—I used to call it a George Washington hat—in knee pants, carrying a scythe. I realized later that he must have been a farmer, but when I was a kid that pointy scythe frightened me."

"I'll have to look for that one," says Michael. "I don't think Mom ever hung it up in Florida. If they kept it, it will be in one of the cartons in our garage."

"Michael, don't put pictures in the garage! The damp will make them all moldy."

"Come on, Judith, don't nag me! I'll get to it. When we got back from Florida, I just put everything in the garage. It was the easiest thing to do."

"Okay, fine. Listen—let me ask you something else. Do you remember if Dad ever told us about any French people he was friendly with?"

"You mean during the war?"

"Of course."

"Sure—the family that gave him the yellow star."

"Yes, but we *know* about them, and they had an older daughter. Dad mentioned her—the young woman who came in to mail a package. But we don't know their *name*. Does 'Duval' ring any bells?"

"Isn't that a very common surname in French?"

"It is. But it's on the back of this photo, in Dad's handwriting."

Michael chuckles. "Sis, if you are trying to track down someone named 'Duval' you're going to be very, very busy. Look, I don't want to discourage you, but this is going to mean a ton of work for you, and—I just hate to see you ending up disappointed."

"Thank you, Michael. But—well, do you remember *anything* that Dad might have said about any friends in France?"

She hears him sigh into the phone. "As I said earlier, Judith, you're the older one. I really don't remember much, other than his taking us out to some French restaurant in New York, when we were kids, and threatening to order frogs' legs just to see the looks on our faces."

"Yes, yes, I remember that! It was in Manhattan, and the first time I had *coq au vin*. I was about seven. There was wild rice with a black cherry sauce."

"What? You amaze me, Ju! How can you remember a specific dish fifty years later?"

"It must have really impressed me, Michael. Who knows? I don't think about it all the time. The memory is just . . . there, stored, and came back when we talked about Dad being in France."

There is a brief silence on the phone as both Judith and Michael pause. Then Michael asks, "He must have had a good time over there and was, I don't know, trying to recapture some of it by going to a French place in New York."

"Maybe."

Michael persists, "Why is finding this family so important to you?"

"I'm not sure. Just that—there are probably things about Dad we don't know."

"Or Mom either. They had lives before we came along, you know."

Judith is quick to answer him, "I know that well! Mom talked for years about the fantastic job she had before I was born, keeping the books for a furniture manufacturer."

"Oh, that," Michael responds. "I remember her talking about that job. And if I remember right, it was the last job she had."

"You remember correctly. Later, when she said, 'I should have gone back to work when you kids were bigger. I should have been a teacher. I should have . . .' I thought she was giving *me* a message. I was so self-centered that I never thought about her own disappointment. But I remember those 'should haves.'"

"Judith, stop. You are just making yourself unhappy," says Michael quietly. "Come on, let's talk about happier things about our parents. For instance," he says, then pauses as he collects his thoughts, "A couple of their neighbors came up to us after Dad's funeral and told us how much Dad had helped people, doing little things like giving them rides or helping them organize their files. They told us how much they appreciated his friendship."

"Sounds like our father! Dad was a good guy."

"I only got to *know* him, really, after he retired. And even then, it was on visits, mostly, or on the phone," Michael says wistfully, then laughs, "which Mom hogged."

"Oh, she wanted to speak to her boy. You were always her favorite," laughs Judith.

"Well, you were the smart one," he retorts. "She was always bragging about you."

Judith snorts, "But you were the cute one, 'oh my little *shayna punim,* you are so adorable!'"

"Ooh, you're good, Ju—you even got her inflection there!" Michael laughs about this, and Judith finds herself grinning. She and her brother really do like each other, and any petty childhood jealousies are decades in the past.

But then she grows thoughtful.

"Michael, you remember what Mom used to tell us over and over when we were little?"

"She told us a *lot* of things, Judith!"

"About how having us was the best thing that ever happened to her?"

"Exactly. I always thought that was such a sweet thing to say. Didn't you?"

"Oh sure, yes. For a while," says his sister.

"What do you mean? She told you something different later?"

She hesitates a bit before she speaks. "You know, for a lawyer, you seem a little thick sometimes."

"What? What do you know that's different?"

"Oh, she really *did* mean the part about our being wonderful—it's certainly better than telling kids you never really wanted children or that they were an 'accident.' But she didn't say anything about Dad when she told us all this."

She hears Michael catch his breath a little, as he pauses in turn: "I'm not sure what you're driving at, Judith. She was just trying to make us, as children, feel loved and secure."

"Yes, yes, and we did. But it didn't occur to me until I was almost a teenager—what about marrying Dad? Wasn't *that* a great thing? Did she ever say anything about how lucky she was to have married Dad?"

There is silence on the other end of the line. "Michael, are you there?"

"Yes. I'm thinking."

"And?"

Michael speaks slowly, as he tries to remember long-ago conversations. "I really can't. Not in those exact words. But she and Dad were always . . . well, you could count on them always to be Mom and Dad. They were a couple. They always celebrated their anniversary. They sent sweet cards to each other—you and I went through a huge pile of cards, didn't we, after Mom passed away?"

"True. Some of them were even a little silly and goofy. Yes, in many ways, I suppose they were a good unit. But there was an edge to her."

"Your evidence?" Now he is talking like a lawyer.

Judith pulls her legs up on the couch and leans back into the cushions.

"This may not be a big deal," she begins, "but I remember it so well that it *may* be a big deal. One Saturday in the fall when we were maybe twelve and ten, or thirteen and eleven, we had spent the day in Connecticut. We went to some little towns, walked along the sound—it was just pleasant, we didn't do anything momentous. We went out to dinner, and that was a big treat. But when we got back to our apartment in Queens, Mom said, 'it was a nice day until we had to come back here.' That was so weird for her to say. We didn't live in a terrible neighborhood. It was ordinary. So I asked Mom why she said that, and she answered 'your father chose this place.' I didn't ask more, because just then Dad came up the stairs with you. I felt uncomfortable, so I just kept quiet. She seemed upset with him. Why would she want to make me upset, too?"

"Judith, I don't remember any of this. Did Mom say this sort of thing to you a lot?"

To Judith, Michael sounds concerned, and she reassures him: "Only that time, as far as I can remember."

"That's got to be, what, a fifty-year-old memory? Are you sure you're even right about it? Anyway, what's so wrong with what she said?"

"Well, why do you think I remember that, after all these years? It made an impression. Mom was dissatisfied, and she blamed Dad. It made me feel . . . sad, awkward."

"Hey, I'm not a shrink! I don't know why this memory stuck with you. But sometimes . . ."—Judith hears him pause—"I think you analyze things too much!"

"And you, the lawyer, don't?"

## CHAPTER FOUR

# The Initial Attempt

I am the daughter of the American soldier in this photograph. This picture was taken in Paris in 1945, and the boy's name is Guy Duval. Today he would probably be between seventy-six and eighty years old. I wonder if you might perhaps be that person—or if you know who he might be. I would appreciate any response or assistance with my quest.

Judith does not know what else to add to the letter, other than her contact information. Using the online directories, she has found an overwhelming number of people named Guy Duval living in France. She has a list of 194, in fact, plus six for a "G Duval." They live throughout France. This is going to be expensive, Judith calculates, with the photo reproductions and the international postage. But it's in the interest of research! Except that no one is giving her funds for this.

When she tells Claudette what she has found, her colleague is not surprised. "Duval is such a common French family name, that I knew you were bound to come up with a substantial list. Let's see what you have written." She takes Judith's note and reads it. "Do you want to add your father's name?"

"No," Judith responds. "The right person will know his name. I also haven't mentioned his military rank, and you can't see the stripes on his sleeve. So the right person may remember that also."

"Good point. No problem here, I can translate this for you easily. I suggest you add your campus address. That will impress some people, that you are a professor, even if they may not have heard of our college. Maybe you ought to include a business card? Some may look up our website, and then they will see your picture—that will look more personal and friendly than if you just send a note with your street address and email."

"Good idea, Claudette."

"And tell me again, just why you are doing this?"

Judith bends her head slightly to the side, saying, "Curiosity."

"Meaning?"

"I want to know more about my father, Claudette. It's strange, but I feel that I didn't really know him that well. Of course, I did, as a father. But I have only a hazy idea of what his pre-*paterfamilias* life was like. Even when I was a young woman, it was my mother with whom I spent the most time. My father was simply there, a part of the background. Does that surprise you?"

"Not at all. With traditional American families I have known, the children, especially the girls, grow up closer with the mother. Of course, today in so many families both parents work. But I understand what you are saying."

The next day Claudette sends the translation to Judith by email, and then on the weekend Judith has copies made and addresses all the envelopes by hand, using information from the online directories she and Claudette have found. She opens Excel and creates a spreadsheet with all the names and addresses so she can keep track of any responses. On Monday morning she carries her stacks of envelopes to the campus post office and sends them off to France.

And then she waits.

Summer session progresses well. She has just two classes, a general British literature survey and a small writing seminar. Judith is happy to have the extra money and a flexible schedule that allows her to work on her own research. She has to work on the paper she plans to give at MLA in a special session on "The New Woman." And she needs to add the next chapters to her biographical study of Elisabeth Shuttleford, the Victorian poet whose intriguing works she has found within the pages of a number of Victorian periodicals. No one, as yet, has done any work on Shuttleford, so this could be a real coup. A good way to crown her career.

Several weeks pass, and classes are nearly over. Judith has used her time efficiently and looks forward to spending a couple of lazy weeks reading the latest fiction and painting her bedroom a soothing shade of pale blue before fall semester begins. Summer, which used to stretch before her like a vast, dry trough, seems to pass rather quickly these days. She doesn't know whether it's a function of age or if she is just having more fun now than when she was younger.

Near the end of August, she starts to get some responses to her mailing. The first few are disappointing. They are all emails, and in French, of course. Judith doesn't want to bother Claudette each time she gets a message. She could pay a French major to translate the emails, but then she'd have to wait for classes to begin, and she is impatient to know what people have written. She finds a language translation site on the internet and makes a promise to herself to take a French course.

The online translation service is a bit awkward in its language use, but Judith understands enough to be discouraged:

> *Dear Madame,*
>
> *I am sorry but I know nobody in the photo. Wishing you luck.*
> *I am Guy Duval, but I have 22 years, so I am not your person. I know not the two women. They are not my family.*
> *There is a story in my family about American soldiers friendly at the war. But my family lives in Toulouse, the south, so probably not us.*
> *I asked my grandmother and aunt, but they do not recognize your people. I am sorry to disappoint you.*
>
> *Goodbye.*

Over the next two weeks, Judith receives a few more messages. Two are handwritten and the rest are emails. There is the same discouraging response. Judith checks her tally; for all the messages she sent, she has received only eleven answers. She knows this is actually a pretty good rate of return. Most people never answer messages that come out of the blue. But all of the responses she has gotten are negative. All of them. This is very disappointing.

Something is wrong. Judith feels like she's hit a dead end. Perhaps the boy in the old photo is no more. There is also the possibility that he has left France. Or maybe he is indeed in France, but under another name, or perhaps he has lost his memory of that time.

A few days after the last message arrives, Judith is sitting at her desk just after lunch when she has a hunch. She reaches over to the mystery photo, turning it over once more and looking again at her father's faded writing. She takes the magnifying glass from the desk drawer and looks again—"Mme Duval" "Mme M" "Guy D"—squinting at the writing. She looks very closely at the name "Duval" and sees what she had not noticed before—the second letter is closed at the top—not completely or darkly, but it is closed.

It is not a U but an A.

She had misread her father's writing. Why didn't I think of this before, she scolds herself. She studies the photo closely under the magnifying glass and sees that, yes, while it looked as if her father had written a U, indeed a pale pencil line crosses the top of the letter, making it an A. The name is actually Daval!

Judith goes back to the computer and looks up the French telephone site Claudette has shown her. She finds just a small group of listings for Guy Daval. Perhaps fifteen in all. None of the addresses match any in her previous database. She decides to look at variations on this spelling, too— what if her father had misspelled the last name? She feels simultaneously discouraged and energized. This could be another blind alley. But she must persevere and will send fresh inquiries.

A few hours later, she goes downtown to have more copies made of the photo and letter, and has addressed the envelopes. Perhaps this time she'll have better luck, she thinks to herself, tossing the envelopes into the out-of-town slot at the post office.

Two more weeks pass. Classes are about to begin. Judith is getting ready for the president's faculty reception when she hears the *ping* of her computer and knows she has a message. She goes into her study to take a look; it's an email from "gjdaval." Quickly, she clicks it open.

*Bonjour, je suis Guy Daval, et j'habite à Bordeaux. J'ai reçu votre lettre au sujet de votre père et la famille française. Désolé de vous décevoir, mais j'ai seulement 45 ans. J'ai montré la photo à mes parents âgés, mais ils ne la reconnaissent. Bonne chance!*

By now, Judith has learned enough words in French to know that this, also, is a no. That word *désolé*—I'm sorry—suffices. He is only forty-five, much too young. No matter; it was the proverbial long shot.

From past experience, she knows that going to the president's reception means she won't have to prepare any dinner later this evening. There will be an open bar, a buffet of cheeses, crackers, olives, smoked meats, and fresh breads. And then the steam tables with lasagna, grilled salmon with rosemary, and roasted vegetables. Once the wine starts flowing, people will talk about their fantastic summer travels and all their grants, and then the conversation will turn to who is sleeping with whom. At that time, Judith will make her way home, where she will sleep soundly with herself.

Much later, when she is deeply and comfortably asleep, the sudden ringing of her phone jangles Judith awake. Reaching for the phone, she glances at the alarm clock—only 5 a.m. Please let it not be an emergency, she thinks.

"Yes?"

There is a voice, but it is not Michael's or Naomi's. There is just a babbling sort of sound, and she cannot make out any words. Now really awake, she is annoyed instead of alarmed. "Who is this?" She sits straight up on the edge of the bed.

More babbling sounds. "Drunk, stupid frat boys," she thinks.

There is a pause on the phone, then: "*C'est moi! C'est moi!*" It is a man, sounding anxious, and also, it seems, crying.

In halting English, he exclaims: "Sergeant Ben! I never forget!"

## CHAPTER FIVE

# Guy

"I can't speak French." Judith is now fully awake, but this is the only thing she can actually say. Inside she is shouting, It's you! It's you! It's really you!

"*Pas de problème.* I have some English."

"How do you know my father's first name and his rank?" Even while asking, she knows that only the correct person will have this information.

"I tell you, I never forget." She hears the man take a deep breath. He sounds like he's been laughing and crying at the same time. "I never see this picture before! Your father, he talk about us?"

"To me? No. I never saw that picture until recently."

"Is your father still . . . he lives?"

"No, I'm sorry. He died last year." There is a brief silence. Judith hears her heart beating quickly. "He was over ninety. And my mother died several years ago."

"All this time."

"I don't understand," says Judith.

The man speaks very slowly. His voice is deep, hesitant. Judith cannot tell if it is language difficulty or emotion that slows his speech. "All this time, I never hear from him. Ever."

"Did he know you well? Who are the women in the picture?"

"Please. Speak slow."

Of course—his English is rocky, but she is excited and speaking too rapidly. "I'm sorry. The women? Who are they?"

"The one with dark hair, this is my *maman*. The other, my *gran'mère*. It was at Pesach."

"My father had Passover with you?"

"He was like a person of the family. He visit us so many times! Yes, yes, we knew him well!"

"I knew he was in France, of course. He spoke about that. We have a yellow cloth star that someone wore."

"Yes, in '42 they make all the Jews wear this."

Judith is tingling with excitement. She wants to stay on the phone, learning more about Guy. "Please, tell me about yourself."

"Nothing important. I am an old man."

"You do not sound old!"

"And how old are *you?*"

"Sixty-one."

"You sound young." There is a pause, and then he says, "So you were born soon after the war."

"Yes. My parents got married after my father returned from Europe. I was born in 1948."

"You have brothers or sisters?"

"One brother, two years younger. He lives with his family in New York."

"Your letter says you live in Ohio. I go to the computer to see where this is. In the middle. Far from anything."

Judith laughs. "Yes, sometimes that's the way it feels. And where are you?"

"Paris. I never leave Paris, but I travel much when I was a young man. Too difficult now."

"Do you remember things about my father? Was he happy, was he kind?"

There is a pause. "He represent freedom. So tall, healthy. What we thought Americans were. He bring things to us, food, soap, things my *maman* cannot get. Sometimes he came to visit with a friend, another soldier."

Judith tries to imagine who this was. The only one of her father's army buddies she ever met was Sol Lipman. But really, it could have been anybody.

"You are Jewish?" he asks.

"Yes, but not religious, really. You are, of course, because you celebrated Pesach."

There is a pause, and then he speaks: "I observe nothing. It is not part of my life."

Judith wants to question him more, but she looks at her clock radio and sees it is already past the time she usually gets up. They talk, in broken bits of sentences, for another quarter of an hour. Finally, Judith tells Guy she has to get ready for work.

"You still work? Why? You can retire?"

"I love teaching, so I keep doing it."

"I retire when it become possible. Benefits in France are very good. But I still work a little bit, so I do not become, how they say, corroded."

At first Judith wonders what he means, then asks, "Rusty?"

"Yes, you know, from not using."

"What work do you do?"

"*Journalisme.* I write. Some politics, some travel. I think you call this free-lance?"

"Exactly, freelance writing. Guy, I really must get ready for work. I can call you tonight."

"Remember, we have different times."

She had indeed forgotten the six- or seven-hour time zone difference. "What about email?"

"Good. I will send you a message. You will see how to reach me. I am very glad to speak with you! I never forget your father!"

"Yes, yes, this is so exciting!"

After she gets off the phone, Judith can hardly wait to tell Michael and Claudette. But right now she needs to concentrate on getting to her class before her students. All through the day she thinks of things she wants to ask Guy: why were there no men in the photo, where was his father? What happened to his mother and grandmother? Has Guy ever been to the US? Does he have a family of his own? The biggest puzzle: why didn't her father stay in touch with the Davals?

As soon as her classes are over, she dashes over to Claudette's office. Claudette is teaching until 4:00. Judith scribbles a note and leaves it on Claudette's door:

"Found him! I need to learn French fast."

Then she goes back to her house and gets Guy's number from the call records in her telephone. It's only 2:30 p.m. now, so given the time difference to Paris, it's not really that late there, and surely Guy is still awake. She dials but is so nervous that she forgets the international access code and has to start all over. Finally, she hears the buzzing ring.

"'Allo?"

"Guy, it's me, Judith. From Ohio."

"Ah, *oui!* I just send you email."

"I did not read it yet. Can we speak for a little bit?"

"I will try. My English, it is weak."

"It is better than my French! I do not speak at all."

"Well, we try, no? I am interested, your father never mention us?"

"No, at least he said nothing to me. Perhaps to his other friends, like the one you mentioned, or to my mother."

"I try to think about this soldier. His name come from the Bible. Solomon, or Saul."

How can he remember such detail over six decades?

"Yes! That has to be Sol Lipman. He was a very good friend of my father's from his army days. You have a wonderful memory! My brother and I even got to know Sol and his wife, Myrna. But they are gone, too. It has been so long."

"Tell me what this Sol looked like."

Judith laughs. "Remember, my memories are from many years after yours. He was tall, and very smart. A deep voice. Curly gray hair, a high forehead. He used to smoke a pipe, just like my dad."

"Also Jewish?"

"Yes, but not very observant. Also like my dad."

"I think I remember. Just a little. I remember your father come to my *bar mitzvah*, and he bring other soldiers with him. One was maybe this tall man. So—tell me about yourself."

"I teach literature at a liberal arts college. In the summers I travel a lot, mostly to England. I have been there many times over the years."

"And you never come to Paris?"

"Once, right after my own college graduation. A lot of kids did that; fares were cheap then. Ten countries in three weeks. My friends and I were in Paris for just a few days. We climbed to the top of Notre-Dame, walked along the Champs-Élysées, visited the Louvre, you know, the regular tourist things."

"And what do you remember?"

"Not too much. How small the Mona Lisa was! Our terrible hotel room—but good bread at breakfast. And also, how expensive everything was."

"Ah, everyone say this! I show you many things here, more beautiful. You have family?"

"I think I mentioned I have a brother, two years younger. He is a lawyer in New York."

"Do you have a husband or children?"

"No. I was married for a short time, many years ago. But that's it. I don't even have a pet."

"I have no animals. They are too much work."

"What about you? Do you have a family?"

"I tell you more another time. This call is expensive for you, no? Go read my letter, I say there."

"All right, then. I will go to my email now, and later I will write to you."

"*Au revoir.*"

Judith excitedly turns on her computer, enters the password, and goes to her email. She has a day's worth in her inbox. Her rule is 'students first,' but she breaks this immediately when she sees a message from 'gdaval' and clicks on it. Interesting, he seemed in a bit of a hurry to get off the phone—and *she* was paying for the call. Perhaps speaking in English is too stressful for him. Or maybe it's just speaking with her.

From context and cognates, Judith can figure out some of his message. But not nearly all. She has to read all of it, and understand it, before she responds. It is entirely in French.

Her phone rings—Claudette. "I saw your note on my door," she says.

"Tell me everything!"

"Do you want to come over? I can make us drinks and dinner."

"Thanks, no. I have to get home. We can have lunch together tomorrow. How do you know he's the right one?"

"He knew my dad's first name, which my letter didn't mention. And remember how I said the right person would know his rank, too? I was correct! He called him 'Sergeant Ben!'"

"Amazing! Well done, Judith!"

"His English is weak. He just sent a long email, but it's in French and I can't read it except for a word here and there. My French is nonexistent. I need to learn, and quickly. Think about it—can you recommend a program?"

"No problem. You want total immersion? Go to France for a year and don't speak to anyone who knows English. Joke. Forward the email to me, and I will translate it tonight. And I'll think about a French course for you. Got to go!"

What would she do without Claudette? They had seen each other at various campus events, but now Claudette was proving to be a real life-saver. Still, Judith doesn't want to take advantage of her. She is sure there must be a translation site online, but Claudette's version will be more reliable, she thinks, as she forwards Guy's message. Then she gets busy with student messages to keep herself calm.

## CHAPTER SIX

# Guy's Message

ear Judith,

    I don't know how to begin except to say that I am very emotional now. Your letter, and of course, the photo, brought back so many memories. It was a sorrowful and also joyous time. I am writing in French, because that is easiest for me. Maybe someone at your school can translate this.

    I am sure you have read a lot about how difficult life was during the war. I was very young when the war started and remember not much, except that suddenly my father and grandfather were not there. My grandmother came to live with us. My mother was very young, and I loved her very much. Whatever she did, she explained why as well as she could.

    During the war I moved around a lot. First, we went to live in another place in Paris. I had Maman and my grandmother but no playmates. I think this made me shy. And I had to remember many rules: there were things I could say and others I could never say. So I was frightened and confused.

I did not know why we had to hide, because we did nothing wrong. My mother said it was because we were Jewish. Back then, I did not even know what "Jewish" was! So I simply said very little.

For a while I lived with friends in a village, away from Paris. My assigned task there was to bring grass or pieces of hay to feed the rabbits they kept in a backyard hutch. This I remember! Sometimes we would have a nice rabbit stew for dinner. During the war, food was scarce, but being in the country was a little easier. Suddenly I had to leave. For a long time I thought I had done something wrong when I stayed there, but Maman told me no, I had been good, but she needed to take me someplace safer. So I worried about the people in the village! Were *they* safe?

My mother took me to a school in the mountains, where I learned skiing and outdoor sports. I loved sports! But it was also very, very cold in the winter. Many nights we wore our jackets and socks to bed. Everything was like a game but this time there were real 'bad guys,' and the teachers were always watching for German patrols. We had practice drills for hiding. And finally, the American soldiers came and told us we were free.

I had a letter from Maman saying to wait for her. So, I missed the Liberation celebrations! But Maman was right to wait—I also missed the battle in the streets.

Liberated Paris was very exciting—everyone seemed happy, but my mother and grandmother, no. Because my father and grandfather never came home. They had disappeared, and so had many others.

And then—like a miracle! Your father came to us, and I saw his uniform and heard Maman and Gran'mère laugh for the first time in a long time. To us, he represented freedom and possibility.

Your father came to our apartment a lot. He became part of our family. He was our own hero! He brought us cans of food, at a time when we

French had so little. He brought soap, and sweets for me. Also, he gave me his American army cap, and I wore it to school with pride, because it was a gift from our sergeant!

I looked forward to his visits so much. He taught me how to play baseball. And he gave me a wristwatch for my *bar mitzvah*. It was my first watch. I wore it for years, right through university.

We were upset when he left, and afterwards, we did not hear from him, never. We knew the US Army had sent him to Germany. Perhaps something happened to him, maybe he had been injured or even killed. Your father had been a special friend to me when I was feeling lonely and lost.

This is a long message, I am sorry. But my memories are pouring out, so I will keep going. Your letter, Judith, came as a relief. Finally I learn about Sergeant Ben! This is why I laughed and cried when I heard your voice. It woke up my memories.

A couple of years after your father left, my mother got married again. Also to a Jewish man. I did not like him much, but it was a decision of my mother. My grandmother died; she had bad health and not seeing a doctor or having medicine under the Occupation made her worse.

By that time I was at university. I became a journalist and wrote for newspapers. I also was married for a while. We had two children, a boy and girl.

Now you know everything about me. I have a quiet life. I read a lot and sometimes practice violin on days when my fingers are not stiff! I still do some writing and reviews, but not much. I hope my message is not boring you and you will write back.

Your friend,
Guy Daval

## CHAPTER SEVEN

# Correspondence

"Claudette, how long did that *take* you?" Judith asks the next afternoon when she reaches her colleague by phone.

"Not that long, really. Remember, I grew up speaking both languages, so I can flip from one to the other easily. This letter would take a good student, a very good student, a couple of hours. How is your friend's English?"

"From our one phone conversation, weak. Still, it is better than my French. So I have to learn. At the very least, I have to be able to converse and read messages."

"Yes, I have been thinking about what you can do in six months to a year. I really think you ought to invest in a program where you can hear French spoken well. This will help you pick up on the pronunciation. And watch French movies online; start with subtitles, then try without them. Next time you come to my office, I will give you some materials to look over."

"*Merci beaucoup,* Claudette!"

*"De rien."*

Judith does not want to wait until she learns more than two words to write to Guy again. She has to let him know she has read his letter, or at least its translation, and that she appreciates it. She must write something, and decides the best course of action is to write in simple, clear English:

> *Dear Guy,*
>
> *Thank you for your long email letter. I have a bilingual friend who teaches here. I will start to learn French, but it will take time.*
>
> *Everything you told me about my father is a surprise. I am glad he was able to bring some happiness into your life.*
>
> *This is all new information, a part of my father's life I did not know. We did not know anything about you or your family. Of course, we (my brother and I) knew what he did during the war for the US Army. But he never told us very much about his life in Europe. He worked for the postal service for a long time after the war. Then he became an accountant.*
>
> *You sound very sad. I am sorry about that.*
>
> *I will write again.*
>
> > *Your friend,*
> > *Judith*

The next morning another message from Guy is waiting in her inbox: "Get Skype on your computer. Then perhaps we can speak that way at the weekend. Meanwhile, I attach pictures from when I was a boy." It's in French but she understands Skype and sees the attachments icon.

She clicks to see a cute boy with blond hair, wearing a dress shirt for what may have been a school picture. His hair is carefully parted on the side, and he smiles shyly. The other picture is an informal outdoor shot; the boy is standing next to an adult woman in a long coat. That must be his mother, visiting him in the mountains, because there is snow on the ground and he is wearing a skiing outfit. Judith looks at the date–November 1943–and she wonders if, behind their smiles, they were both quite frightened.

It is six in the morning. First, Judith hears a melodic binging from her computer. She quickly sits, facing the screen, and presses a button that opens the camera on her side. She sees her own image in a lower corner. In the center of the screen before her is the top of a man's head, and the image adjusts as the man changes the tilt of his own computer.

Finally, she and Guy Daval are looking at each other.

*"Bonjour, Guy! Ça va bien?"*

"Ah, Zhoodeet! You learn two more French words?"

"Yes, my friend here recommended a program and I am listening for one hour each day."

"Can you say all that in French?"

"No."

"Maybe by next week!"

He has a sense of humor, Judith thinks. That's a good sign! She was hoping his sad life story had not turned him into a bitter, pinched old man, a misanthrope.

"Your first time on Skype?" he asks.

"Yes, but I figured it out quickly."

"Ah, good for you! My son recommend it, but he is impatient. I make many mistakes."

"Actually, I asked one of my students to help me. The kids may not be able to spell, but they know everything about technology."

She sees Guy shaking his head from side to side. He looks perplexed.

"Please," he says, "you must speak more slow."

Judith nods and smiles. When she is excited, the New York speed kicks in.

"I am sorry. I will be more careful. I said that my students help me with technology."

"Thank you for speaking slower for me. I need to practice my English. It is bad. So, you see, I have my computer and"—he turns his laptop—"here is the rest of the room where I work. I have a living room and a kitchen, and a bedroom. It is not very exciting."

"What part of Paris do you live in?"

"In the 5th. Do you know how Paris is arranged? It does not have sense if you do not look at a map. The neighborhoods start in the center, next to the Seine, and then go around and around. It look like a snail. Better than your zip codes. The 5th is a nice neighborhood, near the Jardin du Luxembourg. It is called *Rive Gauche,* even though it is more the south. You hear of this?"

"Of course. *Rive Gauche* is the Left Bank, yes? An academic area, many educational institutes, more artsy, lots of students and bookstores. The Latin Quarter, correct?"

They are both speaking slowly and deliberately. Judith wants to speak so Guy can comprehend, and she sees that he is working very hard with English. "Yes, many book shops," he says, "Including one very touristical. All the Americans go there. Shakespeare and Company."

"Everyone who has read Hemingway and Fitzgerald knows about that place!"

"Hemingway! Bah! I do not like him." Guy waves one hand dismissively.

"Why?" Judith does not like him, either, but wants to hear Guy's reasoning.

"His stories, they start nowhere, they go nowhere. It is not because he is American. I do not like Proust either, and he is French. Very—how you say?—overrated. He write about small, not important things as if they are worth a page. I have no patience for this. Hemingway, he also write stupid sentences and small thoughts."

Judith actually doesn't care about these writers. She wants to know more about her father. But she waits for a chance to interject this into the conversation.

"And what do you teach at your little college? It is little, correct?"

"My area is Victorian literature. That is, English. British. I focus on women writers mostly, well known in their time but then forgotten."

"Forgotten why? Because they were not very good writers?"

"No, that's not it. Some were better than others, of course. It's always that way, isn't it? A book is a 'bestseller' today but in ten years no one remembers it. A lot has to do with the publisher, and sales techniques, and whether they wrote about things people at the time cared about. And another thing."

"*Oui?*"

"We prefer to say 'small liberal-arts college.' Small, not little."

"The same thing, no?"

"No. In terms of educational institutions, 'little' suggests trivial, unimportant, while 'small' implies caring, intense. Individualized."

"I see. Maybe I understand. I do not read much American writing. At school I read stories by Poe, and a little Mark Twain. From school I remember *White Fang*, a great adventure story. Have you read any French literature?"

"Some, but in translation, of course. *Madame Bovary, The Count of Monte Cristo.* As a child I read a lot of stories by de Maupassant, mostly because they were short and often had surprise endings."

"Ah, everyone read these."

So far, Judith notices, Guy has been dismissive of almost everything.

He continues, "Your family was from New York the city, yes?"

"Yes. But not Manhattan. One of the other boroughs—these are areas still part of New York, but a little more suburban. It was about an hour from Manhattan. As a child I didn't appreciate how much like a small town it was."

"What do you mean?"

"I went to school about eight streets away. It was so close, I could go home for lunch. We had a library nearby, and a post office. My mother went to the local markets, one shop for fish, one for meat, a bakery for bread and cake. All the shopkeepers knew my brother and me. When we went out, we saw people we knew. It wasn't like a big city. It was like a village."

"Many neighborhoods in Paris are like this, even now. I know which *boulangerie* has the best baguettes. When this baker go on vacation, it is a problem. We have to eat baguettes not so good. There is one shop where I get fruits and vegetables. On days when there is a market, I go to one man for fish, and another for cheese. I know them for a long time, so I trust. You come to Paris, I will show you."

This sounds like fun—and Guy seems to enjoy talking about food. Another good sign.

"I would love to come to Paris. As I said, I only went once, for three days, a long time ago."

"Did you go other places in France?"

"No, just a few days in Amsterdam, a few days in Paris, two days in Zurich, a week in Italy. The typical after-college whirlwind. But three weeks in England."

"England! A very boring place. I go there a few times on holiday. The food is terrible. They produce no wine."

Judith really wants to like Guy. But he is being rather disagreeable. She needs to defend her beloved England.

"It's not warm enough for viniculture. And they do produce excellent cheeses!"

"French cheese, it is better! But"—and he laughs a little—"I do not think you want to talk about French cheese or English cheese, no?"

Guy looks straight at Judith now and his expression becomes more serious.

"No," she answers.

"And what do you want to talk about?"

"I want to learn more about you. And more about my father."

"Your father. When he come to our apartment the first time, it was like meeting our freedom. He come to save us."

"You know my father was not in combat, right? He did not fight."

"I know. He tell us. It did not matter to us. The Americans and the English push the Germans out. They saved us. I had no father to protect me. So I look to your father, and he was so kind."

"What happened to your father? Do you mind that I ask? Will it make you unhappy?"

Guy shrugs, and his face does not register sorrow or anger. "It does not make me happy or unhappy. I do not know what it means, to have a father. I do not really remember him. I was small when he go."

He pauses for a moment, and Judith doesn't know if he has stopped speaking about his father. But then he starts again.

"When I arrive home from the last place my mother hide me, the mountain school, it is a little time after Paris is liberated. I hear about the big Americans, who laugh and have chocolate! And he have chocolate, so I know these stories are true!" He laughs then.

Judith asks hesitantly, "And your father and grandfather? What . . . how did you learn?"

"They never come home, no. But in a way we are lucky. We at least learn something. Most families, they never know, they never learn how their father or mother die, they assume. Most, the gas. But they not know for sure. One day, I think in spring of '45, a man came to see my mother. He look very sick, wearing pajamas. Well, I thought they were pajamas. It was what he had in the camp, he say. He tell my mother that he know my father, and my father killed by the Germans."

Guy speaks very slowly and deliberately. Judith knows he must be translating in his head before speaking. She also has a feeling, from the details, that this story has been repeated before. And these memories—it must be so difficult for him. But she cannot interrupt his narrative. She does not know how often he thinks about this—or if this is the first time in years.

"In Auschwitz."

Just hearing the name gives Judith a sick feeling. Guy has stopped speaking, and Judith has to say something to fill the silence.

"That . . . must have been a tremendous shock to you and your mother."

She sees Guy shake his head. "Maybe to my mother. But no, not to me. I do not remember much about him, my father. I think maybe it would be nice if he come home, so my mother will be happy. But he never come. This other man comes. My mother make him a cup of tea. She want to give him more, but he say no and leave. I do not remember his name now. So, this is my story."

"I am very sorry."

"Do not be sorry," says Guy. "It is a long time over. But now, I have questions for you, too."

"I will tell you anything that I know. But I don't know very much."

"Where did you find the picture that you send?"

"In my dad's papers. Actually, in a box of photos he had stored somewhere out of reach."

"So your father never show you or your brother this picture?"

"No. At least, I never saw this picture before. I'll ask my brother Michael. But the strange thing—this box had photos our dad took over the years, and also some taken by others. But even putting them in this big box—there were pictures from the 1970s, 1980s. He had to have looked at them and remembered. But he never said anything to me. So I know nothing."

Guy pauses before he says: "Something bother me."

"What is that?"

"Your father come to our apartment a lot. Many Friday night dinners. And for the Pesach *seder*, as I told you. And my *bar mitzvah*. He was always there. But after he leave Paris, we hear nothing. Never. Maman and I thought, maybe he die in Germany. Now I learn, he was not hurt, he just went back to New York. I wonder why he never contact us?"

"You mentioned this in your letter," responds Judith gently. "I am sorry, I just don't have any answer."

"When you went on that trip to Europe, after your university time, your father knew you would go to Paris?"

"Yes, of course, he knew where I would go. I had to give my parents a list with dates, so they would know where I was all the time. And I had to telephone them every week. They were very protective."

"And he never ask you to look for us?"

"No, he never said a thing. Guy, I feel terrible about this, but I simply don't have any response to your question. At the very, very least I think my father showed bad manners. Not to write to you or your mother or to call or send a card, *ever?* Very bad. And, actually, not like him at all! He was a kind person."

"Yes, I know. He was very kind to us, at a difficult time."

They are both quiet for a few moments. Then Guy speaks: "It is late here. We are seven hours ahead. I am tired. We talk again, yes?"

"Yes, yes, of course," Judith says quickly.

"*Bien. Au revoir!*"

Guy clicks off. But his image remains on the screen. Judith takes a closer look, because, after all, it's not polite to stare at someone while conversing. Older, of course, but not *wizened* old. Nice head of hair, mostly gray and white, more white on the sides. Wire-rimmed glasses. Tattersall shirt and a blue pullover. A tailored look. Rows of bookshelves behind him. Well, he's a journalist after all. Or maybe he is trying to impress an academic. Or maybe you are thinking too much, Judith.

## CHAPTER EIGHT

# Reflections

Judith has not slept well after her Skype session with Guy. She thinks about her father and is disturbed about why he would cut off a family he obviously liked, and with whom he shared significant times, so abruptly. It was more than poor manners—it was cruel. And she wonders why he told her and Michael many things about Paris and the people he met there—but never about the Davals. Did he forget? Was he trying to hide something? There has to be more to this story, she thinks.

Certainly, this was not like the Ben Gordon she knew, who had the proverbial heart of gold. She remembered many kind things he did for others, especially unasked. In the winters, when they were still in Queens, he would shovel their walk and also the one in front of their elderly neighbors' home. After her parents moved to Florida, her mother recounted how her dad always invited the widows in their building to go grocery shopping with them. When, in the 1990s, Judith visited Bert and Ruth, old friends of her parents, in California, they told her how, decades earlier, Ben kept them supplied with food and money after Bert had lost his job during the McCarthy era. Ben was naturally kind. This was confirmed even by the neighbors at his funeral.

What Guy had told her just didn't seem right; it didn't add up. The thought nags at her: if she had only seen this box when she could have still asked her father!

Judith thinks she has an idea of what transpired. Best case scenario: like many men who realized they might never again have this exciting a time in their lives, or feel so important, he simply decided to close the door on the war. He moved on.

No, not likely—otherwise he would have gotten rid of the photos, his army shirt, his medals, and various other items she and Michael had found carefully folded away in his bureau.

Judith is an expert in analyzing plots and finding plots within plots. Surely she can figure this one out.

All right: alternative scenario, one harder to consider. What if her father had developed strong feelings for Guy's mother? He had certainly spent a lot of time with this family. Perhaps her father and Guy's mother even had a relationship. Things happened during the war. Judith would not have been angry with him even if this had occurred.

How her mother may have reacted? A different story. Judith knew that her Dad's friend Sol had an affair during the war, because in a moment of either honesty or idiocy, he had confessed this to his wife Myrna, who told her friend Sylvia, who had in turn told her teenage daughter Judith as further proof of the general untrustworthiness of men. "Except for your father, of course," Sylvia had said. "*He* would never do such a thing."

Judith does not like where this memory is taking her. She remembers how one of her girlfriends in high school who was sexually active was dumped and miserable. Another left town as a junior, going to live with an aunt in another state, before coming back for senior year. "She got caught," her mother had said to Judith. Those were the dark days before abortion was legal.

"Remember," intoned Sylvia to fifteen-year-old Judith, "You own your honor. It is yours. Don't let anyone take it away from you. Men want just one thing, so you *have* to stand firm."

"But Mom," she remembers asking, "If men are like that, how do you tell the predators from the good guys? There have to be good guys, like Dad and Grandpa."

"Yes, sweetie, of course there are." Her mother had smiled at Judith and explained: "A good guy will ask to marry you."

Ah. That was years before Lawrence the Loser, of course, who *did* marry her but then started an affair with one of his students. And yet at first he had seemed like an ideal partner, and she felt so wonderful with him. She no longer bears him any ill will, but she does hope that wherever he is, he is bald and unappealing.

She never found anyone else afterwards. Perhaps, despite her mother's belief in a "two-by-two" universe, some people were not supposed to marry. They were simply better off by themselves. Aunt Fran had never married; instead, she traveled. Still, Judith was pleased when Michael, during his first year of law school, announced that he and Naomi would marry. A few years later, they produced in quick succession the desired grandchildren, decreasing the pressure on Judith even more. She settled happily into her role as beloved aunt.

The sun is starting to come up, and Judith realizes she will not get any more sleep. She rises, pushes her feet into slippers, and moves into the kitchen to heat water for coffee. Then she drags herself into the bathroom for her morning routine.

Judith laughs a bit as she realizes how far she has drifted in her thoughts from the possibility of her father's being attracted to Guy's mother. There is absolutely no way of knowing at this point. She does have a hard time imagining her father as a gallant lover—he was simply a good guy, a breadwinner for his family, liked by his friends and neighbors. She knows this sounds boring and colorless and remembers with guilt that she and her brother—too caught up with themselves, being young and having their own adventures—hardly asked their parents about the dreams they had once nurtured.

Now Judith feels as though she is peering through a curtain to something of her father's, and her mother's, past. And she has no idea of what she may discover.

Judith returns to the kitchen and glances at the clock—it is no longer too early to call someone. The water is ready, and she pours it into the waiting coffee press. After three minutes she pushes down on the press, then pours herself a cup of strong black coffee. She pulls out her cell phone, where she has Michael on speed dial, and hits the button.

"Michael? I'm glad you're up. Hold on—I'm going to put you on speakerphone so we can yak while I add half-and-half to my coffee."

She presses another button and carries the phone into the kitchen, placing it on the counter.

"Is this good?"

"Your coffee? How would I know?"

"Funny guy—the sound quality."

"Sure, sis. Why are you calling?"

"Do I have to have a reason to call you?"

"At eight in the morning you do!"

"I was just wondering about Mom and Dad."

"What about them?"

"Do you think they loved each other?"

"Why are you asking this, Judith? Where is your brain going these days?"

"It probably has to do with . . ." She pauses to take a sip, "I don't know, they are both gone, we are orphans although we are adults. I am just . . . reassessing."

"What's to reassess? They were happily married for over fifty years. Remember that Golden Anniversary party we gave them? Everyone had such a great time!"

Judith takes a gulp. Nice and strong. She can feel her brain waking up.

"Yes, it was a super event. But you're not answering my question, Michael. Did they love each other?"

"Well, of course they must have. People don't stay married for decades if . . ."

"Oh, yes they do, Michael. Yes they do. Maybe not in our generation, but before that, people stayed married somehow. As Edith Wharton said, 'the not done things are done every day.'"

"Yes, Professor! But, seriously, I can't think of anyone in our parents' set who got divorced."

"That's right. People stayed married, though they might not actually have been in love with their spouses. Maybe some acted on it, as long as they were discreet."

"Wait—what are you suggesting? That our parents may not have been faithful to each other?" She can hear denial in his voice.

"Michael, it's just, well, something I'm mulling over."

"But not every woman in Mom's generation got married, right? Aunt

Franny stayed single."

"Was it because she wanted to?" Judith asks him. "Yes, she was independent to a certain extent, she worked for many years. But she still had to sacrifice something."

"You mean by living with her mother?"

"Exactly. She told me once that she would have liked to marry, to have a home of her own, but that she couldn't. 'I missed my chance,' she once told me. Any potential suitor knew that it would be a package deal: marry Fran and he'd have to take on her mother as well."

Michael sounds incredulous: "Wait—are you saying that Dad married Mom just so he wouldn't have to live with his mother?"

"Not necessarily, but it worked out that way, didn't it? Michael, what I am still trying to learn is whether Dad and Mom really loved each other."

"I guess they did. But remember, by the time we started noticing, they had been married for years and didn't do all kinds of mushy stuff in front of us. Every couple cools off to some extent. Really—I'm not all over Naomi like I was the first five years we were married, and before that. I couldn't keep my hands off her."

There is a little silence.

"Did I say too much? Am I embarrassing you, Ju?"

Judith has been thinking about Lawrence. "Actually, no. I was just thinking about that myself, to tell the truth. Whether I've ever felt like I couldn't keep from touching someone." Another pause. "Must be nice."

"You didn't feel that way with the Loser?"

She pauses, feeling awkward. "No. Maybe that's one reason I found the divorce more embarrassing than painful. I liked being with him. I enjoyed his company, trading witticisms and so forth. The other . . . not so much."

"Wow. You never told me."

"It wasn't the sort of thing you and I discussed."

"Wow."

"I was a little jealous of you and Naomi. The way she looked at you. The way you were touching her all the time . . . little touches."

"Did you ever discuss this with Mom?"

"You mean about me? Of course not! But once, I do remember asking her something. I was probably in high school or even junior high school and was curious because that's all you heard about from your friends, right, about 'love.'"

"What did you ask Mom?"

"I asked her if she felt a little thrill or something, when she saw Dad walking down the street, that sort of thing. And she said, 'I feel very happy, I'm proud that he's mine.' I remember feeling a bit disappointed. I wanted to hear some passionate declaration. What did I know? I was a naïve teenager."

She hears Michael chuckle. "Ah, you were probably reading all kinds of soppy stories. Well, I'll tell you, teenagers today aren't naïve."

"But then—early sixties."

"You're making me remember! I had a similar conversation with Dad, probably when I was seventeen or eighteen. I was starting to look at girls. I asked him how to tell when a girl you meet is The One. Capital letters. And he just said, 'you *know*.' And actually, with Naomi, I did know—within a month of meeting her, I knew she was the one I wanted to marry."

"And look at you—married, what, forty years?"

"Yup, forty years this spring—in fact, we are planning a little party and hope you'll come. We don't have a date for it yet. Too far in the future."

"Sure! Just let me know when."

"Judith!"

"Yes?"

"That's not why you called me at this hour."

"No—I wanted to know if you thought Mom and Dad were truly in love."

"I assume they were. They were devoted to each other. They enjoyed each other's friends. And we had a nice childhood, didn't we? We would remember otherwise if there had been strife—like, if they had had fights. I don't remember anything like that."

"True. But I do remember little things—little digs that Mom made about Dad. Oh, you know—that he didn't push himself enough. That he became a CPA only because she made him go back to college."

"I think we had this conversation before, Judith."

"Well, it's important. He was working during the day, and then taking classes in the evening. So I grew up thinking that Mom did everything for us, but that Dad was a big slacker."

"But he wasn't!"

"I know that!—we just got things from her point of view."

"I don't get it. Why couldn't she have said 'he was working two jobs to support us?' She would still have been important to us without . . . diminishing him."

"I have no idea why she said those things."

"So why are we discussing this now?" Michael asks.

"I have just been thinking. I've been looking at all of those old photos and realizing how little we know of their pre-parenthood lives. To us, they have always been simply Mom and Dad. I guess that's selfish of us."

"It's probably normal."

"But also," Judith goes on, "I learned some really interesting things about Dad from Guy."

"Yeah? You've spoken to him a lot?"

"Email and Skype. Apparently, Dad had a truly big influence on him. He was the first American that Guy and his family met after the Liberation of Paris."

"No kidding! What else did he tell you?"

"General things, like Dad representing freedom. And some specif-ics—Dad would bring food and whatever else he could get to Guy's family. He taught Guy to play baseball and was just a very good friend at a time when Guy was feeling lost and lonely."

"That's really nice to hear! It's a side of Dad we never knew about. I wonder if Mom was aware of all this."

"She never said anything, I don't know. But I liked hearing this, because from Mom . . . well, she complained a lot about how Dad never stood up to his mother. How he had to be pushed to go back to college. That he didn't have strong enough retorts—I remember her saying to him, 'next time, tell them' and so forth. She did that to me, too. Anyway, from *our* mother's perspective, Dad was kind of a weak guy."

"Look, it's all water under the bridge, now that they're gone."

"True, and there may have been issues before you and I were even born. Who knows? After all, how much do Ian and Sarah know about your childhood, or Naomi's?"

"No more than what I've told them. So look—I need coffee and I can smell that Naomi has made a fresh pot. Have I answered your questions for now?"

Judith laughs, "Sure, Michael, thanks! Say hi to Naomi for me!"

She puts the phone down into its holder and thinks. No major reve-lations. Wouldn't it be great to find a diary or some letters? But among their parents' papers, she and Michael had found nothing extraordinary. No mysteries.

No mysteries except, perhaps, one: why did a man who was ordinarily kind and loyal just completely drop a French family he had become very close to at the end of the war?

## CHAPTER NINE

# The Professor Learns

J udith Gordon knows the nineteenth century well. Although trained in the classic Victorian canon—her dissertation was on Dickens—she is proud of having expanded her expertise over the past three decades to include lesser-known but equally compelling authors. She is in the middle of a project to reissue the novels and short stories of Pearl Craigie, an American-born Victorian who originally wrote under the name of John Oliver Hobbes in order to publish. Thanks to the generosity of her school, she has been able to present papers at academic meetings across the US, Canada, and the UK. She even had a trip to Australia paid for because she was an invited speaker. She is proud of her modest contributions to scholarship and has almost memorized the bioblurb she has had to submit for various conferences.

Research is a pleasure; Judith loves poring over old volumes and diaries, getting a special thrill from handling primary sources. Anyone can read the standard reference works and definitive biographies of, say,

Emily Dickinson. But imagine discovering an unpublished Dickinson poem on a hidden scrap of paper tucked into a notebook in a box under some Massachusetts floorboards? Every scholar's dream!

Original research, then, is the life goal of every scholar: to handle something that no one has seen before except the writer. A diary, an unpublished story or letter, or a glimpse into the life of an historic personage—that would be something Judith would prize above all. Of course, she did get the chance when she found the contents of Elisabeth Shuttleford's desk drawers in a storage closet of a university library in the English Midlands. She had been there on a study grant to examine Shuttleford's letters and printed pamphlets, kept in a small room at the end of one corridor. One afternoon, on a whim, Judith peeked into a corner closet, and high up on a shelf was a box marked "E. Shuttleford, desk contents, 1892." From the jumble inside, Judith could see that someone had dumped drawers but had probably not catalogued anything. She carried the box to a librarian to inquire, eventually learning that, indeed, no one had ever inventoried the contents.

Judith remembered her heart thumping as she secured permission to do this very thing. With an assistant librarian present, Judith went through the box carefully, finding among the contents club membership cards (the University Club for Ladies and the Pioneer, in London); two concert programs from 1891 (the Manchester Philharmonic Choral Society, the Central Hall Brass Band); an envelope containing several calling cards (Miss Elisabeth Shuttleford); yellowing paper pieces of, presumably, a shirtwaist pattern; and several letters of response (in franked envelopes!) from magazine editors. Even knowing that the general population did not share her excitement, Judith had been thrilled to make this discovery and write about it for two peer-reviewed journals.

Yet Judith knows that her exploits have been, in the context of all scholarship in all fields, minor. She has discovered nothing that will change the course of life for thousands; she leaves that to the pharmacologists. Still, she has enjoyed going to conferences and connecting her work with that of other researchers. For her, exploring the Victorian period is enlightening and fun. It takes her to a fantasy realm of traipsing over the moors (although, she realized, women in those long skirts couldn't exactly traipse) or alighting from a coach in murky Victorian London. Sometimes she looks up from a book and is surprised to find herself in the present day.

She will admit to holes in her knowledge. The Early Modern period, for instance—the one that was called the Renaissance when she was in college and grad school—is one she gladly leaves to others. Art history—other than sumptuous Victorian painting, of course, and lovely nineteenth century terra cotta architecture—is another area that thrills her not in the least. Math? She knows enough to balance her checkbook, approximately, and do her taxes each year.

All right, then: American history. As a child, she swallowed almost all the stories her teachers fed her. She did get in trouble in fourth grade for insisting that the Vikings "discovered" America, though. Other than that, she learned what was in the textbooks they were given in school. Anything else—about Sacco and Vanzetti, the Triangle fire, Federal troops that fired on the Bonus Marchers—she learned on her own or from her parents' lefty friends. WWII was still fairly recent, but in her high school history classes, it was stressed as a military experience; the Holocaust was never mentioned.

But she knows about it, of course—what Jewish kid growing up in New York during the postwar era didn't know? Judith even learned, in Sunday School, that the term "Holocaust" was not used to describe the civilian genocide of the war until afterwards. She knew the names of the camps, the statistics, and the relationship between what happened to European Jews and the establishment of Israel.

At home, though, Judith's parents never specifically discussed the Holocaust at all. She remembers how, as a fifth-grader, she came across the word "liquidated" in a history book and imagined it as a chemical process in which people were turned into a kind of soup. It didn't make any sense, and she was ashamed to seem ignorant, so she never asked her parents or teachers what this meant.

As a child, when Judith heard her mother speaking Yiddish, she asked about this language and learned that Sylvia was completely fluent, speaking, reading, and writing. "At a club meeting here," she remembered her mother saying just a few years ago, "a man asked me, '*nu*, so, when did you come to America?' My Yiddish was so good that he thought I, also, was a European immigrant!" Because of her ability in Yiddish, Sylvia was the one who, as a teen and young woman, responded to letters from relatives in pre-war Russia and Poland. Judith knew that her grandfather Abe, Ben's father, had a married sister in Poland. Judith remembers asking her mother what happened to them. "One day the letters stopped," was all her mother said. That is where any family discussion ended, and Judith never persisted in asking questions.

But she absorbed. Over the decades, from reading, seeing films, and talking with her friends' parents, she learned. At least once a year she would have a dream where she was hiding from the Nazis, or where she was being pursued. Later, going to various museums and memorials, she expanded her factual knowledge.

Once, in graduate school, she had a dream so vivid that she has never forgotten it. She had been invited to a party being held on Manhattan's

Upper West Side. The location was an old, elegant apartment house with high ceilings and many rooms. The apartment where the party was held, though, had been modernized throughout. At some point in the dream, Judith had needed to use the bathroom and was directed down a hallway. She didn't know the owner of the apartment but knew he was Jewish. The entire bathroom had been updated with wood paneling floor to ceiling. Judith thought, because he is Jewish, he must have one here, and proceeded to tap her fingers on the wood all along the bathroom walls until she heard a hollow sound. Ah, so here it is: his secret hiding place. At that point, she woke up. The idea that every Jew, even in America, needed a secret hiding place was absolutely terrifying.

Thus, Judith knows the topic of the Holocaust fairly thoroughly, and she is informed about the history of anti-Semitism, the growth of German fascism in the 1920s and 1930s, and the cost of American isolationism. She knows about the ship *St. Louis*, about the Nazi obsession with destroying Judaism, about the Nazi plan to create a museum of what was hoped to be an extinct culture in Prague, about the roundups and deportation of Jews, political prisoners, and anyone who displeased the Nazis.

On the other hand, she has never seen anyone with a concentration camp number tattooed on his or her arm. She has never met a survivor who had stories to tell. She has never visited a camp site, nor has she spoken with anyone who had seen one. Most of her WWII knowledge concerns the countries from which her family had emigrated: Russia, Poland, Austria.

So while she is aware of the outlines of the German occupation of France, about the Vichy government and its betrayal of French ideals and citizens, her knowledge of many specifics is imprecise. She knows about the Résistance and the unfounded claims of membership by so many in France at the end of the war. Over the years, she has seen many French films about the war, including *The Sorrow and the Pity, Army of Shadows, Is Paris Burning?* and *Au Revoir Les Enfants*. She remembers being very affected by a book called *A Bag of Marbles*, which she read back in the 1970s when it came out in English. Despite all this, the name "Drancy" evokes only vague negative impressions in Judith's memory.

Judith realizes that as much as she knows, she doesn't know enough. This is the price she is paying, she tells herself, for spending such a long time hiding out in nineteenth century London and Manchester.

She decides to fill in the gaps with research. It is the weekend, and for a change, she has no papers to grade or lectures to prepare or events to attend. So early on Saturday morning—a week after her long discussion with her brother—she fills a big mug with coffee and sits down in front of her computer; later in the day, she will walk over to the college library.

By late Sunday afternoon, she has learned the timetable of the rapid sequence of the anti-Jewish laws the Germans enacted shortly after they invaded Paris. Almost from the moment they arrived, the Germans began issuing statutes depriving Jews of civil liberties, bit by bit by bit. Jews can't be teachers. Jews can't have bicycles. Jews can't change their names. Jews can't move to another residence. Jewish kids can't play in parks. Jews are under curfew. Just as people were reeling from one rule, another was issued.

She learns that the detention camp at Drancy was a tremendous operation, planned well in advance. Nearly all the tens of thousands of Jews deported from France came through here; few returned. It was also a completely French operation, with civilians brought here on French trains and buses that had French drivers; they were guarded solely by French police. Judith had always thought that deporting children to extermination camps was a particularly Nazi barbarity, but in France, this innovation was French.

Guy's father and grandfather might have been caught in one of the many roundups, or *rafles*, eventually, but going voluntarily to "register" set the machinery for their deportation in motion a little faster. Judith learns, by looking at the online register of victims on the website of the Mémorial de la Shoah in Paris, that Guy's father was on the first train convoy from Drancy to Auschwitz.

She wonders if Guy is aware of this.

Judith learns that in France the process of annihilation was vast, involving thousands of people, from local police to city officials, clerical staff, train engineers, track maintenance personnel, lawyers, journalists, physicians and teachers. While the Germans were an occupying force and punished all the French, they concentrated relentlessly on the Jews. As in other countries they occupied, the Germans wanted to beat down and exploit the entire population, but the Jews were particular targets.

She absorbs the fact that, in Paris, as soon as a Jewish family was deported, their apartment was sealed and stripped of all its contents by French moving van companies. (What did these French workers think? They must have known the residents would never be returning.) These goods were brought to a multistoried furniture store in central Paris, where prisoners sorted and refurbished the chairs, desks, beds, tables, linens, pots and pans, lamps, musical instruments, silverware, clothing, and toys–*toys!*–for shipment to Germany. Warehouses at the Gare d'Austerlitz in eastern Paris were crammed full of thousands and thousands of cases of these stolen goods.

Of course, Judith had known about how the Nazis stole artwork from the museums, known that personnel from the Louvre and other places prepared for the German invasion by taking down thousands of paintings and stashing them in hiding places outside Paris. But she had not known that the Nazis arrived in Paris already knowing which well-to-do Jewish families had private art collections, and exactly where they lived, so they could steal those first. The Paris International Exposition in 1937 had offered ample opportunities for spying and advance planning.

And as for how the Germans treated the rest of civilian Paris, the image that came to Judith's mind was one of leeches, gorging on flesh, sucking the lifeblood out of a country. Soldiers covered the city like locusts, eating and drinking the best, creating food and fuel shortages and an illegal but thriving black market. Others surged through the streets, driving Jewish families into a vast net that they drew tighter and tighter.

Judith pushes away from her desk. Enough. She needs a break. Her jogging days are long over, but she still walks at a brisk pace, so she puts on her comfy sneakers and heads out the front door. There is still enough light for a good hour's walk. She heads toward the center of town, past the brick Federal-style public library, the newly opened chocolate boutique, and the used book shop and coffee corner. Ron, the owner, is just locking up and waves to Judith as she strides past; she smiles and waves back.

Inside her head, though, Judith is not smiling. She is lost in what she has been reading all day. She hears Emerson's line echoing: "My giant goes with me wherever I go." The intense reading she has done all day has made historical events seem so immediate—and personal. She cannot stop thinking about the thousands of children, even babies, who had been deported and sent to their deaths.

One source had led to another, as with any research venture, and down the twisting path Judith wandered, propelled by the complex pattern of French heroism and collaboration. She had known previously that some of the French were all too happy to assist the Nazis, but only now discovered that French school texts had declared—until 1983—that the deportations were entirely the work of the Germans.

Basically, the French government had lied for almost forty years.

This walk is supposed to energize her and clear her mind, but instead Judith is more restless. She turns around at the post office, heading back toward her neighborhood with a headache beginning just over her eyes.

It is nearly dark when she returns to her house, so she puts on one small light inside the entryway and goes into the kitchen. She pops a couple of ibuprofen with a glass of sparkling water. Then she lies down on the couch in the shadowy living room.

She desperately needs to rest. But while she is lying in the dark, memories of what she has read creep into her brain again. She thinks about the most infamous of the roundups, originally scheduled to take place on the National Holiday—Bastille Day—of 1942, but moved to a day later by the French police, who were fearful of harmful publicity. An operation this massive must have involved a tremendous amount of logistical advance work, including securing a location large enough to hold thousands of people. Nine thousand policemen, some brought from communities outside Paris, moved in on their targets—families—before dawn. They had hoped to arrest almost 30,000 people but found only half that number because many who believed the rumors about the roundup had hidden or fled, and some sympathetic policemen had also quietly given advance warning.

All the captives—because that is what they were—were crammed into a huge sports arena, the Vélodrome d'Hiver, which had seen bicycle races in the past. This structure, just a few blocks from the Eiffel Tower, became a deadly holding pen. The skylight ceiling, painted black to make it invisible to enemy airplanes, provided no ventilation and in fact made it hotter inside. There was no food or water. Thousands of people had only two toilets, and soon these stopped working. The mid-July heat was unbearable; the place was stifling, the stench overwhelming. A few individuals escaped; several others killed themselves. After almost a week, their health broken, the captives were taken on French buses—the same ones used for the morning commute—to trains, where they were shipped to Auschwitz.

But Judith has known most of this, so why is she so upset now? She is aware of the statistics, that while a quarter of the French Jewish population was murdered, the rest had escaped or been saved. She knows the numbers are much less horrific than those of Poland, or Romania, or Lithuania, or Hungary, all of which had strong Jewish cultures but were, traditionally, dangerous places for Jews. Judith's own grandparents had emigrated from eastern Europe half a century earlier because life there was no longer tolerable. So why is this information about France bothering her so much?

She realizes it's because people like Guy's parents and grandparents thought it was a safe haven. And other Jews, those born in France, assimilated for decades and as French as their neighbors, also felt safe. Yet, daily during the Occupation, they were mocked by the words: *Liberté Égalité Fraternité* carved above the entrance to every public building, every school.

People expected better of France.

Suddenly feeling completely exhausted instead of rested, Judith turns on her side and decides to nap for an hour before going upstairs to bed. She dreams of trying to find a place to hide in her office, under her desk, inside a filing cabinet, behind a framed poster for a conference on "The New Woman." When she awakens, the sun is starting to rise, and she has to scramble to get ready for work.

## CHAPTER TEN

## AUGUST 2011:

# Paris at Last

Guy has asked Judith several times to come to Paris.

She cannot go over spring break—it's really too short a time, and besides, she wants to be able to read and speak French a little better. She tries to study with her online language program for an hour each day. On the weekend, she watches French films on her computer: *Jules et Jim, La Grande Illusion, Amélie, Les Enfants du Paradis, Un Homme et une Femme*. It is so hard not to peek at the subtitles. Claudette invites her to join the college French classes when they have a showing of *Les Misérables* with Jean Gabin.

Guy offers to pay for Judith's travel and a hotel, but she declines graciously. "*Vous êtes très gentil*," she writes to him. "You are very kind. But I can pay for my own travel. *Mais je peux payer pour mon billet d'avion*." They decide to compromise; Judith will pay her passage, and Guy will make a reservation for her at a small hotel not too far from his apartment. "*Bien sûr*, I want to show you many highlights of Paris," he writes, "But this way

343

you will be free to come and go. You do not wish to be every minute with an old man!" Judith has a good chuckle over this as she checks her Social Security page on her laptop.

She decides that the latter part of summer vacation will be best. She has a conference in Washington, DC in July, and then she can go up to New York to see Michael and Naomi and the kids for a few days. She can fly non-stop to Paris out of JFK. August is good, Guy tells her, because it is the time for *vacances*, and many places will be closed because Parisians go away; but even though many tourists come, the streets are relatively quiet. "I will take you to non-touristical places," he says. "If you wish to go to Notre-Dame and stand in long lines with the other Americans, you can go!"

Judith prepares thoroughly for her trip. She has gone through all of her father's photos from Paris, paying special attention to those of him in identifiable places such as the Jardin du Luxembourg, the Trocadéro, on the Pont Alexandre. She knows that the old train station where his post office was located has been replaced by a modern building, but she has her father's pictures of the streets just in front, and these might be the same. She plans to see all of these.

She knows which museums will be open and what exhibitions will be available. And she has made an appointment to visit the library at the Mémorial de la Shoah in central Paris. She does not know if Guy has gone there, and if he has not, whether he would be willing to do so.

The older Judith gets, the less she wants to carry. For fifteen days in Paris, she takes just one bag plus an over-the-shoulder bag. Here she can stow all of the essentials: her wallet, sunglasses, passport case, cell phone, digital camera, and a small notebook. All the clothing she takes can be mixed and is hand washable. A couple of scarves and a string of pearls in case she needs to accessorize and dress up—she realizes she has no idea if she will have any evening events, but she will be prepared. One pair of dressy flats. And to wear, her most comfortable shoes that are not sneakers. She has read enough to know that sneakers would scream "American tourist coming through!" and she would prefer to make a quieter entrance.

Guy tells her he was not doing much driving anyway, and it was so expensive to keep a vehicle in the city that he gave up his car. But he will meet her at Charles de Gaulle airport when she arrives, he promises, giving her explicit directions to their meeting place.

Judith does not rest much during the night flight. She thought flying at night would be ideal because she'd sleep and then be fresh in the morning for the day's exploits. Perhaps she is too excited and keyed up. Instead, she finds she has pulled up assorted memories of that first trip, a couple of weeks after her college graduation. The airport was at Orly then, and the trio of girls—she, Amy, and Ellen—found themselves in Paris without hotel reservations. They could not afford <u>any of</u> the major hotels, and budget accommodations were all full. Finally, they found what Amy called the "last hotel on the last street." It was a small, old place on the Left Bank, with patched walls and old blue carpeting, threadbare in many places. "We are renovating," said the clerk at the desk, but Judith and her friends never saw workmen during the three days they stayed. They had a small room on the third floor with a tiny sink that burbled and spouted tan water each time the hallway toilet was flushed.

She remembers oppressive heat. The girls went to see a French film simply to sit in an air-conditioned theatre. They went to the Louvre and the Eiffel Tower, because, after all, they were young tourists. They saw a play— Judith doesn't even recall the name—at the Comédie-Française without understanding a single word, as they had all taken Spanish. One morning, when Ellen and Amy went to the great department stores, Judith had taken a bus to the Place Vendôme to find a shop her mother had told her to visit and purchase some fragrance for her. Judith smiles now at her recollections. It was so long ago, though, that she cannot remember the details . . . and she drifts off to sleep in the last hour or so of the flight.

The darkened interior of the airplane changes as the lights flash on. The onboard speaker announces that they will land in about forty minutes. The noise rouses Judith, who, disoriented at first, quickly realizes that she will soon be in Paris for the first time in forty years.

After landing, Judith gathers her belongings and disembarks. As soon as possible, she stops at a restroom to repair the damage done by the overnight journey, and then goes off to find Guy.

Although the Charles de Gaulle terminal is busy and crowded, he is easy to spot. Judith remembers his instructions and goes to the meeting place, where she sees Guy leaning against a pillar and watching her. He wears a light-colored blazer and khakis, with a bright, deep pink polo shirt. Judith sees this as a mixture of the conventional and bold and feels pleased for some reason. Guy recognizes her right away as well; not only has he seen her on Skype, but he knows she will have the look of someone scanning the crowd for a specific person. So when she is finally standing in front of him, it is like a meeting of two old friends.

"Ah, Zhoodeet," says Guy, smiling as he bends to give her a light kiss of welcome on each cheek. "You had a good journey?"

"Excellent! I was even able to sleep for a bit."

They both take a step back and gaze at each other, smiling.

"We need to go to the baggage claim?"

"No, I have everything."

"But you are here for two weeks!"

"I don't travel with anything I can't carry. So this is it! *C'est tout!*"

Judith indicates her one small wheelie.

"Ah, but you will want to go shopping while you are here. All the foreign women want to go to the designer boutiques and the *grands magasins*, the big department stores."

"Probably not this foreign woman. But we'll see."

"All right. We will take the bus to the center of Paris, to the *opéra* house. And then we will go by taxi to your hotel. I can take your bag?"

"Thank you, but I can manage."

"Ah. American woman. Independent!" Guy does not insist upon carrying her bag but turns and leads the way outside to a special bus stop. Judith notices that he has a slight limp, but it does not impede his vigorous pace. A large bus with "Opéra" lettered on the front is just pulling up. Guy leads the way and presents the driver with tickets. "I already take care of this. You sit and relax. It will be one hour to Paris."

Judith settles into a seat by the window. There is ample room and a place for her case. As they start to roll out of the airport and toward the city, she suddenly feels a bit shy. What an odd feeling, actually to be sitting next to someone who knew her father more than sixty years earlier. He is a stranger—yet not.

The bus passes through some nondescript suburbs, then the buildings become taller and more dense as they near the outskirts of the city. Signs of urban decay prevail. Graffiti is graffiti, thinks Judith, even if I don't understand what the writing means. Then she wonders if she ought to consider graffiti in the plural, and then it would be graffiti *are* graffiti. She realizes how tired she is.

"*Voilà*," says Guy, pointing. "Look up there on the left, and you can see Sacré-Cœur." As the bus follows the curve of the road, they head right; atop a hill on the left are the white turrets of the church. She recognizes them from her guidebooks and from iconic paintings.

"We are following the northern road around the city," says Guy. "Now we are passing Clignancourt, where there is a big flea market. Save your patience. Don't go there." Judith did want to go there. "Unless, of course," continues Guy, "You wish to waste your time looking at worthless junk or meet a pickpocket."

Now they leave the main road and turn south into the city streets. Judith takes in the street plaques at each corner, large green neon crosses marking the pharmacies, small shops displaying bright fruits and vegetables, a couple chatting over small cups at a corner café, a tiny store marked *Livres Antiques*. The bus is moving too quickly for her to read most other signs, though; then they turn onto a narrow street, and she is amazed how ably the bus driver navigates.

Finally, they emerge at a plaza behind a grand building—this is the Opéra Garnier, where they descend. Guy leads the way to a taxi and holds the door for her. "*Bonjour, monsieur, ça va?*" asks Guy of the driver as they settle into their seats, "*Rue Victor Cousin, s'il vous plaît.*"

"I find you a nice small hotel in the 5th, same *arrondissement* as mine. You can rest and recover from your trip. We have much time to talk!"

"Thank you, Guy. *Merci beaucoup!*"

"Ah, you wish to speak French all the time? You can do this?"

"No, not yet!"

He laughs, and they enjoy the ride down the broad Avenue de l'Opéra, past grand hotels and restaurants. "There," says Guy, pointing, "Excellent *macarons*, though I prefer the ones from Ladureé; and there, if you are homesick for English, a good foreign bookstore!"

This is one of the world's great cities, but what strikes Judith as most impressive here is the huge expanse of bright blue sky that dwarfs everything as their taxi whisks across a bridge over the sparkling Seine. The buildings on either side look clean and welcoming. Within minutes, they stop in front of a tall, narrow yellow building on the Left Bank.

Judith does the paperwork to check in while Guy waits in a lobby armchair, scanning the current issue of *Le Monde*. Judith takes the lift to the fourth floor and is delighted to find that her cheerful room has tall windows framed by flowered curtains, opening onto a small balcony. She can have her morning tea here, watching the neighborhood wake up.

After stowing her bag in the closet, she takes a small album from her shoulder bag. "All right, Dad, you're back," she murmurs, looking briefly at each page. She has filled this album with all of the photos her father took in Paris back at the end of the war. There are fifty, only three inches by about two inches, and many are even smaller than that. She gathered them from the large box of photos she had found, plus a couple from an old album Aunt Fran had left her. She will show these to Guy at a later time; today will be for talking. She places the album on her pillow.

Before going back to the lobby, she washes up in the small bathroom and reapplies her lipstick. She looks into the mirror and thinks: not bad, considering your age. Then she winks at herself.

## CHAPTER ELEVEN

# The Left Bank

"This will be a good practice for you," says Guy. "Do not use the menu in English!"

Judith scans the French menu at the small corner café near the hotel that Guy has chosen. She tries to remember what she has studied so far and understands nearly everything listed.

"*Je voudrais une omelette avec fromage. Je vois qu'il est servi avec une petite salade.* I see that it comes with a small salad. Do I have it correct?"

"Not bad. Though you want to say *au fromage*, not avec. But yes, the rest is fine. You are doing well. We shall do some each day."

"For right now, though, could we speak English, please? I am too tired to think hard."

"Of course! Maybe you need coffee. Do you wish a coffee?"

In French, he asks something of the waiter, who returns a few moments later to place a cup of espresso in front of each of them. Judith stares at the tiny cup.

"Ah, I forget!" says Guy. "Americans drink coffee in giant mugs! Everything must be big!"

"We drink espresso, too. We are not exactly living in the wilderness. But I have always thought of espresso as a late afternoon or evening beverage."

"You can get a *café americano* if you prefer."

"This is fine—as long as I get my jolt of caffeine. You really enjoy making fun of Americans, don't you?"

"Of course. You are a peculiar people. We can always tell who are the American tourists—they talk too loud, they wear sneakers, and they eat big servings of everything, especially meat."

"Have you ever been to the United States?"

"Once. For a conference in New York."

"Do you know any Americans here in Paris?"

Guy thinks for a moment, then shakes his head. "I know one man from Québec, but no, no one from the United States. Why?"

"I was just checking to see where your stereotypes might have come from."

"All stereotypes originate in France!"

"What? How can you say that?"

"Because, *bien sûr*, it is a French word. It means a kind of printing method. Funny, no?"

"Funny, yes." She smiles at him. "But even though I am not wearing sneakers and I don't speak loudly, you are going to hold on to your stereotyped view of my people?"

"Of course!"

Their food arrives, and Judith stars to relax. A little humor can do that, she knows. Yet she also has some serious questions and wonders if she can ask them now, or if it is too early.

"You must have many questions," says Guy as he pours wine into their glasses.

"You know exactly what I am thinking! Naturally I am curious. First, why did my father choose your family to help? Why your family, of all those that survived, how did he choose you?"

"It was not accidental. He come looking for us."

Judith sits up even straighter as this surprise hits her.

"He knew about you?" she asks. "How?"

"My mother have a cousin, a little older than she was, I think. She go to New York just before the war. And she meet your father in the post office, in Brooklyn. My mother explain to me."

"What was this cousin's name?"

"Anna or Anne."

"Do you remember her last name?"

He shakes his head. "No, I do not. Later she return to Paris, marry a Jewish man, and move to the south."

"But you don't know her married name?"

"No—sorry. In Brooklyn she ask your father to look for us if he come to Paris. It was a long time. Paris was not liberated until August of 1944. That was very exciting for me. This day—I never forget it!"

He sits back and looks off into the distance, with a bit of a smile on his face. "It was a big day! It was the same day I return to Paris with my *maman* from the mountain school. We came to Paris by train, and then we walk from the station to our apartment building. It was a little time after the Liberation. There was not much petrol and there were no taxis or buses, just military vehicles. To walk, it take a long time, but I am so happy to be back with my *maman!*"

Judith tries to imagine Guy as a boy in short pants, carrying a school bag, and his mother with his suitcase. August, it must have been so hot. She also imagines that the mother and son do not even notice the heat, because they are happy to be together at last and free without anyone hunting them.

"We come to our building and go up in the little elevator and the door opens! My *gran'mère* stands there with her arms out to hug me—I was so excited to see her!—and your father is nearby in his American uniform."

"You must have been overcome with strong feelings." Judith can hardly believe that this is happening. She is actually sitting at a café in Paris with a Frenchman who has these memories of her father, all those years ago. She realizes that she, too, is overcome with strong feelings.

"Yes! I was so excited to see my *gran'mère!* And our old apartment. I thought I would never be there again. Like when I call you on the telephone—I laugh and cry all together. At the mountain school, the only thing we boys talk about, is 'when the Americans come to save us' and 'when the British come.' And there, in our own apartment, is a real American soldier!" Guy smiles at the recollection. "We felt safe with your father. Maman said the police were our friends now, but I could not trust them. I could hardly look at a policeman's uniform without shaking. But your father's uniform was different. The Americans saved us!"

Guy pauses, taking a sip of wine. Judith sees that his face has become much more warm and animated since beginning this story, and she realizes that she doesn't even care if all of the tiny details are correct; Guy is too good at storytelling.

"It was also a sad time for us. We still do not know where is my father or grandfather. But still, a wonderful time—the Nazis are gone. France is French again. We are safe. There are problems, though."

"What kind of problems?"

"The Germans took so much. My *maman* and *gran'mère* stretch the food, you know, to make it last? We do not have much meat or fresh vegetables at all. The markets do not have much because the Germans took almost everything from the farmers: vegetables, fruit, meat, eggs, cheese. And so the farmers have little to bring to the city. Your father and his army friends help us. They bring many things from their supply store."

He pauses and looks sadly at her.

"I was a lonely boy. I had no friends. I have my family, most of them, but the other children I used to play with—I cannot find anyone. Actually, I cannot remember many at all, after everything. There was one boy I play with in our old building, but after Liberation I cannot find him. I was only eight when my mother take us across Paris. I remember being scared, because I was not supposed to say this, not supposed to say that.

"I remember the day when Jews have to start wearing the yellow stars. I come into class and there are three boys wearing them. The teacher, I want him to say, 'take off your coats, no stars here!' but he does not." He pauses, a stern expression on his face. He does not seem to be looking at Judith, but this memory is obviously painful.

Judith speaks up, partially to relieve the tension. "He was probably afraid to say that, even if he wanted to. Wouldn't someone have reported him?"

"*Bien sûr*. I am sure that may have happen. So we continue. Soon, though, my mother take me out and send me to Hélène—"

"Who is Hélène?"

"Ah, of course. You do not know. A friend of my *maman*, a Catholic woman she know from work before the war. She live in a village, and help us a lot. She got my *maman* the false papers. This save us, because my *maman* could do all the things a Jew could not. Like rent an apartment."

"Your mother sounds like a very brave person."

"Ah, *oui*, brave and very strong. But come now, you must eat and drink, and then you will go to your hotel and rest."

Judith is indeed beginning to feel hugely tired. Just a short nap, an hour or so, will revive her. After they finish lunch, Guy accompanies her to the hotel and tells her he will return at seven o'clock that evening. Judith looks back at him as he walks away down the street and wonders about the cause of his limp.

As she hangs up her pants and top and gets ready to lie down, Judith has a sense of comfort, even though she is in an unfamiliar place. The room itself, all yellow and blue chintz, is lovely, but it is not the source of her feeling of ease.

She sits on the edge of the bed and takes another look through her small photo album. There is her father, in uniform, leaning against the bal-ustrade of a bridge; from photos she has seen of the bridges in Paris, this one is probably the Pont Alexandre; she will check. Another of him, at one of the *bouquinistes* along the Seine. On the back of another, it says, in her father's handwriting, "an idea of the side streets in Paris." He didn't write the name of the street, but there is a large shop called Heyraud, which she has learned is a famous shoe store. A few photos have more informative details: "This is where we work at the Montparnasse RR Station. We sleep on the upper floor." On the back of a picture of a banner-festooned apart-ment house, he had noted: "VE Day in Paris—people all along balconies of houses. Flags all around and over buildings throughout the city." But he had noted no street name. Other locations are well known—the Eiffel Tower, Les Invalides, Notre-Dame—so it doesn't matter that her father had written nothing. But it would have been nice to know what he had thought when he first saw them.

Other photos are a complete mystery: what is the snow-dusted street with a few pedestrians but no vehicles? In front of which Métro station did her father take a picture of another American soldier, who blocks the name? Who are the civilians surrounding Sol Lipman in front of an *épicerie*, a grocery store? She imagines her father, camera in hand, wandering through the streets of Paris, clicking away at places either famous or simply interesting, and at the people he met when he wasn't working. She has found no photos of the post office itself; perhaps because it was a military installation, photographs were not allowed. But from the pictures she does have, she has gained a sense of where her father went in the city.

Judith places the album on the small table next to her bed. Over the next week, she plans to retrace some of her father's steps to see what caught his attention. As she falls asleep, she realizes that when he was in Paris, he was about half her current age.

## CHAPTER TWELVE

# The First Evening

The narrow elevator in Guy's building is a cage-like affair rising from the lobby, and they pass ascending steps that wind around them. Two people can fit comfortably. Just like in a fifties espionage movie, says Judith to herself, when the hero races up the stairs to reach the flat on the top floor, while the villain fires at him from within the elevator. She dares not say this aloud lest Guy start making fun of Americans and their obsession with cinema. Which, he will point out, was of course invented by the French.

Guy lives on the top floor here. "I bought this flat in 1970," he says as they go down a short, tiled hallway. As he unlocks the door, he remarks, "I could never afford it now."

"That's what all my friends in New York say. Property prices in major American cities have become insane."

They step into a sizable living room with tall, curtained windows facing them and a fireplace on the left wall. Judith judges homes immediately by whether books are in the main room. So she is happy to see floor-to-ceiling shelves on the right wall filled with volumes of all sizes, interspersed with framed photos and mementoes; where there is no more shelf space, books are stuffed horizontally. But then, what else did she expect of a journalist?

"While you have been sleeping," he tells Judith, "I have prepared a light dinner. We can relax and talk, and I can tell you what we will see in the next few days."

Judith imagines her mother's reaction to all this. "Judith! He is really almost a stranger. And you're alone with him in his *apartment!*"

Judith laughs to herself as she scans the bookshelves while Guy opens a bottle of wine. He does not feel like a stranger at all, thanks to email and Skype. And she is a grown woman who can handle nearly anything, she feels.

Most of the books are in French, of course, and about history and politics. He also has biographies of de Gaulle, Sartre, Voltaire, Chirac. Literature, art, some fiction—all mixed in without, it seems to Judith, any sort of order.

Guy approaches with two glasses of white wine, handing her one. "*À votre santé!*"

They toast each other and sit at the small glass dining table near the windows, which overlook a park. "Out there, the Jardin du Luxembourg. I will show you the view when it starts to become dark. It is the thing I like best about this apartment."

Guy has set out a mushroom quiche and a salad. Everything is very good. Judith is impressed. Either he is a capable cook (stereotyping again, as she believes everyone in France is a born chef) or, like her, he often uses an outside source for prepared foods.

"Guy," she says, "This is all quite delicious."

"Ah," he responds, and chuckles. "I am happy you like."

"Perhaps tomorrow," Judith begins, "we can add some French to our conversation. But for now, English is just easier for me. Did anyone teach you how to cook?"

"Oh, no, I am French, so I am born with this skill!" he laughs. "Actually, I watch my mother and my grandmother when I can. My grandmother, she make good and traditional dishes."

"How old were you when she passed away?"

"She die just three years after the war end. She was not strong, you know, she have a weak heart. And she was alone all day in the little room my *maman* find us on the other side of Paris. She does not see a doctor, she take no medicine all during the Occupation. Of course, I do not know this when I was a child—I was too small to understand. All I know is, my *gran'mère* is there when I get home, and that she love me."

He smiles a little but looks sad at the same time.

Judith takes a sip of wine, pauses. "Guy," she says, "I don't wish to make you sad—but, if you do not mind, I'd like to know more about your mother and grandmother."

"It is not a problem, Zhoodeet. There are many nice moments to remember, too. My mother, she was brave, as you know. The way she move us and hide us. But we were also lucky. The family in Dreux that keep me, the same people give my mother false papers. Well, they were *real* papers, but a different person's name. A Christian woman my mother's age who died. Also, she go to a priest at a church near our apartment. She hear that this priest give catechism certificates to people. So I get one saying I study in this church and am a good Catholic. When I live in Dreux, I go to a Catholic school and I cross myself and kneel and do everything."

He takes another sip of wine and laughs, "Jewish, Catholic, I do not know the difference then."

"But you knew that you were Jewish, correct?"

"When the war start, I was little. I do not know anything. Later I learn. After the Liberation, we get information, but small pieces. Like a patchwork blanket, you know? A bit here, a bit there. It takes a long time to make a whole cover. *Oui*, I know it was danger to be a Jew. This is all I know as a child."

Guy pauses briefly to refill both of their glasses, and when he begins again, it is with a kind of radiance—or energy—that surprises Judith.

"People who survive start to come back to Paris. This was near the end of the winter after your father arrive. French prisoners of war come back on a train. Other prisoners. They set up a place at the Hôtel Lutetia—you know this place?"

Judith shakes her head no.

"Very elegant, you should see it, it has Art Nouveau design. You like this type of building? In the 6th, not too far from here. The Nazi leaders take it over when they occupy, they get the best rooms, they have the best food when the rest of Paris stay hungry. So after Liberation this become a meeting place. Free prisoners can stay here and rest. Our soldiers, too, prisoners of war. Many are weak, of course. Their names go up on a big board outside the Lutetia, families come and look on the board for people they know. When my mother hear this, she go every day to check. Sometimes I go with her. It is too far for my *gran'mère* to walk.

"We never see my father's name. We look for any name we know. Very, very few Jewish people come back after they were deported. The ones who survive the war are hidden, or live secretly, as we do. Many children were rescued, but their parents were deported and die."

"Did you see any of the people as they returned?" asks Judith. She has only read about this, and here she is sitting with someone who was actually there!

Guy shakes his head. "No, but my mother did. She say the French soldiers who were prisoners, they look tired and dirty but all right. She say people coming from the labor camps, they all look sick. I do not hear everything she tell my *gran'mère*. But later she tell me—like skeletons walking."

Judith speaks quietly. "I cannot imagine what it must have been like."

Guy does not seem to notice her or to hear her. He pauses and simply stares for a few moments, lost in his thoughts. Some of his energy seems to have dissipated. Then he resumes his narrative.

"People tell us how to feel. I remember how everyone say after Liberation, 'We must get back to our normal lives.' But what is normal? I do not know. I do not remember what things are like before the war. I want to make Maman and Gran'mère happy. They say to me my job is to do well in school, go to the *lycée* and then to university. To get my education. So, this is what I do. I work hard, especially in history and languages.

"One day while I am at the *lycée*, this is after the war, after your father left France, my *maman* calls the school office—by now we have a telephone—and ask me to come home right away, fast. So I run and find a taxi. I know this must be about Gran'mère. I told you she was not well all during the war. Now, of course, she can see the doctor, but there is still too much damage to her heart.

"I run up the stairs to our flat, and my *gran'mère* is in bed, same as that morning, but now very pale. She say to me, 'Guy, I wait for you!' And I go over and bend down and give her a kiss. 'Please, Gran'mère,' I say, 'you must get strong again!' She say, 'I am fine now,' and die. Just like that."

Judith and Guy are very quiet. This memory, sixty years old, clearly still disturbs him. She wants to reach over and put her hand on top of his, but she senses that even this small gesture of comfort would be an invasion of his privacy. So she remains where she is seated and simply says, "I am so sorry."

"Yes, I miss her very much. We were close. And she was not old, really. I thought she was old because, well, she was a *grand-mère*. She was not aged, only mid-fifties. But back then, with the war and the rationing, people got old faster."

There is no comparison, but Judith cannot help but think about her own grandmother. And then she speaks, if only to distract Guy from his own unhappy memories. "Yes, you are right. Even where there was no rationing, people just *seemed* older. In my first memories of my grandparents, they looked old. My grandmother had gray hair, which she wore up. She wore shapeless dresses and sensible shoes. But she was only in her early sixties at the time—actually younger than I am now! And I certainly don't feel in the category of 'old.'"

"Well, I am."

"You don't seem that old."

"You flatter. Americans want everyone to be young. You see my gray hair?"

"So?"

"And you notice the way I walk?"

"That's not necessarily related to age, is it? Yes, I have noticed, but it seems very slight."

"It was not there when I was younger. It gets more as I get older. When we live with rationing during the war, I am still developing. Except when I was in the village, I never get enough milk. Children my age, our bones did not get enough milk. So now we have spine problems, difficulty with walking. Many have—I don't know how you say it—*l'ostéoporose*."

"Osteoporosis. People who once were tall get shorter, bent over."

"Yes. I get back to your question. About my mother." He pauses, and when he speaks again his voice is lower. "She was very brave, yes. Otherwise we probably would not survive the Occupation. So I say she give me life twice: once, when I am born, second, when she protect me during the war. I owe her everything. Still . . ."

His voice gets even lower and he pauses, looking sorrowful.

"I spend important years not seeing her. I love her, but I do not have good memories from my childhood. And my father, actually, I do not remember him much at all. I have one or two old photos, that is it. I do not remember his voice, anything he tell me." He stops speaking and covers his eyes for a few moments.

Then he resumes: "After the war ends, my mother keep working. She was a very talented sewer." He pronounces this like the underground pipes, and Judith feels compelled to correct him.

"Guy, I am sorry to interrupt you. This is one of those English words that has different sounds even though the spelling is the same. Sewer has the same letters as sewer, but they mean very different things. Your mother was a sewer, because she sewed clothing."

"Sewer is not right?"

"It means the underground pipes that carry waste from the toilet."

He thinks for a moment, and Judith realizes he is translating in his head. "Ah yes," he says, "I can see where this could be a problem!" He laughs a little. "Both my mother and father were excellent *sewers*. That is what a lot of the poor Jewish people did in the 1920s and 1930s. But they want their children to do something better."

"It was the same in our country. Jewish immigrants worked in the garment industry, or were shop clerks, or did factory work. Both of my grandmothers and one grandfather worked in clothing factories. But the children of the immigrants got an education and became teachers and accountants and civil servants."

Guy nods in agreement. "There was no question—I would go to university. After I finish at the *lycée*, I start at university. By that time, my *gran'mère* is gone, and Maman and I are alone. We mourn for my *gran'mère*—but actually this time in my life is sweet. I love being with Maman, we have not much money, but we feel safe. And I start my university studies, and this I enjoy. Some time later, my mother meet a man, also Jewish; he was in the 'free zone' during most of the war. After the war, he come to Paris to find work. Also he work in garments. He meet my mother and want to marry her. She was still young. Not even forty."

"And from her photo, extremely attractive."

"She ask me, should I marry Martin? I do not want to live with him, because I think he does not like me. If she marry him, my sweet time with her is over. Maybe Martin does not like me because I am from the first husband. Or maybe jealous because I can go to university. But my mother feel she has to decide. In that time, women need to be married, for security. So this was her opportunity; maybe she will not have another. Better to be married, she tell me, than not."

Judith sighs. "My mother said the same thing. Better some marriage than no marriage. She said, 'The world is like Noah's ark, two by two.'"

"Yes, that was the way fifty, sixty years ago. And even later than that. So my mother marry Martin and he take her to live in Toulouse. They start their own clothing business. By the 1960s they are not poor anymore. But I do not see my mother much either."

"What about your children? She must have wanted to see her grandchildren."

He smiles slightly at this. "Ah, yes, she love them, and come to visit a couple of times each year. Once a year, in summer, we drive to the South and see them. But she die in 1981. The children, I think, they do not remember her."

Guy has been lost in his thoughts, but suddenly he sits up and takes notice of the changed light outside. He stands up and motions to Judith to rise as well.

"Step onto my balcony, and you will see Paris at night!"

Guy opens two of the tall windows (in America they are called 'French doors,' Judith thinks, but what are they called in France?). They step out into the cool evening. The sky is a deep blue but there is enough light to see the dark tree line of the park across the street. Melodious guitar music rises from a café five stories below.

"Now," says Guy, "move to your right, where the balcony bends a bit, around a corner of the building. And look."

Judith obeys, and is rewarded with a beautiful sight: in the distance, twinkling with many lights, is the Eiffel Tower.

She inhales and clasps her hands together in delight and cannot helping crying, "Oh!"

"See, I knew you would like this!" Guy, smiling, is obviously pleased that he has provided this source of pleasure.

Judith wants to be a sophisticated academic, to take in stride being in a lovely Haussmannian building within sight of the Eiffel Tower. But her natural instinct is to let go and simply enjoy where she is.

## CHAPTER THIRTEEN

# Being A Tourist

J udith awakens to silence. It is five o'clock in the morning, yet she is absolutely alert. She pads across the thick carpet to the window and looks down at Rue Victor Cousin below. Aside from one truck rolling slowly down the street, it is quiet. The sky is still dark. Not even the birds are up yet.

She cannot sleep. So she decides to go exploring. After putting on dark knit pants, a shirt, and a black pullover to ward off the morning chill, she takes the elevator down to the lobby. *"Bonjour, madame,"* says the man at the desk. She smiles and responds in kind, leaving just as the delivery truck from the bakery arrives with the day's warm baguettes and croissants.

Judith does not have a map with her, but she has a good sense of direction. Parisian streets, she knows, veer off at many angles, so she has to be quite sure of where she goes so she can find her way back. Strolling down the Rue Victor Cousin, she notes the cinemas and bookstores where she might wish to stop later. When she comes to the Rue Soufflot, she turns right and walks another block. Now she comes to a large roundabout where she has a choice of many streets to follow. Traffic is picking up, and it is all zipping around the circle. Judith decides the prudent thing to do is cross where it is zoned for pedestrians and makes her way across the intersection to the park on the side of the circle.

Of course—it's the Jardin du Luxembourg! She recognizes the iron fence, black and tipped in gold, outlining its perimeter from photos in guidebooks. This must be fairly near Guy's apartment, but it was dark last night, and she is not quite sure of the exact street. The area just seems familiar. As the sky gradually becomes lighter, she follows the park's fence to the left and simply enjoys what she observes along the way. A man walking his dog, who insists upon stopping to sniff at every lamppost. A newsagent preparing his shop for the day. A student (she assumes—carrying a backpack but not looking like a tourist), earbuds providing his beat, hurrying to meet some friends for an early coffee.

Then she notices a small plaque close to the ground. Even without her rudimentary French, she understands that this is a memorial. She reads that a young man fell here on August 25, 1944—the very day that Allied troops marched in to liberate Paris. He was only twenty when he died for France, "*mort pour la France.*" The plaque is simple, sturdy marble, placed on a wall with a strong bolt at each corner. It is not new, chipped at one corner, probably placed here not long after the Liberation itself. She imagines the young man crouched in a nearby doorway, perspiring from heat and fear, lobbing grenades at remaining German troops.

She looks around and realizes that all the buildings within her view are likely from before the war. The past is right there, almost tangible.

She continues for a few blocks, musing, and then realizes she needs to head back to the hotel even though there is still ample time for breakfast.

She makes a couple of turns and finds herself on the Rue Gay-Lussac. She passes some interesting shops—*livres anciens*—old books, a florist, a *pâtisserie* that will tempt passersby with rows of fresh multicolored confections, which an employee is arranging in the window—before she realizes that the street is going downhill. She walked downhill to get to the park, so she must be going in the wrong direction now. She turns and heads back up, making a right at Rue Le Goff. Some things are familiar and, sure enough, this street becomes Rue Victor Cousin after the next intersection.

When she arrives at the hotel, several guests are already in the sunlit dining area. Seeing the buffet that has been set out, she understands why breakfast is called *petit déjeuner*, "little lunch." A coffee machine offers six options, and three glass pitchers of different juices are arrayed next to it. Platters of cheeses and bowls of yogurt, applesauce, and peaches greet the diners. Judith sees large glass jars with several types of cereal and bowls full of preserves and butter. At another table, a tall basket holds a dozen fresh baguettes, with a cutting board nearby so guests can slice off the desired length. There are other baskets of *croissants, pain au chocolat*, and . . . plain sandwich bread for toasting. Really? She can't imagine anyone coming to Paris and choosing that over baguettes or croissants!

Judith settles down with orange juice, coffee, apricot preserves, butter, and a generous hunk of baguette. Just then she sees Guy entering the hotel lobby and looking around. He comes into the dining room and approaches her table.

"*Bonjour, Guy! Ça va aujourd'hui?*" She is so proud that she can say, "Good morning, Guy! How are you today?"

"Ah, Zhoodeet!" He kisses her lightly on both cheeks as she rises to greet him. "Would you like today to be an all-French day? I can do this!"

"Perhaps a *little* French. May I get you a coffee?"

She returns with a small cup of black coffee, having noticed that is what he prefers.

"So, Zhoodeet, did you sleep well? Have you just gotten up?"

"I slept well, yes, Guy. But I woke up very early; my body has not adjusted to the time yet. So I went for a walk."

"You have a map?"

"No, but I have a fairly good sense of direction. I wandered around a bit, and did make a wrong turn, but then I got back here as you see."

"Very good! I have some ideas of places to show you today, and where different neighborhoods are located. So we can start with the big land-marks—you can go back later if you wish. You really need to see the opéra house—Palais Garnier. It is a wonderful piece of architecture, and they give tours of the interior. Then we will go to one of the big department stores, where there is a nice restaurant on the roof. From there, you can see almost all of Paris. You know, Paris is not that tall. We have only one, what you call, skyscraper."

"That must be the Tour Montparnasse."

"Exactly. You have done your reading."

"I wanted to learn about the place where my father worked."

"That's right. His post office was in the rail station. They destroy the old station in the 1960s and replace it with a new one, and the Tour. Typical early 1970s horrible, ugly architecture."

"But I am sure it provides wonderful views!"

"The only thing that *monstruosité* is good for! Go and look if you wish. I do not see this. After it is finished, people here, they were so upset, they forbid any more towers. Now, if you want tall, ugly modern buildings, you have to go to the Bibliothèque Mitterrand or to La Défense. They are on opposite sides of Paris, far from the center. They are good only to use for figuring out your direction."

Judith makes a mental note to see the Tour, ugly or not, for the views of the city. For today, she will just follow Guy's lead. They leave the hotel and walk down a few blocks to the Rue Gay-Lussac, where Judith had been just a couple of hours earlier.

"We take the number 21 bus here," says Guy, "It will take us past many important places until we arrive at the opera house."

Guy will not let Judith pay for anything. He has a stack of bus tickets in his wallet. When the 21 arrives, they are lucky to find two seats right near the front with a clear view.

"So you already know this famous garden, yes? You walk here this morning."

"I didn't go inside the park."

"You will have time later. Now we turn right away to the Boulevard Saint-Michel, with lots of boutiques and cafés. See? Even though it is early, many people are out. They are mostly tourists, though."

"How do you know?"

"*Bien sûr,* it is the time for *vacances*, and Parisians go away. So the only ones left are the tourists."

"But you're here."

"I used to go away, in the past. When my children were small, we went to *la plage*, the beach. Now, if they want to go to the beach, they go somewhere else. They do not want an old man with them."

The bus lumbers slowly up Boulevard Saint-Michel, a broad, straight, tree-lined street with sturdy gray stone buildings on either side. Judith wonders about that last comment of Guy's—are his children too busy to see him, or have they distanced themselves? Or has he pulled back and withdrawn from them? He seems friendly enough, but perhaps she is seeing only "company manners."

The upper floors of the buildings on Saint-Michel look almost boring in their solid, quiet elegance and symmetrical uniformity, but at the street level there is flash and color and excitement. At the corner cafés, people are already sitting in red or blue chairs, drinking coffee and gazing out at the passing traffic.

"There, on the right," Guy indicates with his pointed finger, "the Musée de Cluny, very worth your time if you like medieval art."

Judith glances over at the ancient building as they pass, and then Guy calls her attention to something on the left. "Here, the big fountain, you can see Saint Michel with the dragon. This is a famous meeting place."

A huge fountain, about two stories high, and magnificent statuary face the point where the Boulevard Saint-Michel meets another street. On either side of the busy intersection, bookstores with large yellow-and-blue awnings proclaim the name and face of Gibert Jeune. People are browsing at the tables and carts of books in front. The sidewalk seats at the corner café they pass are jammed. Both foot and vehicular traffic have become intense.

"And now, we cross the Seine to the island in the middle—look to the right!"

The towers of the Notre-Dame cathedral rise over everything. Judith thinks about St. Patrick's in New York, dwarfed by the surrounding taller buildings. Notre-Dame has been given space so that it can be viewed from afar in many directions. She suddenly recalls that first visit, when she and Amy and Ellen scampered up the steps of the church and surveyed the city from one of its towers. Amy had posed next to one of the gargoyles, trying to imitate its expression. She silently reminds herself to return but knows her days of scampering are over. As they cross the bridge, Judith gazes quickly up and down the river, the giant expanse of bright blue sky above.

She loves this scale—so human compared with a large city like New York, where forty-story buildings loom over midtown pedestrians.

"On your left, the Palace of Justice . . ." Guy is a real tour guide, but Judith is starting to feel a bit dizzy, turning her head back and forth. "Ah, now we leave the island and go across to the Right Bank. Here, we pass grand theatres where there are performances of drama and ballet, and then we go left onto the Rue de Rivoli, very important street. Here we pass the Louvre."

As the bus passes the massive and ornate building on the left, Judith barely has time to look at what is on her right. Near the end of the Louvre, Judith has just a second to glimpse a large park on the left and the top of a Ferris wheel before they turn right and go up the Avenue de l'Opéra. Judith can hardly believe that it was just yesterday when she and Guy had ridden down this same street.

"See, didn't I tell you?" asks Guy. "The 21 bus is the best, and it goes past the most important places in Paris!"

Just as Guy had promised, the tour of the Palais Garnier's interior is fascinating. Judith is amazed to learn that this building was its designer's first foray into architecture. The massive staircase, the swirling balustrades, the mosaics on the floor, and the paintings on the walls and ceiling are all dazzling. They view several levels of the building, peer into the special royal boxes, and gaze at larger-than-life marble sculptures. It is all very grand indeed, just as Guy had promised. Two hours later, when they emerge on a side portico, Guy inquires, "Do you know about Haussmann?"

"The one who basically redesigned Paris?"

"Ah, you have studied!"

"Was he German?"

"No, French, although it is a German name. His family came from

Alsace, you know this is on the border of France and Germany. He was a *fonctionnaire*, basically, but he has visions of Paris that was more *ordonné*, you know, *méthodique*. So maybe this vision did come from his German roots!" Guy gives a small chuckle. "What you see here"—he gestures with his arm to the broad Avenue de l'Opéra and the uniform buildings lining it—"is what Haussmann imagines. A grand, formal, impressive city! He destroy much of the old Paris to create it. We even have a word for his style: Haussmannian. So. Now we will go to another boulevard, one named for him. It is close."

One part of Judith wants to say that all this is fascinating, but it is not what she came to Paris to learn. She wants to learn more about her father and what he was like as a young man. As far as she is aware, Guy is the only person alive who knew her father back then. He is her last link. If she is going to learn anything new about Ben Gordon, it's going to be now.

But Guy is enjoying his role as guide, showing off his city. So she has to go along with him. Guy leads her past the rear of the opera house and they find themselves on the Boulevard Haussmann. Here, lunchtime throngs are moving slowly in, out, and past many shops. Judith is only vaguely interested, because, frankly, she does not want to buy any clothes. What does she really need at this point in her life? A couple of streets to the left and they come to the large glass windows of a department store.

"This is the famous Printemps. You know what is *printemps?*"

Judith takes just a moment: "Spring?"

"Ah, you are going to get a good mark! Yes, and this is the *magasin,* the store, of eternal youth. I will show you!" Guy is laughing a bit, and Judith can see that he is having a good time.

Once inside, Judith is tempted to look at some of the displays because they are so visually arresting—a mannequin with the body of a woman but with the head of a rabbit! Guy marches ahead resolutely. Judith notes that he moves fairly swiftly for an older man with a limp. He leads her toward one corner to show her a sumptuous Russo-French *pâtisserie* with fancy creations of chocolate and pink mousse and gold swirls that look almost too artful to eat. Then they take the escalator up past more displays of designer clothing, resort wear, children's items, decorative items for the most *chic* of homes, and finally they emerge at the top.

Here a small, elegant buffet opens onto an area of outdoor tables with a panoramic view over Paris. Judith gapes like the tourist she is, and Guy smiles in delight at her pleasure. All the tables near the outside railing are already taken, but from where they sit, the view is likewise spectacular.

"It is very nice, *non?*"

Judith clasps her hands together in delight. "Guy, it's lovely! I can see all the way to Sacré-Cœur from here, and there is the roof of the Palais Garnier—it seems so close!" Further away, and unmistakable in its identity as the sole tall building, is the Tour Montparnasse. "And I never realized how light in color Paris is—especially in the sunshine, so white!"

"That is partly Haussmann, who makes a rule, all his buildings must be the same white stone. And partly—it's the city of light! You will see—when the sun sets, or at night when everything is lit up."

Judith nibbles at her salad, constantly distracted by the views. Guy watches her eyes going here and there. "I knew you would enjoy this," he says, smiling slightly.

"Were these stores open during the war?"

"Of course! You think all commerce stops because we are invaded? *Mais non.* The wonderful world of Parisian fashion continues as usual." He pauses briefly, taking a sip from his glass of white wine. "*Not* as usual. Only 'Aryans' can be designers or owners. Some *couturiers* do not care.

They just want to keep selling their designs. The world must have French fashion! Oh yes, people still buy and sell. Just without Jews."

He stops for another sip of wine, then continues:

"A lot of artisans leave here, and many of those who stay . . . well, they make compromises."

"They collaborated?" asks Judith.

Guy bends his head to one side. "This now, it is a difficult topic. Where is the line between collaboration and doing what you need in order to survive?"

"A collaborator would be *enthusiastic* about accepting the invaders, right?"

"A good way of expressing it. But come, I do not want us to live in the past! Enjoy your lunch and the view, and then I take you to see more of today's Paris!"

Judith has noticed Guy's desire to turn away from bothersome subjects. He has done this in their conversations before her trip, and he continues now. She wants to talk about collaborators; he wants to return to being the genial tour guide. She wants to learn about her father, while he wants to take her to a museum. Guy wanted her to visit, but she is churning up the past, and this, it seems to her, makes him uncomfortable. Totally under-standable—why dredge up memories sixty years old?

And yet he had wanted to meet her, too—a living link to the man he had seen as such a hero. Judith realizes that Guy's curiosity probably matches or even exceeds hers. Perhaps she ought to relax more and wait before she asks more questions.

**CHAPTER FOURTEEN**

# On Her Own

One day early on in Judith's visit, Guy has to attend a journalists' seminar, so she plans to use this time as an opportunity to see places known to her father. Although Judith has been enjoying Guy's company, she tells herself that she really needs to have her own space for a while.

Yesterday had been tremendous fun. After two hours visiting with the Impressionists (the Victorian period, after all, was culturally rich on both sides of the Channel!) at the Musée d'Orsay on the Left Bank, she and Guy had had lunch at the Musée's restaurant with *its* panoramic views. The designers who converted the building, with its soaring ceiling, from a train station into a museum had done so magnificently. Guy and Judith had gone along the exterior walkway, bright in the sun, and he had pointed out various landmarks. Squinting a bit, Judith had been delighted to spot the opera house and had thought she could make out the other rooftop from which they had observed the museum yesterday.

Afterwards they had taken a bus along the *quai* back to the Boulevard Saint-Michel and walked over to Shakespeare and Company. "Here is the bookshop where all visitors must go!" said Guy. "I know you will like this. I wait outside on a bench. Go, go!"

He was being very generous. Judith usually took an hour at least in any bookstore. But these books were all in English, and she knew Guy sat outside because, as a non-English reader, he would be bored. So she gave herself twenty minutes and did a quick once-through. It was rather frustrating, but on this trip, time with Guy was her priority. So she looked long enough to see that she would make a point to return here—she loved the full, piled-on shelves, the cozy nooks, and the framed caricatures of writers on the bright wallpaper. Then she joined Guy outside, where he was waiting patiently on a bench beneath a tree.

Later, over dinner, Guy had wanted to talk about some of his exploits in journalism, so they ended up discussing the 1968 student demonstrations in Paris. He was thirty-six then, approaching the most exciting phase of his career. It was also around the time that he met the woman he would marry. But again, Guy evaded the topic with his "Ah, I do not wish to live in the past!"

Today Judith strikes out independently. By this time she feels more confident about finding her way. Still, she speaks with the hotel's concierge to find the fastest way to her first destination. She carries the album of her father's photos, wanting to see the same places, from the same vantage point. Looking at a map, she decides to start at the Palais de Chaillot, across the Seine from the Eiffel Tower.

The Métro station at Trocadéro brings her out a little behind the Palais. Using her father's photos as a guide, she finds the exact place at which he stood between the two buildings when he took a picture of the row of gilded statues. Then she walks down to the wide area overlooking the Trocadéro Gardens with the Eiffel Tower beyond. Although it is still fairly early in the morning, groups of tourists are already congregating here and taking pictures.

She walks down to the gardens, looking for the bull. One photo shows her father sitting on a stone wall, next to a giant statue of this animal; when she spots it, she realizes that she will be unable to do the same, as fountains block her way. Also, she realizes, when her father was in Paris, he was much younger, and more limber, than she is now.

She will skip the Eiffel Tower today because Guy plans to take her there on Friday. So she heads back to the Métro and goes to the Montparnasse-Bienvenüe station. Here she can look for other places where her father had stood, and then visit the unlovely Tour.

The Montparnasse-Bienvenüe station is confusing; several lines cross here and Judith has to ponder about which way to walk. The labyrinthine underground passages go in all directions at various depth levels; Judith feels she has walked into an Escher drawing. Some stairs head up and others head down; busy commuters who know where they are going hurry past her impatiently; passengers merge in from side passages, while others veer off in another direction. She finally emerges onto the street in front of a sleek, modern building. Now she is in the shadow of the Tour and plans to see the views from the top before she does anything else.

After riding the elevator up thirty-six floors, Judith can see much of her father's city. Looking to the north, she spots the golden dome of Les Invalides, then scans eastward all the way across the Seine and past the Louvre. To the west, the Eiffel Tower, and far beyond it at the edge of the city, the modernist skyline of La Défense. Southwest and very close by lies the new Gare Montparnasse, with what seems to be a garden on its roof. And to the southeast is the Montparnasse cemetery. The views help Judith to get a sense of the proportion of the city and a view of its major arteries, which go, apparently, in all directions. It makes the Manhattan grid look simplistic.

Her father, she reasons, must have spent most of his time in close proximity to his postal station. Looking at the streets directly in front of the Tour, she sees that the buildings facing the site of the former station are much older. She returns to street level and compares her dad's pictures to what she can see.

From one old photo, she can clearly observe the fanning-out pattern of the cobblestone plaza. She wonders if any of the stones are the same as the ones in 1944. Surely most have been replaced—she can see how the stones, in both size and volume, would have made ideal barricade material as well as weapons to hurl. She studies the next pictures, which her father took on V-E Day as he watched people hurrying across the plaza in front of the postal station to hear the announcement of the German surrender. She finds the place where he must have stood because the buildings across the way are exactly the same! Another photo shows her father standing next to an army jeep parked on the Rue de l'Arrivée; behind him, across the narrow street, is a pharmacy. The pharmacy is gone now, but Judith can see that the building she is scrutinizing is the one in the picture.

She begins to walk down the Boulevard du Montparnasse in the direction of the Boulevard Raspail. In her album are a few photos taken at the Café de la Rotonde. Her father and Sol had apparently become friendly with the café's manager, for she has two, taken at different times, that include him. She has checked the address of the café and thinks this will be an ideal place to have lunch. It is nearly one, and the day has become quite hot. She needs to rest and reflect.

Finally seated at a small table under the red awning of the Rotonde, she orders a glass of chilled white wine. She is at one of her father's favorite places in Paris. She smiles and toasts him silently, trying to imagine what he must have felt here in 1944. She also imagines what it was like in 1941, when the seats were filled with German officers and soldiers; she wonders if the waiters served them happily or seethed inside. The scene has probably changed very little since then, she realizes, as the buildings around her are all of the same Haussmannian vintage. (She wonders if her father knew that term.) On the wide sidewalk in front of her pass an elderly and elegant couple (he in a straw boater, she wearing a matching sweater set, both in sunglasses), professionals on their lunch break, and tourists (she can only assume, but they are wearing shorts, sandals, and cameras on neck straps). She sips and sits quietly, enjoying the experience of being a *flâneuse*, a wanderer and spectator. When she can do so discreetly, without being an obvious tourist, she removes her small camera from her bag and snaps some pictures.

To her left is the Boulevard Raspail, which she knows runs down to the Hôtel Lutetia and the Bon Marché department store. She plans to get there at some point. In the middle of this part of the Boulevard Raspail is a leafy traffic island, and in the middle of this island is a tall statue of Balzac. It has been there, she has read, since 1939; although designed in the late 1890s, it was considered too risqué and ugly to be exhibited in public. It would have been a novelty in her father's day, and now it still stands there, hardly noticed. She wonders what he had thought—and whether he had read anything by Balzac. To her chagrin, she realizes that she herself has not.

Judith additionally muses on what her father and his buddies would have talked about while sitting here. Having spent a lot of time in London, Ben had gotten used to a metropolitan area in another country. But here the only English-speaking people would have been other soldiers,

American and British, and some of the French citizens. He could use his fluent Yiddish with Jewish people, but how many did he actually meet? The synagogues in Paris were starting to reopen in late 1944, but did he go to any besides the one where Guy had his *bar mitzvah?* She has read about the first Jewish services held in Paris after the Germans were driven out and what an emotional event it was. But did her father attend? Did his French improve in Paris and allow him to converse with individuals he met? How much had he learned about what the Parisians experienced during the Occupation?

Judith wishes her parents had saved their letters from the war—if only either of them had saved the ones they received from each other. Obviously, they had held onto photographs for her to puzzle over—why not letters, too? Perhaps they, also, did not wish to live in the past.

She remembers a large book her father had kept in the drawer at the bottom of one of the living room bookcases. Its title was *Our Leave in Switzerland*, and its cover featured three uniformed American servicemen leaning against the stone railing of a bridge. She and Michael had been fascinated by the many photographs in the volume—until they realized it was just a souvenir and not personal. Their father's picture was not actually in the book, so they lost interest.

But there *was* something else.

Judith has a sudden, and very clear, recollection of a letter opener she found in his desk drawer. Her father was at work and she was rummaging around after school, looking for a small pencil sharpener she knew he had in his desk. Instead she found a wooden letter opener with a very sharp pointed end and a clear plastic bubble in the center; if you looked directly into the bubble, you could see the tiniest picture of the Eiffel Tower. She doesn't remember ever seeing this letter opener in Florida and wonders what could have happened to it. But she does remember being fascinated by it when she was a child.

Why hadn't she and Michael asked their father anything directly?

The young server asks her something, and she assumes he wishes to know if she would like anything else. She pauses before responding, so he quickly says, "It is all right. You may use English. I can understand."

The extra moment gives her time to think, then say, "*Merci, monsieur, mais je préfère essayer le français.*" Thank you, but I prefer to try French.

"*Bien.* Good!" He smiles warmly at her.

She orders a second glass of wine: "*Je voudrais une autre verre de vin, s'il vous plait.*"

"*Pas mal, madame.* Not bad! Keep at it!"

It feels silly to be proud of uttering a simple sentence, but considering that a year ago she couldn't have done this at all, Judith feels a sense of accomplishment. Still, she has to be very careful when speaking with Guy. If she uses a word incorrectly, he laughs at her. Worse, she might use the wrong word with a different meaning or might communicate a thought incorrectly. She does not wish to upset him. It is one thing to order a second glass of wine, quite another to discuss what may or may not have happened sixty years ago.

Or what may or may not happen now. Why, exactly, is she here? Judith should be (she snorts a bit derisively because she has tried very hard to avoid the dictates of "should" in her life) looking at her retirement options instead of tootling around by herself in a new city while struggling with a new language. But then, *pourquoi pas*, why not? Why should adventure be reserved for college juniors going on a study abroad program, or junior faculty beginning a new research project?

Judith recalls the conversation she and Michael had had when they were clearing out things from their parents' Florida apartment. He had used the term "geriatric ghettoes," and she knew they both thought of retirement not as a longed-for goal but the next-to-last stop. She knows the predictable progression in academia: there is a retirement reception, then someone becomes an emeritus or emerita, perhaps gives a guest lecture or two, then there are fewer sightings around town, until one day there is an obituary in the paper.

So perhaps this trip, thinks Judith, is about the future as well as the past. She hopes to learn more about her father and what he was like before he became her father. And perhaps she will learn what the future holds, for she has absolutely no idea other than not wanting to be pushed toward the exit door.

## CHAPTER FIFTEEN

# The Plaques

**J**udith looks at her watch and finishes her glass of wine at La Rotonde. It is still early, not quite three, and she is not meeting Guy until seven at a restaurant on the Boulevard Arago. She decides to choose a Métro station and then wander back toward Arago, browsing through the streets.

She selects Place d'Italie, which appears to be not too far from Arago, and about half an hour later she emerges from one of its northern exits. At one time, the Place d'Italie may have been a southern boundary of Paris, but today it is a traffic circle. A very large and intimidating traffic circle, with cars and trucks whipping by in a constant whirl. Judith is glad she doesn't have to navigate it in a vehicle. At the far south of the circle are modern buildings and, judging from its large glass walls, what looks like a commercial center. On the north side, a residential and business neighborhood of traditional architecture stretches all the way to the Panthéon in the distance. Judith feels proud of herself for being able to recognize some buildings from their outlines and domes. A large sign on the broad sidewalk indicates local points of interest. This is the 13th *arrondisse-ment*, and nearby is its eighteenth-century city hall, the *mairie*.

She is at the beginning of the Avenue des Gobelins. It actually looks like other neighborhoods she has seen—a wide, straight main boulevard lined with six-story, mostly-white stone buildings, with retail establish-ments at the ground level. Baron Haussmann again.

One of the buildings she passes, however, is not old—it is a modern police station, built to blend in architecturally, ivory in color and of a height similar to the other structures. As she passes, she notices a plaque on the front of the building and stops to read it:

ICI LE 16 JUILLET 1942
FURENT AMENES PAR LA POLICE
DE L'ETAT FRANÇAIS
DES HOMMES DES FEMMES ET DES
ENFANTS JUIFS DU XIIIEME ARRONDISSEMENT
AVANT D'ETRE CONDUITS AU VEL D'HIV,
PUIS DEPORTES AU CAMP NAZI
D'EXTERMINATION D'AUSCHWITZ-BIRKENAU

There are perhaps two words she doesn't quite know, but Judith immediately sees the significance of this memorial plaque. While the extermination camps were run by the Nazis, here the French police are blamed for rounding up this neighborhood's Jewish victims. The plaque looks fairly new, but there is no date. She takes a picture.

Judith looks around her. It's just a neighborhood, with cafés, newsagents, bank branches, food shops. Not wealthy, not poor, just everyday.

Further down she comes to the Gobelins tapestry building. As she translates the informative historical marker in front, she learns there was once a river near here that provided power for the mill. And she realizes that the name of the street has nothing to do with little elves. She turns left onto a meandering side street, taking pictures of interesting signs and doorways. She walks through a large park, past some very new, tall brick apartment houses and some very old cottages. She emerges and walks left, finding herself at yet another five-point intersection. Which way?

She picks the street that passes a bookshop with a bright blue façade and walks toward the elevated train track she can see ahead. That will, at least, be a main thoroughfare. On the left she comes to a building with a patterned tan-and-orange brick façade. Just below its ornately decorated top, the building declares itself an ÉCOLE COMMUNALE, with LIBERTÉ ÉGALITÉ FRA-TERNITÉ proclaimed beneath. The narrow sidewalk in front of the school is separated from the street by a waist-high iron fence, which Judith realizes is designed to protect the arriving and departing children from traffic.

Then she sees another plaque, near the front door:

A LA MÉMOIRE DE LES ÉLÈVES DE CETTE ÉCOLE
DÉPORTÉS DE 1942 À 1944 PARCE QUE NÉS JUIFS
VICTIMES DE LA BARBARIE NAZIE
AVEC LA PARTICIPATION ACTIVE
DU GOUVERNEMENT DE VICHY.
ILS FURENT ASSASSINÉS DANS LES CAMPS DE LA MORT.
PLUS DE 11400 ENFANTS FURENT DÉPORTÉS DE FRANCE
PLUS DE 150 DE CES ENFANTS VIVAIENT DANS LE XIIIEME.

This plaque, she notes, is very new, dated April 2008. Just a few years ago. And there is a message: *Ne les oublions jamais*. Never forget them. But why is there a sixty-year gap between the end of the war and the date on the sign?

As she takes another photo, she notices the brass ring affixed to the wall just below the plaque. She will ask Guy about this. The street is quiet and still. It is summer after all, and the school is closed. Judith imagines there is a similar plaque in each *arrondissement*, as this one mentions specifically how many children from the 13th were deported, although it does not note how many attended this particular school. Certainly students from all over the city, not just this neighborhood, were rounded up. Where did Guy live when the roundups began? More questions.

Then she spots another marker, on the door of an apartment building across the narrow street. But this one—also with a ring beneath it—is older, and, if Judith is translating correctly, raises even more questions:

DANS CET IMMEUBLE S'EST TENUE
LE 13 AOÛT 1944
LA RÉUNION CLANDESTINE
OÙ FUT DÉCIDÉE LA GRÈVE DE LA POLICE
PRÉLUDE DE L'INSURRECTION DE PARIS

Eleven *days* before Liberation! The police had a "secret meeting" here eleven days before Liberation to decide to revolt against their German rulers? Now, were these the same police, or different police, from the ones who rounded up the civilians she read about on the plaque at the police station on Avenue des Gobelins? Were they responsible for what had happened to the children from the school across the street? By August 13, she reasons, people in Paris must have been able to hear the explosions coming from the north. They must have known the Allies were approaching. Did these policemen simply want to be on the winning side and compensate for their earlier *"participation active?"* Or were they the good guys who, until now, did not feel it was safe to rebel against the occupiers?

Judith is rattled and determined to learn more. Such horrific betrayal, and by the people one learned as a child to trust and go to in an emergency. She will ask Guy, but tactfully. She checks her map and sees that she can walk directly north to the Boulevard Arago. It is not far, so she will be on time.

Guy is sitting on a sidewalk bench, reading a newspaper; Judith sees him from a block away. She realizes she has been looking forward to seeing him. During the course of the day, she has actually spoken very little (except to herself). Now she will be able to share her adventures. As she approaches, she also realizes that Guy has a rather distinguished profile.

He suddenly turns his head and spots her, rising to greet her in the French fashion, with a little kiss on each cheek. She feels an unfamiliar rush of warmth to her face.

"I realize this morning I need your cell phone number! What if you are lost in Paris, and I cannot find you?"

"Ha! It would have been like 1980—how did anyone find each other back then?" she exclaims.

"I want to hear all your adventures today!"

"And I had so many. Plus, I have questions for you about things I saw."

"*Bien*—let's go in, have a drink, and we will talk." He holds open the door for her, and they are taken to a table for two.

"I wish I could tell you about everything in French, but I cannot," she begins. "I will try, but then when it is difficult for me, I will have to switch to English."

"*Pas de problème*. No problem. Go ahead, I listen."

And so Judith regales Guy, a little in her elementary French and then in English, with her narrative about retracing her father's visit to the Trocadéro, and then her visit to the Tour Montparnasse, locating where her father must have stood when he took pictures near the postal station. By the time she describes going to the Café de la Rotonde for lunch, and taking the Métro to Place d'Italie, they have nearly finished their entrées.

"You went to the shopping center?" asks Guy.

"No, no—the Métro station. I got out at a very busy street, the Avenue des Gobelins."

"Ah, I see, on the north side of the *rond-point* . . . the roundabout?"

"Yes—mostly it looked like other neighborhoods I have seen: straight streets, older buildings with ornate doors, shops and cafés on the ground level. All except for one building: the tapestry works."

"The Gobelins *tapisseries*—tapestries—have been world famous for hundreds of years! Did you go in?"

"No. It was already past four. I just wanted to walk around." She wants to ask him about something else she saw on the Avenue des Gobelins that is bothering her.

"So here," she continues, "is the part where I have questions. So far, I have seen several memorial plaques honoring people who died in the Liberation, or who were shot by the Germans in Paris. *Mort pour la France*, they read. These are fairly old plaques."

"Yes, they would be from the time right after the war."

"So, almost seventy years ago. But then I saw another plaque on a police station on the Avenue des Gobelins that mentioned the police rounding up Jews for deportation. It was the first time I saw Jews mentioned on a plaque. But the plaque seemed much newer."

"You will see many, many plaques all over Paris," Guy responds evenly. "And yes, a number of them refer to the Jews."

"I saw another in front of a school a few blocks away," Judith continues. "This one mentioned Jewish children who were deported, presumably by the police, and sent to their deaths in the concentration camps. It mentioned the total number of children in France who died this way, and the number from that neighborhood. I know enough French at this point to read them."

Guy sounds, to Judith, rather matter-of-fact as he responds, "You will see a plaque like this near the entrance of every school in Paris that was built before 1940."

"But this plaque I saw had a very recent date—is this a pattern?"

"What do you mean?"

"The heroes of World War II are celebrated all over Paris—street names, station names, yes? But any mention of official complicity in the murder of thousands of Jewish civilians—this did not get discussed for sixty years?"

Judith notices that her own voice is becoming more agitated as she speaks, because what she has seen genuinely irks her. But Guy's voice remains steady and neutral.

Guy stares at his wine glass thoughtfully, and finally he speaks. "It depends, of course, on who was doing the discussing," he says. "I know. My mother know. My father has to 'register' with the French police, and then we never see him again. My mother go to Drancy to look for him and my *gran'père*; she see no Germans. Only French police. Yet when we go back to our apartment and strangers are in it, she go to the police station for help. What is called in English? Irony."

Judith nods. "Irony would be a way of seeing it, yes. What you are saying, then, is that French complicity in the roundups was known by families that were victimized, or their relatives. *They* knew."

Guy's little laugh is not one of amusement.

"*Everybody* know," he responds. "But the official position was: the war is over. It is past. We move on. Even de Gaulle say this. Better to unite the nation than say 'this one did this' and 'this one did that.' *Bien sûr*, it would get complicated." He pauses. "Yes, complicated."

"I understand," says Judith. "Just as the United States protected some Nazis who could be useful to us in our fight against communism, and Nazi scientists who might help the US beat the Russians. More irony."

"*Exactement.* I know this. I am a journalist. Politics can create situations that are cloudy, yes? All the time the leaders say, 'the Nazis do this to France.' Everyone 'forget' the truth, very convenient, this forgetting. The whole country—except for the Jews, but no one listens to them anyway—has amnesia. Finally, when many French families come together, they demand the government accept responsibility. The main voice is Serge Klarsfeld, he is very important."

"I have heard a lot about him. He is the one who tracked down the one called 'the butcher of Lyon,' Klaus Barbie, right? And several other leading Nazis?"

"Yes. He and his wife Beate, they find Nazis and make the French *collabos* very nervous. Mitterrand, when he was president, he look the other way. The first to say, yes, we French did this—this was Chirac. Things change with Chirac. This is why you see a fifty- or sixty-year gap in these plaques."

Judith nods her understanding of the situation.

"How did you feel about this?" she asks Guy.

He shrugs indifferently. "When it was time for my military service, it was also the war in Algeria. But I do not go. I do not want to go, but I have to do service. I do it in France and stay safe. The government say I can do this because my father '*mort pour la France*,' he die for France."

He pauses and frowns. "Ha! Total *merde*. He did not die for France. France *send* him to die. I know this. But I accept the offer because—because I do not want to fight in Algeria."

He stops speaking, then raises his glass and takes a slow sip of wine.

"Now, Zhoodeet, I say this before, but you do not listen. So I say once more, and now you pay attention."

He looks sternly at her and she sees the muscles in his jaw tighten before he speaks again.

"I already tell you. I do not wish to live in the past. It is over. Then I know, and now I know. But what matters is today, yes? I can bring my father back? We can bring those children back? *Non*, so we move on. We do not talk about this anymore."

He moves his chair back a little and signals for the server.

"We move on now, too, we go. I want to go home. I am sorry. We have dessert another time."

Judith feels very awkward about their truncated dinner. Later, back in her hotel room, she reflects on the evening. She realizes she erred in telling Guy about the plaques, even raising the subject. This reluctance to speak on his part: is it the difference between his generation and hers? There is nothing to be done, so just keep moving forward. Or is it just a temperamental difference between them as individuals? He wants to stay busy and matter-of-fact and get things done. She likes to analyze, rehash events, go over things again and again to see if she missed something the first time, or if something could be interpreted another way.

She has met people who went through terrible trauma—for example, a severely wounded military veteran—and afterwards renounced God completely. While someone else, who experienced the same trauma, became more devout. Some vets—her colleague Phyllis Hudson's father is a good example—could not stop talking about their encounters, reliving them through repetition. Others got together with guys at the VFW to talk about this or that battle and comment on today's military leaders. Yet other men simply clammed up and never wanted to talk about their war experiences at all.

Guy seems to want to talk, but then he gets angry when she asks questions. He must be feeling a good deal of inner turmoil. Judith remembers how he both laughed and wept when he first spoke with her on the telephone. The letter and photo she sent him must have released so much emotion that she is not even seeing. She decides to let him resume his role as the genial guide, at least for a while.

And then she realizes that when she usually begins a research project, she is interrogating silent paper and silent books. Unremitting curiosity drives her onward. And because they are non-living things, the books never complain. In the case of Guy, maybe she just needs to shut up.

## CHAPTER SIXTEEN

# Revelations

"I'd like to hear more about your career as a journalist," says Judith the next evening when she and Guy are dining at a small restaurant on the Place des Vosges. The beautifully manicured trees in the square sit motionless. Although it is past seven, it is still hot. A few hardy or oblivious people are actually sitting on benches in the sun.

Guy nods and sips from his glass of white wine. "I worked for different publications, for the newspaper *France-Soir* in the sixties. Then for a couple of magazines such as *Le Point*. Ah, the big student riots of 1968! I suppose the peak of my career was the 1970s, 1980s—it was interesting. I write much on political events, protests and elections and so forth. I still write some guest columns. They call me a 'veteran reporter' now! This means I am old, but I can still put a sentence together."

They both laugh.

"Do you have a favorite topic, or one that you find yourself returning to frequently?" she asks.

He muses for a moment. "I write about so many things. But the most important, probably: colonialism. Yes, colonialism and its evils. Some of the problems France has today come from our history as a colonial power. Imperialism come at a big price."

"So what you are saying," Judith continues, with a bit of a smirk, "Is that what happened historically, even a century ago, affects our daily life today."

"Of course!"

Should she point out the hypocritical nature of his statements? Last night's discussion has not come up today. She must be very tactful.

"And you think the past is not important?" she ventures.

"I never say that! *Non*, I say that I do not wish to *live* in the past. There is a big difference. We have to understand what happened yesterday to plan for tomorrow. But I do not want to—*comment dit-on?* How you say in English? Obsess? Yes—I do not obsess about the past. It happened. But now we have to act on today. Maybe you are a journalist? Or a lawyer? You ask a lot of questions."

"The Socratic method. It's the best way to help someone learn."

"And you think I have to learn something?

"Well, what about the patterns in French history?"

"What about them? Drink more wine."

He refills her glass from the bottle of *cabernet sauvignon* he has chosen. She knows next to nothing about wine, so she happily defers to him.

Guy uses the distraction to change topics. "And your work? Teaching at the little college? You enjoy what you do?"

"Of course!" she responds quickly. "Or I would not have done it for so many years. I could have already retired if I had wanted to. They say when you teach you 'touch the future'—I like this idea. If we can teach students to understand and value things, they can pass this on. In my case, it is literature. Storytelling. We transmit our culture through the stories we tell."

"And your favorite author? American, of course?" He is smirking again, because he thinks he is being funny.

She ignores this and continues. "I tend to like our women authors best. My choices–definitely Willa Cather first. She wrote a lot about the immigrant settlers in the western part of the States. And Edith Wharton, though her interests were a little too patrician for me. But such gorgeous prose!"

"You know she lived in Paris?"

"I do."

"I will take you to see where she lived, if you like. We can stroll through her *arrondissement!*"

"Perhaps. Although I would much rather go to the Rodin Museum."

"*Pas de problème.* No problem, this is one of my favorite museums! I want you to enjoy Paris and see everything you wish. It will be my pleasure. What is on your list? Where else do you wish to go?"

Their entrees arrive, and they take a break from conversation to admire and sample what is on the plates. Judith has ordered grilled salmon and Guy has poached bass. "*Pas mal,*" says Guy after a bite. "Not bad. But I cook this better."

"You will have to cook for me, then," says Judith, almost automatically and unintentionally making herself sound demanding. "And, of course, I will cook something wonderful for you!"

"Ha ha! I do not think so. American food is so wonderful?" He snorts, not too loudly, but definitely derisively.

"You are such a snob! American food is wonderful, because it is a blend of the whole world's influences."

"Hamburgers, hot dogs, big steaks!"

"You love your stereotypes, don't you?"

"And you do not think in stereotypes? All French wear striped shirts and berets, they drink wine and eat baguettes all the time!"

Just then, the server brings a basket with a sliced fresh baguette to their table, and both Guy and Judith cannot help grinning.

"So, what will you cook?" asks Guy as he pours more wine for her, then for himself.

Judith thinks about her repertoire, which is actually fairly limited, but quite good. "*Arroz con pollo*—chicken with rice. Different kinds of pasta— mac and cheese, now there's a great American dish! Topped with buttered bread crumbs, mmm. And then some things my mother and grandmother taught me. Do you know *kasha varnishkes?*"

As though she has said something magical, Guy opens his eyes and audibly inhales. "You make this? I haven't had this since my *gran'mère* . . ."

"I am sure mine isn't as good as hers," says Judith, "But I will be happy to prepare it if I can find all the ingredients."

"It would be wonderful to have some of the old-fashioned dishes," says Guy. "My *gran'mère* did most of the cooking because my mother was always at work. She cook chicken and soup, and *kasha*, and she make her own chopped fish. I forget the name."

"The name in French or Yiddish?"

"Yiddish. Always at home my parents and grandparents spoke Yiddish. Then I start to understand. So they can't keep secrets from me."

"The same for me, growing up," Judith responds. "My parents would speak Yiddish with my grandparents. When they saw I was catching on, my grandparents switched to Russian. But all I learned in Russian was *ya nya panye maya*, because that is what my mother said a lot."

"What does that mean?"

"It means 'I don't understand.' And the name you are looking for is *gefilte* fish."

"Ah, *bien sûr*, that's it!"

"When my grandmother died," remembers Judith, "the first thing I thought of was her soup. And then I cried. Her chicken soup was sweet because she added carrots *and* parsnips. And she added small square noodles. So I do the same." She pauses. "I haven't spoken about my grandparents in so long. I do remember that my grandfather drank his hot tea in a tall glass, not a cup. Russian style. My grandmother would serve the glass to him on a saucer, with a slice of lemon on the side, and a sugar cube."

"When you say your grandparents, you mean your father's parents or your mother's?"

"My mother's. My father's father died many years before I was born, before the war. Actually, I am named for him. He was Avraham Judah."

"Yes, now I remember. Your father tell me this when I learn my own father die."

"He tried to comfort you?"

"Yes. I was a lonely child, also frightened. I try to be strong, to help my *maman*. I had no friends, of course, I move around so much. When we come back to Paris, everyone try to pretend that things are normal now. But they are not normal. It take a long time. But your father, he help me. He teach me baseball, he take me for walks. He talk to me, like a father, to help me understand things. But I tell you this already, *oui?*"

"Yes, most of it. But I like to hear about this, because my father never told me. I like to hear about this side of him."

"This is why, it was . . . we just cannot understand, he was like a family member. Why we do not hear from him ever again?"

This is at least the third time Guy has mentioned her father's lack of communication. Indeed, it is a puzzle. After almost two years of visiting a family and being involved with them so closely, why had her father simply cut them off? Judith has mulled this over for a while.

"Guy? Do you think my father was attracted to your mother?"

Guy looks at her with incredulity. "How would I know? I was just a child!"

"You were not that little—you were *bar mitzvah* age! Kids see things; they notice."

Guy shrugs his shoulders.

Judith looks at him and dabs at her lips with the soft linen napkin. "I have one more theory," she says. "Men like my father, who had rather boring lives before the war and after the war—the lucky ones, who did not see the awfulness of combat—they were important here. I think the war was the high point of their lives. They were heroes."

"Yes, your father was a hero to me and Maman and my *gran'mère!*"

"Well, perhaps these men realized that once they were home they wouldn't be heroes any more, just ordinary working men with families to support. So they simply put the war behind them. They closed the door."

They are both quiet for a few moments. Then Guy asks: "Zhoodeet, when are you born?"

"1948."

"Not much after the end of the war. When your parents get married?"

"Early 1947. A few months after my father returned from Germany."

"He come back from Europe and so fast find someone to marry?"

"Oh no, my parents got engaged before my father went overseas."

Guy stares at her.

Judith thinks he might not have understood all of her words, so she tries another way.

"My mother and father decided to marry before he went to Europe."

Guy continues to gaze at her intently.

"All during the war, he has a *fiancée?*" he asks slowly.

"Well, yes. It wasn't that unusual; a lot of people became engaged and even married fairly quickly, once war was declared. They thought things might end, so this was their way of—"

She suddenly notices that Guy is sitting very still and looking at her with a puzzled expression on his face. Perhaps she has been speaking English too quickly for him.

"Guy, why are you looking at me like that?"

Guy shakes his head. "I am sorry, I do not mean to stare. I just try to remember. Your father, he tell us a lot about his family, his mother, his sister."

"Yes, my Aunt Fran."

"But he never tell us about a woman he promise to marry. My mother, she spend a lot of time with your father. I stay home in the evening with my *gran'mère*, and they go out."

Judith thinks about this for a moment. "Well, they were companions, weren't they? He must have told her he had a fiancée. And also, wasn't this before they knew your father was actually dead? So as far as my father knew, your mother was a married woman. Am I correct?"

Guy shakes his head slowly and slumps down in his seat. "I do not remember. I know your father come to my *bar mitzvah*. This is after I learn my father die. After the *bar mitzvah*, that summer . . . I don't know, I go to visit with the family that keep me, in Dreux."

"You look very sad."

"Yes, it was a bad time. Also good, because I have hope. Then many bad things happen. This is the way it is when I remember too much."

Judith really wants to place her hand on top of Guy's. But she hesitates a bit too long, and he speaks again.

"Your father leave, he go to Germany. Two years later, my *gran'mère* die, yes. A year or two after, my mother marry Martin, and they leave Paris.

By that time I finish at the *lycée* and begin university. I am alone again." He pauses and sits up abruptly. "I do not wish to talk about this. Let us finish dinner and go. I am tired."

Judith glances at her watch. It is nine-thirty, not late at all. But the conversation has been wearing on Guy. Or perhaps he just does not wish to pursue the topic. She, too, feels exhausted. Between their visit to the Rue des Martyrs earlier today and the thoughts aroused by this discussion, too many ideas are swirling in her brain. She really wants to rest.

Outside, on the broad sidewalk of Rue Saint-Antoine, it has started to rain. "Come, we will take a taxi," says Guy, pointing to a taxi stop nearby. "Taxis are difficult to find in the rain, but maybe we are lucky."

They are lucky indeed, and a dark green cab is ready to take Judith to her hotel, and then Guy to his apartment. Guy holds open the car door for Judith, then gives her the customary light kiss on both cheeks. "*À demain,*" he says to her. "Until tomorrow."

"*À vous aussi.*" You, too. She leaves her hand on his shoulder just a second too long, then withdraws it and hurries into the hotel. Once in the lobby, she shakes off the rain that has settled on her hair and wonders if she should look back out onto the street.

Guy is still standing by the open taxi door, one hand on the handle. He looks a bit surprised, then smiles at her as the rain starts to come down heavily, and he gets back in quickly. The cab glides off into the night, and Judith, a bit lethargic from too much wine and too much new knowledge, takes the elevator to her room and the prospect of oblivious sleep.

## CHAPTER SEVENTEEN

# Research Mode

Judith feels tired even in her bones the next morning. It is still raining, and at first she does not want to do anything. Pushing aside the tall draperies, she gazes out onto the gray, shiny street. A few people walk along the pavement below, carrying bright red or yellow umbrellas that make her recall Pound's short verse about "petals on a wet, black bough."

She does have a plan, actually, and wants to accomplish some things alone. She goes downstairs for a quick breakfast and brings a cup of coffee back to her room. Now it's a decent hour. Leaning back against the pile of pillows on her bed, she dials Guy on her cell phone.

"*Oui? Zhoodeet?*"

"*Bonjour, Guy. Ça va bien?*"

"*Non, désolé.* I am sorry, this morning I feel a bit of a cold. *Et je suis très fatigué.* I need to rest."

"*Moi aussi.* Me, too—not the cold part, but I am tired. I think I will do very little today."

"Perhaps you will come over later, if I feel better?"

"*Oui*, perhaps I will cook for you my grandmother's chicken soup, to make you feel better!"

"*Bonne idée!*"

Now her day will have some shape to it. She asks at the hotel desk about the closest food shops and markets, then consults her map to locate her other destination—not far, but in the opposite direction. She will go there first.

Forty minutes later, she is on the north bank of the Seine, at the cross street where the taxi leaves her. It had not been that far, really, but the rain discouraged her from a leisurely stroll. Now she walks up the narrow street, Rue Geoffroy l'Asnier, a short distance from a modern structure fronted by a high steel fence. She goes through a detector in a glass-enclosed security booth and enters the courtyard of the Mémorial de la Shoah, the French Holocaust memorial and library. According to what Judith has read, she will be able to find her answers here.

A few other people enter the courtyard after Judith. They are all silent. The first thing Judith does is examine the group of high stone walls to her left. Inscribed are the names of the 76,000 French Jews deported and killed during WWII. She realizes they are in chronological order, so she looks for the earliest dates. Meanwhile, she notices how huge the listings are for 1942, 1943, and 1944. The Nazis seemed to have bided their time after invading France. After a few moments, she finds them in 1942: Guy's father, listed with his original last name, and grandfather. She touches their names.

Someone has placed a *yahrzeit* light, a small candle in a little glass cup, on the ground next to a specific name. But, in the drizzling rain, it has gone out. Judith walks slowly around the tall walls inscribed in black on both sides. She can see where entire families were rounded up together, assuming the identical surnames are family groups. Birth years are included, and the victims range from the elderly to infants.

She sees given names and understands how easily some individuals would have been the first pulled in, even before the mandated wearing of the stars. These are not traditional French names, but Yiddish and Hebrew names given to children from eastern Europe: Jankel, Leib, David, Sarah, Salomon, Chana, Moses, Isaak, Lazar, Baruch, Avram, and Eliezer. But then others are typically French: Jean-Jacques, Paulette, Benoit, Maurice, Albert, André, Antoine, Jules, Amélie, Philippe, Odette, Thérèse, Henri. There is one little girl ironically named Fortunée. Some family names are Polish or Russian and may be identified as traditionally Jewish; others are not. She takes several photos.

Judith presumes that many people, assimilating into French life, changed their names to something more in keeping with their new country. She knows that if her grandfather had not done this himself, her own family name would be Polish, and would look "foreign," as opposed to the Anglophone Gordon.

The rain is coming down harder now, and Judith is starting to get drenched, so she hurries inside to the museum lobby. There are only a few visitors right now.

"*Bonjour,* may I help you?" asks a friendly young woman in a dark blue suit at the reception desk.

"*Merci, désolé, mais je ne parle pas bien le français,*" Judith responds. She has been finding it helpful to begin conversations by apologizing for her weak French.

"Don't worry," says the young woman, smiling, "we all speak English. In fact, so many people visit who speak English that we have special tours in English. Is this your first visit?"

"Yes. Not my first time in Paris, though; that was a long time ago. This museum was not here in the late sixties."

"Many things were not here then," says the museum worker, laughing. "You have a lot of catching up to do! I saw you looking a long time at the walls outside. Are you trying to find information about lost relatives?"

"I am actually trying to learn about the father and grandfather of a friend in Paris. I found their names outside."

"Your friend has been here?"

"Probably not. He says he does not wish to revisit the past."

"Many people say this. We honor the past, we respect it. Also we provide education, so the past does not become repeated."

"I understand that," agrees Judith. "But my friend does not. It is the same in the US. Many people obsess about the past; they relive it all the time and never enjoy the present. Other people know things but keep silent. I am sure you have seen this."

"Yes, we have," says the woman. "There is also a middle way, and we try to help people with this. Many, as you know, do tell their stories. Now, do you know anything about your friend's father and grandfather?"

"Just their names. And that they both came to Paris from eastern Europe, that they registered early on with the French police, and then were sent to Drancy."

"Drancy, of course. We will open a memorial museum there in 2012. Please come back to see it. Meanwhile, you can go upstairs to the library and look up their names in the large books on the desks, and then cross-check them in the computer that has some photographic records."

Judith takes the glass elevator to the fourth floor and in the library finds the volumes to consult. Each one is very heavy—for good reason, thinks Judith, as she leafs through the pages. Seventy-six thousand names are here, plus addresses, place and date of birth, occupation, and convoy number. Such meticulous records did the Germans keep! A librarian walks over to Judith's table.

"*Madame?* You find what you need here?"

"*Oui, merci*," says Judith. "But—it is one thing to hear about them, and . . . another to see names in print."

"Yes. You know, all this is online. You can find this on the Mémorial website."

"Thank you, I know and did look there and found the names I sought. But it's not the same as looking at the pages and pages here. These books truly display the enormity of what happened here."

The librarian nods. "Almost beyond belief—and right here, in this very city. Now, we are trying to attach a face to every name. You see that computer?" She indicates another table. "Do go over and check. For each name in this book, we try to have a story about the person, and a photograph. Go and look."

Judith does, but finds nothing about Jacques and Samuel, other than their names and addresses, their ages and birthplaces, when they were sent to Drancy, and on which convoys they went to Auschwitz. But she has heard so much from Guy—he must have photos somewhere.

She tells this to the librarian, adding: "I've learned that his father was in the first convoy that went out."

The librarian's eyes widen. "Is he aware of this?"

"I don't know."

"You have heard of the Klarsfelds, Serge and Beate?" asks the librarian, mentioning the renowned Holocaust scholars.

"Of course, the Nazi hunters," Judith responds.

The librarian nods in approval. "They started a group," she continues, "Called Sons and Daughters of the Jewish Deportees, *Les fils et filles des déportés Juifs de France*. There are meetings, and commemorations. Is your friend a member, do you think?"

"I doubt it. He keeps telling me that he doesn't want to live in the past—and then he starts talking about the past again. Also, I don't think he does anything Jewish or with Jewish groups."

"Please," adds the librarian urgently, "Ask your friend to come here. Many children of victims, when they get old, they want to talk and to see their family members remembered in our records."

"I promise," says Judith, taking the woman's card. She can already imagine Guy's response.

Judith stays for three hours, looking at the exhibits on the lower floors. She stops at the desk on her way out to thank the young woman who originally greeted her.

And then she is on the street again, feeling the sun warming her as she walks. She decides to take a bus back to the Left Bank. But her mind is still back at the Mémorial, and on the bus she glances through the program of activities and lectures they offer. If she can, she will revisit it on this trip; she knows she has merely skimmed the surface. She cannot exactly fathom why she wishes to learn more about French Jewry when there is still so much of her own Russian and Polish background she doesn't know.

As she nears her destination, she gets off the bus to find the food shops she was advised to try. Here is another test: will she be able to navigate a grocery store with her modest French? Luckily celery looks just like celery and the place accepts credit cards. The only thing that gives her a problem is the metric system. She enjoys scanning the shelves, looking for products both familiar and not. She finds two dozen varieties of jam, or rather *confiture*, but very little packaged bread as in the States. Of course, it makes total sense; why purchase bread made in a factory when there is a *boulangerie*, a bakery, on nearly every corner?

By six o'clock she is buzzing the keypad on the side of the door at Guy's building. She and her parcels take up almost the entire tiny elevator. He greets her at the top: "Ah, Zhoodeet! *Qu'est-ce que tu as ici?* What do you have here?"

"Soup," announces Judith as she sails into the kitchen. She looks around. Not a bad kitchen for a remodeled old building. Probably vintage 1980s appliances. All she really needs are a cutting board and a couple of pots.

"What you need? I can help you?"

"I need a cutting board, a sharp knife, a large pot and a small one, please. And then you can help by waiting patiently."

"I can do this!"

By half past eight, they have had some chilled white wine, sliced pears, and a small piece of *Tomme de Savoie* that Guy picked up on his last visit to a favorite cheese shop. It's a new taste for Judith, and she enjoys it. Now she ladles out two bowls of steaming chicken soup, thick with onions, carrots, celery, parsley, and parsnips, with just a touch of cumin for seasoning. She has made a small bowl of *kasha varnishkes* as a side dish.

"Ah, it smell so good!" murmurs Guy. "I feel better just inhaling."

"You see? Chicken soup does it again. I don't know whether it's the protein in the soup, or really just the hot steam, but either way this soup seems to improve the health of many."

"My kitchen has not smelled so good in a long time."

"Surely you cook for yourself!"

"Yes, but I do not go to any bother. Chop, chop—too much work! I have a microwave. I want things to be easy. Often I just go to Picard."

"What is Picard?"

"A supermarket with only frozen foods."

"That is such a good idea! There is something like that in England, called Iceland."

"Iceland—now that is very funny! And what do you call it in the United States?"

"As far as I know, we do not have this at all! Supermarkets have frozen food sections, but there is no store just for frozen things."

"Amazing—there are some things that America does not have!"

"We are a primitive country after all."

They enjoy sharing the joke, and then Judith returns to tending the soup.

"How did you manage in this small kitchen," she asks, "when your children lived here? You were in this apartment, right?"

"Oh, it was not bad when they were small. Such a long time ago, it seems. My wife and I take turns cooking. When the children were little, it was easier. When they become teenage, and have different schedules and meal times, it is harder. We manage, but the apartment was always messy. Then one day, quiet again."

"You mean when they went away to university?"

"That, plus my wife leave me. Not all at the same time, but close."

"But you must have loved her at first."

Guy smiles a little. "I knew I was supposed to love someone. My mother say she love my father. Later she say she love Martin. Everyone wait for me to find a woman. Oh, I have girlfriends when I was young. I am normal a little!" He chuckles. "But I do not wish to live with anyone. I spent a long time living with other people, and I want to have my own place. I was busy with work. Also, I travel a lot. It is my habit to be by myself.

"But then, I meet Elena at a party. She was very attractive, young, smart. And I was older and—this was around 1975—well known around Paris. She was impressed, I was flattered. And there—before I know it, we are married and have two babies. Back then I think, oh, this is the way things are supposed to be.”

“But you were happy?”

“I was not unhappy. The children were sweet when they are small. They go to nice schools, in the winter we ski, and in summer go to *la plage*. I think these vacations are boring, but Elena is happy. I think all is fine, then one day, when the children are at university, Elena tells me no, it is not fine. She want excitement. Excitement is expensive, and I am just a writer. Actually I make a good living, but not enough for Elena. She meet a *chirurgien plastique*—how you say, plastic surgeon?—and he has more excitement, so we divorce. You think the 5th is nice?”

“The 5th?”

“5th *arrondissement*. This *quartier*.”

“This neighborhood, here? Why, it’s lovely!”

“But it is not the 16th! The 16th *c’est très élégant.*”

“So? Why are you mentioning this?”

“My ex-wife, she want to live in the 16th. Now, she does. If she is still there.”

“How long have you been divorced?” Hmm, Judith says to herself, the person who does not like to live in the past.

“It was a long time ago, sixteen or seventeen years.”

“But you see your children?”

“Not so much, they live far from here. My daughter is a teacher, she live in Marseille. She is married, with a baby, two years old. My son, he is a *avocat*—lawyer?—in Toulouse, also with a family. We write, we send emails, we speak; but they have other interests and do not worry about an old man.”

"Do they come to Paris?"

"*Bien sûr*, everyone want to come to Paris! They stay here, my apartment is like their hotel, they go to museums, sightseeing, parks. I pay for everything, so they are happy."

"Oh come on, I'm sure they are pleased to see *you*."

"Maybe. If they really like me, they would come more often, no? I was a bad father, always working, always traveling."

Judith grew up seeing her maternal grandparents each weekend. Of course, it was just a matter of an hour's drive, from Queens to Brooklyn, so it is not really a valid comparison.

"What about you?" he asks. "You are attractive, *non?* You must have someone after you get a divorce so long ago."

"Yes, I told you that I was married for a short time when I was just starting out." She has gotten beyond "Lawrence the Loser" and "that bastard Lawrence" because, first of all, it didn't really help to say it, and second, it happened forty years ago. So she will try to keep it brief. "We were both in graduate school in Boston. He finished a year earlier and got a teaching post. I was finishing my dissertation and applying for academic jobs. And then I found out he was sleeping with someone else. So I divorced him."

There, that was simple. That's all she wants to tell him; he doesn't need to hear the sad story of her unsuccessful love life.

"But this must be difficult, to have a divorce at the same time you look for work."

"Tell me about it." She laughs at his puzzled expression. "Oh, that's just another idiom, a saying; I am not really asking you to tell me about it. The problem was that I was ashamed, even though he was the guilty one. I felt I could not focus my job search on Boston, which was too bad because at the time there were many opportunities up there. I felt I needed to get away. So I applied to a small college in Ohio."

"That is where you are now?" he asks.

She nods. "Same place. I thought I could get a good start there, build up my résumé, and apply later for a better position elsewhere. As it turns out, they liked me and offered me tenure a year early. The job market dried out. So I chose the security of the small college, even though I preferred to live in a big city."

She spears an asparagus spear and briefly smiles at the homonym. "What is this in French?" she asks Guy.

"The fork? *Une fourchette.*"

"No," she laughs, "the action," spearing the asparagus again.

"Ah, *lancer.* To spear."

"That is funny—in English we say each piece of asparagus is a 'spear,' using it as a noun."

She relaxes as they switch topics and continue to talk about food and cooking. Guy tells her about the open-air street markets all over Paris, where she can buy fish right from the fishermen, or the best couscous, cooked right there, and special seasonal fruit. "You will taste the *Reine-Claude pruneaux,* they only come once each year!" They will go on Sunday morning.

"You will see how true Parisians buy food. Food is very important to us; the quality must be high. Better to have a small piece of the best cheese than a huge chunk of . . . something *médiocre.* Your people always like to have big, if it is bigger is better, right?"

"There you go with your stereotyping again." Judith feels that Guy is joking, but she is not quite sure. "You think Americans are just a bunch of mindless cows who do not notice if they are being fed swill."

"No? Is not true?" asks Guy with a feigned look of surprise. And then he says, "Now I will be serious—I like this soup very much! And I like that

415

you made it for me, to help me feel better. And *kasha varnishkes*—the last person who cook this for me was my *gran'mère*. I feel happy!"

He takes another spoonful of the soup, smiles, then continues.

"Tomorrow, if the sun is shining, I will want to show you more Paris. We go to Montmartre, yes, and see Sacré-Cœur and the artists who paint *en plein air*, out in the open. It is very touristical, so you will like it."

Judith is pleased both that Guy has enjoyed the soup, and that he is feeling better. Odd, how only a year ago she had no idea he existed, and now she finds herself caring about him. But no way will she consider caring *for* him or make cooking for him a regular occurrence.

The next day is, in fact, quite sunny. Guy telephones Judith early in the morning. "We should go before it is too hot," he says. "We can take the Métro and go up to Montmartre. Maybe we can get there before all the American pilgrims."

"I imagine many religious groups come here."

"No, Zhoodeet, not religious pilgrims. *Tourist* pilgrims who want to see the great sights, and especially Montmartre with its history as a meeting place for the *artistes*, the writers, the *expatriés*. Do you know how Montmartre get its name?"

"Well, anything with 'mont' is a hill or mountain."

"*Oui*, it is the hill of martyrs. According to tradition, Saint Denis, the bishop of Paris, was beheaded here in the 200s. Then he pick up his head in his hands and walk to the top of the hill."

"Charming."

"Yes! We will have a wonderful time!"

## CHAPTER EIGHTEEN

# Drifting Across The City

J udith has never been able to play the placid tourist. She always knows, or wants to know, the story behind what she sees. The first time this occurred was in the mid-1950s when, according to family legend, she and Michael and their parents were visiting George Washington's home, Mount Vernon, in Virginia. It was the largest home Judith had ever seen, and she loudly asked the tour guide, "This place is really big. Who took care of it?" The guide gave some answer, Judith's mother remembered, that deftly avoided the subject of slavery.

So of course Paris is more than a collection of buildings to her, and although the time they spend in Montmartre is indeed lovely, Judith asks many questions. They go early, as Guy suggests, to avoid the crowds. After exiting the Métro at Abbesses, they walk a few blocks on a street that is little more than a corridor of souvenir shops. They take the funicular to the top of the hill—no way either of them was going to attempt over three hundred steps! Wandering through the Sacré-Cœur Basilica, they admire the mosaics and statues encircling the main sanctuary, then stroll behind the church and rest on a bench. Judith asks about the origins of the church and who owned this commanding hilltop, and Guy gives her a lecture about the Franco-Prussian War. They amble past the remaining vineyard and the Lapin Agile cabaret, then back through the Place du Tertre. Judith takes pictures of the square, of an artist at work, of an intricate carving over a doorway. She asks someone passing to take a photo of her and Guy standing under the arched entrance to a passage.

By this time the throngs have arrived, so Judith and Guy need to thread their way around the small square. Neo-impressionist Eiffel Towers, garish pink and aqua Eiffel Towers created with bold brush strokes, minimalist Eiffel Towers made with a palette knife. They watch painters create rapid portraits from life, or sketches of "typical" Parisian scenes—a collection of stereotypes, thinks Judith, but so what? The painters wear berets, the tourists wear white visors. The day is sunny and lovely, full of colors and the laughter of the crowd. An accordion player (of course!) is setting up his music stand at one edge of the Place du Tertre. Within a few moments the strains of *La Vie en Rose* drift over the street. A living postcard, thinks Judith.

Guy indicates a small café off the square where they can have lunch. "This will be a little less touristic," he opines, and Judith has the soup she remembered her father telling her about: onion soup, thick, in a crock, with gruyere cheese melted on top and a few crisp bits dripping down over the sides. Although Judith enjoys the soup and the ambiance of the two-hundred-year-old restaurant, Guy still grumbles, "This place was better thirty years ago!"

"So when did Montmartre change from being a true artists' colony to a stop on the tourist route?" Judith asks.

"This used to be a poor neighborhood. When Haussmann change the city, many poor Parisians had to move further. They come up here. It was a hill, with shacks. Then it become a village. After the church was built, more people come. Artists, also poor. In the twenties it was a good place for artists. Nice views, and cheap. Then the war come. After, people are still poor. But in the sixties come tourists. That is the end for Montmartre."

Guy's simplistic narrative, though, was exactly what happened to the Williamsburg neighborhood in Brooklyn, where Judith's parents were born. She nods, "I know just what you mean. My parents were born at home, in a walk-up flat in an immigrant neighborhood. Later they moved to another part of Brooklyn. Their old neighborhood got even poorer when a highway was built through it. The factories there stood empty. So artists moved in. They couldn't afford to rent studios in Manhattan any more, but Williamsburg was cheap. More artists came, and the area became chic. Now it is so chic the artists cannot afford to stay!"

"Ah, *la même chose!* The same thing."

Afterwards, but before taking the funicular back down the hill, Guy and Judith walk slowly to the overlook at the top of the stairs in front of the church. The sun is straight ahead, and Judith, squinting a bit, wishes she had remembered to bring her sunglasses. The city is spread before them, golden and welcoming. She spots many landmarks, such as the dome of the Panthéon, and far to the distant right, the Eiffel Tower. Just then, she feels Guy's hand move around her back and rest lightly on her shoulder.

"I am glad you like my city," he says, looking not at her but at the city below.

"*Oui, j'aime Paris.* Very much," she answers, turning slightly to look at him. She feels a slight tremor in her shoulder—what is the word? *Frisson.* Another word that English has stolen from French. She suddenly realizes that she hasn't been touched in so long, outside of a family hug or those little French greeting kisses, that she must be overreacting. She wonders if Guy can feel the tremor.

She needs to say something to cover her discomfort: "What is your favorite place in Paris?"

"Ah, you will see. Later."

Over the next week, they walk along the Champs-Élysées not quite to the Arc de Triomphe; that day they head back early in a taxi because Guy's bad leg is giving him trouble. Another day, Judith decides against going to see where Edith Wharton had lived, and instead they go to the Musée Rodin and enjoy lunch overlooking the gardens behind Rodin's studio.

Judith has time on her own, too. Guy, wisely, does not crowd her. She takes the Métro to various *arrondissements* and walks around, using her rudimentary French to order coffee at a neighborhood bistro or buy stamps at a post office. She finds that people are very friendly toward her and do not scoff at her attempts.

"At least you try," says the gray-haired woman with spectacles (*lunettes!* thinks Judith) who works at a bakery, "and I like that." She hands Judith the *pain paysan* she has bought and adds an extra pastry.

## CHAPTER NINETEEN

# The Blue Door

ne golden evening, sitting at an outdoor table at a small bistro overlooking the Seine, Judith tells Guy that she has visited the Mémorial de la Shoah and asks if he has ever been there.

He shows little reaction but continues to focus on the wine in his glass. "No, I never go and do not wish to go. It is over, many decades. Maybe some people want to go there. Not for me. Ever. That time is over."

"But maybe you should—"

Guy looks at her stonily, speaking firmly and quietly, "I say I am not interested. I mean it. It is not for me. The topic is closed. Tell me about something else you see."

If he doesn't want to discuss it, she cannot force him. So instead she tells him about going into a bookstore and finding that the only things she can actually read are stories for children, very young children. This he finds funny.

"Perhaps, in a year, I'll be able to work my way up to *Le Petit Prince*," she says, laughing.

On her solo walks, Judith finds herself repeatedly drawn to the marble plaques in front of every older school building and takes a photo of each. The language is nearly the same on all of them, and she finds herself increasingly angry as she notes the dedication dates: all within the last decade. For fifty years, the neighbors who had vacant apartments next door, the schoolteachers who had empty seats in their classrooms, the shopkeepers who saw that many customers never returned, postal workers with mail that could not be delivered—no one noticed? No one said anything?

A couple of evenings later, Judith arrives at Guy's apartment bearing a bouquet of brightly colored flowers—she knows enough not to bring wine to a French home. Guy has prepared a delicious-looking *salade niçoise*, accompanied by a small cheese platter and a fresh baguette. A bottle of white wine stands ready in the chiller. Guy has set the little table for dinner in front of his open balcony doors.

Judith washes up, and then they sit at the table as Guy pours wine for them and raises his glass in a toast, "*Santé!*"

She joins him in the toast but feels rather subdued. He is sure to notice.

"And so, Zhoodeet, where do your feet take you today?" Guy asks.

Should she tell him? He won't want to hear.

"You are so quiet, Zhoodeet. Where is the American cheerfulness?"

He inclines his head, waiting for her response.

"I don't go out searching for this," she begins, "and I know you have said you don't want to hear about this. But I am absolutely haunted . . . it seems that every time I turn a corner, every time I explore an unfamiliar street, I see a plaque in front of a school."

"Oh, *that* again." He sits back, his expression flat.

"Yes—on a side street near the Hôpital Broca, near the bookshops on the Boulevard Saint-Germain, next to a stairway in Montmartre—they are everywhere. They say the same thing: They mention that the French government worked in collusion with the Nazis and that we should never forget. Sometimes they give the exact number of the neighborhood's children who were deported to the death camps."

"I am aware of this," murmurs Guy quietly.

"These signs—they make me visualize children being swept up, like . . . like so much debris that the Nazis, the French, wanted to toss out. I feel so . . . haunted. Doesn't this *upset* you?" she asks Guy.

"Look, it's all political," he responds impassively. "I told you before." He puts down his fork and knife and stares at her. "This country has a . . . a collective amnesia after the war. This go on for decades. Under de Gaulle it was 'we were divided then, now we are together.' One country. Go forward, not back. Do not live in the past."

Judith persists. "I cannot understand—this doesn't bother you at all? How can you not look at the past? You know this as a journalist, and you have said this—how can you prepare for the future without considering past events?"

"I didn't say 'do not look at the past,'" Guy responds evenly. "I told you. People here chose not to *live* in the past. I include myself. I do not wish to *live* in the past."

He sets his glass down on the table and looks hard at Judith. When he speaks, his voice is quiet but angry.

"You push me. I do not wish to talk about this. I tell you this before. I do not want to talk about the war. You want to. For Americans, a big adventure, right? Not for me, not for me! I live it!"

"I'm sorry . . ."

His voice grows louder. "You want to know more about your father. But you *have* a father, and for a long time! I do not. I do not wish to talk about the past and I do not wish to live in the past. To remember what it was like—too frightening. From the time my father and grandfather disappear, to the time your father appear, what do I feel? Fear. Fear, only fear. I was frightened for years. A scared boy. And most of the time, alone."

Judith feels her face growing flushed. She feels humiliated because she *did* push him. What she has studied, he has lived. Of course he is not a book whose pages she can thumb. She is not naïve enough to think he is a box of documents to be sifted through. But she did begin this quest thinking of him as a source of family information—*her* family.

"When the war end," continues Guy, slowly and more quietly, "I have more than twelve years. There is little difference between having 34 and having 37. But three years is a huge difference in a child. I was very changed, I think, when I come home to Paris. Of course, I was thrilled to be with my mother and grandmother again. But I do not see anyone I recognize from earlier. I have only vague memories of Paris. I spend a lot of time by myself, try to remember places and how to get around."

Judith listens, intent and silent, as Guy continues:

"I was a lonely child, quiet. I was by myself a lot. Below everything, I was very afraid the whole time. That is not unusual, I think, for any child who go through a war, even if he has no wounds.

"My experiences—I cannot talk about this to anyone. Not to my mother or *gran'mère,* certainly. I have no uncles or aunts or cousins. I cannot talk to any teacher. I keep hearing my mother and grandmother say: Be careful. Trust no one. You think that leaves no mark on a child?"

"Of course," she says quietly.

"And all because of being Jewish, which I do not even understand back then. All I know: being Jewish was dangerous. My father and grandfather, they were good people. Always nice to me, and as what is told to me, honest in their work. They do nothing wrong, nothing! They die for being Jewish!"

Now the volume of his voice rises; this is the strongest emotional outburst Judith has seen Guy display.

"You know what else frighten me? Those things my mother *not* say to me. Be careful when you go to the bathroom! Do not let anyone see you down there! Why? She say nothing about *circoncision*. Just that 'Jewish men are different.' You say that to a boy nine, ten, eleven years old? Who is starting his *puberté?* This scare me very much, very much!"

"She was trying to protect—"

"I know! I know she say this to protect me. She have not much education. She do not know how to explain. So as a child, I am very frightened. And I stay frightened because of this for many years, yes. I can ask no one!"

He stares at Judith, then takes a gulp of wine.

"Maybe, if he was here longer, I would ask your father. But I do not. He go away, too." And he looks right at her, accusingly. Her father had helped him, but also—Guy has finally said it—he was another adult who abandoned him.

"So," murmurs Guy, "I just stay afraid."

What can Judith say? She imagines Guy as a young boy, skittish, fretful, unsure of everyone, including other children who played with him.

"It was not so bad at the school in the mountains," Guy says softly, "but before, when I must go to a new school in Paris, it was terrible, terrible."

They have both stopped eating and are sitting quietly. Then Guy resumes his narrative:

"My *maman* take me there in the morning, she kiss me and watch me go inside. But in the afternoon, she is working and I must walk home by myself. By this time, I have ten years, not so little. I wish my *gran'mère* could be there, but I know she cannot. Some boys ask me to come play with them, but I say, no, I must go. Because that is Maman's rule. After some time they do not ask me. I do not have a good friend there. Because I do not speak much, and do not trust."

"There wasn't a teacher you could go to when you were so sad?" asks Judith sympathetically.

"*Mais non*. My *maman*, she tell me, you cannot trust anyone with information about us. You have problems with reading, you can ask. Problems with mathematics, you can ask. Otherwise, safer not to say. At night, I listen hard to my mother and Gran'mère whispering—I hear a little, that people 'report' on other people, who then are taken away. Maybe they are taken someplace like where my father and Gran'père are. I do not know. I just listen. I know there is danger, and I am scared. One time a teacher, she say to me, 'Guy, you look so sad. Please talk to me, tell me what is wrong.' She was kind, very *sympa*, I like her. But I cannot tell things to her. So I just cry a little and say I worry about my father—which was, of course, true. She hug me and tell me to do well in school so he can be proud of me when he come home."

Judith is amazed to hear so many details from Guy about his memories of elementary school. And she feels terrible for him, living in constant fear because of things his mother told him, what she didn't tell him, and what he overheard.

"Guy, I am so sorry . . . you never had a real childhood, did you? And after the war, you never—"

"*Quoi?* What?"

"You never saw anyone?"

"What do you mean 'saw'? I see many people. I do not understand."

He takes another gulp, finishes the glass. Then pours himself some more.

"Did you ever see a . . . therapist?"

Guy looks at her with surprise. She is unsure of what this means, and for a moment she is sorry she broached the subject, that maybe it is too inquisitive, too personal.

Then he bursts into laughter. "A therapist? You Americans! Everyone must see a therapist! You have a problem? Life is not perfect? You are too shy, or your grades are low? Sad because your father disappear? See a therapist! And take a pill. The answer to everything."

"No, it's not the answer to everything. But talking about something can help people cope."

"I cope. I cope," says Guy flatly. "I cope in my way. I work. It is no accident I write about immigrants, hah? I understand them, and their fears. And I tell you something else. You ask me if I will go to a synagogue with you? Bah!" He makes that dismissive *pfff* with his lips. "I do not believe in God. How can God allow this to happen? When I am young, I want to believe in France, but France allow this to happen, also. I believe in a few people around me and that is all. Being 'Jewish' is not part of my life."

"But—you had a *bar mitzvah!*"

Guy's laugh is bitter. "Yes, when I was young. I do this to make my mother happy. Also my *gran'mère.*"

He points an index finger at her, reproachfully.

"And your *père*, your father, too. Maybe he influence my mother about this. And my *gran'mère* too, when they chatter in Yiddish. For me, I do not care. After that day, do I go again to the synagogue? No."

Judith listens and responds quietly. "I think I understand. Everyone was so eager to get back to 'normal' that no one took care of your needs."

"Normal?" Guy asks, quickly downing his glass of wine. "I am not normal. What is 'normal?' I do not know this."

Finding that picture in her father's box of photos has brought Judith to this city, where she has seen physical evidence of what she had known earlier only from books. Seeing these proofs, wherever she has roamed in Paris, has been making her increasingly angry. But Guy himself—a brick wall.

"But to say that Parisians don't live in the past!" she continues to argue. "To me, it seems clear that Paris is totally obsessed with the past! It surrounds you everywhere—monuments, plaques, statues, memorials. Wherever you walk—there are signs at every corner telling you who the street is named for. Reminders even where you do not expect them. I saw one plaque in the courtyard of a building on the Île de la Cité memorializing a group of mothers and their children—infants, babies!—who were deported and sent to the extermination camps. What kind of war makes babies the enemy? What kind of humans are willing to kill babies?"

The tension that has been building in her finally crests, and her voice breaks. She turns her head so Guy cannot see that her eyes have filled.

Guy leans forward and places his hand on top of hers on the table.

"Zhoodeet," he says gently, "will this plaque bring the mothers and children back to us? They are gone and the best we can do is live and make sure it does not again happen. If I think too much about how my life change after my father and my *gran'père* were tricked and murdered, I become crazy. I cannot do this."

Judith vows to herself that she will not pursue this line of inquiry with Guy. But she remains silent, as she does not trust herself to open her mouth.

They both sit quietly for a few moments. Then Guy speaks, telling her a little more about her father.

"I have a very good memory. For people of my age this is a blessing. I cannot remember *everything* that I see and hear my whole life. But I remember the really important things, yes. You see, even if you do not find me or write to me, I still remember your father. I never forget him. When he come to see us that first time, it was so wonderful. He represent liberty and freedom, and when we see him we know it is the end of this terrible period in our life. He was a kind man and he treat me like a son."

He pauses to take another sip of wine, then frowns.

"That is why there is that puzzle. But I never forget him, never."

Judith has recovered enough of her composure to respond.

"The puzzle of why my father never contacted you?"

"Of course."

Ah, she thinks to herself, so it's all right for *you* to perseverate. "Guy, I know this bothers you because you have mentioned it several times. Again, I will ask: do you think he may have been attracted to your mother?"

He takes another sip of wine, thinking.

"So, maybe. They were both young, lonely. But now I learn your father already has a *fiancée*."

"True. I don't know what to think, but not writing to your family at all was . . . just wrong."

"But he keep those photos, yes, all the years? So we were important to him."

If only she had known about that box and examined its contents before he had died! Now that he is truly beyond reach, unless there is a cache of letters stored somewhere, she will never know the real reason for his silence. Judith knows, though, there is no cache of letters.

"I am glad you come to France," says Guy. "I enjoy to meet you, and I like to show off Paris to you. But no more talk of the war. It is over. You must promise. Please."

He is looking steadily at her with a stern gaze. There is nothing she can do except accede to his demand. She nods.

"Good," he says, and his face relaxes a little. "Now, you enjoy yourself these next few days. Do whatever you wish. I will join you for some things, not all. My legs are not so strong. But save your last evening; I have a surprise."

During the succeeding days, while Guy works on an article about immigrants in Paris, Judith continues her explorations. She visits the Parc Monccau just north of the Arc de Triomphe, basically because she has been charmed by a song about it recorded by Yves Duteil. She samples fruit and *tabouleh* at a street market on Rue Monge and relaxes on a bench on the Rue de Rivoli to people-watch. One morning, she takes the Métro to the Place de la République and walks down the Rue de Turbigo until she finds the address she had learned from the large printed list of deported people at the library of the Mémorial de la Shoah. Here she finds the building where Guy and his family had lived, and which her father had visited so many times.

The high blue door is closed; there is a new codebox on the left portal. Judith tries the door anyway, and it opens to her touch. So why not enter? She steps over the threshold to see what her father must have seen sixty years earlier. A tiled, clean hallway leads to a small elevator within a cage. A circular staircase winds around it. She decides to take the stairs. Just as she rounds one curve she meets a man and a woman polishing the brass handrail. The cleaners—so this is why the entry was unlocked.

"*Pouvons-nous vous aider? Qu'est-ce que vous voulez?*"

Of course, they are asking who she is and what she wants, Judith realizes. This will be a real test of her French. She slowly explains as best she can, that her father was an American soldier at the end of the war, the *Deuxième Guerre mondiale*, and used to visit a family that had lived here. She just wants to look. As soon as they hear the phrase about the war, the couple smile and gesture that she is welcome to look around.

Judith mounts to the second floor, coming abreast of a window to the inner courtyard. She imagines Guy as a small boy, playing here. She ascends another flight. The apartments here must have been of different sizes, judging from the doors—some are single, some double. Today they are mostly offices. She has no idea which door once led to Guy's childhood home; it really doesn't matter. The wooden staircase has new carpet, but still Judith enjoys knowing that she is walking the same steps that her father took so many years ago.

She descends the stairs, thanks the cleaners, and emerges onto the busy Rue de Turbigo. Two laughing schoolboys, satchels of books on their shoulders, glide by on scooters. A young couple passes, walking slowly and holding hands. A gray-haired woman wearing stylish red-framed sunglasses strolls past with her little terrier on a red leash. Judith imagines Jacques and Samuel closing the door behind them, nervous, but never imagining it was for the last time, never imagining what lay in store.

## CHAPTER TWENTY

# The Cemetery

On another morning that she has to herself, Judith decides to visit the Père Lachaise Cemetery in the 20th. Not that she is a big fan of graveyards, but she *has* been to Mount Auburn in Cambridge, Massachusetts, to see Charlotte Cushman's resting place, and Highgate in London to see George Eliot's grave–leaving her pen embedded in the earth there with many others. And of course she has been to Elisabeth Shuttleford's when she made her literary pilgrimage. But everyone at home has told her she must see this, one of the oldest, and certainly one of the most famous, cemeteries of Paris.

Judith has heard from her colleagues that Père Lachaise is actually a tourist destination, and she passes couples and groups armed with maps like the ones sold in Hollywood to those seeking the homes of the stars. It is not merely a cemetery with remarkable sculptures, but also the final resting place of many celebrities ranging from Molière to Jim Morrison. Having no map, though, Judith simply wanders. From a gate on the cemetery's eastern side, where she enters, she strolls across a crowded plateau, the leaves of tall trees shielding her from the sun. She passes Simone Signoret and Yves Montand, who sleep under a plain, flat marker. Religious symbols adorn many gravestones—mostly crosses, ranging from simple to ornate, intricately carved Celtic designs, while a few bear the Star of David and Hebrew lettering. These are interspersed among the others, along with an occasional Muslim or Buddhist grave.

Judith bends down and collects small pebbles and stones for remembrance, placing them on the Jewish graves as she wanders through the rows. She realizes she is simply following the ancient custom because she is programmed to do it. I am in a place I have never been, she thinks to herself, and yet I am remembering people whom I do not know. Without realizing it, she is searching for the oldest Jewish graves.

Judith descends carefully along winding paths over a hilly area to a circular garden, and then down more hills to the main entrance. Here she slows her pace, as she would risk a certain fall on the twisting paths that are often crossed by ancient tree roots. She cannot read inscriptions and walk at the same time.

She has read that when Père Lachaise opened at the beginning of the nineteenth century, some people thought it too far from central Paris to be *chic*. No one wanted to be buried there. So a marketing scheme was devised to relocate some 'celebrity' graves. The plan worked, and the new cemetery became the resting place of choice.

She continues meandering, past family tombs with more than one generation interred. Sometimes, all the names are listed on the outside, sometimes not. Judith sees numerous memorials, Christian and Jewish, to sons lost in the Great War. One features a life-size bronze statue of a soldier in uniform, rifle in hand, facing east—toward Germany.

Down another hill she steps and finds an open area encircled by a fence. She walks around it to learn that this is a memorial to those French Jews who have no marked graves–those murdered in the Holocaust.

Judith has been wandering for well over an hour, although she hasn't looked at her watch. She is almost at the edge of the cemetery, for she sees a gateway in the distance.

This is an older part of Père Lachaise, shaded by tall trees whose roots have made the paths uneven and probably have created a jumble beneath the ground.

She is drawn to a large structure in one corner, as it dominates this area. So this is the tomb of Abelard and Héloïse, who died hundreds of years before this cemetery was established. This must be one of the relocated interments, placed here to draw company. The move obviously worked, for this section is crowded with tombs and monuments. Judith spends a few moments among these graves before she realizes they are different from most of the ones she has seen so far.

There are no crosses.

She studies the names and symbols on the graves and family mausoleums. Hebrew lettering and Stars of David indicate that this section of Père Lachaise is predominantly Jewish. She walks the length of this row and approaches a tall, simple, and imposing tomb. There is only one name at the top, but it is a forename, not a family name: "Rachel." Judith wonders if this could be the resting place of the famous 19th century actress, a contemporary of the English Victorian actresses Helena Faucit and Mary Anne Stirling. She remembers that in France, Rachel's reputation rivaled that of Sarah Bernhardt. She pauses and takes from her bag the little notebook she habitually carries, jotting down Rachel's name to remind herself to check later.

Then she turns back to study the names more closely. Several are recognizably Jewish: Cahen, Levi, Levy. Some names refer to the French cities where Jewish families lived when they were ordered by Napoleon to take surnames: Lion or Leon, for Lyon. Many family names have Germanic origins, people who came to Paris from the Austro-Hungarian Empire: Schloss, Heilbronner, Bernheim, Kaufman, Sachs, Gompertz, and Lehmann. Among these is the tomb of the Dreyfus family. This monument, she sees, includes more than one generation, and has a notation—"*mort en déportation*"—for family members murdered in the Shoah. As she moves down the row, Judith recognizes some surnames as Sephardic, such as Amar and Araf, belonging to Jews who came to France from Spain or northern Africa. Again, Judith spots monuments to young men who died in battle, "*mort pour la France.*" She sees that the same family lost two sons in World War I, one at the Somme, the other, younger, at the Battle of the Marne.

Now she finds the oldest Jewish graves. Here is Joseph Henriques Raba, born in Bordeaux in 1793. Not too far away lies Joseph Bernstein, born just a little later, in 1797, in Warsaw. The actual earliest date she finds is 1785—the birth year of a Parisian Jew whose name, on a worn, very old stone, she cannot decipher.

The names Judith reads are as diverse as the places from which their bearers originated.

Oulman, Samuel, Singer, Berl, Nathan, Oster, Maye, Hirsch, Szusterman, Belin, Haas, Schwob, Hernsheim, Cerf.

She remembers seeing some of these same names on the walls of the Mémorial de la Shoah.

Judith has been at Père Lachaise for almost three hours, and now she is very tired. She is exhausted but knows this has little to do with her age and the day's heat. She is overwhelmingly sad. Retracing her steps back to the tomb of Rachel, near the main gate on Boulevard de Ménilmontant, she exits and spots a bench. She sits in the shadiest place she can find. She wishes she had a good friend like Claudette, or her brother Michael, with her now. Certainly she cannot tell anything of what she has seen or feels to Guy.

For two centuries, the Jews of Paris have buried their dead here. Ten generations have become part of the Parisian soil. Many families lost sons, brothers, and fathers defending France in the Great War. Yet in the 1940s, so many thousands—she recalls the many inscribed walls she saw at the Mémorial—were methodically rounded up and deported. How long, wonders Judith, does a person have to live in a place before *not* being considered 'the other?'

She looks down and is surprised to see her hands clenched into fists.

## CHAPTER TWENTY-ONE

# Le Marais

To her shame, Judith has never read *Les Misérables*–not in English, certainly not in French. She does not think seeing her friend's daughter star as Cosette in a school production of *Les Mis* counts. It is a sin of omission equal to that of a specialist in American literature skipping The *Scarlet Letter* or *Moby Dick*. She will move it up closer to the top of her "someday" reading list. Meanwhile, she cannot possibly visit the Victor Hugo museum–in the spacious apartment he rented for many years, here across the Place des Vosges–until she does so.

It is just the beginning of the afternoon on another day when Judith is free to explore Paris alone. She enjoys Guy's company and relies on him for background information, but sometimes she just wants the freedom to make independent observations without his subtitles. This square, for instance– and it is, indeed, a square, unlike others in this city, or in London or New York, which are rectangular, irregular, or even triangular. If squareness and symmetry are desired, this is the example *par excellence*. Enjoying a glass of Chablis outdoors under the arches of Ma Bourgogne, Judith is shaded from the sun and still able to look out over the square with its formal rows of neatly trimmed linden trees, ranged around the central fountain.

She came into the restaurant a little in advance of the midday throng, so she was able to find a seat offering a perfect vantage point of both the elegant surrounding architecture and the individuals in the square. Harmony and balance—the Place des Vosges exudes order, and even if Judith had not read that it was constructed in the early sixteenth century as an exclusive residential area, she would have been able to see it. For almost two centuries after their construction, the buildings surrounding the square were inhabited by the wealthy and powerful—as they are today. But when the Revolution occurred, she learned, the gentry abandoned their symmetrical square and the nearby mansions and *hôtels particuliers*. No longer *chic*, the area filled with workers and immigrants, small businesses, workshops, tradespeople, and the poor. Once-grand homes for aristocratic families were broken down into dwellings for many families. Jews from Alsace settled here in the first part of the nineteenth century, she read, followed by waves of Jews from Russia and Poland after the assassination of Czar Alexander II in the spring of 1881. This was exactly the same impetus for the tremendous influx of Jews to America at the same time. In addition to being Czar of Russia, Alexander II was King of Poland, and Jews living in both places knew that his killing would likely result in riots and pogroms.

Many refugees seeking a peaceful life, Judith's own grandparents among them, looked to America as their ultimate goal, while others went to England or France. Either was preferable, and definitely safer, than Russia or Poland. The flow of immigrants continued through the 1920s, when Judith's great-uncle Jascha had arrived in New York and Guy's father had come to Paris.

Guy had told her how his father, as a very young man, had basically walked with a friend from Krakow to Paris. It took them months, working at odd jobs to pay for food and lodging as they traveled, sometimes hitching a ride on a farmer's wagon for a few miles. If you had a trade, and were good at it, you could manage. So, when Yakov Davidov arrived in Paris, he knew just where to go: the pletzl, the "little place." Here was the center of Jewish life, here he could speak Yiddish, and here he could be surrounded by his countrymen, all while making decent money as a tailor.

Had Yakov once sat in this same square or wandered the nearby streets? Where did he live when he first came to Paris? Did he find work in one of the many garment workshops that filled this area? Judith knows that immigrants from Russia and Poland dominated the garment industry in Paris in the twenties and thirties, and that the workshops and showrooms and wholesale houses had moved up into the 3rd and 11th *arrondissements*. Guy's apartment, the one where his father had a home workshop, and where her father had visited, was in the 3rd. But in general, Judith has no idea of what Yakov's life was like, since what little she knows about him is what Guy has related, and his memories of his father are few.

"All I know, really," he has said, "Is what my mother and my *gran'mère* tell me. My father was a very good workman. Somehow, he meet Samuel— he work in garments, too. I think, all the Jewish immigrants, they all know each other, and they all make clothes! Samuel has a daughter. She has just finished school and is—of course!—working in a dress factory. My father and mother, they meet, they marry, and—*voilà!* Here I am!"

Judith recalls this as she slowly eats her *salade niçoise* and eyes her sliced baguette with its accompanying little tub of fresh butter. Maybe only half. Maybe no butter. Even with her careful eating, the calories can easily insinuate themselves here. She looks up to observe a group on the sidewalk across the street, led by a woman who carries a red umbrella, raised high. But it isn't raining! Aha—it's for visibility. The woman says something, then heads diagonally through the square, the group trotting obediently behind her. They disappear under the covered arches on the other side, and Judith realizes they must have gone to see the Victor Hugo museum.

Two more women come into view, strolling quite close to Judith's table as they make their way around the square. One is looking at a guidebook and tells the other what she is seeing. Judith knows before she even hears their accents: American. Both women wear white shorts, bright flowered T-shirts, and white visors. Visors! Judith finds herself wanting to laugh but is terrified of making a sound and calling attention to herself. Do tourists have a special school, she wonders, where they go to be coached on how to dress like this? An older woman in a gray linen suit, walking a very tiny dog, passes the tourists, who bray with laughter. Oh, if Guy were here, he would mock those Americans for sure! No, she would tell him, it's not because they are *American;* it's because they equate being on vacation with being at a resort. They would dress like this in Manhattan or Boston. She, on the other hand, dresses for a city whether or not she is on a vacation. She hears her mother's voice dispensing decades-old advice: "Dress nicely, and you will be able to walk in anywhere." Perhaps, Judith thinks, that is why no one stares at her or bothers her: she blends in. Or maybe she is simply, like so many other older women she knows, invisible. Fine, she thinks. This allows her to remain ever the observer, watching and taking notes.

After paying for her lunch, Judith wanders through the square herself, then out by the southernmost archway, where only one block ahead rumbles the crowded and busy Rue de Rivoli. She joins the mighty stream of shoppers, workers on their lunch hour, tourists, and students as they make their way toward wherever they are going. Occasionally a group of two or three young women stop in front of an attractive shoe display in a shop window, and all the sidewalk traffic has to flow around them. Just like Fifth Avenue in the middle of the day, thinks Judith, except that here the buildings are lower, often older, and frankly, prettier.

Now on the left there is a large church, and a more open area—indeed a "little plaza"—where several streets converge. Shops, cafés, the Saint-Paul Métro station entrance where hawkers distribute flyers to people as they come up the steps, souvenir vendors—all add to the general atmosphere of noisy bustle. This changes as Judith turns right onto the narrow Rue Pavée. Why name a street "paved," she wonders, unless this was an unusual feature? She will ask Guy later.

Here the atmosphere becomes—Jewish. On her right, Judith sees signs in Hebrew and Yiddish proclaiming the delights of the falafel restaurant inside; there is already a line at the door. A little further along is a synagogue with an atypical wavy façade. She sees the name of the architect on an outside corner of the structure: Hector Guimard. The same man who designed those distinctive Art Nouveau "Métropolitain" entrances! Curious, she decides to go in, and she rings at the gate. Whoever is inside can see her, and she is buzzed in. The people inside speak no English at all, but Judith manages a bit with her weak French and is allowed to roam a bit in the sanctuary. She sticks to the women's balcony—after all, this is Orthodox, and she is not here to make any waves. But she also has the advantage of an excellent perspective from there, noting the plain and austere seating and the marvelously ornate railing handles.

Outside again, she is across Rue Pavée from one of the *hôtels particuliers*, a former mansion from the seventeenth century, behind whose high doors is now a . . . what? It remains a mystery, as there is no sign. She knows that other former mansions in the area have been turned into museums. But this one is a mystery.

Beyond this building is an intersection with the beginning of a new street, the Rue des Rosiers. Here there is no mystery. This narrow street, paved with cobblestones and barely wide enough to accommodate one car, is the heart of the old Jewish area of Paris.

One of the first places she sees is a former trade school for boys, where underprivileged children could learn a trade. She looks at showcases with photos of the boys and examples of their work. Two thoughts compete in Judith's head. First, how lovely that the community took care of its own, trying to feed and educate the young and get them started in life. Second, what easy pickings. An occupying force bent on destroying a group of people could just come to the Rue des Rosiers and scoop up the children.

Of course, that is exactly what they did. But not all at once. No, they tightened the noose bit by bit and took their time.

In other parts of Paris, Judith has seen those plaques on the fronts of schools. But on this street, with its newly opened *chic* boutiques, there are many. She stops and reads them all. No one else on this hot summer afternoon is doing so. Perhaps Guy is right: what good is it doing for her to read and feel troubled?

At number 16, there is a small plaque above the doorway to a set of apartments. Unlike most of the memorials she has seen, this one mentions specific names. From this building, between 1942 and 1944, were taken a twelve-year-old girl, Rosette, along with her father; a couple named Esther and Henri; and a woman named Rywka and her children, Victor, a toddler of two, and Paulette, just one month old.

The decisiveness of Guy's mother overwhelms her. She was so lucky to have formed a friendship with a Christian woman who gave her those papers. But then she had to rely on her own instinct, to listen to her own gut. So she simply walked away from a vulnerable neighborhood to live underground while remaining visible. What courage that must have taken—to know that she could never be contacted by husband or father even if they managed to escape. To live one life at home and another at work. Always thinking one step ahead.

But what had this all meant to Guy as a small boy? This is something Judith can barely imagine, but that Guy has tried to convey. He loved and trusted his mother, knowing she would protect him. But this protection had come at a cost. If his mother had not acted swiftly, or had not possessed those papers, Guy would have ended up like Rosette or the other 11,000 children who were deported from France to Nazi extermination camps. As it was, he survived with an ever-present sense of fear, a distrust of uniforms, anxiety about his own body, and a string of losses.

Judith looks about and spots some wide steps in front of a building; she can at least sit for a while as she watches people go past on the Rue des Rosiers.

Guy's interest in refugees is definitely no coincidence. He has much in common with the frightened and threatened individuals he has met. He has been able to listen seriously to their concerns and has examined the causes of their anxiety. That, Judith supposes, has been his therapy.

And then there is his lifestyle, which is, as far as Judith can see it, more or less solitary. His phone rarely rings. He has never mentioned personal friends. Once she asked, and he had laughed and shaken his head.

"Ah, friends, mostly they leave," he had said. "They are like me, old. So either they move to be near to their children. Or they die."

Judith is thinking that, perhaps, she could offer the friendship and trust he needs. But then she is distracted by boisterous shouting. A group of boys has arrived at the doorway of the bakery just next to the apartment building with the plaque over its door. The boys, who all seem to be young teens, are jostling each other noisily about who gets to enter the small shop first. Then Judith notices that they all wear *kippot*, and some have *tallis* fringes hanging out from beneath their shirts. There must be a *yeshiva* nearby where they study, and this is break time, so they have run over for a snack.

Smiling to herself, Judith rises from her perch, deciding to bring some treats back for Guy. Maybe she will ask the boys which they like best.

## CHAPTER TWENTY-TWO

# The Seine

O n the last evening of her visit, Guy reveals the surprise he has been planning for Judith. He stands up, smiling, to greet her in her hotel lobby, wearing a linen blazer in a warm tan over a russet shirt and a striped tie. He looks rather dashing. She feels a sudden and unexpected rush of blood in her arm as he takes her elbow to guide her toward a waiting taxi. They ride through the Latin Quarter to the north bank of the Seine just off the Pont de l'Alma, and then walk along the embankment to where the *Bateaux Mouches* are moored.

"Oh these boats!" exclaims Judith. "I have seen them only from the bridges. They look like so much fun!"

Guy beams at her. "They are—I even go on them a couple of times when I was younger. Of course, they are very touristic. Many Americans and Italians come here. You will not hear much French spoken, except by the staff. And by me, if you choose. But I think you will like this a lot."

It is early evening, and by the time the boat leaves its berth and starts to glide along the Seine, the sun has begun to drop. Judith and Guy, each holding a glass of white wine, stand on the deck and watch the light gilding the buildings they pass. The towers of Notre-Dame gleam; on the opposite bank, people dance in a park as the music travels over the water. Later, this will be what Judith remembers best: watching a group of people expressing their *joie de vivre*. The riverbanks are busy and full of life, with knots of people on the steps and quays.

Judith waves to a couple enjoying a private picnic beneath a quayside tree, and they wave back. She feels happy and young, and she wants to wonder why, but it seems like too much work. She has not had enough wine to feel lightheaded—and she knows she will never catch up to Guy's capacity, nor does she wish to. But on the whole, she has enjoyed the trip and getting to know this witty, sardonic, damaged man who drinks too much.

The boat moves slowly, and they are called down the stairs for the first course. The food is excellent (grilled salmon with a fig *confit* and potatoes roasted with rosemary), but Judith hardly notices—she is entranced by the views through the long glass windows of the golden spires of the buildings they pass, the stately archways of the bridges they glide beneath. The ride is timed perfectly—dessert is served, and then, with darkness, the boat glides past the Eiffel Tower. Guy and Judith go up to the top deck with everyone else to enjoy the scene as they float past. As they come abreast of the Tower, it begins to blaze out flashing lights. The cries and squeals of the passengers indicate who is a first-time visitor.

Judith loves every second of the trip. "I feel like such a tourist!" she says to Guy.

"*Alors*, you *are* a tourist!"

"Guy, you are absolutely right—I love this evening! It's such a treat, and a wonderful way to conclude my trip. I have seen so much, both with you and on my own. Still, I am sad about all the things I have not had time to see."

He smiles at her. "That is always the way on a trip. You must leave something for la *prochaine fois,* the next time."

Judith likes the sound of that phrase. She is standing quite close to Guy—in fact, their shoulders nearly touch. She is acutely aware of the weave of his linen blazer, the faintly spicy scent of his cologne. It would be perfectly natural, she thinks, to give him a hug right now. Perhaps even a kiss—not the light customary greeting on each cheek, but a nice soft kiss that tells him she likes him, cares about him. But she is afraid of being too forward, or impetuous, or violating some code. He could hug her but does not. They continue to stand, close and almost touching, for a few moments.

"We are here," he says, extending his arm gallantly, "So be careful not to trip on the steps as we get off the boat."

Then they are docking, and any chance for spontaneity is over.

## CHAPTER TWENTY-THREE

# Returning

The interior lights of the plane dim a bit to give passengers the illusion that they are in sleep mode. Judith settles back in her seat by the window. Even with the small print she bought from an artist at the Place du Tertre, she still managed to have only one carry-on bag, which is stowed beneath her seat. She bought the picture very quickly, almost impetuously, because Guy tried to pay for everything during her visit.

On the other hand, she, of course, had found him, had made contact, and had made the trip. He must have been so pleased by this, although he seemed to take it in stride. Well no, at the very beginning he was quite emotional.

Judith tries to relax and enjoy the flight, but right now she is too—she is not sure of the exactly correct word. Nervous? Edgy? No, these are descriptions of younger people. She is the collected and consummate professional. What is it, then? She will make a list, as is her habit on return trips, and from her bag she takes out her small black notebook. First, she will jot down her 'to do' tasks for when she arrives: collect the mail from the post office, make sure the titles for her fall classes have arrived at the college bookstore, water the plants, make an appointment to see the chair.

That accomplished, she starts another list. This one is of all the places in Paris she visited with Guy and on her own. The Opéra, the Musée d'Orsay, the Tour Eiffel (of course!), Notre-Dame, the Tour Montparnasse, the Café de la Rotonde. The Boulevard Haussmann and a couple of the department stores. The bookshop, Shakespeare and Company. Very nice, she chides herself—any tourist could compile this list.

The other things are what made a difference: ascending the stairway to where Guy's childhood apartment had been located, following her father's footsteps along the Rue de Turbigo, seeing the interior of a synagogue where he might have sat at one time, sipping a glass of wine at his favorite café and watching the afternoon crowd drift past. And the highlight of course: meeting Guy. The "*petit garçon*" of the 1945 photograph. Who would have thought this possible, sixty-six years after the picture was snapped?

Judith cannot rest at all. This has not been just another trip, a conference appearance that will add an extra line to her résumé. She has an exhausting conversation with herself.

So how old are you now, Professor?

Mid-forties sounds about right—enough time since graduate school to have gained experience in research and teaching, but plenty of time left for additional projects and conference appearances.

But wait—you've been at the college for the past thirty years!

Oh, you want the *factual* age. Then I am sixty-three.

Really! You could have fooled all of us—you look ten years younger! What is your secret?

Besides good genes, which we cannot do anything about, I think it's doing work that you truly love. Yes, that's it. Staying out of the sun, gallons of face cream, no smoking, that can help. But for the most part, I have really enjoyed the academic life. You know how Thoreau wrote about lost people living lives of "quiet desperation?" If I had a life of quiet desperation I would look and feel old. Oh no, I have kept any desperation at bay by going to conferences, developing an international network of friends I enjoy seeing. Going out to dinner with former students and colleagues in Boston, New York, Los Angeles, Seattle, London. And I have never missed having my own children, really. I love Ian and Sarah very much, and it's been a pleasure watching them grow to adulthood. Of course, their parents have done all the really hard work; I just get to enjoy the fruits of their labor.

So, Dr. Gordon, what would you say has been the major accomplishment of your career?

Her seatmate is asleep, but Judith knows she will not get any shut-eye on this trip. She buzzes for a flight attendant and requests a glass of white wine.

Glass in hand, she sips while mulling the best response. Over the years, she answers her invisible interviewer, I estimate that I have taught approximately 6,000 students, nearly all undergraduates. I hope I have instilled in them, if not a love of the Victorian era, at least an appreciation of literature and the skills associated with close textual reading. Oh, that sounds so pretentious!

That's all right, Professor, but can we go back for a moment to something you said a bit earlier?

Oh, and what was that?

That you have kept "desperation at bay"—desperation for what?

Your questions are getting a bit too pointed now. Perhaps I ought to take a nap.

Answer the question!

Fine: if you must know, I have never completely felt that I was . . . quite good enough. Good, yes; very good, at times. But truly excellent? I have had to keep proving myself, over and over. I'm tired of it, all right? I'm at a college that is a lovely place, but it's not a top research school. I've applied for other positions when they come up elsewhere. And I always get rejected—I have a folder of letters to prove it. I have been flown halfway across the country for interviews, but ultimately I am not chosen. Why? Because there is always someone better, trendier, younger, who has won more prizes, has more publications, or has better connections. Yes, I have won awards. But I have never won a "genius" grant, so I'm not a genius. Has my work made any difference? It doesn't matter now. I am nearing retirement age, only staying on because I like my work and have nothing better to do. Also, the longer I work the more I can piss off my department head. What am I going to do—join a book club, take up knitting, or start tending a garden? Please.

You know, Dr. Gordon, a lot of people do enjoy this time of life. They don't have to show up at work at a certain hour, they don't have to deal with administrative blather, they don't have to publish or grade papers—they do what they like, when they like. So why can't you?

All right, then—what *do* I like?

She tries to keep the creepy thoughts away, such as how she imagines being nothing more than a footnote in someone's paper fifty years from now. That, just as she skips over out-of-date books from the fifties and sixties as she scans the shelves in the college library, she knows someday someone will pass hers, giving her work no thought.

Really, Judith, she asks herself, how important was Elisabeth Shuttleford?

What, so all scholarship should cease because you decide what is important and what is not? The inner dialogue exhausts her, as it always does. She polishes off her glass of wine and tries to sleep.

Eighteen hours after her arrival at JFK, she is collecting her accumulated mail in the faculty lounge and exchanging greetings with her colleagues. Lounging in a leather armchair next to the journal-covered coffee table is her department head. She must pay homage.

"And how has your summer been, Charles?"

"Beautiful, Judith. Each year I congratulate myself on buying that cottage in Maine twenty years ago. So quiet. I got a lot of writing done, almost an entire book!"

"That's wonderful!" she enthuses. "Good for you! I hope it is as successful as your last book." If she praises him, he'll find it harder to criticize her. She just has to be careful and not lay it on too thick.

"Well, I had a wonderful time in Paris," she says, trying to sound nonchalant. "And I think I have a couple of new research projects to tackle."

She thinks she notes one of his eyebrows rising slightly. "Really? Such as?"

"Gertrude Atherton spent some time in Paris, and . . ."

"Oh, one of your 'New Women?'" he asks, paying attention yet managing to be dismissive at the same time. He has no way of knowing that she no longer cares what he thinks.

"Exactly. She did volunteer work in France during World War I and wrote about it. I'd like to do some work on this."

"Yes, well that sounds quite interesting. Ah, Robert—good summer?"

He turns away, which is fine with Judith as she has done her duty and now can concentrate on the people she has truly missed. She will meet Claudette for lunch, have dinner with some other friends, and later tonight she will call Michael to give him a full report.

## CHAPTER TWENTY-FOUR

## JANUARY 2012:

# Bonne Année

W hen she arrives this time, it is the middle of winter, and she is prepared for snow on the ground. She had emailed Guy from JFK that she did not want him to come out to the airport; she can do it on her own and will take the Roissybus to the Palais Garnier.

"*Comme tu veux*," he had written back. "As you wish."

She manages to sleep a little on the plane. The last couple of weeks have left her happy but exhausted. She gave a successful conference paper at a panel on underrepresented writers, and this generated additional interest in Elisabeth Shuttleford. Maybe a couple of the doctoral students who attended will work on her. She has agreed to write a chapter for a proposed collection of studies on unheralded women writers. Then she had gone to her brother's for a week, which included a Chanukah party featuring Michael's potato *latkes* and Naomi's famous *sufganiyot*, sugar-dusted, jelly-filled pastries.

Later that evening, washing dishes after the guests had left, Judith had told Michael and Naomi about her travel plans for the rest of winter break. Michael had said jokingly, "Oh, so you are moving on to Paris now? Had enough of nineteenth-century London and Manchester?"

"Oh Michael, I was in Paris for only two weeks last summer. How much can one see in two weeks?"

"I assume you will see Guy again?"

"*Pourquoi pas?* Why not?"

"Aha! Remember what they used to say when a guy went out with a much, much younger woman? 'Robbing the cradle.' And you, sis, are just the opposite!"

"Oh, stop! We're just good friends."

"Whatever you say." He was actually pleased that Judith had found Guy and had returned home with some stories of their father's activities in Europe. He, too, is mystified by Ben's seeming abandonment of the family he had obviously cared for. It just didn't seem like his dad to act that way.

Judith loves her family, but holiday parties and going to the theatre and out to dinner had proven a grueling routine. She remembers wishing, in the guest room at Michael and Naomi's house, that she could drift off into sleep like the little girl in *The Nutcracker* ballet.

Now, a few days later, she is coming into Paris on the airport bus. Although the streets are clear for the most part, snow still clings to roof-tops and open spaces, patches of ice covering shady spots on the sidewalks. An elderly couple inches along, he pushing a wheeled wire shopping cart ahead of him, she clutching the sleeve of his puffy winter jacket. As the bus approaches the center of the city, along narrow commercial streets, past the twirling red "*Tabac*" signs and flashing green pharmacy crosses, she tries to remember the route to that same small hotel where she had stayed last summer. Stepping carefully off the bus, she makes her way to the taxi stand across the intersection from the Opéra.

The taxi goes the same way she and Guy rode last summer. Seeing the city in a new season is a novel experience. Right away she can see that the streets are not quite as thronged as they were during the high season. But there are still tourists, many of them, perhaps, university students on winter break.

As the taxi moves down the wide Avenue de l'Opéra, she notices that many shops have large signs in the windows reading *"Soldes."* Of course— the post-holiday sales; she'll have to check on that. On the left, in front of the Comédie-Française, is a little park she recalls filled with people—tourists, street musicians, and vagrants—sitting around the central fountain. Homeless people had stowed their bedrolls under the benches. Now the benches are empty, the fountain frozen.

Past the Louvre she goes, and over the bridge across the Seine, which sparkles in the midday light; it all looks so familiar and friendly. She feels pleased, anticipating an enjoyable few days. Guy has emailed to tell her he has tickets to both the *opéra* and the theatre, and also he knows there is an exhibit at a small museum that she may like. Normally, she almost bristles if she is not at least consulted about what to see, but this is Guy's city and she knows he wants to impress her. So why not?

Of course she wanted to return to Paris. She has already compensated, she feels, for her father's lack of communication. She has written, emailed, and phoned. She and Guy have spoken a number of times. Her French has improved, although Guy has said: *"Pas mal.* Not bad. You make mistakes only in vocabulary, case, and tense."

She enters the lobby of the hotel with her one small bag, greeting the receptionist in French. She has arranged for a room a bit smaller and less expensive than the one Guy treated her to last summer. She signs the register and then turns to go to the elevator; she has promised Guy she would phone him as soon as she was settled in the room.

But he is already at the elevator.

"Guy! I thought—"

He clasps her shoulders and gives her the twin Parisian kisses.

"*Bienvenue!* Welcome! I know from your email about when your plane would arrive, and think I will come straight here. It is so nice to see you!"

Just as abruptly, he drops his hands and waves her toward the elevator. "Go! Put your bag away and then I take you out!"

Judith is not used to being told what to do, except by her chair and dean, and for the most part she ignores them and does what she likes. She isn't disagreeable, it's just that when she turned fifty, she decided she had little patience for attending pointless meetings where people mainly talked about themselves or filled out forms no one needed.

But she has been looking forward to seeing Guy, and once she is in the room she quickly puts her one bag in the closet, splashes cool water on her face, and refreshes her lipstick, bought on her previous Paris trip. She takes a quick look at herself in the mirror and is glad she lost those pesky ten pounds.

In the lobby, Guy looks up and gets to his feet.

"We go for a nice walk now, and have a very French *déjeuner*, yes? And then if you are still awake, we can see a museum."

The sun is bright, and it is really not too cold. Guy looks quite jaunty in a tweed coat with a tartan scarf at the neck. He has everything planned, thinks Judith.

The day turns steely gray and chilly, but Judith and Guy do not notice because they are indoors at the Musée Jacquemart-André in the 8th *arrondissement*. Guy has taken them to lunch at the Musée's restaurant, which, formerly a dining room, is painted a deep scarlet and lined with large paintings framed in gilt curlicues. Huge tapestries fill one wall.

"What do you think?" Guy asks, indicating the room with a flourish of his hand.

"*A bisl ungepatcht*," she had replied, and they had both laughed. Unless people understood Yiddish, no one sitting near them would have known she had said "a little overdone" and been insulted. Minimalist tastes would have been overwhelmed by so much gold-encrusted decor, but Judith enjoys seeing these Beaux Arts excesses.

She also enjoys discovering works of art she has never seen before as they wander from room to room in the nineteenth-century mansion. They stop frequently so Guy can rest his leg. When they finally leave the museum in the late afternoon, the sky is completely leaden, and the frozen air is sharp.

"Cold weather wants for a hearty dinner," says Guy, as they walk down the Boulevard Haussmann toward the Miromesnil Métro station. "I have prepared a delicious *bœuf bourguignon* that we can have later."

"When do you find time to do all this?"

"Ah, the secret is to prepare it the day before. Before you get into your airplane, I chop and simmer!"

When they reach Guy's apartment, they hang their overcoats in the hall closet and Guy pours them each a glass of sherry. "To warm up," he says, instructing her to make herself comfortable. He draws the heavy curtains across the windows to keep out the chill air, telling Judith to choose a CD and put it in the player while he sees to their dinner. She selects a Brahms quartet, settles herself on the sofa, and thumbs through the current issue of *L'Observateur* lying next to her. Part of her feels jet lag taking hold, but she feels awkward doing nothing.

"May I help you?" she calls.

"*Non*," comes the answer from the kitchen, "You are my guest. I work, you relax."

In a few moments, the aroma of the *bœuf bourguignon* drifts from the kitchen as Judith finishes her sherry and fights sleepiness while wandering about the living room. She browses the titles of some of the books and notices a whiskey tumbler on one of the shelves. She quickly looks back toward the kitchen, and then sniffs the tumbler's contents; it's mostly water, probably melted ice, but the strong alcohol aroma is still there. She moves to another set of shelves, where she finds a small framed photo of a smiling young man sitting on a stone wall, the sleeves of a blue pullover draped over his shoulders, with the sea in the background. Perhaps this is Guy's son Jacques? Another framed photo displays a young man and woman with an infant of perhaps a few months; this must be Guy's daughter Mireille with her husband and child.

Interspersed among the books and leather-bound journal volumes are other photos, showing a younger Guy holding a notebook and standing next to a man with a goatee, who wears a Nikon with a telephoto lens on a strap around his neck. She is just about to read the inscription on a brass award plaque when Guy emerges from the kitchen, carrying a steaming bowl.

"I see you find my little gallery," he says.

"Are these your children?"

"Yes, my son, you see, Jacques. And Mireille with her family. They all come to see me in December. Mireille is moving."

"Where to?"

"To Israel, Netanya."

"I had no idea your family is, well, that Jewish."

"Mireille not so much. But her husband, Yves, he is more observant.

He feels they can life a better life as Jews in Israel, not in France."

"Why is that?"

"You know why, I am sure. The anti-Semitism here. Nothing new, of course. It was quiet for a while, but no more. It is louder now."

"Unfortunately, no, it is not new. There is anti-Semitism everywhere. If people are unhappy about something, blame the Jews. Even in the United States."

Guy looks sadly at the photo of Mireille and her family. "I never see them again," he says quietly, "Unless they come back to France."

"Why do you say that? There are nonstop flights from Paris to Tel Aviv."

He sighs. "I am too old to travel."

Judith helps him set the casserole on the table. "Don't be silly. People older than you travel. And you are not that old. Cut it out."

"Cut what out?"

She laughs. "Sorry, another idiom. It just means: stop."

"Americans! You want everybody to be young forever."

"That's right. If you won't join our cult of youthfulness, we won't talk to you."

"You will talk to me after you try this."

Judith sits, and Guy serves them each a bowl of the *bœuf bourguignon*. A green salad and a cheese plate await on the side. Guy uncorks a bottle, swirls a bit in his glass, and with an approving "ah!" pours for each.

"*Bon appétit!*" says Judith.

Guy raises his wineglass: "*L'chaim!*"

"Since when have you become so Jewish?" Judith asks, with a smirk.

"I say this to please you. Are you pleased?"

"Thank you, yes I am." She takes a bite, and her eyes widen.

The meat is soft because it has been cooked slowly for a long time, but it is not overdone. It is rich, flavorful, and meaty. She can taste the wine, but it is subtle, not overwhelming. The small white onions, carrots, and other vegetables and herbs arc distinct and just right. Altogether, this is an excellent dish. And she says so.

"You know," says Guy after a while, "I like that you come to visit. But also when you visit, it disturbs me."

Judith is taken aback. "Have I done or said anything that has upset you?"

"No, no. Nothing, neither." He pauses thoughtfully and sips his wine, staring into the glass. "But you remind me of a time in my life when I was both very sad and very happy. Happy to be back in Paris, with my *maman* and *gran'mère*. Happy not to have to hide any more. But sad because I learn for sure that my father and grandfather were killed. Your father, he help to make me happy again, to see that life continues, yes?"

"I'm glad of that, that he was good to you."

"After he left, life became sad again. But that first feeling, of freedom, it was joyful."

"I know it was difficult afterwards, with rationing and the cold."

"This got better after a while. After my mother marry Martin, I am alone a lot. Then I just study, study, I have little pleasure."

"Were you expected just to pick up and keep going as though nothing had happened? Or did you think this would happen? But how could it? You had no childhood! Your father and grandfather were murdered, and you had to spend the rest of the war basically hiding. That is major trauma."

"How do you know about these things? You just teach about books. You are a psychologist, too? You are going to send me a big bill for this!"

Here he goes again, thinks Judith. He is going to lead me into something and then say he doesn't want to talk about it, despite that little chuckle. Oh hell, she'll just give it to him.

"You think that because I teach about literature I don't see real life? I've taught for thirty years. I've had students come crying to my office because they found a story too painful—it reminded them of a childhood illness, or even a recent assault. I had a young woman in one of my classes who had never truly coped with the death of her father, and when we read a novel by James Agee she just snapped. Everything comes out in a literature classroom, and if not in the classroom, then in my office. I have heard everything. We are sensitized to this. We have to watch for students who may turn violent, even suicidal."

"You speak too fast, Zhoodeet, I am not used."

"I am sorry, Guy. I forgot."

"*Pas de problème*. Just a little slower for me, please."

"Don't worry about it—you just have a mistaken idea about teaching. Or perhaps what teaching is in my country. Perhaps it's just me—but we *listen* to students. What if I said you just wrote some little stories for some newspaper?"

"I write about major national and international issues!"

"Of course you do. I read up on you. I read some of your pieces, too, about the French treatment of the Algerians who fought on their side, the Harkis, and the fallout from that law in 2005 that so many called 'cultural revisionism.'"

Guy raises one eyebrow. "You read these in French?"

"As much as I could, yes. And I have a Larousse."

"I am impressed. You have done your research."

"I am impressed, too, by yours. Also, you cook well."

He makes a little self-deprecating gesture, waving his hand. "Ah, anyone can do this. It is nothing."

Amazing—they have evaded an argument about the past.

They finish the meal and bring the dishes into the kitchen. "Leave them," says Guy. "I will take care in the morning."

Judith peers at her wristwatch. "Look at the hour! I really ought to be going."

"I will walk you," offers Guy. "You will say no, independent American!"

"You are very gallant, but it's only five or six blocks."

The music ends. Only then do they note the silence outside. Guy draws aside the curtain over the window.

"*Alors!*" he exclaims. "There was no *prévision* of this."

Snow is falling heavily and there is already considerable accumulation on the pavement. Very little traffic passes. A bus that was probably already out is trying to complete its run, moving very slowly up the street. One man, who has apparently just gotten off the bus, gingerly crosses the street and bends to face the wind.

It was simply cold earlier, but Judith certainly is not prepared for snow; she looks down at her black leather flats.

"You cannot walk in those shoes," says Guy. "Or in this snow."

There is a moment of awkward silence, and then Guy continues, "So you stay here. I will fix up the couch for you."

Judith has a vague thought somewhere in the back of her brain, or perhaps not so far back, that a snowstorm outside would provide a wonderful excuse for staying in bed and mindlessly watching French TV. She wonders what Guy is thinking, but there isn't even a hint of a leer on his face when he returns with a set of linens, a pillow, and an extra comforter.

"I can do this," she says, taking the linens from him.

"Ah, but you will need nightclothes," he says, rather matter-of-factly, Judith feels. She waits to see what he returns with. If it's a negligee left over from when his wife lived here almost two decades ago, Judith thinks she will unhesitatingly run outside and choose to ruin her flats.

But Guy comes back with a set of his pajamas, neatly pressed and folded. "I think these will fit you, yes?"

"They will do nicely, Guy, thank you."

"All right then. I will use the lavatory and after you can take your time."

Judith returns to the magazine she was reading earlier. In a little while, Guy emerges from the bathroom and says good-night.

"*Bonne nuit, Guy, et merci.*"

Now Judith is alone in the quiet living room. She fits the pale blue sheet on the couch, puts two pillowcases on the burgundy throw pillows. She presses down, finding the couch very comfortable to her touch. She changes into the pajamas in the small tiled bathroom and washes up. Guy has thoughtfully supplied a set of towels and a spare toothbrush, still in bubble packaging. Does he have overnight guests a lot, Judith wonders. He seems to be well supplied.

Judith is so tired that she feels she can't lie down fast enough. She falls into the little nest she has made and feels the coziness creeping into her body from the duvet. It must be down-filled, she thinks, to warm me up this quickly. Perhaps she dozes for a while. The warmth and the wine combine to lull her quickly into sleep.

Later she wakes. She glances at her watch; it's only been two hours since she lay down. She lies inert, thinking, looking up at the ceiling high above and at the unused chandelier medallion at its center. She wonders about the generations of inhabitants who may have lived in this flat. Whether anyone from this building was deported or disappeared. Whether any intrigue or illicit rendezvous was carried on here, or maybe someone living here merely had a quotidian existence. Got up, went to work in an office, came home, in the summer went to the beach, perhaps, during the annual *vacances* in August. She tries to imagine what this place was like when Guy's two children were small and ran around.

Now Judith cannot sleep. She wants to see if it is still snowing. She pads silently toward the high French doors that open to the wrought-iron trimmed balcony. Pushing the curtain aside, she sees the snow, still falling silently, sometimes horizontally, then swirling around on the whim of the wind. She can barely see the buildings on the other side of the street. Whatever brightness there is comes from a street lamp on the corner, its light shifting as the snow eddies around it.

The whole scene before her reminds Judith of the Zeffirelli production of *La Bohème*, which she saw a couple of years ago at the Metropolitan Opera in New York. There was that magical scene in the snow at night—then she reminds herself that the opera was set in an earlier Paris, in the 1830s, so the Haussmannian buildings would not have been here. Neither, for that matter, would the electric streetlight. And anyway, *La Bohème* was a tragedy, and she doesn't want to think of any sad stories right now.

But seeing Paris in the snow at night—she has never had this experience, and she feels magically alone in the city; no one is walking down there on the street, all is hushed. She quietly and slowly opens the latch and steps out onto the balcony, just a little way. Now she can hear the wind and snow, whipping around the corners of the buildings, whooshing upwards over the rooftops with their many chimney-pots. She stays entranced for a few minutes, watching the snowflakes whirl back and forth across the yellow glow of the streetlights.

"Zhoodeet?"

She turns quickly with a little surprised gasp. She hasn't even heard Guy come into the living room.

"You are all right? You feel well?" He steps closer, a look of concern on his face.

"Yes—I just—couldn't sleep, so I got up to look. And thought I would feel the snow, just for a bit."

"Ah, well, I feel the cold air come in the flat, so I worry that the wind has pushed open the door and you will be chilled."

"I am so sorry that I woke you. But look, isn't it pretty?"

He chuckles, "I have seen snow outside this window so many times that I no more get excited. To me, it is a *nuisance*. You—you act like a child! An open door and no shoes!"

"Well, I didn't exactly plan to be here without my slippers."

"I am a bad host if I let you catch a cold," he says, stepping past her and latching the doors to the balcony. The room grows quiet again. She shivers involuntarily.

"You are cold," he says, "So take this."

He takes off his heavy robe and places it around her shoulders. "Better, yes?"

She turns as he places his robe on her shoulders and leans her face against his chest.

"What is this?" he asks at last.

She remains pressed against him but turns her head enough so that she can speak.

"In America, we call this affection."

He says nothing, though he keeps his hands on her shoulders and rubs them lightly through the robe.

"I am an old man."

"I am not a young woman."

"You are younger than I am."

"Not by that much."

"Almost a generation."

"*Ah, fermé la bouche.*"

"Your French, it is terrible."

They remain standing like this for some moments. Judith tries not to think of anything, but then she feels the jet lag kicking in again.

"Guy, if I do not lie down, I'll collapse."

He guides her back to the couch and takes back his robe, saying, "*Oui*, Zhoodeet, I also cannot stand for long time, because of my leg. Sleep well."

"*Bonne nuit.*"

In a few moments, she is asleep.

## CHAPTER TWENTY-FIVE

# The Next Day

J udith is hiding deep in a cave. She thinks the cave is in a forest. It is very dark, but now she hears some sounds coming from outside. She has to keep still, so still. She hardly breathes; the slightest sound or movement could give her away. "I know you are in there." She hears a voice, then tries not to hear it. She is almost suffocating, but she cannot move. The roof of the cave is very close, almost touching her face. The voice again: "Are you going to come out?" They know she is in here. Should she simply burst out, fighting, or remain quiet and hidden? Then she smells something—are they building a fire at the entrance of the cave, to trap her?

No, it's a good smell: coffee. Why are they making coffee in the forest? To lure her out.

Judith blinks awake. She is in the dark and something soft is on her face. She has no idea where she is, so she remains still while her brain resurfaces. She actually does smell coffee and realizes she is under a down comforter that is pulled up over her head.

Peering out from under the comforter, she sees a bright yellow room and the sun blazing in through two tall windows. Striped curtains have been pushed to either side. She hears a scraping sound, then a distant motor, and then remembers everything in a flash. She realizes she is hearing shovels clearing sidewalks, and a snowplow coming down the street.

Guy emerges from the kitchen. "You are awake finally! *Bonjour!* I make you a coffee."

He reappears in a moment, smiling, with a small cup of espresso for Judith, gives it to her, and sits on the edge of the couch.

"Where is it?" asks Judith. "I see only a thimble."

"I am sorry," says Guy. "It is winter. I do not have a beach bucket."

This is now a joke between them, and they both laugh.

"It is very good, really. It will wake me up."

"So, you slept well?"

"Falling asleep was nice," she says, smiling at him. "Later in the night, though, I had some disturbing dreams."

"I am sorry to hear that. Do you remember anything?"

He doesn't need to hear this, Judith thinks.

"Nothing in particular. I'll forget about it if I don't talk about it. I see that the weather has become nice and sunny!" She can change topics, too.

"Yes, the sun and our plows will take care of most of the snow. By this afternoon everything will be passable. It is actually almost afternoon now! But Paris, in the snow—oh, you can get many good photographs."

She is surprised to see that it is almost noon. She takes another sip of the strong, black espresso. "This is really good. I can feel the caffeine taking effect."

"What do you wish to do today?"

"I don't have an agenda. But I think at some point, I'd like to go back to that bookshop, Shakespeare."

"Ah, yes. The English books. Touristical. But of course, it is your vacation." He pauses and looks at her. "I have an idea, too."

"Yes?"

"I thought . . . perhaps . . . you might like to go to the Marché aux Puces, the flea market. But not with the snow, no."

Judith feels he was about to suggest something else, but then changed his mind. But she responds as though his was a sincere suggestion. "You know, twenty years ago, I would have jumped at the chance, but I really don't need to collect any more stuff. On the contrary, I need to get rid of some of the things I've collected over the years. Still, if it were a nice day, it would be fun just to go and people-watch. But not today."

He smiles and, to her imagination, looks relieved.

"I like your idea of using the snow as a reason to take some pictures. Where do you suggest we go?"

"I think you ought to go to the Île de la Cité, Notre-Dame, the Île Saint-Louis, all around the little streets on the islands."

"And you will come with me?"

He shakes his head. "No, not before much of the snow is gone. I am very afraid I will fall. Though I use a walking stick sometimes, I could slip on a patch of ice. And then it is over."

Judith understands completely and simply nods. When you're a child and there is ice, you think of skating; when you're an adult, you think of ice as an annoyance and a possible driving hazard; but when you are old, an icy slip can mean a broken hip and then a final descent. Ice is to be greatly feared.

"You have more sturdy shoes than the ones you have yesterday?" Guy asks.

"Oh yes, back at the hotel I have ankle-high boots."

"Good! So I suggest you change into those and go take your pictures. Then I meet you at a café about four o'clock. By then there will be much melting. It will be safer for me to walk later."

"Then I would like to change, please."

Guy is a little embarrassed and flustered. "Of course, yes! Do you wish to dress in here, or the bath? Whatever you are comfortable with."

"Thank you. I'll just gather my things and use the bathroom." She has finished her little coffee. Now she adjusts the pajamas and swings her legs off the couch. She feels the cold as soon as her feet touch the bare wooden floor.

"Take your time. I just wait here," says Guy.

Judith reaches over to the chair where she had placed her clothing in a neat pile after changing into the pajamas last night. She wonders if Guy has had women stay over often. She gathers her garments, goes into the bathroom, and emerges about fifteen minutes later, dressed, washed, and refreshed.

"*Voilà!*" she says.

"You are quick," Guy observes. "I am not so quick anymore."

"I am in Paris for only a few days," Judith responds, "so I don't want to waste time. I have already wasted half a day!" She longs to nap some more but wants to see if he is truly eager for her to leave, or if he will ask her to stay.

She goes to get her coat from the closet near the door of the apartment.

"Wait," Guy says. He is holding a slip of paper. "I have made a reservation here. I meet you at four, yes? I can get a taxi if it is too icy."

She takes the paper with an address on the Rue des Grands Degrés.

"You have a good map of Paris? *Excellent.* I see you later. Go take your pictures, while there is sun."

The streets are already fairly slushy by the time Judith begins her walk back to the hotel. By keeping to the middle of the road, watching carefully for cars, and then walking on the sunny side of cleared pavements, she manages to keep her flats from becoming soaked. Still, her feet are chilled when she enters the lobby. She takes the elevator to her room and immediately changes into warmer socks and her sturdier ankle boots. Now she has a couple of hours for taking pictures.

Judith uses a simple digital camera. People tell her she has quite a good sense of composition. Still, she is no professional, and she needs an easy-to-operate instrument that takes high quality shots with a minimum of expertise. Someone once advised her to "frame" her photos, so she will look through doorways and arches to find subjects, or she will stand in the entryway of an apartment building to get a shot of the street outside. She enjoys taking multiple pictures of the same subject from different points of view. That's probably the feature of digital photography she likes best: the ability to pick and choose later which shots to keep, which to delete. The other reason she likes this particular camera is that it is so small. Judith wants to be an unobtrusive photographer, unlike those who wear huge Nikons around their necks. She wants to be able to keep the camera in a side pocket so as not to be immediately labeled a tourist, which of course she is. But she still likes being able to blend in.

In her small shoulder bag, she carries a thin booklet purchased last summer at BHV, a map of Paris by *arrondissement*. She consults it now to find where she is, and where she is to meet Guy later. She decides to walk in the direction of the Sorbonne and then let her steps take her wherever they choose, to whatever looks interesting on this side of the Seine. Then perhaps she will go over to Notre-Dame—perhaps the weather has dissuaded many visitors. If it is open, there might not be a very great line, and she could go inside.

Heading up the hill approaching the Sorbonne, Judith finds herself only half-noticing which shops are open and which are not. Instead, she watches carefully for automobiles going too quickly, which might splash her with snowy slush. She wanders through the narrow streets of the Latin Quarter, thinking about education, and wonders whether the *lycées* and universities are equally concerned with passing French culture to the next generation and encouraging criticism and reassessment of this culture. She has heard the phrase "passing the torch" in American academia so often that it has become a cliché. But this is what the best teachers should be doing, rather than making things all about themselves. In this way, Judith knows she has done a conscientious job.

But who had passed the torch to her? Where did her own interests originate? Mom and Dad hadn't been able to complete their educations because of the Depression, and Dad's continued studies were delayed by the war. They were thrilled that she and Michael were simply able to study whatever they wanted. Michael has been very practical, Judith thinks, in getting his law degree. She, however, had piddled along in graduate school mostly because she enjoyed reading and having discussions about books and ideas with her undergraduate students. Her real learning had come later, as she started researching the lives and thwarted publication hopes of several neglected writers.

The bright sun reflects blindingly on patches of snow in the small open spaces as she crosses the broad Rue des Écoles. She is sorry she didn't think to wear her sunglasses. She goes into a small bookshop, mainly to rest her eyes, finding herself pleasantly diverted. Good thing her reading skills in French are so rudimentary, or she would be tempted to buy several titles and then would be schlepping around with a heavy bag. She recalls with a smile her very first trip to Europe, when she bought a book here and there, until at the end of six weeks she had accumulated so many that she could not fit them into her suitcase. For the return flight, she had packed all the books into her one suitcase and then put on all of her clothes, layer upon layer. It was July, and she was perspiring furiously when she waddled off the plane at JFK as her parents stared in puzzlement.

Judith continues to work her way to the river along small back streets so narrow that even one car would have difficulty navigating its way. Bollards on the sidewalk prevent anyone from parking. She passes a closed antiques shop, a designer's studio behind a rehabbed orange door, a bicycle shop where a technician can be seen in the window working on a chain. At the corner there is a *papeterie,* with racks of brightly colored postcards on the newly swept sidewalks; Judith is surprised at the comparatively high cost of these cards. Really, those generic, 'famous sights' cards sell ten for a dollar, printed in Italy, at the tourist shops along Broadway; here, the equivalent cards cost a couple of dollars each. It's just a momentary thought that flits in and out of Judith's consciousness as she walks along the river.

Here it is much colder, with an icy wind blowing across the Seine. Judith pulls her wool scarf a little tighter around her neck. Still, the day is gorgeous, with a cerulean, cloudless sky. Despite the cold and the fact that it's off-season, there are still packs of visitors strolling along the walks and people streaming over the bridges across the river to Notre-Dame. Students on winter break? Office workers hurrying because they have only one free hour?

Judith watches out for traffic and then crosses carefully to the sidewalk overlooking the river walk. She snaps a photo of a man walking his dog—they are both sporting red coats—next to the water. A barge moves along slowly, a puff of smoke drifting upwards from a pipe near the stern. She leans against the gray stone wall and looks out over the scene. She takes a deep breath, feeling very relaxed. If she could just remain this way for more than five minutes! But she is exhausted from the inner dialogue she has been having over the last half hour, covering so many topics: her role as an educator, her discovery of neglected writers, what her parents had hoped she would study, the books she bought on her first trip to Europe, the price of postcards, the centuries-long stream of visitors to Notre-Dame, and her discovery of Guy. Get it all down on paper, and it would be stream-of-consciousness writing.

Turning, Judith sees three young women exclaiming over something one of them has found at the riverside bookstall they are visiting. Judith moves closer. The girls are not speaking French—it's Italian. They are looking at fashion magazines from the 1960s, pointing and laughing. Judith has a photo of her father next to a *bouquiniste's* stall, but she has no idea what is in the bag he holds in one hand. She has seen enough to know that some of the stalls specialize in antique prints, some in old magazines, some in paperbound books, and some in tacky modern souvenirs. Perhaps she'll take a closer look on another day.

She hears music drifting from her left, and there, on the other side of the road and a little below the level of the street where she is walking, is Shakespeare and Company, its name emblazoned on a large yellow sign above the green shop exterior. She had wanted to go in anyway and approaches the little plaza in front of the shop. A lone flutist is standing near the entrance, piping a cheerful ditty; he is wearing gloves that have just the tips of the fingers cut off so he can still play. He sees Judith's eyes following him as she approaches the bookstore.

"To answer your thoughts," he says as she comes abreast, "Yes, the flute does get rather cold, but I don't play for more than twenty minutes at a time."

"That's exactly what I was thinking," she responds, laughing.

A few people are sitting on the bench outside the shop, and several are browsing through the volumes on the shelves and tables outside. In warm weather, Judith knows, the little flagstoned plaza with its Wallace fountain and two trees in front of the shop will be packed with tourists and readers, and many people will be both. She steps inside where it is cozy and warm. Last summer when she visited, she did not spend nearly as much time here as she would have liked; Guy was waiting patiently outside, and she did not wish to take advantage of him. He simply thought she ought to see one of the largest draws in Paris for English-speaking people.

"You know it is not the original one," he had said.

"Yes, I know."

"Now it is all a touristical place!"

Judith didn't care if the shop, located here for over half a century, was seen as a tourist stop as well as a magnet for the literati. Any temple to the printed word was valuable, as far as she was concerned, and if it got people to read more, wonderful. Now she takes her time, browsing the contemporary offerings on the first floor before venturing up the stairs, past the wallpaper decorated with drawings of well-known American and English writers, to see the tumble of assorted nooks and reading corners above.

The upstairs windows, overlooking both the open area at ground level and Notre-Dame, offer a wonderful vantage point for a few more pictures. Then Judith returns the small camera to her pocket and settles in for a closer look at a book on Proust. But she cannot concentrate; she keeps thinking of the other issues pecking at the corners of her brain for attention.

When she glances at her watch, Judith is surprised to see that it is already half past three, and she has only thirty minutes before she is to meet Guy. She returns the book to its place on the shelf and makes her way downstairs. Her second visit and she still does not have enough time! But during this time, however, she has gleaned some ideas for a new course.

Checking the BHV map guide, she realizes she does not need to go very far along the street, here called the Quai de Montebello, to reach her destination. Judith has to laugh. The Rue des Grands Degrés has such an impressive name but is such a short street that would be easy to miss. Like so many other small streets in this *quartier* untouched by Haussmannian symmetry, it is very narrow, built for pedestrians and small carts. She walks up and back the entire length, passing an antique bookshop and decorators' shops selling tapestries and needlepoint kits. Taking a few steps back from the buildings, she notices that one has an elaborate frieze above the second floor, depicting women at work, painting and designing. Judith heads back toward the small street in time to see a taxi rolling up to her destination.

Guy, stepping out, sees her right away. "Ah, Zhoodeet! Such perfect timing!"

"I didn't realize how close this was to Shakespeare and Company."

"You went there to commune with the spirit of Hemingway?"

"He's not talking to me ever since I said out loud that he is overrated."

They enter the tiny restaurant where Guy has made a reservation. He has obviously been here before, for the staff greet him warmly, as an old friend. The dining room is very narrow, decorated with oversized mirrors in heavy gilt frames that enlarge the space. The simplicity of their surroundings calls the diners' attention to the true focus: the food. The server greets them both, but then he and Guy have a rapid-fire conversation in French, and Judith cannot even try to keep up.

Finally, Guy addresses her. "I hope you don't mind. I ordered something you will like, that is a specialty here. *Canard*. Duck. You will see.

Meanwhile, let us start."

The server has poured chilled white wine into their glasses. Judith raises hers and says "*À votre santé.*"

Guy smiles at her and lifts his, "*Tchin-tchin!*" He takes a sip, pauses, and continues. "So, tell me about your day and where you went."

"Really," she says, taking a small sip, "Four hours is a short time when you include a bookshop."

"Ah, yes, the shrine of English!" he laughs.

"Go ahead and laugh, but it does have an excellent collection, and I've gotten some good ideas for a course proposal. I'll make one more trip there before I go home."

"Please yourself."

"Oh, I will." She enjoys their repartee. Aha, another French word that has made its way into English. No wonder he feels so linguistically superior. She decides to ask him the question that has been nagging at her.

"Guy," she begins slowly, "Earlier today, when you asked me whether I wanted to see the flea market, did you *really* mean to ask me that?" There is a brief pause.

"No."

"Ah. Then what did you truly mean to ask me?"

He pauses again and turns a little pink. Unless he has been drinking all morning, it can't be the wine. "I think—perhaps—you might like to—well, your visit last summer was short, and this visit now is short."

"True. That is an observation, not a question."

"Americans! Always rushing! Wait—I am not finished speaking. I thought, I think—maybe you wish to plan a longer visit? But then I say to myself, oh that is too bold."

She cannot help but laugh, genuine mirthful laughter.

"You see?" he says quietly, looking downcast and serious. "You laugh at me. As I was afraid."

"'But at my back I always hear / Time's wingèd chariot hurrying near.'"

Guy frowns as he looks at her. "*Quoi?* What?"

"It's from a poem. English, from the 1600s. It means there isn't much time. *Carpe diem.*" He still looks a bit puzzled.

"I am not laughing *at* you. It was a happy laugh. Yes, I *do* wish to stay longer. I need a really long visit."

He smiles and his shoulders ease downwards as he relaxes. "Ah, good, then I can really show you so much of *mon cher Paris!*"

Now she feels her face flushing, too. Their meal is served, and surely it is delicious, but Judith doesn't remember a single bite.

## CHAPTER TWENTY-SIX

# Les Printemps

"The pussy willow is coming out early!"

Judith smiles as she joins her colleagues in the meeting room and catches this bit of conversation. With all that is going on, someone thinks it remarkable enough to mention the blooming of the pussy willow.

"Well, Serena, when does it usually appear?" asks Tom, one of the new assistant professors.

"Not until late March, usually. So, spring is ahead of time this year."

It is only the end of February, and Judith has been back from Paris for a month. She has a lot to do over the next twelve weeks. She has a checklist in her datebook and takes another look as Charles calls the meeting to order, beginning in his usual way by speaking of the New Opportunities of a New Year and All They Will Accomplish Together. She wishes the department would choose a new chair, if only to vary the speeches. But it's not really her worry anymore.

The talk moves to class registrations becoming final after the drop/add period, with confirmations to be sent online to the secretary. They confirm the date in April of the guest lecture by a Harvard professor, and all the local arrangements are being taken care of by Serena and Tom. Judith wonders vaguely if the pussy willow will still be available for use in a centerpiece.

The meeting continues, covering mundane matters such as who is scheduled to teach during the summer session, how many entries have been received so far in the poetry competition, and whoever is organizing the pre-spring break potluck must see to it that there are not ten macaroni and cheese casseroles. Faculty are reminded that proposals for any new courses must be received by the chair one week from today.

It has taken less than an hour, which is comparatively good. Judith gathers her papers and goes up to Charles. "Do you have a few moments? I'd like to discuss my course proposal with you."

He gives her a look of surprise over the top of his bifocals. "A *new* course, Judith?"

"How did you guess! I'm always exploring, you know. Want to stay fresh!"

Careful, careful, she tells herself. Just because Charles is stodgy and uses the same lecture notes from year to year you don't have to rub it in.

"Yes, yes, let's talk for a moment in my office."

They go into the department office. The sun is coming through the blinds and highlights dust motes in the air. Charles's office is just beyond, off to the left, and Judith settles into one of the burgundy leather arm-chairs facing his desk. She knows that Charles could easily plop down on the small, upholstered sofa and invite her to sit there as well. But Charles, she thinks sadly, doesn't plop and never relaxes. He needs to sit behind that desk and use it to remind everyone else that he is in charge. This, also, is not her worry.

"Judith, I have been so busy that I don't think I've even had a chance to speak to you since MLA. I hope you had a good turnout for your paper."

"Thank you, I did. The session was quite well attended, and I do hope some more interest in Shuttleford will result. And how did your panel turn out?"

"Oh, nice indeed! The participants were wonderful. My panel, as you might recall"—she does not—"on 'Double Metaphors: Tautology and Trope in the Poetry of the Lake District' went brilliantly, and we had quite a lively discussion at the conclusion. Yes, quite lively."

"I am so glad for you. All that work getting an appreciative audience!"

Oh, Judith, she says to herself, you've laid it on rather thickly, haven't you? But he's got to be in a good mood now.

Charles leans back in his swivel chair, his arms on his vest-covered tummy and his fingertips touching.

"So—tell me about your proposed course."

Judith clears her throat. "I have been reading Shari Benstock's *Women of the Left Bank*, about all the expatriate women writing in English who found a haven in Paris. Well, I'd like to do a course on expatriate women in Paris. All of the emphasis has been on male figures like Hemingway and Fitzgerald. This would be different, and I would also include many less familiar women in other fields, such as Josephine Baker."

"But the course would be primarily dealing with literature that is accessible to students?"

"Definitely."

"Well, it does sound interesting. Do you have a proposed syllabus?"

Judith leans forward to give him a printed page.

"Excellent—thank you. Now, this would be for this coming fall?"

Judith remains leaning forward to deliver her major message. "Charles,

I have been giving a lot of thought to that phased retirement offer you mentioned last year."

"Oh?" he says. His eyebrows rise, and she imagines him calculating how many instructors he can hire with her budget line.

She continues: "I like the idea of taking a semester off, then coming back, and later doing the full retirement. But right now, I am not quite ready to stop teaching. So I am proposing to teach the course next spring."

"I think this can be arranged, Judith. Oh my. So you will be leaving us. Certainly, we'll have to plan a big to-do for you!"

Judith imagines him drooling over the opportunities conjured up by the thought of getting rid of a longtime teacher.

"Well, we *will* have to start advertising now for one or two leave-re-placement faculty," he says thoughtfully. She knows he is thinking of five or six part-timers.

"Charles—please don't exploit any adjuncts."

"They cost less."

"Think of the college. We don't want the reputation of using and discarding talented teachers. Just my two cents."

"Well, thank you, Judith. I will consider what you've said and discuss it with the dean."

As she leaves, Judith thinks to herself, Charles will do what Charles will do. If they hire adjuncts at low pay, she can at least offer to rent her home to them at a low cost.

The next three months pass in a dizzying schedule of teaching, advising honors theses, grading papers, and packing. She puts jewelry and valuables in her safety deposit box, checks insurance policies, and puts what she doesn't need to use in one closet. She has contacted the Mémorial de la Shoah about volunteering. Through the internet, she has located a small furnished apartment not far from the Jardin du Luxembourg. It has a lift. Guy has difficulty on stairs and, face it, on some days she does too. She speaks often to Guy and advises him of his plan.

"But this is silly," he says early on, "As we discuss in email. Why do you wish pay rent for a flat when you can stay in my flat at no cost?"

"It is so kind of you to offer," she has responded. "But think about it, Guy. You and I have each gotten used to coming and going on our own. We have lived alone for decades. This way we each have our own space and privacy, and then we can meet . . ."

"*Bien súr*, yes, yes, I understand. You just let me know what I can do!"

In May, the department hosts a "Bon Voyage" party for her with a French theme. And then she is flying to New York to spend a few days with Michael and his family before her summer and fall semester in Paris. She wants them all, but especially Ian and Sarah, to visit while she is abroad, so she can show them everything, including the places visited by their grandpa Ben.

It never fails to impress Judith how the pilots manage to steer a huge metal pipe through thousands of miles of empty sky. When she looks out her window many hours later, they have crossed the Atlantic and are already over land. She sees a brightly lit train, its headlights shining, racing along beneath them. The tracks must bend several times near here, Judith thinks, because the path of the train seems erratic. It disappears and then blazes forth again. Watching in amazement, she soon realizes there is no train; what she has been seeing is the reflection of the moon in streams and rivers below. Just the magic of the night, and of the mind.

When they land—again those miraculous pilots, bringing their craft out of the void and down onto a specific patch of ground—she knows exactly where to go. It seems that she left from this terminal only weeks earlier. On the bus to the Opéra, she realizes she is smiling at nothing.

As Judith is deciding exactly how to get to her hotel, the bus comes to a stop across from the Palais Garnier. She gathers her purse, slips on her small backpack, grasps her wheelie, and steps down from the bus to the sidewalk.

The day is gorgeous, the overhead sun warm, and there is a vanilla-scented breeze brushing her face. Perhaps the door of a perfume shop is open.

"*Bonjour, madame, peut-être je peux vous aider?* Perhaps I can assist you?"

Standing there, smiling, is Guy. He is wearing a jaunty straw cap and tips it gallantly. "Shall we get a taxi?" In his linen blazer and khaki slacks, he looks positively dashing. And his smile, she knows, is for her.

"*Mais non,*" she responds. "We can just take the 21."

# Bibliography

Adler, Jacques. *The Jews of Paris and the Final Solution*, 1985.

Atkinson, Rick. *The Guns at Last Light: The War in Western Europe, 1944-1945*, 2013.

Beevor, Anthony and Artemis Cooper. *Paris After the Liberation, 1944-1949*, 1994.

Belth, Nathan. *Fighting for America,* 1944.

Chandler, Adam. "Florence Waren: Hiding in the Spotlight, *Tablet*, August 6, 2012.

De Fontette, François. *Histoire de l'Antisémitisme*, 1982.

Diamond, Hanna. *Fleeing Hitler: France 1940*, 2007

Dreyfus Jean-Marc and Sarah Gensburger. *Nazi Labour Camps in Paris*, 2011.

Feuchtwanger, Lion. *The Devil in France*, translated by Elisabeth Abbott, 2009.

*Restricted: French Phrase Book*. United States War Department, September 1943.

Gildea, Robert. *Marianne in Chains*, 2002.

Glass, Charles. *Americans in Paris: Life & Death Under Nazi Occupation*, 2009.

Gottschalk, Max. "Report on the Jewish Situation in France, September-October 1945," confidential report to the American Jewish Committee, October 19, 1945.

Grobman, Alex. *Rekindling the Flame: American Jewish Chaplains and the Survivors of European Jewry, 1944-1948*, 1993.

Gutman, Israel, editor-in-chief. *Encyclopedia of the Holocaust*, 1990.

Henry, Patrick. *We Only Know Men: The Rescue of Jews in France During the Holocaust*, 2007.

Hershco, Tsilla. "The Jewish Resistance in France During World War II: The Gap Between History and Memory," *Jewish Political Studies Review*, March 2007.

Hitchcock, William I. *The Bitter Road to Freedom: A New History of the Liberation of Europe*, 2008.

Hobson-Faure, Laura. *Un 'Plan Marshall Juif:' La Présence Juive Américaine en France Après la Shoah, 1944-1954*, 2013.

*How to See Paris: For the Soldiers of the Allied Armies*. Commissariat Général au Tourisme, Paris, n.d.

Humbert, Agnes. Resistance: *A Woman's Journal of Struggle and Defiance in Occupied France*, 2004.

Hyman, Paula. *The Jews of Modern France*, 1998.

Jackson, Julian. *France, The Dark Years: 1940 – 1944*, 2001.

Josephs, Jeremy. *Swastika Over Paris: The Fate of the Jews in France*, 1989.

Kaiser, Hilary. *WWII Voices: American GIs and the French Women Who Married Them*, 2005.

Kaufer, Cecile and Joe Allen. *Goodbye for Always: The Triumph of the Innocents*, 1997.

Kurlansky, Mark. *A Chosen Few: The Resurrection of European Jewry*, 1995.

Lipton, Eunice. *French Seduction*, 2007.

Marrus, Michael R. *Vichy France and the Jews*, 1983.

Moore, Deborah Dash. *GI Jews: How World War II Changed a Generation*, 2004.

Neiberg, Michael. *The Blood of Free Men: The Liberation of Paris, 1944*, 2012.

Nemirovsky, Irene. *Suite Francaise*, 2007.

Ousby, Ian. *Occupation: The Ordeal of France 1940-1944*, 1997. *Paris Guide for Leave Troops*. United States Army, n.d. (1944).

Paxton, Robert O. *Vichy France: Old Guard and New Order, 1940-1944*, 1972.

Poznanski, Renee. *Jews in France During WWII*, 1994.

Riding, Alan. *And the Show Went On: Cultural Life in Nazi-Occupied Paris*, 2010.

Roberts, Mary Louise. *What Soldiers Do: Sex and the American GI in World War II France*, 2013.

Sebba, Anna. *Les Parisiennes: How the Women of Paris Lived, Loved, and Died Under Nazi Occupatio*n. New York: St. Martin's, 2016.

Shaw, Irwin and Ronald Searle. *Paris! Paris!*, 1976.

Sinder, Henri. "Lights and Shades of Jewish Life in France 1940-42," in *Jewish Social Studies*, IV, 5, 1943.

2770th *Engineer Base Company*. Paris: Communication Zone, ETO, 1945.

Vinen, Richard. *The Unfree French: Life Under the Occupation*, 2006.

Wilt, Brenda J. "War Brides," *America in WWII*, August 2005.

Wyman, David S. *The Abandonment of the Jews: American and the Holocaust*, 1984.

Zaretsky, Robert. *"La Difference," Tablet*, March 7, 2012.

Zuccotti, Susan. *The Holocaust, the French, and the Jews*, 1993.

# ──◆ About the Author ◆──

*Jane S. Gabin*

 native of New York City, Jane S. Gabin earned her earned her BA at Queens College of the City University of New York and her PhD in English from The University of North Carolina at Chapel Hill. An independent scholar, she has participated in numerous academic conferences and lectured extensively in the United States and abroad, spending considerable time in England and France.

Professionally, Jane is an experienced teacher and educational counselor. Her extensive teaching ranges from high school to college to lifelong learning. Most recently, she has taught at the Osher Lifelong Learning Institute at Duke University. She has also worked for many years in university admissions and in college counseling, and is a member of the Southern Association for College Admission Counseling, the Victorian Society of New York, and the Alliance Française.

She has published three academic books with university presses, two on 19th century expatriate American women and one on the musical career of Southern poet Sidney Lanier. *The Paris Photo* is her first novel.